Henry Gibson

Catechism Made Easy

Being A Familiar Explanation Of The Catechism Of Christian Doctrine In Three Volumes - Vol. 2

Henry Gibson

Catechism Made Easy
Being A Familiar Explanation Of The Catechism Of Christian Doctrine In Three Volumes - Vol. 2

ISBN/EAN: 9783337391737

Printed in Europe, USA, Canada, Australia, Japan

Cover: Foto ©Andreas Hilbeck / pixelio.de

More available books at **www.hansebooks.com**

CATECHISM MADE EASY,

BEING

A FAMILIAR EXPLANATION

OF THE

Catechism of Christian Doctrine,

IN THREE VOLUMES.

BY THE

REV. HENRY GIBSON,

Late Catholic Chaplain to the Kirkdale Gaol and Kirkdale Industrial Schools.

VOL. II.

"EXCEPT YOU UTTER BY THE TONGUE PLAIN SPEECH, HOW SHALL
IT BE KNOWN WHAT IS SAID? FOR YOU SHALL BE SPEAKING
INTO THE AIR."—I. COR. XIV. 9.

LIVERPOOL

PRINTED BY ROCKLIFF BROTHERS, 44 CASTLE STREET.

LONDON:

R. WASHBOURNE, 18 PATERNOSTER ROW.

MDCCCLXXIV.

CONTENTS OF VOL. II.

CONTENTS.

TO THE READER.

After an interval of some years, occasioned by a long and severe illness, which involved the necessity of absolute repose from all mental labour, the author is at length, with God's blessing, able to offer the second volume of "Catechism Made Easy" to the Public. It contains the explanation of that portion of the Catechism which treats of the Commandments of God and of the Church. The Sacraments and the remainder of the Catechism will form the subject of the third volume, which is now in course of preparation, and will complete the work.

It will be remarked that the chapters of this volume are, for the most part, considerably longer than those of the first. This arises from the nature of the subject, which regards the moral law, and usually requires greater development, while, at the same time, it is capable of more copious illustration than that which relates to dogma. The average length of the catechetical lesson has been adhered to, as it is generally found necessary, in teaching the Catechism, to go through the whole of it in a limited number of lessons, while, on the other hand, it is easy for those who avail themselves of this explanation, to omit such points as are of minor importance, and to make their own selection among a number of examples.

In conclusion, the author begs to thank his Very Rev. and Rev. Brethren for the general approval with which they received his former volume, and for the many kind letters of inquiry and condolence which cheered him in his sickness, and have encouraged him to devote his returning health to the prosecution of his unfinished task.

BELMOUNT, AMBLESIDE,

1st May, 1874.

CATECHISM MADE EASY.

On the Commandments of God and the Church.

FIRST INSTRUCTION.

CHAPTER IV.—*Charity. The Ten Commandments. Their Promulgation. Their strict Obligation.*

Q. How many commandments are there?
A. Ten.

We come now, my dear children, to a most important part of the catechism, namely, that which treats of the commandments of God and his Church. It is most necessary that we should be well instructed on this point, since it is by his commandments that God teaches us what his Holy Will is, and it is only by doing his Will that we can hope to be saved. Hence our Blessed Lord himself says, "Not every one that saith to me, *Lord, Lord*, shall enter into the kingdom of heaven; but he that doeth the Will of my Father who is in heaven, he shall enter into the kingdom of heaven." * Attend, therefore, carefully to this and the following chapter, which contain a full explanation of the commandments. First of all, the catechism speaks of those commandments which God himself has given to man, and which he has

* Matt. vii. 21.

appointed the Church to teach and explain to us. Then, in the next chapter, it goes on to speak of the Commandments or Precepts of the Church, that is to say, of those rules which the Church, guided by the Holy Ghost, has laid down to enable us better to fulfil the commandments of God, and thus work out our salvation.

You will remember to have noticed at the top of the second chapter of the catechism, in which the Apostles' Creed is explained, the word *Faith* printed in large letters, while the next chapter, which is about Prayer, was headed with the word *Hope*. I told you that the reason was, that the Apostles' Creed teaches us what we are to *believe*, while Prayer is the expression of our *hope* or trust in God. The chapter that we have now come to is headed with the word *Charity*, which means, as you know, the love of God. Can any of you tell me why the word *Charity* is put at the head of the chapter which treats of God's commandments? It is because the keeping of his commandments is the very way in which we show our Charity or love towards him; just as we show our Faith, by believing what he teaches, and our Hope by praying to him. Hence our Blessed Lord expressly says, "He that hath my commandments and doeth them, he it is that loveth me."* If, then, you wish to find out whether you love Almighty God or not (and you know that without loving him you cannot enter into heaven), examine yourselves to see whether you keep his commandments. If you keep them well, you love God much; if you keep them badly, you do not love him at all; but if you are trying to keep them better than you have done, then you are beginning to learn to love God.

You see now, my dear children, that Faith, Hope

* John, xiv. 21.

and Charity are like three sisters who are sent by God to conduct us to heaven. Faith lights us on our way, showing us the road by which we are to journey; Hope strengthens and nourishes us with the Divine Grace which we obtain by the devout use of Prayer and the Sacraments; while Charity takes us by the hand and leads us to God. For Charity conducts us by the sure road of the Divine commandments to the kingdom of heaven, where she finally unites us with God in a loving and eternal embrace.

We now go on to speak of the commandments of God, which are ten in number. Hence they are sometimes called the *Decalogue*, which means the ten words of God to man.

Q. Say the ten commandments.
A. I am the Lord thy God, who brought thee out of the land of Egypt, and out of the house of bondage.

1. Thou shalt not have strange gods before me. Thou shalt not make to thyself any graven thing, nor the likeness of anything that is in heaven above or in the earth beneath, nor of those things that are in the waters under the earth ; thou shalt not adore them nor serve them.

2. Thou shalt not take the name of the Lord thy God in vain.

3. Remember that thou keep holy the Sabbath day.

4. Honour thy father and thy mother.

5. Thou shalt not kill.

6. Thou shalt not commit adultery.

7. Thou shalt not steal.

8. Thou shalt not bear false witness against thy neighbour.

9. Thou shalt not covet thy neighbour's wife.

10. Thou shalt not covet thy neighbour's goods.

Yes, my dear children, these are the Ten Commandments, by which Almighty God makes known to us his Divine Will, and instructs us in the duty which we owe to him, to our neighbour, and to ourselves. They contain in themselves a short summary of all our obligations, and are the rule by which we should form our lives and direct all our actions. They are just, they are holy, they are true, they are unchangeable; for they are the commands of God, who is Justice, Holiness and Truth itself, and in whom, as the Apostle says, "there is no change or shadow of alteration." * They are the light of our pilgrimage here below, they are the path to eternal life, they are the source of all happiness here and hereafter. Hence the Psalmist beautifully cries out—

" Oh, how I have loved thy law, O Lord !
It is my meditation all the day.
Thy word is a lamp to my feet, and a light to my
　　paths.†
The law of the Lord is unspotted, converting souls ;
The testimony of the Lord is faithful, giving wisdom
　　to little ones.
The justices of the Lord are right, rejoicing hearts ;
The commandment of the Lord is lightsome, en-
　　lightening the eyes.
The fear of the Lord is holy, enduring for ever and
　　ever ;
The judgments of the Lord are true, justified in
　　themselves.
More to be desired than gold and many precious stones,
　　and sweeter than honey and the honeycomb :
For thy servant keepeth them, and in keeping them
　　there is a great reward." ‡

Let us, my dear children, imitate the pious David in his love for the Divine commandments. Let us try to understand them well and keep them faithfully, and we shall find by our own experience the truth of what holy David says, that they fill the heart with a sweet consolation, which all the false joys and pleasures of the world can never bestow,

* James, i. 17.　　　　　　　　 † Ps. cxviii. 97, 105.
‡ Ps. xvii. 8-12.

and that they draw down upon those who faithfully observe them the most abundant blessings from God, both here and hereafter.

I told you just now that it is by keeping the commandments of God that we show our love to him. But whoever loves God truly, loves his neighbour likewise for the sake of God; for no one can love the Creator without loving the creature, the work of his hands; nor can any one love our Blessed Redeemer without loving his fellow man, whom our dear Lord died to save. Now, it is the ten commandments which teach us how to practice this double love, the love of God and of our neighbour. The first three commandments show us how to love God, and the last seven how to love our neighbour. Hence it is that they were written by God on *two* tables of stone—the one containing the first three commandments, which treat of our duty to God, and the other the remaining seven, which instruct us in our duty to our neighbour. Hence, also, our Blessed Lord declares that the whole of the commandments may be reduced to these two, the love of God and our neighbour; for, being asked by the Pharisees, on a certain occasion, which was " the great commandment of the law," he made them this beautiful answer, " *Thou shalt love the Lord thy God with thy whole heart, and with thy whole soul, and with thy whole mind.* This is the greatest and the first commandment. And the second is like to this, *Thou shalt love thy neighbour as thyself.* On these two commandments dependeth the whole law and the prophets." *

You have said the ten commandments for me as they come in the catechism, I will now teach you them in verse. Perhaps you will remember them better in this way, and when you grow up will be

* Matt. xxii. 35-40.

able to teach them to others. For, notice, my dear
children, that it is a great charity to teach the commandments to those who do not know them; it is
like pointing out to them the road which leads to
heaven. Listen now, and I will tell you the verses.
Each of the commandments is contained in two short
lines—

1. I am the Lord, and thou shalt serve
    No other God but me;
2. Thou shalt not take God's name in vain,
    Nor swear unlawfully.

3. Remember that thou always keep
    The holy Sabbath day;
4. Thy parents honour, serve and love
    And cheerfully obey.

5. Thou shalt not kill, nor do those things
    Which oft to murder lead;
6. Do not commit adultery
    By unchaste word or deed.

7. Thou shalt not steal, nor waste, nor cheat,
    And all thy debts repay;
8. False witness thou shalt never bear,
    And calumny unsay.

9. Thou shalt not covet thy neighbour's wife,
    Such sinful thoughts confess;
10. Thou shalt not covet thy neighbour's goods,
    Nor aught he may possess.

We come now to speak of the giving of the commandments on Mount Sinai.

Q. Who gave the ten commandments ?
A. God gave them on Mount Sinai.

Yes, *God gave them* to Moses and the Children of
Israel *on Mount Sinai*. They were spoken by the

mouth of God himself in the hearing of all the people, and they were written by him afterwards on tables of stone, that the Jews might have them always before their eyes, and might not be able to plead ignorance as an excuse for breaking them. But do not think that they were given to the Jews only, or intended for them alone. They were given through the Jews to all mankind, for they contain the unchangeable law of God, which all men are equally bound to obey. Nay, even before God gave the commandments on Mount Sinai, man was still bound to keep them. But you will say, "How could he be bound to keep them, if he did not know them; and how could he know them if God had not spoken them?" My dear children, the commandments of God were engraven on the hearts of men, even before they were spoken on Mount Sinai, or written on stone tables. For when we are born, we have a *natural* knowledge of right and wrong imprinted on our souls by the hand of our Creator. We know, for example, that it is wrong to steal, fight, or tell lies, and that it is right to adore God, obey our parents, and to be truthful and honest, long before any one tells us, or before we can read and learn our catechism But how is it that we know this before we are taught it? It is by the light of our *Reason*, that noble gift which God has given to man to guide him to his duty, and by the voice of our *Conscience*. Our reason teaches us what is good and what is evil, and our conscience tells us when we do it. You have often heard, I am sure, your conscience whispering in your heart when you have done wrong, telling you that you have committed sin and offended God. How unhappy you then felt! The voice of your conscience was like a sting in your soul, making you feel wretched and miserable until you had forgotten your fault, or,

what is better, had become sorry for it and come to
our Blessed Lord, in the person of his priest, to
confess it.   On the contrary, when you had done a
good act, for example, given something to the poor,
overcome a bad temper, forgiven an injury, or done
a kind turn to a companion, your conscience made
you feel very happy, telling you that you had done
a good deed, and that God would reward you.   You
see, then, that we have got a law engraven on our
hearts, teaching us our duty, as well as a law written
in the Holy Scriptures.   This law, which we have
within us, is called the *Natural* or *Unwritten Law*,
and by it the world was governed from the Creation
until the time of Moses.   It was this law, which
caused Cain to know and feel that he had done a
very wicked thing when he killed his brother Abel.
It was this law which made the brothers of Joseph
say to one another, when they fell into misfortune,
" We deserve to suffer these things because we have
sinned against our brother Joseph." *   You will now
understand what we mean by the *Natural* or *Unwritten*, and what by the *Written Law*.   The Natural
Law is the light of our reason and the voice of our
conscience, which are a part of our nature, and teach
us what is good or evil, and when we have done it ;
the Written Law teaches us the same thing in
words, written by the finger of God himself.

At first, as I have told you, after the creation of
the world, mankind were governed only by the
Natural or Unwritten Law.   Two thousand five
hundred years passed away before the will of God
was made known to man in express words.   It is
true that God did speak at times to mankind, for
example, to our first parents, Adam and Eve, in the
garden of Paradise, and in later years to the holy
patriarchs, Abraham, Isaac and Jacob, but it was

* Gen. xlii. 21.

principally to reveal by degrees the great mystery of the Incarnation of his Divine Son, by whom the world was to be saved. And when he did speak to man to reprove him for his crimes, as in the case of our first parents, and that of the murderer, Cain, he did not lay down any set commandments for man to obey, but left him still to be guided by the same Unwritten Law engraven in his heart. Unhappily mankind, blinded by their passions, refused to be governed by this law, and gave way to the most guilty excesses. The world became steeped in sin through the universal corruption of mankind, and was by the just anger of God swept with the waters of a mighty deluge. Of all mankind, Noah and his family alone were saved, being preserved by God in the ark, which floated on the top of the angry waters. A new race of men, sprung from the three sons of Noah, new peopled the earth, but they, in like manner, shut their eyes to the light of reason, and their ears to the voice of conscience, preferring to live like beasts, which have no understanding, slaves to their own appetites and passions. Almighty God then chose a single nation to preserve the knowledge of the true religion, and to hand down to future ages the promises which he had made regarding the coming of his Divine Son. This nation was that of the Jews, descended from Abraham, whom God called out of the land of Mesopotamia into that of Chanaan, which he promised to give to his descendants to be their country and abode. Very many years, however, passed away before this promise was fulfilled. During this time the Jews gradually grew into a great nation, but had no country of their own. They dwelt in the land of Egypt, where the kings or Pharaohs, as they were called, were at first kind to them, but afterwards cruelly oppressed them. God did not, however, forget his people, or the promise which he had made to their forefathers. He sent them a deliverer in the person of Moses, and forced the Egyptians, by means of ten terrible plagues or scourges, to let the Israelites depart from the land. Moses then led them into the neighbouring desert, while the Angel of God went before them, in the form of a bright cloud by day, and a pillar of fire by night. Having brought them to the . borders of the Red Sea, where they were closely pursued by Pharaoh and the army of the Egyptians, Moses, by the command of God, raised his wand over the waters, which immediately divided so as to allow a passage to the Israelites, but when they had passed through returned to their natural course, and swallowed up the army of their pursuers. They now advanced into the sandy Desert that lay between the Red Sea and the rich and fertile land of Chanaan, which God had promised to give them. Here they began to murmur against Moses and his brother Aaron, complaining that they had led them out to starve in the wilderness. Almighty God was angry with his ungrateful people; nevertheless, in his goodness he worked a fresh miracle to relieve their distress. By his Almighty Power he caused a delicious food called Manna to be rained down each night from heaven, which continued to support them during the whole period of their wandering in the Desert. He, moreover, bade Moses strike the hard rock with his wand, and there issued forth a clear stream of water to allay their thirst.

You would imagine that after all these favours the Jews would, out of pure gratitude and love to God, have served him faithfully according to the light and knowledge which they possessed. But alas! they proved faithless to their Divine Benefactor, and preferred to follow their blind passions and sinful appetites rather than to be guided by the law which he had planted in their hearts. Then it was that Almighty God determined to deliver to them his Divine commandments in express words, and at the same time to set before them the terrible consequences of disobedience to his law, and the rich rewards which he had in store for those who faithfully observed it. Knowing the Jews, however, to be a hard-hearted and stiff-necked race, he determined to deliver his commandments to them in a manner that would strike terror into their hearts, and fill them with the deepest awe and reverence. Accordingly, three months after their departure from Egypt, he assembled them at the foot of Mount Sinai, and ordered them to encamp about the mountain, but at a respectful distance. He then bade them keep three solemn days of preparation, spending the time in prayer and fasting, and purifying themselves from all uncleanness. Meanwhile, by his command, Moses drew round the foot of the holy mountain a boundary which none were permitted to pass under pain of death.

The third day dawned, the sky was clear and serene, and the rising sun lit up with its bright rays the summit of Sinai. Suddenly, however, the scene changed; a black cloud overshadowed the mountain, dreadful peals of thunder rolled through the air, and vivid flashes of lightning sped from side to side through the gathering darkness. Then did the Lord descend in fire upon the steep summit, and call to him the prophet Moses. Meanwhile, the whole of the mountain appeared involved in thick smoke, in the midst of which an incessant stream of flames arose as from a glowing furnace. The shrill and swelling clangour of a loud trumpet was heard at the same time; the people trembled, and kept within their tents. Summoned, however, at the command of God, to stand about the foot of the mountain, they trembled still more when they heard the voice of God declaring to them, as it were, in tones of thunder, the ten commandments—-

" I am the Lord thy God, who brought thee out of the Land of Egypt and out of the house of bondage.

1. *Thou shalt not have strange gods before me. Thou shalt not make to thyself a graven thing, nor the likeness of anything that is in heaven above, or in the earth beneath, nor of those things that are in the waters under the earth. Thou shalt not adore them nor serve them.*

2. *Thou shalt not take the name of the Lord thy God in vain;* for the Lord will not hold him guilt-less, that shall take the name of the Lord his God in vain.

3. *Remember that thou keep holy the Sabbath day.* Six days shalt thou labour and shalt do all thy works. But on the seventh day is the Sabbath of the Lord thy God; thou shalt do no work on it, thou, nor thy son, nor thy daughter, nor thy man servant, nor thy maid servant, nor thy beast, nor the stranger that is within thy gates. For in six days the Lord made heaven and earth, and the sea, and all things that are in them, and rested on the seventh day, therefore the Lord blessed the seventh day, and sanctified it.

4. *Honour thy father and thy mother,* that thou mayst be long lived upon the land which the Lord thy God will give thee.

5. *Thou shalt not kill.*

6. *Thou shalt not commit adultery.*

7. *Thou shalt not steal.*

8. *Thou shalt not bear false witness against thy neighbour.*

9. *Thou shalt not covet thy neigbour's wife;*

10. Nor his house, nor his field, nor his man servant, nor his maid servant, nor his ox, nor his ass, nor anything that is his.

" And all the Israelites," continues the Holy Scripture, " when they heard these words, and beheld the flames, and the Mount smoking, were exceedingly terrified, and stood afar off. And they said to Moses, *Speak thou to us and we will hear, let not the Lord speak to us lest we die.* And Moses said to the people, *Fear not, for the Lord is come to prove you, and that the dread of him may be in you, and you may not sin.*" *

Such, my dear children, is the account handed down to us in the Sacred Writings of the giving of the ten commandments, from which we see how important and how sacred they are, since the Great God of heaven gave them in person to mankind, and gave them in a manner so solemn and so awful. Let us bear them ever in our hearts, and shew them in our conduct. Let us, with the royal prophet, frequently reflect upon them, and set them before us as the rule by which we are to form our lives. We shall find them, as he tells us, " a lamp to our feet and a light on our path " to heaven. Though hard in appearance they become sweet and easy in practice, and, what is the most consoling, they are the sure road to eternal life. Listen to what God himself said to the Jews about the care with which they should cherish and meditate upon the commandments—

" These words which I command thee this day shall be in thy heart. And thou shalt tell them to thy children, and thou shalt meditate upon them, sitting in thy house, and walking on thy journey, sleeping and rising. And thou shalt bind them as a sign on thy hand, and they shall be and shall move between thy eyes. And thou shalt write them in the entry and on the doors of thy house." †

* Exodus, xx.; Deut. v.   † Deut. vi. 7-9, and xi. 19, &c.

Q. Are we bound to keep them?

A. We are; for our Lord says, "If thou wilt enter into life, keep the commandments."—*Matt.* xix. 17.

We come now to speak of the strict obligation we are under of keeping the commandments of God. It seems hardly necessary to prove that we are bound to do this, for our reason tells us that it is the part of God to command and of man to obey. As, however, we so often fail in this duty, it will be well for me to remind you why it is that we are so strictly bound to keep the commandments of our Good God.

It is related in the Holy Scripture that when Almighty God delivered the ten commandments to the Jews on Mount Sinai, he began by uttering these solemn words which you are taught to repeat at the beginning of the commandments:

"I am the Lord thy God, who brought thee out of the land of Egypt and out of the house of bondage."

In these words God himself has shewn us why it is most just and reasonable that we should give a willing and entire obedience to all that he commands us.

In the first place he is *the Lord our God*, that is to say the Great Being who created, governs and preserves the whole universe, and who is the Supreme Lord or Master of us and of all things. For we all are the work of his Divine Hands, made out of nothing, and made for the very purpose of loving and serving him. This is one of the best and strongest motives for keeping the commandments of God; for it would be monstrous if we should refuse to obey him who gave us our being, and who continually preserves and supports us. If you were to make anything, as I once told you, would you not expect it to do that for which you made it? How just, then, that you should obey God who made you out of nothing, and who made you for this very end, that you might do his Will, or, in other words, keep his commandments.

In the second place, Almighty God is not only entitled to our obedience because he is our Sovereign Lord and Master, but also because he has *brought us out of the land of Egypt, and out of the house of bondage.* You think, perhaps, that these words were spoken to the Jews only, and you are ready to acknowledge that it would have been very ungrateful of them not to keep the commandments of that Good God who had just before brought them in safety out of a land where they had been so harshly treated, and which had been to them, in very truth, a house of cruel slavery. But, my dear children, has not God done far more for *us* than for the Jews, and has he not, therefore, a still better right to *our* love and service? We, too, were slaves to a cruel tyrant, one far more cruel than the Egyptian Pharaoh, namely, to the devil, who kept us bound by the chains of original and actual sin; nor could we ever have recovered our liberty or entered the promised land of heaven, had not the Son of God, in his Infinite Goodness, come down to redeem us with his own Blood and conduct us to eternal life. This great work of our redemption he has accomplished by dying for us on the cross, becoming thereby our true Paschal Lamb, of which that slain by the Jews on coming out of Egypt was but a type and figure. And now he conducts us to the promised land by the guidance of the ministers of his Church, feeding us, in our passage through the desert of this life, with the heavenly manna of the Blessed Eucharist, and the living water of his Divine grace. Ah! if the Jews were ungrateful for not keeping the law of their Divine Benefactor, a thousand times more so are Christians if they refuse to obey the commandments of God from whom they have received still greater graces and more precious favours.

You see now why justice and gratitude require that we should keep the commandments of God, but there is another reason which our Lord sets before us to encourage us to observe faithfully the Divine Law. It is contained in those words of our Blessed Saviour, which you have repeated from the catechism, *If thou wilt enter into life keep the commandments.* In other words, he here declares that those, and those only, who keep his commandments shall obtain eternal life. These words were spoken by our Lord in answer to that young man who came and put to him the question, "*Good master, what good shall I do, that I may have life everlasting?* And Jesus said to him, *If thou wilt enter into life, keep the commandments.* He said to him, *Which?* And Jesus said, *Thou shalt do no murder. Thou shalt not commit adultery. Thou shalt not steal. Thou shalt not bear false witness. Honour thy father and thy mother,* and *Thou shalt love thy neighbour as thyself.*" * By these words our Blessed Lord has taught us that the commandments are the high road to heaven. He who keeps the commandments is secure of his salvation as long as he continues to observe them; but he who keeps them not will surely be lost, unless he returns to the right path by a true and sincere repentance.

But some one will perhaps say that the commandments of God are hard and difficult to keep. I will grant that they are hard, and yet our Lord says, "My yoke is sweet and my burden light." What, then! is the yoke, that is the law of God, sweet and easy too? Yes, for our Lord says so. But how is it that the same commandments are hard and difficult, and at the same time sweet and easy? I will tell you. They are *hard* to nature but *easy* to

* Matt. xix. 16-19.

Divine grace. They are *difficult*, nay impossible for man to keep if left to himself, but *easy* if assisted by Almighty God. But is God always ready to give his grace? Yes, to those who seek it. And how must we seek it? By prayer and the Sacraments. You see now why prayer and the Sacraments are so much spoken of in the catechism. They strengthen and enable us to walk in that road, which is the only one that leads to eternal life, viz., the way of the Divine commandments.

I am now going to relate to you the history of two travellers who set out together on a distant journey. You must try and find out the meaning of what I tell you.

STORY OF THE TWO TRAVELLERS.

Two travellers undertook a journey to a distant city. The way by which they had to travel was narrow and difficult. At one time it lay across a dreary and sandy plain, at another over desolate and rugged mountains. They had, however, the consolation of knowing that the road was a direct one, that it was perfectly safe from the attacks of robbers, and that, as long as they followed the plain and easy directions with which they were furnished, they could not possibly go astray. They were, moreover, supplied with provisions and everything necessary for the journey.

Thus provided, they set out one fine Spring morning. The elder of the two travellers, with staff in hand, walked steadily onwards, carrying his provisions in his wallet suspended over his back. The younger, on the contrary, stopped continually to look back or gaze about him, and, at times, cast a longing eye on a smiling tract of country which lay towards the left hand at a little distance from the road. At length he became weary of carrying his stock of provisions, and, in order to ease himself, opened his wallet and threw the contents first on one side and then on the other, until he had exhausted the whole. His companion reproved him for his folly, and warned him that he would soon stand in need of refreshment, for that the heat of the day was now approaching, and the most difficult part of the road still remained to be traversed. His young friend, however, paid no heed to his advice, and laughed at his friendly warning.

Mid-day had now arrived, and the two travellers, oppressed with heat, sat down to rest and refresh themselves. The elder, who had prudently preserved his provisions, renewed his strength by a substantial meal, and was soon ready to resume his journey with fresh vigour. The younger, on the contrary, already wearied with the route, now felt faint and hungry from the want of food. Having rested, however, for a while, and swallowed a few crumbs which he found in a corner of his wallet, he rose to his feet and endeavoured to drag himself along the road which at length brought them to the foot of the mountain. The elder traveller began vigorously to surmount the steep ascent, while the younger, at the sight of it, became thoroughly disheartened, and sat down to look about him and divert his mind from the difficulties which remained to be encountered. His eye reverted to the smiling meadows which he had before observed, and which appeared still more charming now that they were lit up by the bright rays of the midday sun. While thus idly gazing, he perceived a path leading from the main road to the object of his admiration. Without allowing himself a moment for reflection, he immediately rose and began to follow it. His companion, seeing him, turned and called after him. " My friend," said he, " do you not know that the road which you are quitting is the only one which will lead us to our journey's end ? " " I know it," replied the other, " but I prefer those charming meadows to this rough and difficult ascent." " But," rejoined his companion, struck with amazement at his folly, " of what use will it be to you to wander through those pleasant fields, if, so far from helping you on your way, they only lead you further from your destination ?"   " I grant that it will not help me on my road," returned the other, " but I do not feel able to get up this steep hill. I would sooner walk along the broad and easy path that leads to yon meadows, where I see many beautiful flowers, and shall, no doubt, find sweet and delicious fruits."   " Foolish man," replied his friend, " those fruits, as you well know, contain a deadly poison, and bring certain death to whoever tastes of them; while the path you speak of leads to a frightful abyss, situated in the midst of those verdant plains."

The words of the prudent traveller were lost upon his companion. He followed the tempting path, eat of the poisonous fruits, and was seized with a fatal languor, under the influence of which he incautiously approached the brink of the abyss, and fell headlong into it. Meanwhile, his companion steadily pursued the rugged mountain path, and arrived safely before night closed in, at the city to which he was journeying.

My dear children, do you understand the meaning of this history, which is what is called a *Parable*, that is, a story told to convey a useful lesson? You yourselves are the travellers who are journeying to a distant city, the heavenly Jerusalem. The road by which you are to arrive there, and it is the only one which leads to your journey's end, is the way of God's commandments. As long as you follow it you are perfectly safe from all danger. The wicked spirits, who are ever watching to rob you of your treasure, the love and friendship of God, can never succeed in doing so unless you turn aside either to the right hand or the left. Moreover, you are supplied with abundant food to support and strengthen you on the road. This food is the grace of God, which we can obtain at all times by Prayer and the Holy Sacraments. The foolish and thoughtless make little account of this food, nay they trample it under foot by their neglect, and the consequence is that they grow every day weaker and more languid in the service of God. They begin to cast a longing eye at the pleasures and vanities of the world, and at the first great difficulty which they meet with on their route, in spite of the voice of their own conscience, and the warnings of the ministers of God, they abandon the path of virtue, and follow the broad and easy road of their passions. Each step they take leads them further from God and nearer to the abyss of hell, but they heed it not amid the false joys and empty pleasures of a worldly life. Instead of the heavenly food of God's grace, they now nourish themselves with the forbidden fruit of sin, which produces in their soul a fatal languor and insensibility, overcome with which they at length sleep the sleep of death, and, by a just judgment of God, fall headlong into the abyss.

Meanwhile, the prudent Christian steadily pursues

his path to heaven, without allowing his attention to be diverted to this side or that by the allurements of vice. Supported by the grace of God, with which he constantly nourishes his soul in prayer and the Sacraments, he surmounts all obstacles, and, persevering to the end of his life, happily arrives, when the night of death closes in, at the term of his labours, the eternal possession of God amid the joys of heaven.

SECOND INSTRUCTION.

What the Commandments teach us.   The First Commandment. What it commands. Faith, Hope, Charity, and Religious Worship.

Q. What do these commandments teach us ?
A. They teach us to avoid evil and do good.

The commandments *teach us to avoid evil and do good*, in other words, they both forbid and command ; they forbid us to commit sin, and they command us to practise virtue. For it is not sufficient for us to keep from doing evil, we must also *do good*, or we should shew very little love to Almighty God. You would not say that a boy really loved his father if he contented himself with not doing what his father forbade him, and never troubled himself about performing what he enjoined him.

There are some people who make the great mistake of thinking that it is sufficient to avoid evil in order to get to heaven. They will say, for example, " Oh, such a person was a very good man ; he never cursed or swore, he never got drunk, he never quarrelled with or cheated his neighbour; surely he is gone to heaven." They forget that the commandments teach us to do good as well as to avoid evil. He may not have cursed or sworn; but did he go to Mass and frequent the Sacraments? He may not have been a drunkard; but did he keep the fasts of the Church? He may not have quarrelled with or cheated his neighbour; but did he relieve the poor? did he forgive his enemies? did he love his neighbour as himself? Hence our Blessed Lord tells us, that at the last day he will judge us not only for the evil we have done, but for the good we have left undone, "I was hungry and *you gave me not* to eat," &c.* And again he tells us in the parable, that the unprofitable servant who hid his master's talent will be cast out into exterior darkness, not for having made a bad use of his master's money, but for not having turned it to good account.† So will our Blessed Lord condemn us also, not only if we have abused his gifts to commit sin, but also if we have not employed them to fulfil the duties which we owe to God and our neighbour.

Listen, and I will tell you a little history, from which you will see how those who keep the commandments of God, besides securing their own salvation, are often the happy means of helping others on the way to heaven.

EXAMPLE THE BEST SERMON.

During the cruel persecution of the Chinese Emperor, Hien Fong, A.D. 1850, a Christian convert named Yin, came to settle at the pagan town of Lo-kia-tien, where he began to work at his trade, which was that of a tile maker. He had not received much instruction, and was by no means clever, though fervent and pious; hence he made no attempt to

* Matt. xxv. 42, &c.   † Matt. xxv. 24, &c.

announce the Gospel to his new neighbours. Being, however, a man of simple manners, and pure, innocent and upright life, he preached much by his example. He heard those around him cursing and swearing at each other, *he* never cursed any one. He saw them quarrelling and fighting, *he* was never seen in a passion or at variance with his neighbour. They got drunk, *he* was always sober. Moreover, he regularly observed certain days of fasting and abstinence, and recited without fail his morning and evening prayers.

A course of life so different to that of his neighbours excited the curiosity of some gardeners who lived near him. To satisfy themselves they came to visit him. "How is it," said they, "that you do not live as we do? You are not like us; what sort of man are you?" "I am a Christian," he replied, "and I do nothing but follow the teaching of my religion." "Your religion!" said they, "what is your religion? and what is its teaching?" Explanations followed, and his religion was acknowledged to be good because *he* was good. In a short time eighteen Pagans expressed a wish to become Christians. Yin at once sent for the Catechist of the district, who instructed and encouraged the catechumens, and assisted them to build a small chapel, where they might assemble to sanctify the Sunday and learn the truths of religion. Thus was laid the foundation of a flourishing Christian mission, which bore good fruit in the course of the following summer, when several of the new converts suffered the most cruel torments before the tribunal of the Chinese mandarin, rather than consent to trample on the Cross of Christ.—*Annals of the Propagation of the Faith*, vol. xiv. p. 79.

Q. What is the first commandment?

A. Thou shalt not have strange gods before me. Thou shalt not make to thyself any graven thing, nor the likeness of anything that is in heaven above, or in the earth beneath, nor of those things that are in the waters under the earth; thou shalt not adore them nor serve them.

We come now to speak of the first of the ten commandments, which teaches us to render to Almighty God the homage and worship due to him. We should not, indeed, need any commandment to induce us to offer to that Great and Infinitely Perfect Being, who created and continually preserves us, frequent acts of adoration, praise and thanksgiving; but, alas! man is too apt to neglect the plainest duties, and too often repays the love and blessings of God with the blackest ingratitude. This commandment recalls us to our duty; it teaches us in what manner God requires us to worship him, and forbids us to perform any act that is contrary to the worship which we owe him.

What, then, is the first commandment? *Thou shalt not have strange gods before me.* It is Almighty God who here speaks, and he speaks to the people of Israel. As if he would say, "*Thou,* my chosen people, on whom I have bestowed so many favours, and whom I have delivered from so many evils, shalt not be guilty of the grievous sin of adoring *strange gods,* like the other nations around thee. *Thou shalt not,* like them, *make to thyself any graven thing,* that is, any idol, carved or moulded by the hand of man, *nor the likeness* or figure *of anything that is in heaven above, or in the earth beneath, nor of those things that are in the waters under the earth,* in other words, either of bird, or beast, or reptile. And if I forbid thee to make them, it is only that thou art not to make them for the purpose of giving them that Divine worship which is due to me alone, for *thou shalt not adore them nor serve them.*" This is the great and awful commandment regarding the homage due to himself, which Almighty God gave to the Children of Israel, and gives through them to us.

You will wonder, perhaps, why the whole of the first commandment is taken up with forbidding us to commit a crime, which seems too foolish and wicked for any one to fall into, namely, that of idolatry, or the worship of false gods and idols. The reason is, because the crime of idolatry is directly opposed to the worship of the One, True, and Living God, and also because it is the sin into which the Jews, owing to the example of the neighbouring nations, were in the greatest danger of falling.

But notice that the first commandment, in forbidding us to worship *false gods*, as a matter of course commands us to worship the *True God*, and in the manner that he prescribes.   It commands us to perform certain duties which we owe to God as our Sovereign Lord and Master, and it forbids us to commit certain sins which are opposed to those duties.   The catechism first tells us what the duties are which we are bound by this commandment to practise.   Tell me then—

Q. What are we commanded to do by the first commandment ?

A. We are commanded to believe in the one true and living God, to hope in him, to love him, and to serve him all our days.

From this answer you see that there are four distinct duties taught us by the first commandment. We must *believe* in God, *hope* in him, and *love* him ; in other words, we must practise the three virtues of Faith, Hope and Charity, and lastly, we must *serve* God, that is, adore and worship him.   Faith, Hope, Charity and Religious Worship are, therefore, the four duties which we are here commanded to fulfil.   And when we come to speak of the sins forbidden by this commandment, you will find that each of them is opposed to one or other of these four duties.   So that you see, if you wish, in preparing for Confession, to find out what sins you have committed against the first commandment, you have nothing to do but to think of these four duties, and see whether you have fulfilled them or done anything contrary to them.   Thus, for example, if you have neglected to learn your catechism or denied your religion, you have sinned against the virtue of Faith ; if you have despaired of God's mercy, you have sinned against Hope ; and so of the rest.

Let us now see, my dear children, what we must do in order to fulfil these four duties. And first, as regards the duty of *Faith.*

What is Faith? The catechism tells you that Faith is *to believe without doubting all that God teaches and the Church proposes.* In other words, it is to receive and firmly hold fast, on the authority of God himself, all those truths that he has revealed to man, and proposes to our belief by means of his Church, which he has appointed to teach us in his name. This great virtue of Divine Faith is the foundation of all religion, and of all the other virtues; hence it is the very first duty which God teaches us by his commandments. Faith is a gift of God, which he bestows upon us at our Baptism; by this commandment we are commanded not only to *have* faith, but to put it to a proper use. For there is a great difference between *having* faith, and *making use of* this precious gift. A man may be a carpenter by trade, but he is a worthless one, if he never handles his tools. Again, a person may be clever enough to be able to carve a statue or paint a picture, but of what use is he if he never uses his talent? So, also, a person may be a Christian by being baptised and having the gift of faith, but he is an idle unprofitable servant if he never turns this great gift to account by making acts of faith.

You will ask me, perhaps, what I mean by *acts of faith.* What is an act of faith? It is simply declaring our belief, either by word or deed, in the truths, or in any particular truth that God teaches us. For example, if you say, "O my God! I believe all that thou teachest me by thy Church," you make an act of faith in all the truths of religion; and again, if you say, "I believe that there are three persons in one God, because God has revealed it," you make an act of faith in the mystery of the

Blessed Trinity. Moreover, if you express your belief in any truth of religion by some outward act, even though you say no words at all, you make a real act of faith in that truth. For example, if you take off your cap in passing a Catholic Church, or bend your knee before the tabernacle, you make an act of faith in the real presence of our Lord in the Blessed Sacrament, since by this outward act of reverence you shew your belief in this mystery. And finally, if you do all your actions in the presence of God, remembering that his Eye is always upon you, you are living in the continual exercise of the virtue of faith, for it is by faith you know that God is everywhere present, and thus in every action you perform there is an act of faith implied, though not expressed in words. This exercise of a continual remembrance of the presence of God is most pleasing to him, and of great profit to our souls; whence St. Paul says, that " the just man liveth by faith." *

You will now understand what is meant by an act of faith. I will therefore go on to tell you when it is that we are strictly bound to make such acts, and when to neglect making them, would be a grievous sin against the first commandment.

In the first place, we are bound to make an act of faith, *as soon as we come to the use of reason,* for it is fitting that as soon as we are able to know anything, we should submit our understanding to those truths which Almighty God teaches us.

Secondly, we are bound to make acts of faith *frequently in the course of our lives.* To neglect to do so would be to abuse the great gift of Divine faith which God has given us at our Baptism. I do not mean, however, that we are obliged to say the long act of faith, which comes in your prayer book and catechism. The " I believe," which you say

* Heb. x. 38.

every day in your morning and night prayers, is an act of faith, and indeed every act of religion may, as I have already shown you, be considered in a certain sense as an act of faith, since we should not worship or pray to God unless we believed in him. So that you see there is no fear, if you have attended to your religion, of your not having fulfilled this obligation.

In the third place, we are obliged to profess our faith, *whenever the glory of God or the good of our neighbour requires it.* The martyrs, for example, when questioned by their persecutors, whether they were Christians, could not have denied their religion without committing a grievous sin.

Fourthly, we are bound to make an act of faith *whenever we are grievously tempted against that virtue, and cannot well overcome the temptation in any other way.* For though it is better generally to despise such temptations, and turn our thoughts to something else, or make a little act of the love of God, yet sometimes, when the temptation is very strong, we shall find it the best remedy to make an act of faith, saying, for example, " O my God, because thou art the very Truth, I believe all that thou hast taught and the Church proposes."

Finally, we are bound to make an act of faith *when we come to die,* for it is fitting that we should end life as we have begun it, with the submission of our understanding to God and the expression of our firm belief in those mysteries which will soon be revealed to us in another life.

We have a beautiful example, related in the Holy Scripture, of the courage with which we should profess our faith, even at the cost of our lives, whenever the glory of God or the good of our neighbour requires it. I mean the history of the martyrdom of the virtuous Eleazar.

MARTYRDOM OF ELEAZAR.

During the cruel persecution with which Antiochus afflicted the Jews, in the hope of inducing them to abandon the worship of the true God, a venerable old man named Eleazar was brought before the judge and ordered to eat swine's flesh, as a proof that he abandoned the observance of the law of Moses. On his refusal, they strove to force it into his mouth, but, as he manfully resisted, preferring death to the violation of the Law, he was ordered be to led to execution. On his way, those who accompanied him, moved with pity for him and respect for his old age, took him aside, and begged him to eat at least of some food which they brought him, and which was not forbidden by the Law, that in appearance he might be considered to have obeyed the king's orders, and so save his life. But he bravely made answer, " It doth not become our age to dissemble, whereby many young persons might think that Eleazar, at the age of fourscore and ten years, was gone over to the life of the heathens. And so they, through my dissimulation, should be deceived, and hereby should bring a curse and stain upon my old age. For though, for the present time, I should be delivered from the punishments of men, yet should I not escape the hand of the Almighty, neither alive nor dead." Having spoken thus, he was forthwith carried to execution. But when he was now ready to die with stripes, he groaned and said, " Oh Lord ! thou knowest that, whereas I might be delivered from death, I suffer grievous pains in body, but in soul am well content to suffer these things, because I fear thee." Thus did he die, leaving to the whole nation an example of virtue and fortitude.—2 Mach. vi.

You see now, my dear children, from what I have told you, that we are bound by the first commandment to exercise continually the gift of faith which God has bestowed upon us at our Baptism. But there is another obligation which the duty of believing necessarily carries with it, and it is that of *knowing* what we are bound to believe, in other words, the obligation of being instructed in the truths of religion. Whoever, therefore, neglects religious instruction, and grows up in ignorance of the great truths of religion, is guilty of a sin against this commandment. You will remember that I once told you * that there are some truths which it is so strictly necessary to know and believe that it is thought by many that no one can be saved who is ignorant of them. These truths are, that there is one God, that there are three Persons in God, that God the Son became man and died to save us, and that God will one day reward the good and punish the wicked. But besides these four great and *necessary truths*, there are certain other things in which it is the strict duty of every Christian to be instructed. Indeed, whoever remains wilfully ignorant of any of them, commits a mortal sin, and cannot be admitted to the Holy Sacraments. Thus every one is strictly bound to know—

1stly, The commandments of God, and those of the Church which especially concern him.

2ndly, The particular duties of his state or condition of life.

3rdly, The seven Sacraments, and the meanings of them, especially the use and meaning of those which it is his duty to receive, namely, Baptism, Confirmation, Holy Eucharist and Penance.

4thly, The Our Father, Hail Mary, and I believe.

These, my dear children, are the most necessary and important points of our instruction, but we ought also to obtain a fuller knowledge of our religion, as far as opportunity is afforded us. If, therefore, you neglect to learn your catechism, stay away from instruction, or do not pay any attention to it, you are guilty of a sin against the first commandment, of which you should accuse yourselves when you go to Confession. To neglect to learn all that we can

* Vol. I. p. 88.

about Almighty God and the truths that he teaches us, would be a mark of ingratitude to that Good God who has given us the gift of Faith, and has caused us, in preference to millions of others, to be born of Catholic parents, and to be made by Baptism members of the One, Holy, Catholic and Apostolic Church which his Divine Son has established upon earth to teach us the way to heaven. Let us thank God for so great a grace, and shew our gratitude to him by our eagerness to learn, and readiness to profit by those Divine truths which he has taught us.

We come now to speak of the second duty which we are taught by the first commandment to practise, namely, that of *hoping* in God; in other words, Almighty God commands us not only to believe in him, but to place in him all our trust and confidence. *Hope*, my dear children, follows close upon Faith; for it is what we believe about God which causes us to hope in him. Faith teaches us that God is All-powerful and can do whatever he pleases, also that he is infinitely Good and Merciful, and finally, that he has promised to hear our prayers, and grant us whatever is necessary for our salvation, if we make use of the proper means to obtain it. *Therefore* we hope in him; we trust to his Goodness, we rely on his Power, we place an unbounded confidence in his Divine promises. It is this beautiful virtue of Hope which comforts us in all our troubles, which supports us in all our trials and temptations. Without it the world would indeed be a dreary desert, while hell itself would be robbed of half its terrors, if Hope could ever enter into that abode of torments.

The virtue of Hope, like that of Faith, is implanted in our souls by the ever-Blessed Trinity at our Baptism, but we are bound by this commandment to cherish, preserve and increase it by continual acts. Thus it is our duty to make an act of Hope, as well as an act of Faith, *as soon as we come to the use of reason, at the approach of death,* and *frequently in the course of our lives.* We are also bound to make an act of Hope, *whenever we are strongly tempted against this virtue,* for example, in temptations to despair, and indeed *when we are in danger of being overcome by any temptation.* For it is only by God's help that we can secure the victory in temptation, and this help he has promised that he will never refuse to those who trust in him. We do, however, make an act of Hope whenever we *pray* to God, for why do we pray to him, except that we hope to obtain what we ask, because he is able, and willing, and has promised to grant it?

I must now say a few words about the sins which are opposed to the virtue of Hope, for they are, of course, forbidden by this commandment, though they are not mentioned in this part of the catechism; they are chiefly these two—*Presumption* and *Despair.*

Presumption, my dear children, is hoping either that God will give us what we have no right to expect, or that he will give us what we may indeed hope for, but without our taking the proper means to obtain it. Now this is hoping *too much.* Almighty God has promised only to give us what is good for us, and this on condition that we take those means to obtain it which he has provided. For example, he has promised to give us grace to overcome temptation, but he has not promised us the gift of working miracles or speaking in strange languages. For these gifts are not necessary, and, most probably, would not be good for us; therefore it would be Presumption to expect them. Again, he usually requires certain conditions on our own part before he grants us what is really good for us, so that if a person, for example, were to hope to keep from sin without praying to God for his grace and avoiding dangerous occasions, or, if he were to expect pardon for his sins without going to Confession, he would be guilty of the sin of Presumption, in hoping for these graces without doing what God requires of him.

The other great sin against the virtue of Hope is that of Despair. I have told you that Presumption is hoping *too much*; now Despair is just the contrary, it is hoping *too little*. In fact, it is giving up all hope, and is a most heinous sin against God; for it is as if we doubted the Infinite Mercy or Power of God, or disbelieved his Divine Promises. A person is guilty of Despair when he goes on in his sins, thinking that they are too great to be forgiven, or that his temptations are too strong to be overcome. It was into this terrible sin that the murderer Cain fell, when he said in his heart, " My iniquity is greater than that I may deserve pardon ;"* and it was in this way that the devil deceived the traitor Judas to his ruin, when he tempted him to give up all hope, and end his miserable life by his own hand.

The third duty which we are commanded by this commandment to practise is that of *loving* God.

Charity, or the love of God above all things, and of our neighbour as ourselves for the sake of God, is of all virtues the most noble and excellent. It is by Faith that we submit our *understanding* to Almighty God and the truths that he teaches us, but it is by Charity that we unite to him our *heart* and our *will*, which are the most noble part of our being. To love God and our neighbour is a strict duty, because God has so commanded us, but it is also a supreme honour and the source of all happiness. Hence St. Augustine beautifully cries out, " What art thou to me, O God, and what am I to thee, that thou shouldst command me to love thee, and shouldst be angry with me if I do not love thee,

* Gen. iv, 13.

and shouldst threaten me with great miseries! Is it then a small misery not to love thee?"* Yes, my dear children, it is indeed true that not to love God is the greatest misery that can befall us.

This beautiful virtue of Charity is implanted in our souls at Baptism, along with the virtues of Faith and Hope, and we are bound by the first commandment continually to exercise it during our lives. It is our duty, indeed, to make acts of the love of God more frequently than acts of Faith or Hope, because it is a nobler virtue, unites us more closely with God, and we have, moreover, received a special commandment to practise it. Thus Almighty God said to the Jews in the Old Law, "Thou shalt love the Lord thy God with thy whole heart, and with thy whole soul, and with thy whole strength."† And our Blessed Lord, repeating the same to his disciples, declares that in the love of God and our neighbour are contained the whole Law and the Prophets, that is, the whole of the commandments which God has made known to man.‡ Hence we are bound to make acts of this virtue, not only *at our coming to the use of reason, at the approach of death*, and *when it is necessary to overcome a strong temptation*, but also *when we approach the Sacraments, when we have fallen into grievous sin*, and *very frequently in the course of our lives*. Notice, however, that you do make an act of the Love of God, not only when you say the act of Charity which comes in the prayer book, but also when you make an act of sorrow for your sins by which you have offended God, when you do anything to please Almighty God, when you bear any suffering or trial for his sake, and when you try to prevent others from offending him by sin. For in all these things there is an act of the love of

* St. August. Confes. I. 5. † Deut. vi. 5.
‡ Matt. xxii. 37, &c.

God implied though not expressed, since the love of God is the motive for which you do them. In the same way you make acts of the love of your neighbour when you forgive injuries, when you relieve others in distress, or do them any act of kindness, as long, at least, as you do these things for the sake of God. Thus, you see, we may be making acts of the love of God and our neighbour all the day through, though we may not be thinking of doing so, or reading the act of Charity in our prayer book. It is useful, however, often to make direct acts of Divine Love, such as, " O, my Jesus! I love thee," or, " O, my God! I love thee with my whole heart, and for thy sake I love my neighbour as myself." We should also frequently ask of God to give us the grace of his holy love, saying to him, for example, when the clock strikes, " O, my God, teach me to love thee in time and eternity." Thus will the flame of Divine Love burn each day more brightly in our hearts, cleansing us more and more from sin, and urging us on to the practice of every good work. It is only by loving God here upon earth that we can hope to love and possess him for all eternity in heaven.

As we are commanded by the first commandment to love God above all things, and our neighbour for the sake of God, so we are forbidden by the same to do anything contrary to this double love. All sin, indeed, is contrary to the love of God, for no one can love God truly who wilfully offends him; but there are some sins which are especially contrary to the precept of charity, and are therefore especially forbidden by this commandment. For example, if we love riches, honours or pleasures more than God, we do not fulfil the duty of Charity, since by it we are bound to love God *above all things*. Again, if we never thank God for his benefits, if we never seek to please him, if we murmur at the trials and sufferings which he sends us, we sin against that tender love which we owe him. As the sins which are opposed to the love of our neighbour are especially forbidden by the other commandments, we shall speak of them later in their proper place.

We come now to speak of the fourth duty, which we are commanded by the first commandment to practise, viz., that of *serving* or worshipping Almighty God, all the days of our life. The duty of worshipping God is so deeply imprinted on the heart of man by God himself, that there has never been found a people or nation, who, however much they may have erred about the nature of God, have failed to follow some form of *Religious Worship*. For Almighty God being the Creator of all things, and the Sovereign Lord and Master of the universe, it stands to reason that we should adore him as such, praise and glorify him for his Infinite Perfections, thank him for his blessings, and implore from him those graces which we stand in need of. Now it is in these four acts, namely, in adoration, praise, thanksgiving and supplication, that Religious Worship consists. The most perfect way of worshipping God is by the *Holy Sacrifice of the Mass*, because in the Mass we offer to God his own Divine Son, who alone can adore, praise and thank him as he deserves, and whose supplications for man, being of infinite value, cannot fail to be heard. But as we cannot be always hearing Mass, we are also bound to render to God the worship due to him by frequent *prayer*, which we offer in the name of Jesus Christ, and in union with his merits. For it is only by the merits of our Blessed Lord that our prayers become pleasing to God, so pleasing indeed, that they cannot fail to be heard, if offered with proper dispositions. We are commanded, therefore, by the first commandment to pray, and to pray often. *When we come to the use of reason, in danger of death, when attacked by strong temptation, when we approach the Sacraments,* and *very frequently during our lives* we are bound to pray to God, to whom alone we can look for those graces that we continually stand in need of. Without God's grace we cannot be preserved from sin, and without prayer we cannot hope to obtain his grace. Prayer is thus, as it were the support and nourishment of the soul, without which it would soon grow faint and languid, and die the death of sin. Hence we are taught from our infancy to worship God each day of our lives by morning and evening prayer. Be faithful, my dear children, to this important duty, and try to perform it with attention and devotion. If you always say your morning and night prayers, and say them well, you may be sure that the blessing of God will attend you both day and night, that you will be preserved from innumerable sins, and receive many precious graces, of which you would otherwise be deprived.

There is another duty connected with the worship of God, which we are bound by this commandment to fulfil, viz., that of *receiving the Holy Sacraments,* and receiving them worthily. It is by the Sacraments that we are cleansed from sin, united to God, and provided with abundance of grace for the performance of all our other duties. I will say no more, however, about the Holy Sacraments now, because we shall speak about them later in another part of the Catechism.

When you come to Confession, you should examine yourselves carefully with regard to the manner in which you have said your prayers and approached the Sacraments. Thus, if you have neglected your morning and night prayers, said them badly, stayed away from the Sacraments or received them unworthily, you have been guilty of sins which are opposed to the duty of Religious Worship, and of which you should accuse yourself, under the first commandment.

I have now explained to you the four duties, which we are here commanded to render to Almighty God, namely to *believe* in him, to *hope* in him, to *love* him, and to *worship* him. If you wish to see an excellent example of the fulfilment of these duties, you will find it in the life of the holy king David.

EXAMPLE OF KING DAVID.

The holy King David, of whom the Sacred Scripture says, that he was "a man according to God's own heart," fulfilled, in an eminent degree, the fourfold duty of this commandment. His lively *faith* made him ever walk in the presence of God, look upon himself as the humblest of his servants, and deem himself happy in being able to contribute to the dignity and splendour of his worship. When his wife, Michol, mocked and derided him for dancing before the ark of God on its entrance into Jerusalem, he made her this beautiful answer, "Before God I will both play and make myself meaner than I have done, and I will be little in my own eyes." * His faith taught him that it was a greater honour to assist, in the most humble capacity, in the solemn services of religion, than to be the ruler of the kingdom of Israel.

Hope, or confidence in God, is the natural consequence of a lively faith. David's faith in the Divine Goodness and Power, led him to throw himself into the arms of Providence with the most unbounded confidence. "The Lord is my protector," he says, "and I have hoped in him." † "In God have I hoped, and I will not fear what man can do to me." ‡ Behold him, in his youth, advancing to the combat with the mighty giant Goliath, "Thou comest against me with a sword, and with a spear, and with a shield, but I come to thee in the name of the Lord of hosts." § Behold him also fleeing from the pursuit of Saul, or, in his old age, again a wanderer in the desert, while his son Absalom usurps his throne. Never, for a moment, does he waver in his unbounded confidence in the Divine Goodness and Providence.

The flames of Divine *love* burnt also brightly in the heart of David. His psalms and canticles are full of the sweetest expressions of praise, gratitude and love to God. "As the

* 2 Kings, vi. 21, 22.   † Ps. cxliii. 2.
‡ Ps. lv. 11.   § I. Kings, xvii. 45.

hart panteth after the fountains of water, so my soul panteth after thee, O God." *　And again, "What have I in heaven, and besides thee what do I desire on earth?　For thee my flesh and my heart hath fainted away: thou art the God of my heart, and my portion for ever." †　Tender, gentle and compassionate to all, David shewed the sincerity of his love to God by his love of his neighbour.　When Almighty God had sent a severe scourge upon the people, in punishment for David's sin, the latter wept bitter tears over their affliction, and besought God to spare them, begging him rather to turn the arm of his indignation upon himself, who was alone guilty.

Finally, where shall we find a man more zealous for the worship of God, more faithful in prayer, more exact in the duties of *religion*, than holy King David?　"O Lord," said he, "I have loved the beauty of thy house, and the place where thy glory dwelleth." ‡　"Better is one day in thy courts above thousands." §　And again, "Seven times in the day I have given praise to thee.　I meditated on thy commandments which I loved.　In the night I have remembered thy name.　I rose at midnight to give praise to thee.　I prevented the dawning of the day that I might meditate on thy words." ‖　Could we have a more perfect model of a life of prayer?

Another beautiful example of the practice of the duties of the first commandment will be found in the life of the virtuous Tobias.

HISTORY OF TOBIAS.

Tobias was one of the Israelites carried into captivity to Nineve by the Assyrian king, Teglathphalasar.　Though involved in the ruin of his country, he was no sharer in the crime of his people, which had drawn upon them this severe chastisement.　For the Holy Scripture says of Tobias, that "when all went to the golden calves which Jeroboam, king of Israel had made, he alone fled the company of all, and went to Jerusalem to the temple of the Lord, and there adored the Lord God of Israel, offering faithfully all his first fruits and his tithes." ¶

In a strange land, and in the midst of an idolatrous people, Tobias continued equally firm in his faith, and faithful

---

* Ps. xli. 1.　　　† Ps. lxxii. 25, 26.　　　‡ Ps. xxiii. 8.
§ Ps. lxxxiii. 11.　　　‖ Ps. cxviii.　　　¶ Tobias, i. 5-6.

to the practice of his religion. While the companions of his exile all fell away from their duty, and, contrary to the strict command of the Jewish law, "eat of the meats of the Gentiles, he kept his soul," as the Holy Scripture tells us, "and never was defiled with their meats." *

The virtues of Tobias, and his faithful observance of the duties of his religion, excited the admiration and gained for him the favour of the Assyrian king, who granted him a degree of liberty, along with other privileges, that was not allowed to the other captives. Tobias availed himself of these advantages to relieve his afflicted brethren. "He daily went among his kindred," as the Holy Scripture informs us, "and comforted them, and distributed to every one as he was able, out of his goods. He fed the hungry, and gave clothing to the naked, and was careful to bury the dead and those that were slain." † These works of mercy drew upon him the displeasure of the cruel King Sennacherib, who had now succeeded to the throne. He ordered Tobias to be slain, and took away his substance. Tobias, however, escaped with his life, and remained in concealment till the king's death, after which he continued to practise the same works of mercy towards his suffering countrymen, undeterred by the danger he had run, or the prudent advice of his friends, for, as the Holy Scripture says, "he feared God more than the king." ‡

We have seen Tobias firm and stedfast in his Faith, faithful to the duties of his Religion, and zealous in the performance of works of Charity. But a new trial now awaited him, to put to the test his hope and trust in God. Wearied with his labours in burying the dead, he laid himself down one day to rest beneath the wall of his house. As he was sleeping, the hot dung from a swallow's nest fell upon his eyes, and deprived him of his sight. Far from murmuring and repining under this severe trial, he bore it with invincible patience, and, like holy Job, thanked God in the midst of his affliction. The insults of his friends, and the reproaches of his wife, did not disturb the peace of his soul. When asked by them, in derision, " Where was now the hope for which he had given alms and buried the dead ?" he made them this noble answer, "Speak not so ; we are the children of the saints, and look for that life which God will give to those who never change their faith from him." §

The virtues of Tobias were not left by God, even in this life, without their reward. The great Archangel, St. Raphael,

* Tobias, i. 12.   † Ibid. i. 19-20.
‡ Ibid. ii. 9.   § Ibid. ii. 15, &c.

was sent from heaven to be the guide and protector of the young Tobias, and to heal and comfort his aged father. Restored to sight, Tobias lived happily for many years in the bosom of his family, until at length, at an extreme old age, rich in virtue and full of good works, he went to receive the reward which God has promised to his faithful servants.—*Tobias.*

THIRD INSTRUCTION.

The First Commandment continued. What it forbids. Idolatry, False Religions, Infidelity, Superstition and Sacrilege.

Q. What does the first commandment forbid ?

A. The first commandment forbids us to worship false gods or idols, or to give to any creature whatsoever the honour which is due to God.

We come now to speak of the sins which are forbidden by the first commandment, and which, as I told you, are all opposed to one or other of the four duties: Faith, Hope, Charity and Religious Worship, which we are enjoined by this commandment to practise. The Catechism does not here speak of all the sins against these duties, but only of a few which are opposed to the duty of Faith and Religious Worship. The other sins against this commandment, such as Presumption, Despair, Neglect and Profanation of the Sacraments, Distractions in prayer, &c., are spoken of in other parts of the Catechism.

The first sin here mentioned is the grievous crime of *idolatry*, which is, as the Catechism says, the *worship of false gods or idols,* or *the giving to any creature whatsoever the honour which is due to God.* This heinous sin is directly opposed to the two duties of Faith and Religious Worship; for by the one we are bound to *believe* in one only True and Living God, and by the other to *worship* him in the manner he has taught us. Idolatry is a sin, my dear children, which happily you are in no danger of committing, enlightened as you are by the light of Faith, and the teaching of the Church of God. It is a crime, however, which was very common before the coming of our Blessed Redeemer, and which even yet exists in many parts of the world. You would think, perhaps, that no one can be so foolish as to worship as gods, images made of wood or of stone, which, as the Holy Scripture says, can neither see, nor hear, nor help us,* but alas! there is no crime, however much it may be opposed to reason or the Divine teaching, of which man, when blinded by his passions, is not capable. After our first parents, Adam and Eve, had fallen into sin, and had been driven out of the Garden of Paradise, their descendants soon became corrupt, and gave way to grievous crimes and excesses. In punishment of their wickedness God permitted them to fall into deplorable ignorance. They lost the knowledge of the true God, and began to worship as gods the very creatures, which God had made for their use and benefit. At one time they adored the sun, the moon, and the stars; at another the earth and the sea; at another their fellow men; and sometimes even the very animals or vegetables. Then, as if these false gods were not enough, they made for themselves figures or images of clay, of wood, of stone, or of metal, and set them up, and adored them. Thus were they guilty of a most grievous outrage against the Divine

* Ps. cxiii. 5, &c.

Majesty, for what could be more heinous, than to turn the gifts of God against the giver, and to set up as gods, creatures made by the hand of God, and made for the use of man !

Such was the unhappy condition of mankind, before the coming of our Blessed Redeemer, who, by his own Divine teaching and that of his Apostles, has scattered the dark cloud of ignorance with which the whole world was covered before his coming. For at that time the Jews were the only people who preserved the knowledge and worship of the true God; the Gentiles, that is all other nations, were buried in the darkness of idolatry. Now *we are the* children of the Gentiles, and if we now enjoy the blessing of the true faith, it is to the Infinite Goodness of our dear Lord, and the merits of his bitter Passion and Death that we owe this greatest of all graces. Let us frequently thank him for it, and pray that he will extend the same blessing to those nations among whom idolatry still exists, bringing them by his powerful grace, and the preaching of his zealous missioners into the bosom of his Church.

I will now relate to you the beautiful history of St. Eustachius, who, with his wife and children, suffered a most cruel martyrdom rather than be guilty of an act of idolatry.

THE MARTYRDOM OF ST. EUSTACHIUS.

In the reign of the Emperor Trajan there lived at Rome a nobleman named Eustachius, who was no less renowned for his birth and riches, than for his courage and military exploits. One day while engaged in hunting, he was favoured with the vision of an image of our Lord crucified, which appeared to him, darting forth bright rays of light between the antlers of the stag that he was pursuing. At the same time he heard a voice saying, that, if he wished for happiness, he must abandon the worship of idols, and seek for instruction in the truths of the Christian religion.

Eustachius, being converted by this vision, was baptised with his whole family, but soon after began to experience the displeasure of the Roman Emperor. Stripped of his vast possessions and reduced to a state of extreme poverty, he was compelled to withdraw to a distant spot, where God tried him still further by the loss of his wife and children, who were separated from him by sudden and unforeseen disasters.

In the meantime the Roman army, pressed by the enemy, bewailed the loss of their favourite general, and loudly clamoured for his recall. The Emperor at length consented, and Eustachius was sought for and discovered in his retreat, where he was quietly employed in the pursuit of husbandry. At the Emperor's command he again put himself at the head of the troops, and led them once more to victory. Eustachius was now restored to his former high position, and, being again united to his wife and children, whom he had long believed to have perished, nothing seemed wanting to complete his happiness. Meanwhile the victory was celebrated with great rejoicings, and Eustachius was ordered by the Emperor to take part with his troops in the idolatrous sacrifices, which were offered in thanksgiving to the false gods of the country. Eustachius firmly refused, for he well knew that he owed a higher duty to God than to any earthly monarch. In vain did the Emperor strive alternately to win him by promises or to terrify him by threats, he remained unshaken in his resolution, and nobly declared that he was ready to die rather than sacrifice to idols. The Emperor, enraged, ordered him along with his wife and children to be thrown to the lions, but as these savage beasts refused to touch them, he commanded that they should be shut up in the body of a brazen bull, which should be placed, until it became red hot, over a glowing fire. The sentence was executed, and Eustachius and his family singing the praises of God to their latest breath, like the three children in the fiery furnace, accomplished in this manner their glorious martyrdom.—*Roman Breviary, Sept.* 20.

Q. What else is forbidden by the first commandment ?

A. All false religions, and all disbelief, or wilful doubt of any article of faith.

As the first commandment commands us to believe without doubting all that God has taught us by his holy Church, and to worship him in the manner that he has appointed, it consequently forbids *all false religions*, as well as *all disbelief* of the truths of our faith, and even a *wilful doubt* of any doctrine which the Church proposes to our belief. These three sins are all opposed to the virtue of Faith, and the first of them, namely, false religions, is also contrary to the duty of Religious Worship. All these sins are very grievous in the sight of God, as they are a direct rebellion against his teaching.

But what do we mean by *false religions*, which is the first of the three sins here mentioned? We mean of course every religion, except the one true religion established by Jesus Christ, namely the One, Holy, Catholic and Apostolic Church. For it is the Church which God has appointed to teach all nations what they are to believe about him, and how they are to worship him. Moreover, it is to the pastors of the Church that our Lord has said, "He that heareth you heareth me, and he that despiseth you despiseth me,"* and in another place, "If any man will not hear the Church, let him be to thee as the heathen and publican."† Whoever therefore follows any other religion, except the religion or Church established by Christ, despises the teaching of our Lord himself, and strays from the one road that leads to eternal life. Hence you see that we ought to be ready to make every sacrifice, and suffer everything rather than abandon our religion, or take part in any other form of worship. Thus, for example, no human motive, such as the fear of offending others, or the hope of obtaining any temporal advantage, should be able to induce us to deny our faith, to attend a Protestant church, or to take part in the services or prayers of any other religion than our own. Were we to act otherwise, we should be unworthy of the name of Catholics, and should disgrace the memory of our forefathers, who willingly sacrificed

* Luke, x. 16.   † Matt. xviii. 17.

their fortunes and their liberty, and cheerfully underwent the most cruel tortures, nay, even death itself, rather than abandon their faith or conform to a false worship.   Listen while I tell you what one of them had to undergo less than three hundred years ago, simply for confessing to a Catholic priest, and refusing to attend Protestant service.   It is but one example taken out of hundreds.

HISTORY OF JOHN RIGBY.

Among the glorious martyrs, who suffered for the faith in England during the cruel persecution of Queen Elizabeth, was a Lancashire gentleman of a good but reduced family, named John Rigby.   Having been obliged in consequence of his straitened circumstances to take service in a gentleman's household, he was unhappily prevailed upon through fear and human respect to frequent occasionally the Protestant Church.   At a later period, however, entering into himself he bitterly bewailed his past weakness, and was reconciled to God in the Sacrament of Penance by the Rev. Mr. Jones, at that time a prisoner for the Faith.   Sometime afterwards, having occasion to present himself at the Old Bailey to answer for his mistress, who had been summoned on grounds of religion, but was unable through sickness to appear, he was himself charged with being a Catholic, which he gladly acknowledged, and was accordingly condemned to death in virtue of an unjust law lately enacted, which made it treason to be reconciled to God by the ministry of a Catholic priest.

Upon hearing his sentence read, which condemned him to be hung, cut down alive, bowelled and quartered, he cried out with great joy, "Thanks be to God.   It is all but one death, and a flea-bite in comparison of that which it pleased my sweet Saviour Jesus to suffer for my salvation."   Though he was repeatedly offered his life in case he would consent to go to the Protestant Church, he always courageously refused, saying, "It is not lawful, and I will not go.   I desire and look for the day of my execution, but think myself unworthy to die for so good a cause."

It is related in the history of his trial that upon one occasion when he was brought before the judge, the latter ordered him to be loaded with a pair of heavy shackles.   The shackles were brought, and the holy confessor of the faith kissed them, and signed them with the sign of the cross before they were riveted about his legs. After he had stood in them awhile the irons fell to the ground, at which he smiled, and bade his keeper rivet them on faster. Soon after they again fell off, upon which he told them to make them faster still, "for," said he, "I esteem them as jewels too precious to be lost." This extraordinary circumstance, which was considered at the time miraculous, he looked upon as a token that his soul should soon be set free from the prison of the body. And so in fact it happened, for his execution, which had been long delayed, took place two days afterwards.

Having arrived at the place appointed for his execution, which was in Southwark, near the river Thames, he knelt down and recited aloud the Our Father, Hail Mary, I believe, and I confess. He then mounted the cart, and, making the sign of the cross, kissed the rope which the executioner adjusted to his neck. To the latter he gave a piece of gold, saying, "Take this as a token that I freely forgive thee, and all others that have been accessary to my death." No sooner was he turned off the cart, than he was immediately cut down, and standing on his feet, exclaimed, "God forgive you. Jesus receive my soul." He was then thrown to the ground, and one of his murderers placed his foot upon his neck, while his body was ripped open, and his heart and bowels were torn out. Thus did this noble and generous soul, this faithful imitator of his Divine Master, accomplish his glorious sacrifice.—*Challoner's Missionary Priests.*

Let us, my dear children, never fall off from the noble example of our forefathers, but be ready, like them, to make every sacrifice for that faith which they have preserved to us at the price of so many sufferings. Let us often say from our hearts, in the beautiful words of our hymn—

> "Faith of our fathers, holy faith !
> We will be true to thee till death."

The second sin mentioned in this answer of your catechism is the sin of *disbelief,* which is a refusal to believe any of the truths revealed by God to man, and proposed to our belief by the Church. To call in question any particular truth taught by the Church is the sin of *heresy;* to deny all revealed truth is the still more grievous crime of *infidelity.* You can easily understand how great a sin it must be to deny anything which God, who is truth itself, has taught to man. Such an act is a direct rebellion of the understanding against Almighty God, and can only spring from an excess of human pride. The infidel and heretic set up their own weak and erring judgment in opposition to Divine Revelation, and prefer their own ignorance to the Divine Wisdom. The heart of man must be very corrupt to fall into such an excess of pride and folly. Indeed we find that those who have made profession of infidelity have been, for the most part, men of the most abandoned lives ; and that those who have fallen away from the Church, by the denial of any of her doctrines, have done so for the sake of some worldly motive, or in order to indulge their passions more easily, by throwing off the restraints of religion. Thus did the wicked king Henry VIII. deny that the successor of St. Peter was the head of the Church, and compel his subjects, under pain of death, to do the same, because the Pope would not allow him to break the Divine Law by marrying a second wife while the first was living.

The last of the three sins here spoken of is *wilful doubt of any article of faith!* For, if it is forbidden to *disbelieve* a doctrine, it is no less forbidden to *doubt* of it, since faith requires that we should firmly hold fast, without a moment's doubt or hesitation, what God teaches and the Church proposes. But notice, my dear children, that it is one thing for a doubt to enter into our minds, and another for us to give way to it. What is forbidden by this commandment is a *wilful* doubt ; that is, a doubt which comes into our mind and which we do not put away when we notice it, but which we dwell upon on purpose. If we dislike these doubts, and do our best not to think of them, we do not commit any sin, but, on the contrary, gain great merit. We are forbidden, however, to do any thing which might bring these doubts into our mind, for example, to read Protestant or irreligious books, to go to Protestant schools, or to frequent the company of those who talk against or mock at our religion. For our faith is a precious gift of God, which we are bound, by every means in our power, to guard and cherish. Sometimes you will perhaps meet with deluded but well-meaning persons, who will offer to give or lend you religious tracts or Protestant bibles. Be always firm in refusing to receive them. Tell these parties that Catholics have books and bibles of their own, and that you do not require them. If they offer you, along with the books, clothes or money, tell them that you value your faith too highly to sell it for any temporal advantage. Esteem yourselves happy in being able to make a sacrifice, however small, for your faith, and doubt not that God will reward it. Finally, never forget the words of our Blessed Redeemer, " Every one that shall confess me before men I will also confess him before my Father who is in heaven. But he that shall deny me before men I will also deny him before my Father who is in heaven." *

Q. Does the first commandment forbid anything else ?

A. Yes; dealing with the devil, and inquiring after hidden things, or things to come by fortune-tellers, or superstitious practices.

Q. What other things are forbidden by this first commandment ?

A. All charms, spells, and heathenish observations of omens, dreams, and such-like fooleries.

* Matt. x. 32-3.

In these two answers, my dear children, are mentioned several sins which are forbidden by the first commandment, inasmuch as they are opposed to that religious worship which is due to God. All these sins are included under the common name of *superstition*, by which we mean a " false worship rendered to God or his creatures." We give a false and superstitious worship to God, when we worship him in a manner contrary to his revealed Will; and we give a false worship to his creatures when we shew them an honour and reverence which is due to God alone, or seek to obtain from them what we ought to look for only from God. Hence you see that idolatry is a kind of superstition, since by it we give Divine honour to idols or other things, which are only the creatures of God; and the sins here mentioned are also forms of superstition, since by them we try to obtain from creatures help or knowledge which depend on God alone.

The first sin which is here spoken of, namely, *dealing with the devil*, is so heinous a crime that the very name of it is sufficient to inspire us with horror. For what greater wickedness can we imagine than for man, the creature of God, redeemed by the Blood of the Son of God, and receiving daily innumerable blessings from the hand of God, to seek to have any dealings with that wicked spirit who rose in rebellion against God, and is ever striving that God may be dishonoured and that man, for whom the Son of God died, may be eternally lost. And yet, alas! there have been found men who, by giving way to their passions and vices, have at length arrived at such a height of wickedness as to give themselves up, body and soul, to the power of this wicked spirit, in the hope of obtaining from him, what a Good and Loving God thought well to refuse them. Such a one was the magician Simon, who lived at the time of the Apostles, and whose history I will relate to you, for it will show you how the devil, who was a liar from the beginning, always deceives to their ruin those unhappy men who, abandoning the protection of God, put themselves, of their own accord, in the power of their most bitter enemy.

SIMON, THE MAGICIAN.

One of the earliest converts to the Christian faith in the time of the Apostles, was a celebrated sorcerer or magician of the name of Simon. Having seen the miracles worked by the Apostles, and in particular the visible signs, which frequently followed the conferring of the Sacrament of Confirmation, he came to St. Peter, offering a sum of money, and saying, " Give me also this power, that on whomsoever I also lay my hands, he may receive the Holy Ghost." But St. Peter said to him, " keep thy money to thyself, to perish with thee, because thou hast thought that the gift of God could be purchased with money. Do penance for this thy wickedness, and pray to God, if perchance the thought of thy heart may be forgiven thee." Simon, thus baffled in his design, shortly after abandoned the Christian religion.

Giving himself then up entirely to the practice of the magic arts, he entered into a compact with the devil, who assisted him to perform various wonderful feats, which caused his fame to reach the ears of the Emperor Nero. In order to eclipse if possible the fame of the miracles of the Apostles, he engaged to fly through the air in presence of Nero and his whole court, on condition that St. Peter, who presented himself in the amphitheatre, was securely bound during the performance. This being done, he began by means of the magical arts, which God permitted to have effect for his greater confusion and punishment, to mount into the air, promising the people as he ascended, that he would shower down upon them good things from heaven. His momentary success was loudly applauded by the people, who clapped their hands, and raised shouts of exultation. Hereupon St. Peter, pitying their blindness, betook himself to prayer, earnestly beseeching God to confound the efforts of the devil, and not to permit him to obtain so signal a triumph. At the same moment Simon, abandoned by the wicked spirits that held him, fell with a loud crash upon the ground, amid the laughter and derision of the populace. In his fall he broke both his legs, "so that he," says St. Maximus, "who had undertaken to fly in the air, in a short time was not able to walk on the ground."—*Butler's Lives of the Saints.*

The second sin here mentioned is *the inquiring after hidden things or things to come by fortune-tellers or superstitious practices.* But whom do we mean by fortune-tellers? We mean those cunning cheats, who make their living by imposing on weak and silly people, persuading them that they can tell them whatever they wish to know, as if God had revealed his secrets to *them*, or made known to *them* the hidden things of the future. To consult a fortune-teller is a folly of which, I trust, none of you will ever be guilty; but besides being a folly, it is a sin, since it is an attempt to learn what God has wisely concealed, and to learn it by means which he has expressly forbidden. For Almighty God says in the Holy Scriptures, "Let there not be found among you any one that consulteth soothsayers, or observeth dreams or omens, neither let there be any wizard nor charmer, nor any one that consulteth pythonic spirits or fortune-tellers, or that seeketh the truth from the dead. For the Lord abhorreth all these things." *   And in another place he orders those who practised these forbidden arts among the Jews to be put to death without mercy, "dying let them die, they shall stone them, their blood shall be upon them." †

But some persons will perhaps say, that if they go to get their fortunes told, it is only for fun and as a harmless joke, and not because they believe in such folly. My dear children, he would be a bad Christian indeed, who should seek for fun in offending God, or call that a harmless joke which God has said that he abhors, and which he has expressly forbidden. Besides, though those who consult for-

<hr>

* Deut. xviii. 10-12.   † Levit. xx. 27.

tune-tellers may not believe them, yet they encourage
those whom they consult in their wicked trade, and
are thus guilty of the sin of scandal, by causing
others to offend Almighty God.

There are other ways, besides consulting fortune-
tellers, which foolish ignorant people sometimes practise to discover hidden things. For example, you
will sometimes hear of persons so silly as to imagine
that by tossing cups, that is to say, watching the
dregs of the tea leaves in a tea-cup, they can read
the history of their lives. Others, again, are guilty
of a like folly in pretending that, by cutting a pack
of cards, they can tell any one who asks them
whatever he wishes to know. All these and other
sinful and foolish tricks come under the common
name of *superstitious practices,* and are strictly forbidden by this commandment.

We come now to speak of *charms* and *spells,* which
are the next sins here spoken of. These two words,
charms and spells, have much the same meaning.
A *charm* is anything done, or used, or worn, to produce an effect which we have no natural reason to
expect from it; and a *spell* is a word, or number of
words, spoken, or written and carried about with us
for a similar purpose. I will explain to you what I
mean by an example. Let us suppose that you have
a toothache which causes you great pain. You go
to a druggist, who gives you something to cure you.
There you are taking a proper means of curing
yourself, and you have reason to hope that you will
be better, for it is the natural effect of medicine to
cure disease. God has given it to us for this purpose.
But let us suppose that instead of going to the
druggist, you go to some old witch, who tells you,
that, if you take a flat stone with a hole in the
middle, and hang it round your neck, it will cure
you : then, if you are silly enough to do what she

tells you, you make use of a *charm ;* for there is no reason to suppose that a flat piece of stone with a hole in the middle can cure disease. In the same way if you imagine that by saying some idle jargon of words, or wearing about you some sentence written on a scrap of paper, you can cure yourself from sickness, or preserve yourself from hurt and harm, you would be guilty of the sin of believing in *spells*, and would grievously offend Almighty God.

You will sometimes hear Protestants say, that Catholics make use of charms and spells by wearing medals, scapulars, Agnus Deis and Gospels, especially as we hope to be preserved from many evils by wearing them. But you will easily see that there is an immense difference between the use of charms and spells, and that of pious objects, blessed by the prayers of the Church for a particular end. Whoever wears a charm thinks that there is some virtue in what he wears, which has power to preserve him or bring him luck; but the Catholic who makes use of a blessed medal or Agnus Dei, looks only to God for the effect that he hopes for, trusting that the prayers of the Church and his own good desires will be mercifully heard by God in his behalf, whenever he makes a devout use of that sacred object.

The next sin mentioned in the Catechism, as forbidden by the first commandment, is the observing of *omens*, by which we mean the folly of attaching importance to trifling occurrences, believing that they are signs of the future and betoken good or evil. The observing of omens is called in the Catechism a *heathenish observation*, because it is a practice which was very common among heathen or idolatrous nations, but of which Christians, enlightened by the true faith, ought surely never to be guilty. If you read the history of the Greeks or Romans for example, you will find that they regulated almost all their concerns, both private and public, by the observation of omens. The flight of birds, the pecking of the sacred fowl, the appearance of the entrails of the victims slain for sacrifice, and accidental events of the most trivial nature often decided the question of peace or war, and determined the erection of cities, the passing of laws, and the most important affairs of the state. Such detestable superstition has been in a great measure happily dispelled by the light of the true religion ; but still there linger in some parts, even of Christian countries, and in some weak minds, superstitions of a similar nature. For example it is a common but foolish saying that a single magpie is a sign of sorrow, two of mirth, three of a wedding, and four of a birth; that to spill salt at table is a sign of misfortune; that it is unlucky to sit down to table in a company of thirteen, &c. But you, my dear children, who are better taught, know very well that God does not make the future depend on such foolish trifles.

We come now to speak of believing in *dreams*, which is quite as foolish and sinful as the observing of omens. This sin is also called in the catechism a *heathenish* practice, because it was very common among the pagans, who foolishly imagined that dreams are so many signs or forebodings of the future. Such a belief is, however, a detestable superstition, strictly condemned, as you have seen, by Almighty God, and forbidden by the first commandment. For dreams come from merely natural causes, being produced by the rambling of the brain at a time when the body and most of the powers of the mind are lulled in sleep. Things that we have seen or heard, or feared or hoped for, then pass through the mind in a disorderly and unconnected manner, especially if the body be out of health, or the mind disturbed by any violent emotion. Such idle wanderings of the brain cannot, it is plain, have any power to unfold to us the future, the knowledge of which God has reserved to himself alone.

It is true, however, that there *are* dreams which come from God, such as those we read of in the Holy Scriptures and in the lives of some of the Saints. For God, who can make use of any means that he pleases to accomplish his adorable ends, has sometimes made use of dreams to make known to man the events of the future. Such were the dreams, which he sent to the patriarch Joseph in his youth of the twelve stars and twelve sheaves of corn, whereby he shewed him his future greatness. Such, also, were the dreams of Pharaoh of the seven ears of corn and the seven fat and lean kine, by which were signified the seven years of plenty and the seven years of famine, which were about to be accomplished. Then, again, you will remember the famous dream of the Babylonian King Nabuchodonosor, who saw in his sleep a vast statue, the limbs of which were made of different materials, and betokened the great empires that were to succeed each other after his death, in preparation for the establishment of the Church. These and many other dreams of a similar nature were really sent by God, and were in truth signs of the future. But notice, that they were only sent on extraordinary occasions, for especial ends, and that God usually sent an inspired prophet or saint to interpret them—that is, to explain their meaning. To believe in these dreams was no sin, but to believe in the idle, foolish fancies of our brain—for God does not speak to us by dreams—is a wicked superstition, by which the devil has deceived many to their ruin.

The sins which are named in these two last answers of your Catechism, and which I have now explained to you, are the principal sins of superstition ; but all *such like fooleries*, or foolish practices, by whatever name they may be called, are in general forbidden by this commandment. I will now tell you a little story from the life of St. Bernard, from which you will see the horror in which the Saints of God held the sin of superstition.

ST. BERNARD'S HEADACHE.

The great St. Bernard, in his youth, was at one time afflicted with a violent headache, which deprived him of all rest, and which all the remedies that were prescribed were unable to relieve. Thereupon some of the attendants bethought themselves of a woman, who was reported to have the power of healing diseases by means of certain charms applied to the sick person. They accordingly introduced her into his chamber, but no sooner had the holy youth perceived her intention than he leaped from his bed, and drove her hastily from the room. Having done so, he again lay down, but this time fell into a refreshing slumber, on awaking from which he found himself entirely cured.—*Life of St. Bernard.*

I have now explained to you all the sins that are mentioned in the Catechism as forbidden by the first commandment. There are many others, some of which I have already named in speaking of the four duties—Faith, Hope, Charity and Religious Worship which this commandment enjoins, for, as I told you, whatever is opposed to any one of these duties is here forbidden. But there is one sin which I have not yet mentioned, and of which you ought to know the meaning, as you will often hear it spoken of— I mean the grievous sin of *Sacrilege.*

What then is sacrilege ? It is the profanation of any place, person or thing that is consecrated to the service of Almighty God. Whatever is consecrated to God is worthy of a certain degree of religious reverence, for the sake of him to whom it especially belongs. Therefore when, so far from respecting, we outrage or profane it, we are guilty of a grievous transgression of the duty of religious worship, and therefore of a mortal sin against the first commandment. For example, if a person were to turn a consecrated church into a shop, that would be a sacrilege, because a church is *a place* set apart for ever by the solemn act of consecration to the Divine worship. In the same way, if any one were to kill or injure a priest or a nun, he would be guilty of sacrilege, because priests and religious are *persons* especially dedicated to Almighty God. Again, if any one were to turn a chalice into a common drinking cup, it would be sacrilege, because a chalice is *a thing* consecrated by the Bishop for the purpose of holding the Precious Blood of our Blessed Lord. But the worst of all sacrileges is to receive the Holy Sacraments unworthily, especially the Sacrament of the Blessed Eucharist, for there is nothing, my dear children, more sacred in religion than the Sacraments, and he who receives Holy Communion in mortal sin profanes and outrages, as far as he is able, not that which is merely dedicated to God, but God himself in the person of his own Divine Son.

While speaking on this subject, I may mention that there is another kind of sacrilege, called *Simony*, which consists in selling or buying that which is sacred, and which appertains to the service of God— for example, any sacred office or spiritual grace. This is the sin which Simon Magus committed when he wanted to buy from the Apostles the gift of working miracles, and it is from him that this crime receives its name.

There are many terrible examples recorded in the Holy Scriptures of the judgments of God on those who have been guilty of the sin of sacrilege. Listen and I will relate to you one or two of them.

THE BANQUET OF KING BALTASSAR.

It is related by the prophet Daniel that during the captivity of the Jews in Babylon, Baltassar, the king of that country, made a great feast to which he invited a thousand of his courtiers. In the midst of the entertainment, being drunk with wine, he ordered the sacred vessels of gold and silver, which his father Nabuchodonosor had carried off from the temple of Jerusalem, to be brought to table, in order that he and his guests might drink therefrom, in honour of their false gods. It was done as he commanded, but Almighty God did not allow his sacrilegious impiety to remain long unpunished. "In the same hour," says the prophet, "there appeared fingers as it were of the hand of a man, writing upon the surface of the wall of the king's palace; and the king beheld the joints of the hand that wrote." Struck with terror and dismay, Baltassar called for his wise men to interpret the mysterious writing, promising, at the same time, the most magnificent rewards to any one who should succeed in doing so. No one, however, was found among them able to read the writing, much less to explain its meaning.

By the queen's advice, Daniel was now summoned into the royal presence, to whom the king repeated the promises which he had previously made. The holy prophet, inspired by God, while he rejected the splendid offers of the king, declared himself, nevertheless, willing both to read and interpret the writing. After reminding Baltassar of the numberless blessings which he had received from the hand of God, and which should have made him eager to reverence everything connected with his Divine worship, he reproached him for his sacrilegious profanation of the sacred vessels, and declared to him the awful judgments which were about to fall upon his head.

"This," said he, "is the writing that is written—*Mane, Thecel, Phares.* And this is the interpretation of the word. *Mane :* God hath numbered thy kingdom and hath finished it. *Thecel :* thou art weighed in the balance and art found wanting. *Phares :* thy kingdom is divided and given to the Medes and Persians."

That same night the mysterious sentence was fulfilled. The armies of Darius entered the city of Babylon, overthrew the mighty empire founded by Nabuchodonosor, and established on the ruins thereof the kingdom of the Medes and Persians. The impious Baltassar perished by the sword.—*Daniel,* v.

PUNISHMENT OF HELIODORUS.

We read in the Second Book of Machabees that Seleucus, king of Syria, hearing that a large sum of money was deposited in the temple of Jerusalem, despatched Heliodorus, one of his officers, with a sufficient guard to seize upon it and convey it to the royal treasury. Having arrived at the holy city, Heliodorus acquainted Onias the high priest with the object of his mission, and demanded the surrender of the treasure. Onias, however, firmly refused to comply with his demand, declaring that the money in question had been dedicated to God for charitable and pious purposes, or had been deposited for greater security under the Divine protection in the holy places. To this Heliodorus replied, that what he refused to surrender at the king's order, would be taken from the temple by force.

Meanwhile the whole of the people, with Onias at their head, earnestly implored Almighty God to avert so great a sacrilege. At length, upon the day appointed, Heliodorus, accompanied by his guard, entered the holy places, and ordered his men to lay hands upon the sacred treasure. At the same moment, God sent forth his holy Angels to protect his sanctuary, and punish the sacrilegious attempt. All who ventured to obey the orders of Heliodorus, were struck by the hand of God, and lay fainting and trembling on the ground, while he himself met with a still more severe chastisement. "For," says the sacred writer, "there appeared to them a horse with a terrible rider upon him, adorned with a very rich covering ; and he ran fiercely and struck Heliodorus with his fore feet ; and he that sat upon him seemed to have armour of gold. Moreover, there appeared two other young men beautiful and strong, bright and glorious, and in comely apparel, who stood by him on either side, and scourged him without ceasing with many stripes. And Heliodorus suddenly fell to the ground, and they took him up covered with great darkness, and, having put him into a litter, they carried him out. And he indeed lay speechless and without all hope of recovery. Then some of the friends of Heliodorus forthwith begged of Onias that he would call on the Most High to grant him his life. So the High Priest offered a sacrifice of health for the recovery of the man. And when he was praying, the same young men, in the same clothing, stood by Heliodorus, and said to him, *Give thanks to Onias, the High Priest, because for his sake the Lord hath granted thee life. And thou, having been scourged by God, declare unto all men the great works and the power of God.* And having spoken thus, they appeared no more."

This signal punishment produced a salutary effect on the mind of Heliodorus. After offering a sacrifice to God, in thanksgiving for his merciful preservation, and returning thanks to Onias for his charitable intercession, he returned to the king, publishing everywhere the wonderful events which had occurred. The king was at first anxious to pursue the attempt, and requested Heliodorus to name some one to whom he could entrust the conduct of the enterprise. Whereupon Heliodorus boldly and candidly made answer, "If thou hast an enemy or traitor to thy kingdom send him hither, and thou shalt receive him again scourged, if so be he escape. For He that hath his dwelling in heaven is the visitor and protector of that place, and he striketh and destroyeth them that come to do evil to it."—*II. Mach.* iii.

SACRILEGE AVENGED.

In the year 1834, upon the eve of the Assumption of Our Blessed Lady, the Puritan population of Charlestown in the United States, being excited by some fanatics, rose up against the Catholics, and, with cries of fury, rushed towards the Ursuline convent of Mount Benedict. It was night-time, and the inmates of the convent were reposing in peaceful slumber, from which they were aroused by the shouts of the mob and the smashing of the outer doors. Before the pupils had time to dress, the kindling flames flashed over their peaceful dwelling, and it was with difficulty they made their escape, while their invaders were engaged in plundering the church and convent.

In the midst of the tumult, one of the ringleaders ascended the altar, seized the Ciborium, and, horrible to relate, emptied the precious particles into his pocket. He then repaired to an inn at Charlestown, where, surrounded by a throng of eager listeners, he related his sacrilegious exploit. In the midst of his recital he suddenly recognised among his audience an Irish Catholic, who was listening with intense horror. On perceiving him he drew from his pocket several hosts, and, holding them forth, said in a sneering tone, "Here, behold your God! Why need you go any more to seek him in the church?" The Catholic stood dumb with horror. At the same moment, however, the blasphemer turned pale, and feeling himself seized with a sudden colic, left the apartment. A quarter of an hour, half an hour elapsed, yet he returned not. A vague fear fell upon the bystanders. They followed him to the closet to which he had retired, and there found him—a corpse. He had died the death of Arius.—*Annals of the Propagation of the Faith,* vol. viii. p. 347.

FOURTH INSTRUCTION.

———

The First Commandment continued. What it does not Forbid. The Making of Images—Praying to the Saints and Angels — Honour paid to Relics, Crucifixes and Holy Pictures.

Q. Does the first commandment forbid the making of images?

A. The first commandment does not forbid the making of images, but the making of idols; that is, it forbids us to make images to be adored or honoured as gods.

When Almighty God says in the first commandment "Thou shalt not make to thyself any graven thing, nor the likeness of anything that is in heaven above, nor in the earth beneath, nor of those things that are in the waters under the earth," he *does not forbid* altogether *the making of images*, but only of such images as are intended to be set up as *idols*, that is, which are made *to be adored or honoured as gods*. For the meaning of the words, " Thou shalt not make to thyself any graven thing," is explained by the words which follow—" Thou shalt not adore them or serve them." If it were not so, it would be wrong for us to make a statue to be set up in a public square, or the figure of a horse or dog to put upon our chimney piece, or even a doll for a child to play with. But we know that there is no harm in any of these things.

We are forbidden, therefore, to make images to *adore* or *serve* them, but not forbidden to make them for any other purpose; for example, for use or ornament, or to inspire religious reverence and devotion. Hence God himself in the old law commanded images to be made and used for religious purposes; for example, the two golden Cherubim placed on each side of the ark of the covenant in the Holy of Holies, whose extended wings formed, as it were, the Mercy Seat of God, from which he made known his Will to the Jewish people.* What God himself ordered the Jews to do, the Catholic Church does likewise, placing in her temples the images of the angels and the Saints, and, above all, that of Christ crucified and his Blessed Mother. These sacred images serve to fill the mind with holy thoughts, to instruct and arouse our faith, to excite our hope, to move us to love and sorrow, and finally to fill us with a holy zeal to imitate the virtues of those whose images we contemplate. For in the same way as men erect in the squares and public places of our cities the statues of kings, and warriors, and statesmen, though but sinners like themselves, as well to honour their memory as also to excite the zeal of others to imitate those great deeds which they have performed for the good of their country, so also does the Church of God place in her temples the images of our Divine Redeemer, his Virgin Mother, and his Blessed Saints and Angels, not only in order to shew a loving reverence to those whom they represent, but also to lead us to walk in their footsteps by the imitation of their virtues.

I told you just now, that it is strictly forbidden by the first commandment to make any graven image for the purpose of idolatrous worship. Listen, and I will relate to you the history of five noble martyrs, who chose rather to sacrifice their lives than to be guilty of this heinous sin.

* Exod. xxv. 18, &c.; ib. xxxvii. 7; Numb. xxi. 8, 9.

DIOCLESIAN AND THE SCULPTORS.

In the reign of the Emperor Dioclesian there lived at Rome five clever sculptors, whose works of art had obtained for them a high place in the Emperor's favour. Their names were Claudius, Nicostratus, Symphorianus, Casterius, and Simplicius—the last of whom had been converted to the Christian religion by the piety and edifying example of his companions. Never did these holy men commence their work without devoutly invoking the holy name of Jesus, and such a blessing from heaven attended this pious practice, that each succeeding work they executed served to raise them higher in the Emperor's favour.

About this time Dioclesian was engaged in the erection of a costly edifice, and as he was anxious that the decoration should be as perfect as possible, he sent for the five sculptors to execute the difficult piece of carving which was to ornament the front of the building. The design exhibited the figures of various animals, which were to be carved in marble; the centre of the piece was to be occupied by the images of certain pagan divinities. In the course of a short time the Emperor came to watch the progress of the work. He found the carving complete, with the exception of the vacant space which was to be occupied with the images of the pretended deities. Dioclesian praised the sculptors for the skill with which they had executed a portion of the work, but blamed them for their delay in completing the remainder. "Sire," replied they, "we are Christians, and we are not permitted by our religion to execute any work which may contribute to the superstitious worship of idols." The Emperor, enraged, ordered them to be delivered up to the judge, to whom he gave secret orders to use every effort to induce them to renounce the faith, that he might not lose, by their martyrdom, the services of such skilful workmen. The judge displayed before their eyes the most frightful instruments of torture, and strove, by alternate threats and promises, to induce them to submit to the will of the Emperor. His efforts proving unavailing, he caused them to be inhumanly scourged. As they still remained constant, the Emperor condemned them to be enclosed alive in a vast leaden coffin, and thrown into the river Tiber. The sentence was executed, and they thus sealed their noble profession of faith by a glorious martyrdom.—*Lives of the Saints.*

Q. Is it forbidden to give honour to the Saints and Angels ?

A. It is forbidden to give them supreme or divine honour, for this belongs to God alone.

Q. Is it allowable to give them any kind of honour ?
A. Yes ; it is allowable to give them an inferior honour, for this is due to them, as the servants and special friends of God.

From these two answers you see that while *it is forbidden to give the Saints and Angels that supreme* or highest kind of *honour*, which *belongs to God alone, it is* both *allowable* and pleasing to God that we should give them *an inferior* or lesser kind of *honour*, which indeed *is due to them* as being his chosen *servants and special friends.* For an honour, paid for the sake of God, passes to God himself; nor could we honour God rightly if we did not also honour those whom God has himself honoured and placed about his heavenly throne. You will easily understand this, my dear children, from what happens here below. We honour the Queen as the sovereign ruler of the State, but we also, for her sake, honour her ministers, her generals, her judges. Were we wanting in respect to them, we should be dishonouring the Queen herself. And why ?. Because by their very office and position they are entitled to be treated with respect, as possessing her confidence and bearing the marks of her authority. Yet notice, that the honour we pay to them falls far short of that which we render to the Queen in person. We salute them with respect if we meet them, but we do not kiss their hand on bended knee, as those do who are presented to the Queen. We call them by the titles they hold, if we speak to them, but we never say to them "Your gracious Majesty." So is it also in the court of heaven. To God alone we pay *Divine* worship, but to the Saints and Angels we shew a *lesser* reverence for the sake of God, whose friends and servants they are. Thus we *adore*

God, but we do not adore them; we *ask God to pardon our sins*, but we do not ask pardon from the Saints and Angels; we *beg blessings and grace from God*, but we only ask the Saints and Angels to use their power and favour with God to obtain for us from him what we stand in need of. Hence you see there is a wide, and indeed an infinite distance between the honour we pay to God and that which we render to his Saints and Angels—as great a distance as there is between the Creator and the creature.

You will often hear it said by those who differ from us in religion that the honour, paid by Catholics to the Saints and Angels, is an injury done to God, and takes away from the honour due to him. You see now, from what I have said, that this cannot be the case, since the honour which we pay to them is of a totally different nature from that which we give to God, and is given only for His sake. On the contrary, it is plain that we honour God the more, the more we reverence those who are his friends and favourites. For it is God only who has made them what they are; and when we extol their glory, their power, their holiness, their sublime virtues, we extol His gifts and graces. Take, for example, the Virgin Mother of his Divine Son, the greatest, the noblest of the creatures of God, excepting only the Sacred Human nature of our Blessed Lord. Who is it that has made her what she is—so pure from every stain of sin, original and actual, so humble, chaste and gentle, so high in dignity and so excellent in glory, the creature yet the Mother of God, and the Queen of Angels and of men? It is to God, and God alone, that Mary owes all, as she herself tells us in her beautiful canticle of thanksgiving, the Magnificat, " He that is mighty hath done great things in me, and Holy is his Name." Therefore, when we praise and shew reverence to Mary, when we recommend ourselves to her protection and ask her intercession, we glorify and acknowledge the Infinite Power, and Wisdom, and Goodness of God, as manifested in her. In the same way is it with the other Saints and the Angels of God; they are his friends, his favourites, or his ministers to execute his Divine decrees; but all their honour, their holiness, their power with him come from God himself, and are the gift of his Goodness. In praising them, therefore, we praise Him; in begging their prayers, we shew our belief that He loves them, and will not refuse to grant them what they ask.

Cherish, therefore, my dear children, always in your hearts a tender devotion to the Blessed Angels and Saints of God. Especially love and honour the Blessed Mother of God, who is our own Mother also, since our dear Lord gave us to her to be her children before he expired on the cross, and bade us look upon her henceforth as our mother. Oh how many precious graces shall we not obtain, if we practice, during life, a tender devotion to the Blessed Virgin! She will be our comfort in affliction, our strength in temptation, our sure refuge in every danger. Be faithful, therefore, in performing some little devotion daily in her honour. Love to pray before her image, to sing her praises, to adorn her altar, but, above all, strive to practise those virtues of which she sets you so beautiful an example, especially these three— humility, obedience and holy purity. Believe me, there is no more powerful means of advancing in virtue, and no surer sign of perseverance, than the practice of a true devotion to the Blessed Virgin.*

After our Blessed Lady, do not fail to love and honour St Joseph, for his power is very great with Mary, his Virgin Spouse, and with the Divine Child,

* See vol. 1. p. 282, &c.

of whom he was the guardian and protector on earth. St. Joseph is especially the patron of the young and the patron of the dying. He will guide your steps in the path of virtue, guard your innocence from danger, and obtain for you the greatest of all graces, namely, that of a happy death. I would recommend you to say some little prayer daily in his honour.*

You should also have a special devotion to your Patron Saint, that is, the Saint whose name you have received in Baptism or Confirmation, or whom you have particularly chosen as your model and protector. You should read his life, try to imitate his virtues, and frequently recommend yourself to his prayers. He on his part will intercede for you before the throne of God, and guard and help you in all the trials of life.

> "Holy Saint whose name I bear,
> Guard me from all danger here ;
> Till at length I come to be,
> Safe in heaven with God and thee."

There is one kind friend and protector, of whom I have not yet spoken to you, but whom you should never forget, for he is ever by your side, watching over you with a tender and constant love, guiding your steps aright, assisting you in every necessity, protecting you in every danger. I mean, of course, your Guardian Angel. For you know that is a pious and universal belief in the Catholic Church, that when God gives each of us our being, he at the same time chooses out from among those glorious spirits who ever minister about his throne, one to be our special guardian and protector throughout life. Hence, holy David says beautifully, in one of the Psalms, "He hath given his Angels charge over thee, to keep thee in all thy ways. In their hands they

* See vol. i. pp. 75, 271, &c.

shall bear thee up lest thou dash thy foot against a stone." *   And again, our Blessed Lord, warning his disciples against the grievous sin of scandal, reminds them that the Guardian Angels of those whom they lead to sin will bear witness against them before the throne of God: "I say to you that their Angels in heaven always see the face of my Father who is in heaven." †   Oh, my dear children, how many graces do we not owe to the watchful care and tender love of these blessed spirits! It is they who shield us from danger, and strengthen us in trial and temptation, comfort us in affliction, and breathe into our souls pure and holy thoughts. How true, indeed, are those beautiful words of the hymn—

> "But I have felt thee in my thoughts
>   Fighting with sin for me,
> And when my heart loves God, I know
>   The sweetness is from thee.

> "Yes, when I pray thou prayest too,
>   Thy prayer is all for me ;
> But when I sleep thou sleepest not,
>   But watchest patiently."

Preserve, then, ever in your hearts a tender devotion to your good Angel. Always remember his presence, and never grieve this pure and holy spirit by defiling your soul, which he loves so dearly, with the guilt of wilful sin. Often invoke him in your temptations, for he is especially appointed by God to help you in such moments of need. You could say to him, for example, this little prayer, "My dear Angel Guardian defend me ;" or this longer one, to which an indulgence is attached, "Oh, my good Angel, whom God has appointed to be my Guardian, enlighten and protect me, direct and govern me."

There is a beautiful history related in the Holy

* Ps. xc, 11-12.   † Matt. xviii. 10.

Scripture, which shews with what lovingkindness and tender care our Guardian Angels watch over those committed to their charge, and guide their steps through life. I mean the history of—

ST. RAPHAEL AND THE YOUNG TOBIAS.

When the elder Tobias was now old and blind, and thought that the day of his death was not far distant, he called to him his son, and, after giving him his last advice, bade him seek out some trusty guide to conduct him to the city of Rages, there to receive a sum of money due to him by one Gabelus. The young Tobias, going out to fulfil his father's commands, was met by a youth of comely aspect who was girded ready for a journey. In answer to his inquiries, the stranger told him that he knew the way to Rages, and was acquainted with Gabelus; he added, moreover, that he was ready to guide him on his road. Full of joy, Tobias brought in the young stranger to his father, who asked him his name, little thinking that it was the great Archangel St. Raphael, whom God, to reward his piety, had sent to take charge of his beloved son. The youth replied that his name was Azarias, for this was the name that he had assumed, and he assured the old man that he would undertake to conduct his son in safety to Rages, and bring him back again to his home.

The two travellers accordingly set out, and rested the first evening by the banks of the river Tigris. Here Tobias went into the water in order to bathe his feet, when suddenly a monstrous fish came rushing forwards to devour him. In great terror he called out to his companion, who told him not to be afraid, but to take the fish by the gill and draw him to the shore. He did so, and, having brought the fish to land, set aside, by the direction of his guide, a portion of it as useful for medicine; the rest they cooked and carried with them as provisions for the journey.

Thus they travelled on till they arrived at the house of an Israelite named Raguel, a friend of the elder Tobias. Now, it happened that Raguel had a daughter named Sara, who had been espoused to seven different husbands, all of whom had been slain by Satan on the first night of their nuptials. The angel bade Tobias ask her in marriage, assuring him that such was the will of God. Tobias did so, and obtained her father's consent. The marriage was celebrated with great rejoicing, and the holy couple sanctified it and drew down on themselves the protection of heaven by spending the first three nights of their union in fervent prayer. Meanwhile, Azarias proceeded to Rages, and received the money owing by Gabelus.

Soon after, the young Tobias, with his virtuous spouse and faithful guide, set out on his return home. As they drew near to their journey's end, the dog, which had accompanied them throughout, went running forwards with signs of joy, as if to announce their return. Tobias rose hastily, and, leaning on a servant's arm, ran, with stumbling feet, to meet and embrace his son. After the first joyful greetings were over, the young Tobias, by the direction of Azarias, took of the fish's gall, and applied it to the eyes of his father, who immediately recovered his sight. With hearts overflowing with gratitude, both father and son raised their voices in praise to God for so signal a favour, and then, turning to the young guide, begged him to accept of half of their substance as some return for his services. Upon which Azarias declared who he really was, and how he had been sent by God to guide the son, and to console and heal the father.

"Bless ye the God of heaven," said he; "give glory to him in the sight of all that live, because he hath shewn his mercy to you. For I am the Angel Raphael, one of the seven who stand before the Lord. Peace be to you, fear not. For when I was with you I was there by the will of God. It is time that I return to him that sent me, but bless ye God and publish all his wonderful works.

"And when he had said these things he was taken from their sight, and they could see him no more. Then they, lying prostrate for three hours on their face, blessed God, and rising up they told all his wonderful works." *

Tobias lived to an extreme old age, and died, happily, in the arms of his children and grandchildren.—*Tobias.*

OTHER EXAMPLES FROM HOLY SCRIPTURE.

The holy patriarch Jacob, being on his death-bed, called his twelve sons around him to give them his last blessing. His son Joseph brought also his two children, Ephraim and Manasses, to their grandfather's bedside, and Jacob, stretching out his hands to bless them, prayed thus to his good angel, "The angel that delivereth me from all evils bless these boys." †

* Tobias, xii. 21-22. † Gen. xlviii.

When Almighty God spoke to Moses upon Mount Sinai, he told him that he had appointed one of his holy angels to guide and protect the people of Israel, and conduct them safely into the promised land.

"Behold," said he, "I will send my angel who shall go before thee, and keep thee in thy journey, and bring thee into the place that I have prepared. Take notice of him and hear his voice, and do not think him one to be contemned ; for he will not forgive when thou hast sinned, and my name is in him. But, if thou wilt hear his voice, and do all that I speak, I will be an enemy to thy enemies, and will afflict them that afflict thee. And my angel shall go before thee, and shall bring thee " into the promised land.*

While the holy prophet Daniel was mourning over the continued captivity of the Jewish people with whom he had been led to Babylon, and was praying fervently to God for their speedy deliverance, there appeared to him an angel, probably the holy Archangel St. Gabriel, who told him that his prayer was heard, and that God had sent him to announce its speedy accomplishment. The heavenly messenger informed him that the prince, or Guardian Angel of the Persians, had resisted him in this matter for one and twenty days, when St. Michael, the Guardian Angel of the Church of God, came to his help, and their prayers prevailed with God. No doubt, the blessed Angel of the Persians was unwilling that the nation entrusted to his charge should be deprived of the presence and example of a people who followed the true religion, not worshipping false gods like the Persians, but the one true God of heaven. The angel added, that the Guardian Angel of the Greeks had appeared also, when he came forth to the prophet, so that he would return to continue the combat. He feared, probably, that the Angel of the Greeks, whose empire was soon to be established on the ruins of that of Persia, would be equally anxious that the Jews should remain in that country for the spiritual good of the people committed to his charge, and would join with the Angel of the Persians in imploring this grace from God.†

During the cruel persecutions raised by King Herod against the early Christians at Jerusalem, the holy Apostle St. Peter was thrown into prison, where he was bound with chains and guarded by a band of soldiers. In the middle of the night an angel appeared to him, loosed his chains, and led him forth into the street, where he disappeared from his sight. St. Peter, being now at liberty, directed his steps to

* Exod. xxiii. 20-23. Dan. x.

the house of Mary, the mother of St. Mark, where the faithful were assembled together, praying for the speedy deliverance of the great Apostle. Having knocked at the door, a servant maid named Rhode came cautiously to listen ; recognising, however, the voice of St. Peter, she ran in haste to tell the disciples that it was St. Peter himself who was without. They, knowing that the Apostle had been cast into prison and placed under a strong guard, did not at first believe her, but thought that perhaps it was his Guardian Angel come to console them in his absence. "Nay," said they to her, "it cannot be St. Peter, surely *it is his Angel.*" Upon opening the door, however, they found that it was the great Apostle himself who related to them the manner of his miraculous deliverance.[*]

From these examples, my dear children, you easily see how the Jews believed, no less than we do, in the protecting care of Guardian Angels, and how this belief is in exact accordance with the teaching of Holy Scripture.

Q. And is it allowable to honour relics, crucifixes, and holy pictures ?

A. Yes ; with an inferior and relative honour, as they relate to Christ and his saints, and are memorials of them.

Q. May we pray to relics or images ?

A. No, by no means ; for they can neither see, nor hear, nor help us.

We come now to speak of the honour paid by Catholics to *relics, crucifixes, and holy pictures.* From these two answers of the catechism, you see that it is allowable to *honour* them, but not to *pray to* them. We honour them because *they are memorials,* that is, objects which remind us *of Christ and his Saints ;* but we do not pray to them, because they are without life or sense, and *can neither see, nor hear, nor help us.* Moreover, the catechism tells you that the honour which we pay to them is of an *inferior* or lesser kind, and is only *relative ;* that is, given to them not for their own sake, but for the

---

[*] Acts, xii.

sake of our Blessed Lord and his Saints to whom they in some manner *relate*.

From this simple explanation, you see how foolish is the charge of idolatry sometimes brought against Catholics by ignorant people, on account of the respect which we shew to relics, crucifixes, and holy pictures. Idolatry is, as you know, the giving Divine worship to an image or false god. But who can be so foolish as to suppose that we worship as gods the *relics*, that is, sacred remains of the departed Saints; or that we adore pious pictures or the *images* of Christ crucified? The simplest Catholic child knows that the respect which we pay to these pious objects is only a means that we take of shewing our reverence and affection to those whom these objects represent, or to whom they have in some manner belonged.

But it will be said that we place these objects in our churches, that we adorn them with lights and flowers, that we wear them about our necks, that we kneel and pray before them. Assuredly we do. But does not a child cherish with the same fond reverence the memorials of a departed parent without ever being blamed, much less charged with idolatry for so doing? Let us suppose you have lost a beloved mother in your early childhood. You remember well her watchful and patient care, her loving words, her gentle smile. She was taken from you by the hand of God, no more to meet or embrace you till that day so full of happiness for the good, the day of the final resurrection. But perhaps you have the good fortune to possess a lock of her hair, the letters she has written to you, or some other object which once belonged to her. Can any one blame you if you prize these relics, as they really are, of a dear departed mother above all else that you possess, if you carry them about with you, if you kiss them with filial tenderness? Or let us suppose that you have a picture or likeness which recalls to you the features of that beloved parent. Does any one charge you with the black crime of idolatry if you set it in an honoured place in your little room, if you adorn it with flowers, if you water it with your tears, or if, in moments of temptation, you kneel and pray before it, recalling to your mind the gentle warnings and prudent counsels given you in years gone by by that dear departed one? Nay, so far from blaming you, would not any one that saw you say, "There is a good child, who truly loved his mother." And shall it not be lawful, then, to shew the same affectionate reverence to the memorials of our loving Saviour, of our Heavenly Mother, or of the Blessed Saints and Angels, that we do to those of our departed earthly parents? Surely the more holy and exalted that the person is whom the image or relic recalls to our mind, the greater is the reverence with which it should be treated. You will understand from this, I am sure, why it is that the Catholic Church shews such respect to relics, crucifixes, and holy pictures.

As you will no doubt remember better what I have said, if I tell you a little story to impress it on your minds, I will now relate to you the history of

THE ABBOT STEPHEN AND THE EMPEROR'S IMAGE.

About seven hundred years after Christ, a violent heresy arose in the East, which was directed against the veneration that had always been paid in the Catholic Church to crucifixes and sacred images. The fanatics who embraced this heresy overran the country, everywhere tearing down and defacing the pictures and statues of Christ and his Saints, from whence they received the name of Iconoclasts or "Breakers of images." The Emperor Constantine Copronymus, who was a violent partisan of these heretics, treated with the greatest cruelty all who remained stedfast to the Catholic faith.

Among others whom he summoned before him was the holy Abbot Stephen, whom he ordered to trample upon the crucifix, if he wished to save his life. Stephen declared that he would rather die than be guilty of so great an irreverence towards his Blessed Redeemer. "Stupid and ignorant man," rejoined the Emperor, "do you suppose that by trampling upon his image you trample upon Jesus Christ?" Upon this the Saint, drawing from beneath his robe a piece of money, asked the Emperor whose image it was that was engraved upon it. "Whose can it be," replied he, "but my own?" The holy man then turning to the bystanders said, "What treatment, think you, would he deserve who should trample underfoot the Emperor's image?" "A most severe and exemplary punishment," replied all with one voice. "What!" said the Saint, heaving a deep sigh, "shall it be esteemed a grievous crime to trample under foot the image of a mortal king, and none to outrage that of the King of Heaven!" Constantine felt the force of this reasoning, but did not yield to it. Falling into a violent passion, he ordered the heroic martyr to be beheaded.—*Butler's Saints' Lives.*

There are many among you, I dare say, who wear about your necks a blessed crucifix, medal, scapular, Agnus Dei or Gospel. The relics of the Saints are also worn in the same manner. As it is well that you should understand the meaning of what you wear, I will give you a short explanation of these sacred objects.

The *crucifix* is the image of our Blessed Lord nailed to the cross, so that you see there is a difference between a crucifix and a cross. A cross is simply a piece of wood, metal, &c., with a shorter piece placed across it; but a crucifix is a cross with the figure of our Lord upon it. By wearing the crucifix devoutly, we are reminded of the infinite love of our Blessed Saviour in dying for us on the cross, we are taught to place all our hopes in the merits of his Passion and Death, and are encouraged to follow him generously, bearing our cross after him by patiently submitting to the trials and afflictions which he sends us.

The *medals*, which we wear as objects of devotion, are pieces of metal stamped with some sacred image, such as the figure of our Blessed Lady, of our Guardian Angel, or of our Patron Saint. There are also medals of the Sacred Heart of Jesus, of the Precious Blood, of First Communion, Confirmation, &c. By wearing respectfully these sacred medals, we shew our devotion to that Saint or Mystery which they represent, and obtain, no doubt, many graces through the pious sentiments which they inspirè and the prayers which are offered up over them in the name of the Church when they are blessed. There are also many indulgences, which have been granted by different Popes to those who wear or make devout use of crucifixes and sacred medals; but in order to gain these indulgences, it is necessary that these pious objects should have been blessed by some priest who has received power for this purpose from the Pope.

The *scapular* is a sacred badge, consisting of two small pieces of cloth joined together by two strings and worn about the neck. The first mention of the scapular is found in the life of St. Simon Stock, General of the Order of Mount Carmel. This holy monk earnestly besought our Blessed Lady to bestow on the religious of his Order some pledge of her special care and protection. The Blessed Virgin granted his request, and, appearing to him, presented him with a scapular which she held in her hand, at the same time promising that she would watch over and guard in a special manner all who should wear it in her honour. Since that time many religious· orders have worn it over their habits, and numbers of the faithful also wear it under their ordinary clothing. The scapular most commonly used is the

Brown Scapular of our Lady of Mount Carmel, but there are many others besides this. There is the Blue Scapular in honour of our Blessed Lady's Immaculate Conception, and the Black Scapular in honour of her Seven Dolours. There is also the Red Scapular in honour of the Passion of our Blessed Lord, and the White Scapular in honour of the Most Holy Trinity. In order to gain the graces and indulgences attached to the wearing of the scapular, it is necessary that we should be invested with it by a priest who has received power for the purpose. We must also wear it constantly, recite the prescribed prayers, and fulfil the other conditions laid down. But let us remember that it will avail us little to wear the badge or livery of our Blessed Lady or our Divine Lord, if we do not honour the sacred habit with which we are clad by a good and holy life.

The *Agnus Dei* is made from the wax of the Paschal Candle mixed with the Sacred Chrism, and is worn in honour of our Blessed Redeemer. It receives its name of "Agnus Dei," or "Lamb of God," from the figure of a lamb stamped upon it in memory of our dear Lord, who shed his blood like a meek and gentle lamb for our salvation. Sometimes it is worn about the neck, in which case it is covered with silk, out of respect; sometimes, also, it is enclosed in a frame or silver case to be hung in our rooms or oratories. No one but the Pope can bless an Agnus Dei, and he performs this ceremony but once in seven years upon Easter Thursday. In this solemn blessing he prays that those who use the Agnus Dei devoutly may be preserved from pestilence, earthquakes, shipwrecks, and sudden death : also that they may receive many spiritual and temporal blessings. Although those who wear the Agnus Dei are not strictly obliged to recite any prayer, yet it is recommended to say daily some little prayer in honour of it. A very suitable one is the prayer repeated three times by the priest in the Mass, "Lamb of God, who takest away the sins of the world, have mercy on us."

Gospels are of very ancient use in the Catholic Church. They consist usually of a written or printed copy of the beginning of St. John's Gospel, the same part that is read by the priest at the end of Mass; and they are used as a protection against various diseases and other calamities. By wearing them devoutly, we express our firm belief in the truths revealed to us by God in the Holy Gospel, the unbounded confidence which we place in his Goodness, and our ardent love of Him, the true Word of God, who "was made flesh and dwelt amongst us."

By *relics*, we mean the remains of the Saints; for example, portions of their bones, of their hair, of their clothes, or of whatever has belonged to them during life or touched their bodies after death. These relics are usually enclosed in silver cases, sealed with the Pope's seal, and are accompanied with a written paper certifying that they are true or genuine, otherwise it is not permitted to expose them for public veneration. The honour paid to relics is as old as the Church herself. No sooner had the Apostles and early Martyrs laid down their lives in the midst of cruel torments for the love of their Divine Master, than the Christians eagerly sought out the remains of their sacred bodies, and preserved them with the utmost reverence. During the times of persecution they hid these precious relics in the catacombs, or secret passages beneath the surface of the earth, to which they had to fly for safety; but when peace was restored to the Church, they erected over them magnificent altars and costly churches, to which the faithful flocked to pray before the tombs of the martyrs, and implore their intercession in presence of their sacred remains. The same veneration has in all ages been paid by the Church to the relics of the Saints, and this not only through respect for the Saints themselves, but still more in reverence to God. For as the bodies of the Saints were during their lives upon earth the chosen temples of the Holy Ghost, and will hereafter be glorified for all eternity in heaven, so does the Church feel that any honour paid to their remains redounds to the glory of God, who has blessed and sanctified them for his own Divine service.

You will now understand, my dear children, that these pious objects, the meaning of which I have explained to you, are so many helps given us by God to arouse our faith and excite our devotion. In making use of them, we hope to obtain many graces, and to be preserved from many dangers through the prayers of the saints in whose honour we wear them, or through the blessing which the Church has pronounced over them. Were we to expect help from the objects themselves, or to imagine that the mere wearing of them would be sufficient to save us, we should be guilty of the sin of superstition. But you all well know, that it is to God alone, through the merits of his Divine Son, that we look for every grace ; and that we cannot hope for salvation if we do not believe what he has taught and practice what he has commanded. We hope, indeed, to obtain the Divine assistance more speedily and surely, through the prayers of the Saints and the blessing of the Church, but we are very far from believing that crucifixes or medals, or scapulars or Agnus Dei's, or even the relics of the Saints, have, of themselves, any power to help or save us.

In the Lives of the Saints and other pious books you will find an account of many wonderful graces obtained from God by the devout use of these holy objects. I will relate to you one or two examples of the use of relics taken from the Holy Scripture.

RELICS OF ELISEUS THE PROPHET.

The holy prophet Eliseus, who inherited, along with the garment, the miraculous powers of his great master Elias, was no less remarkable for his holy life than for his wonderful miracles. At his death he was buried, according to the custom of the Jews, in a tomb or small cavern hollowed out of the rock, the door of which was closed, no doubt, with a large flag or stone, as we read in the history of our Lord's burial. Shortly after his death, the Moabites, a neighbouring nation who were often at war with the Jews, made an incursion into the land of Israel. It happened that a party of Israelites were at this very time carrying the body of a man to the place of burial, the road to which lay past the tomb of Eliseus. Seeing, however, the Moabite rovers approaching, and fearing for their lives, they hastily uncovered the sepulchre of the prophet, and cast in the body. No sooner had the corpse touched the bones of Eliseus, than the soul returned to it, and the man stood upon his feet alive and well.—*IV. Kings*, xiii.

GARMENT OF OUR BLESSED LORD.

" And behold a woman," says the Evangelist, " who was troubled with an issue of blood twelve years, came behind Jesus and touched the hem of his garment. For she said within herself, *If I shall touch only his garment I shall be healed.* But Jesus, turning and seeing her, said, *Be of good heart, daughter, thy faith hath made thee whole.* And the woman was made whole from that hour."—*Matt.* ix.

RELICS OF ST. PAUL.

" And God," says the Holy Scripture, " wrought by the hand of Paul more than common miracles, so that even there were brought from his body to the sick handkerchiefs and aprons, and the diseases departed from them, and the wicked spirits went out of them."—*Acts*, xix.

The Church of God, which is ever watchful in guarding her children from all danger of superstition, or of paying veneration to unworthy objects, requires that no public honour should be paid to relics, which have not been properly examined and declared by her to be true and genuine. You will understand how careful she is on this point from the following little history.

ST. MARTIN AND THE ROBBER GHOST.

In the time of St. Martin, bishop of Tours in France, there were, at a little distance from that city, an altar and chapel built over the body of a pretended martyr whose relics were held by the people in great veneration. St. Martin, suspecting that their devotion was misplaced, carefully examined into the origin of this sanctuary, and questioned the oldest of his clergy on the subject. Not receiving any satisfactory explanation, he one day repaired to the spot, attended by his clergy, and, standing over the tomb, earnestly besought Almighty God to shew him who it was that was there buried. Then, turning to the left, he saw near him a pale ghost of fierce aspect, whom he commanded to speak. The ghost told him his name, and it then appeared that the body was that of a robber who had been executed for his crimes, but whom the people revered as a martyr. None saw him but St. Martin, the rest only heard his voice. St. Martin, accordingly, ordered the altar to be removed, and thus freed the people from the superstition.—*Butler's Saints Lives.*

THE WOOD OF THE TRUE CROSS.

St. Gregory, another bishop of Tours, who lived in the sixth century, and on account of his many miracles is surnamed Thaumaturgus, or the Wonder-worker, says, in his writings, that he once received a present of an old silk veil, which the donor assured him had been wrapped round the wood of the true cross. "In my simplicity," says St. Gregory, "I had a difficulty in believing it ; nor could I imagine how he could have merited so great a favour, knowing, as I did, that on the days when the sacred wood was exposed, it was not only impossible to obtain any relic of it, but that the greatest care and even violence was employed to keep the crowd at a respectful distance. The person related to me, however, that he had received it at Jerusalem, along with other relics, from the Abbot Photinus, an ecclesiastic in high favour with Sophia, the Empress of the East.

"On receiving the veil," continues St. Gregory, "I washed it in water, and gave certain persons, who were suffering from fever, the water to drink. In a moment, by the effect of the Divine power, they were cured. I gave a portion of the veil to a certain abbot, who, coming to see me two years after, assured me that he had cured with it three possessed persons, three who were blind, and two paralytics. One day, he informed me, he put the veil into the mouth of a dumb man, but scarce had it touched his teeth and tongue, when his voice and speech were restored."—*Rohrbacher. Vies des Saints.*

Miraculous cures, similar to those related by St. Gregory, no doubt frequently accompany, even in these our days, the devout use of relics or other pious objects. For the arm of God is not shortened, nor is his Power diminished; while his Goodness and Mercy are equally ready now, as they were in the days of the Apostles, or in any age of the Church, to reward the faith and loving confidence of those who have recourse to him, if he sees that the favour they ask will conduce to the salvation of their souls.

Before we go on to speak of the second commandment, there is one other remark which I wish to make, and it is this. In wearing the image of Christ crucified, or of his Saints, in placing them in your little oratories, in adorning them with lights and flowers, you should never forget that what you must principally aim at is, to imprint in your heart the virtues of those whom they represent. The crucifix, meditated upon, will preach you a continual sermon. In moments of temptation it will keep you from sin by the remembrance of what our dear Lord has suffered for our salvation. In sorrow and sickness it will animate you to patience and resignation, by the example of his patient suffering. It will teach you to be meek and humble of heart, to forgive all who have offended you as Christ forgave his enemies on the Cross, and to be obedient, in all things, to your parents and superiors as he was obedient to his Heavenly Father even unto death. In like manner, the pictures of the Saints will animate you to fight against your passions, to despise the world and its empty pleasures, and to walk in their footsteps by the imitation of their virtues, keeping your eyes constantly fixed on heaven, where they are now awaiting you. Oh, my dear children, how happy will you be if you learn such lessons from these sacred objects! Encouraged by the example of the Saints, and helped by their prayers, you will not fail one day to arrive at the same eternal happiness.

ST. BONAVENTURE AND THE CRUCIFIX.

The great St. Bonaventure, who on account of his many learned and pious writings is numbered among the Doctors of the Church, was one day visited by St. Thomas of Aquinas, who asked him what books he had chiefly made use of in composing so many excellent and learned works. St. Bonaventure pointed to his crucifix, all tarnished with the many kisses he had imprinted upon it, saying, " This is the book from which I have collected all that I have written ; this has taught me all the little that I know."—*Life of St. Bonaventure.*

DEATH OF MARY, QUEEN OF SCOTLAND.

The gentle and unfortunate Mary Stuart, having taken refuge in England from her rebellious subjects, was thrown into prison by her cousin, Queen Elizabeth, and kept for many years in close confinement. After the mockery of a trial, she was condemned to death, and at length the fatal warrant was signed by Elizabeth. Mary prepared herself for her end with edifying piety, and walked with firmness to the scaffold, bearing the crucifix in her hands. Upon her arrival at the place of execution, she offered a fervent prayer for the pardon of her sins, and for a blessing on the Church, her son James, and her cousin Queen Elizabeth. Then, holding up the crucifix before her eyes, she exclaimed, " As thy arms, O God ! were stretched out upon the cross, so receive me into the arms of thy mercy, and forgive me my sins." " Madam," said the Earl of Kent, " you had better leave such Popish trumperies, and bear him in your heart." She replied, " I cannot hold in my hand the representation of his sufferings, but I must, at the same time, bear him in my heart." So saying, she laid her head upon the block, and gave up her soul into the arms of her crucified Lord.—*Lingard's History of England.*

KING BOLISLAUS AND HIS FATHER'S IMAGE.

Bolislaus IV., King of Poland, caused the image of his father, for whose memory he entertained the greatest veneration, to be engraved upon a golden medal, and always wore it round his neck. Ever after, when about to say or do anything of importance, he took the image into his hand and kissed it, saying respectfully, "Dear father, let me not do anything unworthy of your name."

How much more guarded would Christians be over their words and actions, were they to wear about their necks the image of Jesus crucified, and look at it when tempted to stain their souls with sin, saying, in the words of Bolislaus, "Dear Saviour, do not allow me to do anything unworthy of the name of Christian."

====

FIFTH INSTRUCTION.

The Second Commandment. What it commands. Reverence in speaking of God and holy things. Fidelity in keeping our lawful oaths and vows. What it forbids. Swearing, cursing, blasphemy, and profane words.

Q. What is the second commandment?
A. Thou shalt not take the name of the Lord thy God in vain.

We now come to speak of the second commandment, in which Almighty God strictly enjoins us not to take his holy and adorable name in vain, "for the Lord," he adds, " will not hold him guiltless who shall take the name of the Lord his God in vain."*   From this we see how grievous in the sight of God is the profanation of his holy name, since he has added to this one only among all the commandments a special threat in case we disobey him—" the Lord will not hold him guiltless;" that is to say he will consider him guilty of a great and a grievous crime.

Let us first see what we are *commanded* to do by this commandment, and afterwards what sins it *forbids* us to commit.

Q. What are we commanded by the second commandment ?

A. We are commanded to speak with reverence of God and all holy things, and to keep our lawful oaths and vows.

From this answer you see that there are two particular duties pointed out to us by the catechism, as enjoined by this commandment.

The first is *to speak with reverence of God and all holy things*, that is of all that relates to God.

The second is *to keep* faithfully *our lawful oaths*, and the lawful *vows* or promises which we have made to God.

I need not, I think, give you any reasons to shew that it is our duty to speak with becoming reverence of Almighty God. If you only consider for a moment who *He* is and who *we* are, you will easily see that we are bound by every motive to speak of Almighty God with the most profound respect. *He* is the Sovereign Lord and Master of all, the Great Creator of heaven and earth. *We* are his creatures and the work of his hands. *He* is Infinite in Goodness, Wisdom, Power, Holiness, and every perfection. *We* are poor little worms of the earth, full of sin

<hr>

* Exod. xx. 7.

and corruption. *He* is our continual Preserver, our constant Benefactor, our tender Father, and our loving Saviour. *We* are in everything dependent upon him, and receive every moment fresh marks of his Goodness and Love; moreover we are his adopted children, redeemed from the power of the devil by his own most Precious Blood. Surely, then, we are strictly bound by every motive, whenever we speak of God, to do so with the most profound reverence. We read in the history of the Jews that, out of respect to the most holy name of God, they abstained from uttering it, and used in place of it the word "Adonai," or Lord. God, however, does not forbid *us* to utter his holy name; nay, on the contrary, like a tender father, he loves to hear us pronounce it, as long as we do so with hearts animated alike by love and reverence.

But we must not only speak of God himself with respect, we must do the same of *holy things,* inasmuch as they relate to God. Hence we are bound to speak with reverence of the Blessed Virgin, who is the Immaculate Mother of God; of the Angels, who minister about his throne; of the Saints, who are his friends and favourites; of the Church, which is the Spouse of his Divine Son; of the Sacraments, which are the channels of his grace; of the Mass, which is the Sacrifice of the Body and Blood of Jesus; of the Bishops and Priests, who represent him upon earth; of the Holy Scripture, which is his Divine word; of the sacred offices and ceremonies of religion; in a word, of all that appertains to God and his worship. You can easily understand that to speak of those things that relate to God in a light, and much more in a disrespectful manner, is an outrage offered to God himself.

In the second place, we are commanded by this commandment *to keep our lawful oaths and vows.*

An *oath*, my dear children, means "calling God to witness that we speak the truth." It is the same as *swearing*; to take an oath and to swear mean one and the same thing. For example, if a person says "I take God to witness that what I say is true," that is an oath; in other words, it is swearing by the Holy Name of God. But it is not necessary that a person should use the Name of God to make it an oath; it is an oath if he swears by the Saints, by Heaven, by the Holy Scriptures, his own soul, &c. And why so? Because all these relate to God; They are the noblest of God's creatures, and therefore if we call them, it is like calling God himself to witness the truth of our words. You will now understand what we mean by *swearing* or *taking oaths*; it is a very different thing from *cursing*, which I shall explain to you just now.

The catechism here tells us that we are bound by this commandment *to keep our lawful oaths*; in other words, if we have promised to do anything which is lawful, and have called God to witness the truth of our promise, we are strictly bound to fulfil it. If you simply *promised* a person to do anything, it would be mean, dishonourable, and unjust to break your word, at least without very good and sufficient reason; but if you have *sworn* to do it, you are bound by a much stricter tie, since you have taken God himself as your witness that you will do what you have promised, and therefore if you break your word you commit the terrible outrage of making him, who is Truth itself, witness to a lie. Hence to break an oath is justly considered a grievous insult to God, and one of the greatest of crimes. This detestable sin, which is called *perjury*, was in former ages punished with death, both by the Jewish law and by the laws of many Christian nations; and though a lesser penalty is inflicted now, we cannot doubt that this crime continues to meet with the most severe punishment from the justice of an outraged God.

So far, my dear children, we have been speaking of *lawful* oaths, but what must we do about those which are *unlawful?* For example, if a person had sworn to revenge himself, or to keep a thing secret which it was his duty to tell, what must he do? Must he keep his oath and commit the sin, or must he break the promise which he has called God to witness? Most certainly he must break it, for though he committed a grievous crime in swearing to do a bad thing, he would commit a fresh sin if he actually did it. Thus, for instance, the forty Jews who, as we read in the Holy Scripture, had all sworn not to touch food till they had slain St. Paul, were not bound by their wicked oath. They were guilty of a great sin in taking it, but they would have added to this the grievous crime of murder if they had fulfilled it. This double crime Herod really committed in the case of St. John the Baptist, who fell a victim to the sinful observance of a rash and unlawful oath. I will relate to you the history of his martyrdom.

MARTYRDOM OF ST. JOHN THE BAPTIST.

"Herod," says the Evangelist, "had sent and apprehended John, and bound him in prison for the sake of Herodias, the wife of Philip, his brother, because he had married her. For John said to Herod—*It is not lawful for thee to have thy brother's wife.* Now Herodias laid snares for him, and was desirous to put him to death, and could not. For Herod feared John, knowing him to be a great and holy man, and kept him, and when he heard him did many things, and he heard him willingly.

"And when a convenient day was come, Herod made a supper for his birthday for the princes, and tribunes and chief men of Galilee : And when the daughter of the same Herodias had come in, and had danced and pleased Herod and them that were at table with him, the King said to the damsel, *Ask of me what thou wilt and I will give it thee.* And he swore to her, *Whatsoever thou shalt ask I will give it thee, though it be the half of my kingdom.* Who, when she was gone out, said to her mother, *What shall I ask?* But she said, *The head of John the Baptist:* And when she was come in immediately with haste to the King, she asked, saying, *I will that forthwith thou give me in a dish the head of John the Baptist.*

"And the King was struck sad. Yet because of his oath, and because of them that were with him at table, he would not displease her : But sending an executioner, he commanded that his head should be brought in a dish. And he beheaded him in prison, and brought his head in a dish, and gave it to the damsel, and the damsel gave it to her mother. Which his disciples hearing, came and took his body, and laid it in a tomb."—*Mark* vi.

We come now to speak of *vows*, which the catechism tells us we are bound to keep whenever they are *lawful*. But what is a vow? It is a solemn promise made to Almighty God. Thus you see a vow is very different from an *oath*, which is calling God to witness the truth of what we say, or of some promise that we make. It also differs from a *good resolution*, which is simply an intention of doing something pleasing to God; whereas a vow is a strict engagement, which we freely take upon ourselves, binding ourselves before God to do something or to leave something undone. For example, it was very common in past ages for a king or general going out to battle to promise to build a church or monastery, or offer some rich gift to God, if victory blessed his arms. Again, we read in the lives of the Saints of many who devoted themselves by vow to serve the sick, to visit and ransom prisoners, to embrace the state of holy virginity, to enter a religious order, &c.; in other words, they promised Almighty God to do these good works in his honour. Such promises or vows are, of course, strictly binding; to break them would be a most grievous outrage to the God to whom they are made. For if it be considered among men an insult and injustice to others if we break the word which we have pledged, how great an outrage must it be to the Lord of Heaven and earth if we violate the solemn promise which we have made to him! Wherefore the Holy Scripture says, "If thou hast vowed anything to God, defer not to pay it; for an unfaithful and foolish vow displeaseth him. And it is much better not to vow, than after a vow not to perform the things promised." *

We must notice, however, that *unlawful* vows are not to be kept any more than unlawful oaths. In other words, if a person were so wicked as to insult God by promising him to do a sinful thing, he would, of course, commit a fresh sin by doing it.

To make a vow, or promise to Almighty God to do some work of piety or charity in his honour, is in itself an act of religion, and no doubt pleasing to God when done with proper prudence and discretion. But as it imposes upon him who makes it a strict obligation of fulfilling it, a vow should certainly not be made rashly, or without the advice of a confessor. For example, you wish to honour our Blessed Lady by the daily recital of her rosary or litany. Make a *good resolution* to perform this act of devotion, but do not make an express *promise*, for if you do, you bind yourself by a strict obligation, and are guilty of sin if you omit it. Remember the words of the wise man, "It is much better not to vow, than after a vow not to perform the things promised." If, however, a person has made a rash or imprudent vow, or one which he finds himself unable to fulfil, a confessor has in most cases power to dispense with it, or to commute, that

* Eccles. v. 4, 5.

is, change it into some other good work which his
penitent is better able to perform.

Q. What does the second commandment forbid ?
A. The second commandment forbids all false, rash,
unjust, and unnecessary oaths ; as also blaspheming, cursing,
and profane words.

In this answer, my dear children, you find four
different sins mentioned as forbidden by this commandment, namely,

1. Swearing, whenever the oath which we take is
    either false, rash, unjust, or unnecessary.
2. Cursing.
3. Blaspheming, and
4. Making use of profane words.

These sins are all opposed to that reverence which
we are bound by this commandment to use in
speaking of God and everything that is sacred and
holy.

In the first place we are forbidden to *swear*, whenever the oath which we take is either *false*, *rash*,
unjust, or *unnecessary*. For to swear, that is, to
call God or his Saints or holy things to witness the
truth of what we say, is not a sin in itself ; on
the contrary, it is an act of piety and religion,
whenever we fulfil the conditions which are necessary to render it good and pleasing to God. Hence
Almighty God said to the Jews in the old law,
" Thou shalt fear the Lord thy God, and thou shalt
swear by his name."* Thus the king swears to rule
his people justly, the soldier to be faithful to his
prince, the judge to pass sentence according to the
laws, the witness to speak the truth in a court of
justice ; and neither king, nor soldier, nor judge, nor
witness commits any sin by so doing ; on the con-

* Deut. vi. 13.

trary, they perform an act good in itself and pleasing to God. And why so? Because they fulfil all the conditions which are necessary to render an oath lawful. What, then, are these conditions? The Holy Scripture tells us by the mouth of the prophet Jeremias, "Thou shalt swear in truth, in judgment, and in justice."* Whoever, therefore, swears with *truth*, with *judgment*, and with *justice*, commits no sin; but if his oath is wanting in any one of these conditions, he is guilty of a sin against the second commandment.

You will wonder, perhaps, what is the meaning of these words, "Thou shalt swear in truth, in judgment, and in justice?" I will tell you. To swear in *truth* is to be sure, if you assert something upon oath, that what you say is true, and if you promise something, that you are both able and intend to do what you promise; moreover, you must actually perform it. To swear in *judgment*, is to swear only when you can form a prudent judgment that there are good and sufficient reasons for taking an oath, as in the case of the examples I have just named to you of a king, a soldier, &c. Finally, to swear in *justice*, is to swear to do what is good and just.

If you will now look at the four kinds of oaths, which the catechism tells you are forbidden by this commandment, you will find that they are all wanting in one or other of these conditions, and it is for this reason they are sinful. Thus false and rash oaths are opposed to truth, unjust oaths to justice, and in taking unnecessary oaths we swear without that prudent judgment which we are obliged to form of their necessity. All such oaths are therefore sinful, but they are not all equally grievous in the sight of God. Thus a false oath is a greater sin

* Jerem. iv. 2.

than a rash one, and an unjust oath is far more grievous than one which is simply unnecessary.

I told you just now that to swear or take an oath is to call God, or his Saints, or holy things to witness the truth of what we say or promise. From this you will see how great is the guilt of him who takes a *false* oath, or, in other words, commits the crime of *perjury*. He comes before the great God of heaven, that God who is the very Truth, with a lie on his lips, and asks of God either himself, or by his Saints, or by the sacred things of religion which immediately relate to him, to bear witness to the lie which he speaks. Can you imagine a more grievous outrage to God than this? Truly it is a wonder of the Divine Goodness that God, who holds the life of the perjurer in his hands, does not strike him dead in the very act of offering him so heinous an insult.

Rash oaths are the next kind of oaths here mentioned. To swear rashly is to swear without thought or reflection, not thinking, in fact, whether that which you swear is true or false. People who have the unhappy habit of swearing, continually take rash oaths, and thus they expose themselves to the danger of taking false ones. And although it is not so grievous a sin to swear rashly, as it is deliberately to call God to witness a falsehood, yet it is undoubtedly a great insult to him to ask him to witness the truth of what *may* be a lie, since we have not taken the trouble to reflect whether it be true or false. The condition of truth necessary for a lawful oath requires that we should be absolutely certain of the truth of what we swear to.

The third kind of oaths forbidden by this commandment are *unjust* ones, that is, oaths in which we swear to do something sinful. Unjust oaths are a most grievous sin in the sight of God, for what can be more horrible than to call God to witness that we will not obey him? For example, a man receives an injury ánd swears to revenge himself. In other words, he calls God to witness that he will do what God has strictly forbidden—namely, revenge himself on his fellow-creature. He thereby denies the right of God to govern him, sets himself up in his stead, and calls God to witness that he does so.

The fourth and last kind of oaths here spoken of are *unnecessary* ones—namely, those which are taken without just and sufficient reason. Though not so grievous in the sight of God as those which are false, rash, or unjust, they are, nevertheless, very displeasing to him. For the Holy and Adorable Name of God is not to be treated as a mere bye-word, nor is the great Lord of Heaven and Earth to be called upon to witness every trifle. An oath is a holy and a sacred act, and is only to be taken when the glory of God or the good of our neighbour requires it, as in the case of those oaths which are administered by public authority. So few, indeed, are the occasions when it is lawful to swear, that our Blessed Lord expressly forbids it in the Holy Gospel in these plain and severe words :—

"You have heard," said he to the Jews, "that it was said to them of old, *Thou shalt not forswear thyself, but thou shalt perform thy oaths to the Lord.* But I say to you, not to swear at all, neither by heaven for it is the throne of God, nor by the earth for it is his footstool, nor by Jerusalem for it is the city of the Great King; neither shalt thou swear by thy head, because thou canst not make one hair white or black. But let your speech be, Yea, yea; no, no ; and that which is over and above these is of evil."*

These words of our Blessed Lord do not, however,

* Matt. v. 23-37.

apply to those oaths which fulfil the necessary conditions of truth, justice, and judgment, but to those false, rash, unjust, and unnecessary oaths which are forbidden by this commandment.

We come now to speak of the second sin forbidden by this commandment, which is the grievous crime of *cursing*. To curse is to call down some evil upon ourselves or others; for example, if a person were to say, "May you be struck dead," or "Bad luck to you," those are curses. You see it is different from merely *wishing* some evil to others in your heart, it is praying that that evil may happen. There is always a prayer either expressed or implied in a curse. Indeed it is this which makes cursing a sin against the second commandment, otherwise it would only be a sin against charity, that is, against the love we owe our neighbour for the sake of God. But when we pray that some evil may happen to him, besides not loving him and wishing him well, which charity requires, we do also what is most injurious to the Holy Name of God, by calling on Him to execute our guilty wishes. Almighty God says to us in the Holy Scripture " Revenge is mine, and I will repay ;" * that is, " Leave all vengeance to me. I shall punish those who injure you with strict justice unless they sincerely repent." But what does the curser say? " No, O Lord; revenge is not yours, it is mine. At least it is for me to will it, and for you only to execute my will. You must not give this man time to repent; you must punish him at once, because I wish it. You, who loved to give sight to the blind and to raise the dead to life, must strike this man blind and that other one dead because I say so. You, who shed the last drop of your blood to save the poor sinner from hell, must condemn this enemy of mine, nay, per-

* Rom. xii. 19.

haps this wife, this child of mine to eternal damnation, and give them no further hope of salvation." My dear children, you are horrified, and no wonder, at such terrible impiety. You think, perhaps, that it is impossible that any one could dare thus to speak to God. Alas! it is what the habitual curser says, perhaps twenty times a day, whenever, for example, he uses such words as these—"God strike you blind! God strike you dead!" &c. Ah! how much it is to be feared that a just and outraged God will cause the curses of the wicked to fall with tenfold weight upon their own heads!

It happens not unfrequently that the habitual curser, besides invoking the curse of God on his work, his cattle, his neighbours, his children, his wife, actually in as many words calls it down upon his own head; in other words, he prays God, who is infinitely just and infinitely powerful, to send him bad luck, to strike him dead, or to damn him for all eternity. This kind of cursing is what the Jews were guilty of in the desert, when they murmured and cried out, " Would to God that we may die in this vast wilderness !" *   And they were guilty of the same when they sought our Lord's death, calling out to Pilate, who strove to release him, " His blood be upon us and upon our children !" †   Almighty God heard their wicked prayers and granted them.   Of the mighty multitude who came out of Egypt, all who had attained the age of manhood, except only Josue and Caleb, perished in the wilderness; and you know how the innocent Blood of the Lamb of God, shed by the hands of the Jews, has drawn down the Divine vengeance on this guilty nation. Driven from their country, and scattered over the face of the earth, they are a living monument of the Justice of God on those who insolently brave

* Numb. xiv. 8.   † Matt. xxvii. 25.

the Justice of God. And so it will be, no doubt, with those wicked sinners who have the habit of invoking the Divine vengeance on their own heads. Often, as we read in history, has God heard their prayer, and granted them the evil they asked for, even while the words of their curse were yet upon their lips ; and if sometimes in his Mercy he delays his vengeance, there is no doubt that, if they do not sincerely repent, the punishment will fall upon them with still greater severity either in this or in the next life.

Sometimes you will hear the curser excuse himself by saying that he curses by habit, and that he does not really wish any evil from his heart, nor intend what his words imply. Almighty God accepts of no such excuse. If a person curses by habit, he is guilty of a grievous sin in having formed so wicked a habit, and is equally guilty and accountable for what he says as long as he does not sincerely strive to correct it. This he can always do by the grace of God, which is all powerful, but he must take the proper means to obtain it. He must pray earnestly to God for grace to overcome this wicked practice, carefully examine his conscience each evening, making sincere acts of sorrow for past sins and fresh resolutions for the ensuing day, and approach often to the Holy Sacraments. He must also avoid the company of cursers, watch carefully over his temper, and try to check his anger by a little prayer whenever he finds it rising. Let him do this, and he will soon find that each day the number of his curses will grow less and less, till at length he will have cured himself entirely of this unhappy sin, which is the cause of the eternal damnation of so many souls.

I will now tell you a little story on this subject, which is handed down to us by the historian Eusebius, one of the earliest writers of Church history.

THE THREE CURSERS.

It is related that three men, who were addicted to the sin of cursing, were in the habit of uttering imprecations on their own heads in order to make people believe their assertions. One used to pray that he might be burnt alive if his words were not true, the second that he might be seized with a fit of sickness, and the third that he might be struck blind. In a short time they all obtained what they asked. The first was burnt alive with his whole family; the second was afflicted with a frightful disease from head to foot; and the third was so touched with fear at the sight of the judgments which had fallen on his companions, that he sincerely repented, and by reason of the abundant tears which he shed over his past sins, lost the use of his sight. Thus did Almighty God, while he punished each for his sin according to the words of his curse, make that very punishment turn to the eternal salvation of him who sincerely repented.—*Euseb.*, Bk. vi. c. 9.

STORY OF EARL GODWIN.

When St. Edward the Confessor sat on the throne of England, his younger brother Alfred, whom he tenderly loved, was one day cruelly and treacherously murdered. The perpetrators of this foul deed remained undiscovered, but several historians attribute the guilt of it to the powerful Earl Godwin, who was the father of the queen. Some years after, when the king was seated at table with his nobles, the conversation happened to fall on the death of Alfred. St. Edward declared that he would always regard with horror those who had been guilty of so black a crime. As he uttered these words he cast his eyes towards Earl Godwin. The latter, fearing that he was suspected, took up some bread, saying, " If I had any hand in that foul deed, may this be the last morsel I ever swallow." No sooner had he uttered these words than he fell dead from the table with the morsel in his mouth.—*English History.*

The third sin here spoken of is the grievous crime of *blasphemy.* By blasphemy we mean speaking injuriously of God, or his Saints and Angels, or sacred things. This is, indeed, a crime which we should expect to find only among the devils in hell.

For can it be possible that man, the creature of God, redeemed by the Blood of the Son of God, receiving daily his existence and innumerable benefits from the hand of God, should be found capable of speaking injuriously of God, or what immediately relates to him ? And yet, unhappily, it is so. Many, indeed, blaspheme that which they know not; for example, those who, not belonging to our holy religion, and misled by prejudice and false teachers, misrepresent Catholic Doctrine, mock at the ceremonies of the . Church, or speak disrespectfully of our Blessed Lady, or the Saints, or the Holy Sacraments; but there are others, alas! Catholics in name only, who blaspheme that which they do know, by murmuring against the Justice or Providence of God, jesting about holy things, or mocking at the ministers of the Church. You can easily understand how heinous this crime is in the sight of God. In the Old Law the blasphemer was, by the command of God himself, sentenced to death, and stoned in the sight of all the people, and in the laws of many Christian nations we find the severest punishments enacted against this crime ; as, for example, in the laws of St. Louis, King of France, who ordered the tongue of the blasphemer to be pierced with a red hot iron. Many instances are likewise recorded, in which God has, in his Justice, taken upon himself at once to avenge his own honour, and struck the blasphemer dead in the very act of insulting him.

THE BLASPHEMER STONED TO DEATH.

" And behold," says Moses, in the Book of Leviticus, "there went out the son of a woman of Israel and fell at words in the camp with a man of Israel. And when he had blasphemed the name, and had cursed it, he was brought to Moses. And they put him in prison till they might know what the Lord would command.

"And the Lord spoke to Moses, saying, *Bring forth the blasphemer without the camp, and let them that heard him put their hands upon his head, and let all the people stone him. And thou shalt speak to the children of Israel, ' He that blasphemeth the name of the Lord dying let him die; all the multitude shall stone him, whether he be a native or a stranger.'*

"And Moses spoke to the children of Israel, and they brought forth him that had blasphemed without the camp, and they stoned him. And the children of Israel did as the Lord had commanded Moses."—*Levit.* xxiv. 10-23.

THE PUNISHMENT OF SENNACHERIB.

The holy king Ezechias, who ruled over the kingdom of Juda shortly before the time of the Babylonian captivity, was on one occasion besieged in Jerusalem by the Assyrian general, Rabsaces, who had been sent by King Sennacherib to demand the surrender of the city. Rabsaces, in the name of his master, uttered horrible blasphemies against the God of heaven, who, he assured the Jews, would be no more able to protect his people than the idols whom they worshipped had been able to protect the neighbouring nations. Being compelled to abandon the siege, in order to lead his army against the King of Ethiopia, he wrote a letter to Ezechias, in which he repeated his former blasphemies, and threatened, upon his return from his expedition, to destroy the holy city, if it did not appease his master's anger by a timely submission. The pious Ezechias was struck with horror at the words of the letter, and, carrying it into the temple of God, he there spread it open, and, with many tears and fervent prayers, begged of the Lord to avenge the insult offered to him on the head of the blasphemer. He then repaired, for consolation and advice, to the holy prophet Isaias, and was assured by him, on the part of God, that the blasphemies uttered against the Lord should not remain unpunished.

"And it came to pass that night," says the sacred writer, "that an Angel of the Lord came and slew, in the camp of the Assyrians, a hundred and eighty-five thousand. And when he rose early in the morning, he saw all the bodies of the dead. And Sennacherib departing, went away, and he returned and abode in Nineve. And as he was worshipping in the temple of Nesroch his god, his sons slew him with the sword, and Asarhaddon his son reigned in his stead.—*IV. Kings,* xviii., xix.

THE BLASPHEMER STRUCK BLIND.

A few years ago the town of Nottingham was visited with a most awful thunderstorm, the effects of which were most disastrous. The lower part of the town was flooded, and the poorer classes, who inhabited cellars, as well as many shop-keepers, suffered severely. Among those who sought shelter from the pitiless storm in the Milton's Head public-house, was a young man, a lace-maker by trade. For some time he amused himself with ridiculing the fears of the company, but his language, which was from the first light and unbe-coming, became, at last, impious and profane. He used the Holy Name of God in the most blasphemous manner, and, with bitter oaths, expressed a wish that a thunderbolt might come down and strike the company blind. Then, raising himself, he looked through the skylight over the room in which they were sitting, and, with profane gestures, defied the lightning. At that moment a vivid flash entered the room, and in an instant he was lying speechless on the floor. He was taken up by the trembling bystanders, none of whom were injured, and laid upon a couch. The first words he uttered, on recovering his speech, were, " God forgive me ! " He remained, however, blind, and was removed to the general hospital.—*Catholic Weekly Instructor.*[*]

THE BURIED CRUCIFIX.

About the beginning of the present century there lived in Lancashire, among the Aughton congregation, a good religious Catholic woman named Mrs. Ann Spencer, who occupied a farm-house on the Prescot road. In the same neighbourhood there dwelt with his father a young farmer named Charles King, who died a few years since at an advanced age, in the adjoin-ing parish of Lydiate. The following history was related by Mr. King to the priest who attended him on his deathbed,[†] and is given in his own words.

" About sixty years ago it happened that my neighbour, Mrs. Spencer, had a boat load of manure to be carted from the canal. It was customary then, as indeed it is now, for the neighbours to help with their teams, in order that the work might be got through speedily. I accordingly brought

[*] The names of the parties concerned are given in full in the original.
[†] The brother of the author. The latter, also, was well acquainted with Mr. King, a fine old Catholic farmer, full of interesting reminis-cences of his early days.

my father's team to assist, but, having to go to Liverpool in
the afternoon, I did not stay for the dinner given on such
occasions. The next morning I went again, and found Ann
Spencer very indignant at some impiety which her company
had been guilty of the previous day. It seems that, after
dinner, when most of the party had left, there remained
five young men, Protestants, in the room. Now there happened to be a crucifix over the chimney-piece, which they
took down and began to ridicule. They said it was the
Papists' God, &c. 'Let us go,' said one, 'and bury it, and
see if it will rise again in three days.' They carried their
blasphemy into effect, and actually dug a hole in the ground,
into which they thrust it. Mrs. Spencer, who was engaged
in another part of the house, did not hear of the profanity
till afterwards. In relating it to me she was very much
moved, and said, 'Mark my words, not one of those who took
part in this blasphemy will die in his bed.' I did mark her
words, and have lived long enough to witness their exact
fulfilment. These men are all dead, and not one of them
died in his bed. Two were brothers (he mentioned their
names) ; one was killed by falling out of his cart, the other
cut his throat in a barn. A servant-man of theirs was also
present, and he was killed by his team. Another drowned
himself in a pit, and the fifth died in his chair."

Among the many impostures and superstitions of
this *enlightened* age is the doctrine of Spiritualism,
or a belief that we can communicate directly and in
a palpable and material manner with the spirits of
the departed. The following awful event which has
just happened, and has been recorded in almost every
newspaper throughout the land, shews us at the same
time the impious tendency of such attempts, and the
severe judgments which the sin of blasphemy, even in
this life, frequently calls down from the hand of God.

" DIED BY THE VISITATION OF GOD."

In the month of November, 1873, a *seance* or spiritualistic
service was held in the Athenæum Assembly Rooms, in Bir-
mingham, which was attended by the principal believers in
spiritualism residing in the neighbourhood. Among the rest

was a tradesman of the town, who was well known among the spiritualists as a successful medium, and who addressed the meeting on the subject of his past experiences. Among other things, he declared to them that at a certain *seance* he had shaken hands with the Apostle Peter, and that he had on that occasion felt the Apostle's hand firmly clasped within his own. From this he went on to argue that it was very easy to understand how the Apostle Thomas put his hand into our Lord's side, or rather into that which was a representation or personification of our Redeemer. No sooner had he uttered this awful blasphemy than he fell back upon his chair a corpse. This terrible judgment produced a vivid impression on all who were present, and the meeting broke up in the wildest excitement.

At the inquest, held a few days after, over the body of the deceased spiritualist, the usual verdict was declared, the words of which, in such a case, cannot fail to strike the mind as having a special and terrible significance, "Died by the visitation of God."—*See Liverpool Mercury and other Journals.*

The last sin which is here mentioned is that of speaking *profane words*. By profane words, we mean those bad words which are neither oaths nor curses, and which contain nothing blasphemous or indecent, but which are, nevertheless, unbecoming in the mouth of a Christian—such, for example, as the words "what the hell, bloody, devilish," &c. Almighty God warns us in the Holy Scripture that we shall have at the day of judgment to render an account of every idle word, how much more, then, of those which are actually profane! To these we may add the profane use of the Holy Name of God; for instance, when a person has a habit of saying in common conversation "O God, O Lord, O Christ!" &c. Such expressions, though not mortal sins, are most displeasing to God, for his Holy Name should never be taken *in vain;* that is, without due cause and proper respect. Some children are so foolish as to imagine that it makes them look big and like men if they season their speech with profane words. This is the mark of a weak mind; for a modest, simple, and candid way of speaking is one of the most pleasing ornaments of youth.

I have now, my dear children, explained to you in full the different sins forbidden by the second commandment. Listen while I repeat them to you in short. They are four in number—

    1st, *Swearing*—that is taking oaths, whenever the oath is either a false, rash, unjust, or unnecessary one.

    2nd, *Cursing*—that is praying bad prayers on ourselves or others.

    3rd, *Blaspheming*—which means making use of any word or expression injurious to God, or what immediately relates to him.

    4th, *Profane words* and the profane use of the Holy Name of God.

SIXTH INSTRUCTION.

The Third Commandment. What it commands. The obligation of hearing Mass. Sunday a day of rest. What it forbids. Unnecessary servile work. Profanation of the Lord's Day. Innocent recreation not forbidden.

Q. What is the third commandment?
A. Remember that thou keep holy the Sabbath Day.

The third commandment instructs us in the obligation we are under of devoting one particular day in the week to the worship of Almighty God— *Remember that thou keep holy the Sabbath Day.*

Every day, indeed, belongs to God, since man is
the creature of God and time is God's gift; hence
the catechism tells us that we are bound to serve
God *all our days*. It is, however, fitting that besides
rendering to him this general service by daily prayer
and the keeping of his commandments, we should
also devote certain days in a special manner to his
worship. Upon these days we *rest*, that is, abstain
from our daily work, and we do so in order to be
able to spend a portion of our time in adoring God,
thanking him for his daily favours, and imploring
from him those helps and graces which we continually stand in need of both for soul and body.
Hence the day set apart for the worship of God is
called the *Sabbath*, which means the day of rest, and
this is the name which God himself has given to it
in the Holy Scripture.

The institution of the Sabbath, my dear children,
is as old as the world, for it was immediately after
the Creation that God commanded Adam to set apart
this day as a day of rest from his ordinary labour,
in honour of his own Divine rest from the work of
the Creation. "For in six days," says the Holy
Scripture, "the Lord made heaven and earth, and
the sea, and all things that are in them, and rested
on the seventh. Therefore the Lord blessed the
seventh day and sanctified it." * In obedience to the
Divine commandment the holy patriarchs, who lived
before the time of Moses, devoted the seventh day
of the week to the worship of God, spending it with
their families in prayer and the offering of sacrifices.
It was not, however, till the time of Moses that
Almighty God, in giving his commandments on
Mount Sinai, explained in express words the manner
in which the Sabbath was to be sanctified to his
service. "Six days shalt thou labour," he said,

* Gen. ii. 2, 3.

" and shalt do all thy works. But on the seventh day is the Sabbath of the Lord thy God : thou shalt do no work on it, thou nor thy son, nor thy daughter, nor thy man-servant, nor thy maid-servant, nor thy beast, nor the stranger that is within thy gates." * And again God commanded Moses that on the seventh day of the week a special sacrifice of two lambs without spot or blemish should be offered up, in addition to the daily morning and evening sacrifices which were prescribed.†

When our Blessed Lord came down upon earth, he confirmed and established the law respecting the strict observance of the Sabbath, which Almighty God had already delivered to the Jews. He shewed them, however, that they had fallen into some mistakes regarding the manner of keeping it, and that the exact observance of it did not prevent the performance on that day of works of necessity or works of charity. He also, no doubt, instructed the Apostles as to the manner in which the Sabbath was to be observed in the Christian Church, and how it was to be sanctified, as soon as the old law and the ancient sacrifices should be done away with by the offering of the Holy Sacrifice of the Mass.

You will have noticed, my dear children, that the day on which we keep the Sabbath is not the same as that on which it was observed by the Jews. They kept and still keep the Sabbath upon Saturday, we upon Sunday ; they on the seventh, we on the first day of the week. Hence the Jews close their shops and attend their synagogues upon Saturday, but Sunday is observed as the day of rest by all Christians, even by those sects who are separated from the Catholic Church. You will ask, what is the reason of this ? It is because the Apostles, who were the first pastors of the Church, by that authority which

* Exod. xx. 9, 10.   † Numb. xxviii. 9, 10.

they had received from our Blessed Lord to regulate all that regards his public worship, changed the day appointed for the keeping of the Sabbath from Saturday to Sunday—from the seventh to the first day of the week. And why did they do so? To honour the glorious Resurrection of our Blessed Lord and the Descent of the Holy Ghost upon the Apostles, both of which mysteries were accomplished on the first day of the week. From this we may understand how great is the authority of the Church in interpreting or explaining to us the commandments of God—an authority which is acknowledged by the universal practice of the whole Christian world, even of those sects who profess to take the Holy Scriptures as their sole rule of faith, since they observe as the day of rest not the seventh day of the week commanded by the Bible, but the first day, which we know is to be kept holy, only from the tradition and teaching of the Catholic Church.

Q. What are we commanded by the third commandment?
A. We are commanded to keep the Sunday holy.

Q. How are we to keep the Sunday holy?
A. By hearing Mass, and resting from servile works.

We are commanded, my dear children, by this commandment, *to keep the Sunday holy.* Now the catechism teaches us that there are two things which we must do in order to fulfil this duty—*we must hear Mass, and* we must also *rest* or abstain *from servile work.* It is by hearing Mass and resting from servile work that we consecrate and set apart this day to the service of God.

In the first place, *we must hear Mass.* The Holy Sacrifice of the Mass is, as you know, the most sacred, the most solemn, and the highest act of religion. Man cannot worship God in any way that is so worthy of him and so pleasing in his sight as by offering up or assisting at Mass. And why so? Because the Mass is the sacrifice of the Body and Blood of Jesus Christ, the Second Person of the Blessed Trinity, and the Beloved Son of the Eternal Father. Hence it is a sacrifice of infinite value, and one with which Almighty God cannot fail to be well pleased. In no way, therefore, can we honour God so profoundly, atone for our sins so effectually, or obtain his grace so securely, as by hearing Mass devoutly and uniting our prayers and intentions with those of the priest. For this reason the Church teaches us that one of the chief means of sanctifying the Sunday is to assist at the Holy Sacrifice of the Mass, and has moreover laid upon us a strict injunction, which you will find among the commandments of the Church, not to be absent from this duty *under pain of mortal sin.*

But notice that we are bound not only to be *present* at Mass, but to assist at it with *attention* and *devotion.* To do this we must banish from our minds all wilful distractions, and spend the time of Mass in fervent prayer and good and holy thoughts. We should also assist at Mass with profound *reverence,* kneeling respectfully in body and prostrate in soul before that Lord of heaven and earth who is present upon the altar. Ah, if we could only see with our eyes what we know by faith takes place at the holy Mass, we should be lost in admiration, reverence, and love! We should behold the Son of God, equal in all things to his Eternal Father, coming down, as it were, from his throne of glory, concealing the majesty and splendour of his Godhead and of his Glorified Body under the form of a little host, and offered to God for the sins and wants of man by the hands of the priest. And all around we should behold the Angels bowing in profound adoration, while they sing with heavenly voices that song, which cannot be heard by mortal ears, but which we hope one day to sing with them in Paradise, " Holy, holy, holy, Lord God of Sabbaoth. Blessed is he that cometh in the name of the Lord." Oh! my dear children, never profane these awful mysteries by any bad behaviour at the time of Mass, for example, by playing, looking round, whispering or talking. Remember that our Blessed Lord sees you from the altar, and that you grieve him and prevent him from bestowing his grace upon you by such conduct. The Angels also see you, they are struck with horror, and would, out of a holy zeal, severely punish you, did not the Mercy of God restrain them.

There is another point which we must take notice of in regard to the obligations of hearing Mass, and that is that we are bound to be present during the *whole* of the Mass; for it is the Mass, and not a part of it only, that we are bound to hear. If anyone, therefore, comes late to Mass or goes away before it is finished, he is guilty of sin, which is mortal or venial according to circumstances. If he has been wilfully absent from a considerable portion of the Mass, or from an important part of it, he has been guilty of grievous sin; but if he has missed only a small part of the Mass he is still guilty of sin, though the offence is only venial. You will ask me, perhaps, how late a person must be to cause him to miss Mass and commit a mortal sin. This is very difficult to determine. It is commonly thought, however, that if a person comes in to Mass after the Gospel is ended, he does not fulfil the obligation, and is consequently guilty of grievous sin. Such a one, if it be possible, must stay to hear another Mass, or go elsewhere for the purpose, so that he may be able to fulfil the law of the Church. I may remark that persons who are in the habit of coming late to chapel through their own fault are very often guilty of grievous sin, for though they may come in before the Gospel is ended, yet they expose themselves to the imminent danger of missing a considerable portion of the Holy Sacrifice. When, therefore, you come to Mass, take care to be at the chapel a few minutes before the Mass commences, not only that you may be in no danger of being late, but also that you may have time to recollect yourselves and prepare your minds for the great mysteries at which you are about to assist. Nothing can be more unbecoming, irreverent, and disedifying than for people to make a practice of crowding in when the Mass is already commencing, or of leaving the chapel before the end of it, or while the priest is yet at the altar.

You see, my dear children, from what I have told you, how strict is the obligation of hearing Mass upon Sunday. There are, however, certain occasions in which it would be no sin to be absent from it. For example, if you were laid up at home by serious illness, or were at such a distance from chapel that you could not be present at Mass without great difficulty, you would be excused from attending. Again, it would be no sin for you to miss Mass if you had to stay at home to nurse a sick person, or to keep the house while the rest of the family went to church. In such cases, however, an arrangement should be made by which the members of the family might take it in turn to hear Mass Sunday about, or if there is more than one Mass, by which some might go to the early and some to the later Mass, and thus all be able to fulfil the obligation. With regard to sickness and distance from chapel, we must always remember that it is not a slight sickness or a moderate distance which will excuse us, but such an illness or distance as will render it a serious difficulty to be present. If you be in doubt whether you are really excused, be guided by the advice of your confessor, if you are able to consult him, or otherwise of some pious and prudent person.

We read, in the Lives of the Saints, a beautiful example of the fidelity displayed by the early Christians in fulfilling this duty, even at the peril of their lives. It is the history of

ST. SATURNINUS AND THE MARTYRS OF AFRICA.

During the cruel persecution of the Empress Maximian, forty-nine Christians had assembled in a private house at Abitina, a city of Africa, to assist at the holy Sacrifice of the Mass, which was said by the priest Saturninus. The officers of justice broke into the house during the celebration of the Sacred Mysteries, arrested those who were present, and conveyed them before the public tribunal under a guard of soldiers. By order of the judge, they were sent to Carthage, the capital city of the province, where they were again examined and cruelly tortured. Being asked by the proconsul why they had assembled together in spite of the decrees of the Emperor, St. Saturninus answered in the name of the rest, "It is because we are not permitted to be absent from the Sacred Mysteries. This is the commandment and teaching of the Divine Law. This Law we faithfully observe, and for this we lay down our lives." In the midst of their torments they prayed as follows, "O Lord Jesus Christ, we are Christians, and thou art our hope." The judge, unable to shake their constancy, sent them back to prison, where most of them died of starvation, martyrs for their faithful observance of the third commandment.—*Rohrbacher. Vies des Saints*, Feb. 11.

To keep the Sunday holy, it is not, however, sufficient to hear Mass, we must also, as the Catechism says, *rest from servile work.* "Thou shalt do no work on it, thou, nor thy son, nor thy daughter, nor thy man servant, nor thy maid servant, nor thy beast, nor the stranger that is within thy gates." But, you will ask me, what is meant by *servile work*, which is what Almighty God here forbids. By servile work we mean *manual labour*, in other words, hard work done with the hands, such as that which servants, labourers, mechanics, &c., usually perform. Thus, for example, digging is servile work, so also is ploughing, haymaking, building, joinering and working in the coal pit or factory. Again, it is servile work to follow the trade of a baker, butcher, watchmaker, tailor or shoemaker. There are other works, also, which are usually performed by females that are servile by nature, for example, sewing or knitting, scouring, washing and ironing. All these employments, and others of a similar nature, are strictly forbidden upon Sunday; if they were not, Sunday would be no longer a day of rest, but a day of labour. There are other kinds of works, however, which are not servile, because they are performed with the mind rather than with the body, and which are therefore not forbidden upon Sunday. Such are reading, writing, drawing and painting; I mean painting pictures, not walls or houses. Such works as these do not break the Sunday, because there is no great bodily labour attending them.

ANECDOTE OF SIR THOMAS MORE.

When Sir Thomas More was imprisoned in the tower of London by King Henry VIII. for refusing to acknowledge him as the head of the Church, it was remarked that he took as much care to dress himself in his best upon Sunday as he had done during the time that he was at liberty. Being asked why he was so particular about his dress now that there was no longer any one to see him, he replied, "I did not dress myself in my best when I was in the world through human respect or to please the world, but out of respect to God and in honour of his sacred day."—*Life of Sir Thomas More.*

Q. Why are we commanded to rest from work ?

A. That we may have time and opportunity for prayer, going to the Sacraments, hearing instructions, and reading good books.

From this answer you see that Almighty God, in ordering us to abstain from bodily labour upon Sunday, does not intend us to spend that day in idleness or pleasure. If we are commanded to rest from servile work, it is in order *that we may have* that *time and opportunity* which we could not well secure on other days of the week *for prayer, going to the Sacraments, hearing instructions and reading good books*, in other words, for the service and worship of God. For Sunday is, as you know, *the Lord's day*, a day which he has especially reserved for himself, " the seventh day is the Sabbath of the Lord thy God." Let us now consider what those works of piety are, to which Sunday should be principally devoted.

In the first place, the Catechism teaches us that Sunday should be especially a day of *prayer*. It is by prayer, my dear children, that we converse with God, acknowledge him for our Lord and Sovereign Master, thank him for his past blessings, implore his pardon for our offences, and beg of him all those graces which we stand in need of both for soul and body. No exercise can, therefore, be more suitable for Sunday than that of prayer. The most perfect form of prayer is, as I have told you, the holy Sacrifice of the Mass, which we are bound to assist at under pain of mortal sin ; but a good Catholic will not be content on Sunday with hearing Mass ; he will also be present at the other services of the Church, namely, the afternoon or evening prayers and Benediction of the Most Holy Sacrament. The beautiful service of Benediction is, indeed, after the Mass, one of the most excellent of all devotions, for in it we gather together at the feet of our Blessed Lord, present upon the altar, to lay before him our sorrows, our trials and our wants, to enjoy the sweetness of his presence, and receive his loving blessing.

Never, if you can help it, be absent from Benediction; to assist at it devoutly, you will find, brings peace and joy to the soul, and is the source of the choicest graces. Those, however, who, through distance from chapel or other causes, are unable to attend the afternoon or evening service, will do well to supply for it, as far as possible, by reciting at home the rosary or other devout prayers.

In the second place, the catechism teaches us, that we cannot better sanctify the Sunday than by approaching to *the holy Sacraments.* For it is by Confession and the Holy Communion that our souls become purified from sin and united to God, nor can we certainly keep the Lord's day in a manner more befitting, than by inviting the Lord himself into our souls, and entertaining him there by a devout and holy Communion. Oh, how sweet and happy are those Sundays which we consecrate to God by approaching worthily to the holy Sacraments! To such days may the words of the Psalmist be well applied, " Better is one day in thy courts, O Lord, above a thousand." May you, my dear children, who have made your first communion, often enjoy this happiness. Nourished frequently with the Bread of Life, you will grow strong in the grace and love of God, you will learn to despise the world and its vanities, to fix your thoughts and affections on heaven, and to keep yourselves pure and innocent in the midst of a wicked world. And do you who have not yet received our Blessed Lord, beg of him earnestly, whenever you assist at holy Mass, to come at least spiritually into your hearts, and to prepare them by his grace for that loving visit which he is about to pay you on the great day of your first Communion.

The third means of sanctifying the Sunday mentioned in the Catechism is attendance at *religious instruction.* I have already told you, in explaining the first commandment, that it is the duty of every Christian to be instructed as fully as possible in the truths of religion. Now, there is no day more suitable for the fulfilment of this duty than Sunday, when our minds, being no longer distracted by worldly occupations, are better able to fix themselves on the things of God. The Church has wisely provided for this want by the establishment of Sunday Schools, and the public catechism, which it is the duty of every Catholic child to attend. Neither are grown-up persons excused from the duty of obtaining religious instruction. The sermon at the late Mass, and the discourse at the evening Benediction, are the principal means afforded to them of fulfilling this obligation. Hence those Catholics who content themselves with hearing an early Mass upon Sunday, and through sloth or indifference attend no other service, cannot, generally speaking, be excused from sin on account of their wilful neglect of religious instruction.

I may here remark, my dear children, that there are some young people who, when they have been admitted to their first Communion, think that they have no longer any occasion to attend the Sunday School, or assist at Catechism. They forget that the truths of religion cannot be too deeply impressed upon our minds. Moreover, there is always something fresh to be learned about Almighty God, and the more we know of him the better shall we love him, and the more faithfully shall we fulfil our duty to him. Follow, therefore, in this the wishes of your parents and the advice of your pastor. And when at length you have grown up and completed your instruction, many of you will, I trust, be able to show your gratitude and love to God by helping in the work of the Sunday School, and instructing those who are ignorant of the truths of religion, whenever opportunity offers. How happy will you be if you are able to assist in teaching others how to know and love our Good God ; and how great and glorious will be your reward in the next life, according to the words of the prophet Daniel, " They that instruct many to justice shall shine as stars for all eternity ! " *

In the last place, we are taught to make the reading of *good books* one of the chief exercises by which to sanctify the Sunday. For there is hardly anything that is likely to make a deeper impression on our hearts, or lead us more powerfully to the love and service of God, than the attentive perusal of works of piety—such, for example, as those in which the life of our Blessed Lord or of his Saints is set before us for our imitation, or in which we are taught to meditate on the truths of eternity, or are instructed in the doctrines of our faith. I would earnestly advise you all to provide yourselves by degrees with a small library of good religious books. Among others, I would recommend the New Testament, the History of the Bible, that excellent little work the Think Well On't, the Poor Man's Catechism, and the Sufferings of Jesus, by St. Alphonsus Liguori. To these might be added a few volumes of the Lives of the Saints, and the Glories of Mary or some other book of devotion to our Blessed Lady. These excellent works are not like the silly tales and magazines of the day, the greater part of which do nothing but fill the mind with idle and dangerous thoughts, and are only read to be thrown aside ; they are full of spiritual wisdom and useful instruction, and every time they are read they bring fresh profit to the soul. It is impossible for any one to go far astray who is fond of reading

* Dan. xii. 3.

religious books, for the good instructions they contain will powerfully serve to restrain him from sin, and keep him in the path of virtue. There are many Saints now in heaven who owe to the reading of some Saint's Life, or other religious book which Providence threw in their way, their conversion from a sinful and worldly life to one of penance and heroic virtue. Of this you will see an example in the history of St. Ignatius Loyola, whose conversion I will now relate to you.

CONVERSION OF ST. IGNATIUS LOYOLA.

The great St. Ignatius Loyola, founder of the Society of Jesus, was born of a noble family, and followed in his youth the profession of arms in the service of the king of Spain. The character of Ignatius was open, generous, and courageous ; he was, however, vain of his personal appearance, fond of pleasure, and full of worldly and ambitious thoughts. He ardently longed to distinguish himself in the service of his king, and to gain for himself the esteem and applause of the world. An opportunity soon occurred to put his courage to the test. The city of Pampeluna was besieged by the French army, and, owing to the death of his superior officer, it fell to the lot of Ignatius to direct the defence. On this occasion he gave proof of great and noble qualities. Though at the head of but a small force, he scorned every proposal to surrender, encouraged the drooping spirits of the soldiers, and led them in person to attack the besiegers. In the engagement he was wounded by a cannon ball, which shattered his leg, and he was carried back helpless to the fortress. After the surrender of the city he was permitted by the French to retire to his own home, the Castle of Loyola, where he remained for many months helpless and confined to his bed. To while away the time, he desired his attendants to bring him some romances or tales of chivalry, but they could find no such books in the castle. They brought him, however, a volume of the Lives of the Saints, which they had met with in their search. Ignatius at first laid it impatiently aside, as ill suited to his taste ; seeing, however, that no other book could be procured, he at length opened and began to read it. By degrees his attention became awakened, and he could not help admiring the noble generosity of men who had sacrificed

fortune, worldly honour, and even life itself in the service of
God. He soon began to compare their lives with his own,
to reflect on the emptiness and vanity of all that passes with
time, and to understand how wisely the Saints had acted in
preferring the service of the God of Heaven to that of an
earthly king. From that time Ignatius resolved to occupy
himself no longer with the vain pursuit of earthly glory, but
to devote himself to the great work of obtaining the victory
over his own passions and promoting the glory of his
Heavenly Master. Accordingly upon his recovery he retired
into solitude, where he gave himself up to the practice of
penance and prayer. Soon after he laid the foundation of
the illustrious order of the Jesuits, the members of which,
by the great works which they have performed for the education of youth and the preaching of the Gospel, have so well
fulfilled those words which St. Ignatius took as the rule and
motto of his life, "Ad majorem Dei Gloriam"—all to the
greater Glory of God.—*Life of St. Ignatius.*

ST. AUGUSTINE'S EXPERIENCE OF THE USE OF GOOD BOOKS.

A certain courtier, a friend of St. Augustine, was one day
walking near the city of Triers with three of his gay companions, when two of them, who were officers in the Emperor's
army, chanced to enter a cottage which was the dwelling-
place of some devout servants of God. Here they perceived
upon the table a copy of the life of the great St. Anthony
the hermit, which one of them opened through curiosity.
Attracted, says St. Augustine, by something which caught
his eye, he began to read, and reading to admire, and admiring, to burn with the desire of imitating so noble and heroic
an example. At length inflamed with what he read, and
burning with a holy zeal, he cried out to his companion,
"Tell me, I pray, with all the pains we take, what does our
ambition aspire to? Have we any greater hopes at court
than to arrive at the friendship and favour of the Emperor?
And when this is obtained, how long will it last? But behold,
if I please, I can become this moment the friend and favourite
of God, and remain such for ever." So saying, he paused;
but having read a little further he again exclaimed, "Behold,
now, I bid adieu to former hopes, and am fully resolved to
have no other pursuit but that of serving God. I begin
from this very hour, in this very place. For you, if you do
not imitate my example, at least do not hinder my resolu-

lution." The other replied that, so far from hindering him, he wished to stand by his side in so noble a warfare for so glorious a reward. Accordingly, taking leave of their other companions, who had now rejoined them, they remained in the cottage ; upon receiving news of which, the two young ladies to whom they were espoused consecrated their virginity to God.

This example, which was related to St. Augustine by his friend Pontitianus, one of the four, at a time when his mind was still wavering between the force of truth and the violence of his passions, raised immediately a mighty conflict within his breast. Agitated by his feelings, and drawn by the grace of God, he retired into the garden to pray. Here he poured forth the anguish of his heart with bitter sighs and tears, when suddenly he heard the voice of a child frequently repeating these words, " Tolle lege ; tolle lege "—take and read ; take and read. Upon this, rising up in amazement, he went to fetch the book of St. Paul's Epistles, which he had left hard by, and opening it, he lighted upon the words, " Put ye on the Lord Jesus Christ, and make no provision for the flesh and its concupiscences." He read no further, nor had he need ; for at the end of these lines a new gleam of confidence and security streamed into his heart, and all the darkness of his former hesitation was dispelled. He immediately went in and told the good news to St. Monica, who was transported with joy. He then put himself under the care of St. Ambrose, who shortly after conferred upon him the sacrament of Baptism.—*Life of St. Augustine.*

Q. What does the third commandment forbid ?
A. The third commandment forbids unnecessary servile work and all profanation of the Lord's day.

We come now to speak of the sins which are forbidden by the third commandment. There are two mentioned in the catechism, namely, *unnecessary servile work* and *profanation of the Lord's day.* These sins are opposed to the two duties of resting from servile work and devoting the Sunday to the worship of God, which we are commanded by this commandment to practise.

I told you, my dear children, that Almighty God, in appointing the Sabbath as a day of rest, has forbidden all manual labour upon that day—" Thou shalt do no work thereon." Hence, when he sent the Manna from heaven to feed the Israelites in the desert, he strictly forbade them to gather any on the Sabbath. To prevent the necessity of their doing so, he told them to collect on the day before the Sabbath what would be sufficient for the wants of that and the following day. Moreover, he ordered that those who broke the third commandment by working on the Sabbath should be most severely punished. Thus we read in the Old Testament that on one occasion, while the Jews were in the desert, it happened that a man was found gathering sticks upon the Sabbath day. He was brought for punishment to Moses and Aaron, who consulted Almighty God as to what was to be done with him. The answer which God gave, shews us the grievous nature of this sin and the severe punishment which it deserves. "Let that man die," said Almighty God, " and let all the multitude stone him without the camp." Now, if the crime of that man in gathering a few sticks upon the Jewish Sabbath was so great, and the punishment which he received so severe, how much greater must be the guilt of Christians, and how much more terrible will not their punishment be, if they profane or cause others to profane by servile work the Christian Sabbath—a day consecrated to God in honour of such sublime mysteries !

There are two reasons, however, which excuse the performance of servile work upon Sunday, and render it no longer sinful. These works are *necessity* and *charity*. We are permitted to do on Sunday work which is of absolute necessity, and which cannot be performed upon a week day. We are also allowed in certain cases to work, out of a motive of charity to our neighbour. I will explain to you what I mean by two examples taken from the holy Gospels.

THE DISCIPLES OF JESUS AND THE EARS OF CORN.

It happened one Sabbath day that, as our Blessed Lord was walking through a corn-field with his disciples, the latter, being hungry, gathered a few ears of corn and began to eat them. In doing so they did not commit any theft, since it was the custom of the country and allowed by the law, that whoever should pass through a corn-field or vine-yard might eat of the corn or of the grapes as he passed along, provided that he did not stop or go aside to gather. Now it happened that some of the Pharisees, having heard of this, took offence and came to our Lord to lay a complaint against his disciples as breakers of the Sabbath. "Behold," said they, "thy disciples do that which is not lawful to do on the Sabbath day." Our Blessed Lord, however, took up their defence, and shewed that they were to be excused, inasmuch as they had acted through hunger and necessity.

"Have you never heard," said he, "what David did when he had need, and was hungry himself and those that were with him? How he went into the house of God under Abiathar the high priest, and did eat the loaves of proposition, which was not lawful to eat but for the priests, and gave to those who were with him?" And he said to them, "The Sabbath was made for man, and not man for the Sabbath."—*Matt.* xii. 1, &c. ; *Mark* ii. 23, &c.

From this example you see how a strict necessity excuses the performance of servile work upon the Sabbath, since, as our Blessed Lord shewed the Jews, it excused in David and his followers a greater violation of the law, viz., the eating of the consecrated shew-bread. From the following history we shall learn that charity, or the performance of some great work of mercy, likewise excuses us from the observance of the law in this respect.

THE INFIRM WOMAN HEALED BY OUR LORD.

"And he was teaching," says the Holy Scripture, "in their synagogue on the Sabbath. And behold there was a woman who had a spirit of infirmity eighteen years, and she was bowed together, neither could she look upwards at all. Whom when Jesus saw, he called her unto him and said to her, *Woman, thou art delivered from thy infirmity.* And he laid his hands upon her, and immediately she was made straight and glorified God.

"And the ruler of the synagogue being angry that Jesus had healed on the Sabbath, answering, said to the multitude, *Six days there are wherein you ought to work. In them, therefore, come and be healed, and not on the Sabbath day.* And the Lord answering him said, *Ye hypocrites, doth not every one of you on the Sabbath day loose his ox or his ass from the manger, and lead them to water? And ought not the daughter of Abraham, whom Satan hath bound, lo, these eighteen years, be loosed from this bond on the Sabbath day?* And when he had said these things all his adversaries were ashamed."— *Luke* xiii. 10, &c.

Although, as we have seen, necessity and charity often excuse the performance of servile work upon Sunday, we must remember that this is to be understood of a strict necessity and a pressing call of charity. For example, some sudden accident occurs upon the railway. If the damage done to the line be not repaired at once, all traffic will be interrupted, and the lives of many endangered. The machinery breaks down at some large manufactory. If not set right on the Sunday, hundreds will be thrown out of employment on the Monday morning. Again the fires must be kept up at some kiln or furnace, or else the material which is being manufactured will be all spoiled. In these and similar cases it is allowable to work, because there is a real necessity for it, and great evil would arise and serious loss if the work were not done. But we must be careful not to excuse ourselves too easily, or to imagine that there is a necessity when really there is none. Those who are negligent and careless in the performance of their religious duties often make excuses for themselves which certainly Almighty God will not admit. A tailor, for example, works upon Sunday to complete an order required upon Monday, but which by a little extra effort during the week or by engaging more hands, he might have already despatched. A woman washes and mends her children's clothes on the Sunday morning. She says that she *must* do it, for that the children cannot go dirty or ragged to chapel. But could she not, by a little foresight, have provided for this by washing and mending them during the week? Again, a shoemaker works at his trade, and makes or mends shoes upon a Sunday. He says that he cannot support his family unless he works on Sunday: they are poor and in want, and he must do his best for them. I answer, better a thousand times be poor than profane that day by servile work which God has commanded us to keep holy. Better the little you earn during the week with God's blessing, than great earnings made upon Sunday with his curse. But indeed Sunday's earnings never did enrich any one nor ever will, for they have the blight of God's curse upon them. It is a common but a very true saying that money badly got never caused any one to thrive. You will understand what I mean from the following little story.

THE SHOEMAKER AND THE MERCHANT.

At the beginning of the present century there lived at Lyons a poor shoemaker named Berthier, who was to be seen working at his stall every Sunday morning. In the same street, and opposite to his house, dwelt a wealthy merchant, who, being a good Catholic, was grieved to see that his poorer neighbour neglected the duties of his religion, and determined, if possible, to reclaim him. Accordingly one day he spoke to him on the subject, and represented to him how much he offended God by working on a Sunday. The shoemaker replied that it was necessity that compelled him to do so. "You that are rich," added he, "can well afford to be idle one day in the week, but as for me, I could neither finish my work nor support my family if I did not labour on the Sunday." "My good friend," replied the merchant, "all I ask of you is to give my advice a fair trial. But I do not wish that you should be the loser by so doing. Promise me that you will do no work and will attend your Mass on Sunday for the next six months, and I engage on my part to make good all the losses you sustain by following my advice. Do you accept my offer?" "Willingly," replied, Berthier. "It is much easier for me to rest than to work, so that, as I am not in any case to be the loser, it is a bargain."

At the end of the six months the merchant paid another visit to the shoemaker. "My friend," said he, "I have been delighted to see that you have kept your promise. Tell me, now, the amount of your losses, for I have engaged to make them good." "Ah, sir," replied Berthier, "it is I that am in *your* debt, not you in *mine*, for I have been the gainer by our agreement." "In what way?" said the merchant. "I will tell you," replied the shoemaker. "At first I found a little inconvenience in not having my work completed, but as I was determined to keep up to my promise, I learned to push on matters during the week, and not to undertake more than I could accomplish. Soon I found that, by resting on the Sunday, I was so much refreshed and strengthened in body and mind as to be able to do as much work in the six days as I had before done in the seven. Meanwhile I attended church regularly with my family, and there heard many excellent instructions, which shewed me the danger in which I had been of losing my soul for a paltry gain. Accordingly I began to prepare for my confession, which I had long neglected. I made it to the best of my power, and received Holy Communion. I need not say that the peace and joy which I have felt since is far beyond any temporal gain ; but indeed I have lost nothing, for, somehow or other, I am quite as well off as I was before." "I am delighted to hear it," said the merchant ; "but tell me, how are matters going on now between yourself and your wife, for formerly, as every one knows, there was not a day without a quarrel?" "It is too true," said Berthier, "and I used to think that my poor wife was always in fault ; but when I became better instructed I began to see that she was not always wrong, neither was I always right ; so when we went to confession together we made it up to bear with each other and live peaceably for the time to come. Since that time peace and happiness have reigned in our house, and we have now time to devote ourselves to the care of our children." "I congratulate you on your happiness," said the merchant, "and I must acknowledge that I am not really in your debt, since you have derived profit rather than loss from my advice. But see, here is the money which I intended for you ; take it as a mark of my friendship. I am only too happy in having been the means of shewing you how true it is that no one ever loses by what he does for God."—*Power's Catechism.*

We come now to speak of the other sins forbidden by this commandment, which are included in these words of your catechism, *all profanation of the Lord's day.* The sin we have just been speaking of— namely, doing servile work upon Sunday—is one way of profaning the Lord's day, but there are many others. For example, those who spend Sunday in drinking, gambling, sinful amusements, or in riotous and disorderly conduct, profane the Lord's day ; so also do those who buy, and sell, and trade as they would on a week day, unless they are excused by some good and sufficient reason. All who act in this manner are guilty of a sinful profanation, since, instead of making Sunday truly the Lord's day, by devoting a considerable portion of it to his Divine worship, they make it a day of mere amusement and sinful indulgence, or else a day of worldly business and profit.

You will sometimes hear it said that Catholics are not sufficiently strict in this respect, and that they allow games and amusements upon Sunday, a thing which Protestants have often a great horror of. It is true, my dear children, that the Church does allow innocent recreation upon Sunday, as long as we have fulfilled the duty we owe to Almighty God by giving a due proportion of the day to his Divine Worship. For piety does not consist in a long face, but in a pure and loving heart; and our good God does not wish to be served in sadness and melancholy, but in joy and gladness. Moreover,

God has expressly given us the Sabbath as a day of *rest* ; that is, a day on which we may relax the mind and refresh the body, to prepare ourselves to enter with renewed vigour on the work of the succeeding week. Hence there is no harm, after you have performed the religious duties of Sunday, in your enjoying an innocent game at play with your companions, or a pleasant walk in the country. But we should be careful to avoid any amusement which is unbecoming the holiness of a day consecrated to the worship of God, or which, owing to the habits and prejudices of those among whom we live, can reasonably become to them an occasion of offence or scandal.

To buy and sell, to barter and traffic upon Sunday is, as I have said, a profanation of that day which God has commanded to be kept holy and consequently free from the cares and anxieties of daily life. But there are certain cases in which such dealings are permitted on the ground of necessity or charity. For example, a druggist commits no sin by selling upon Sunday medicines required for the relief of the sick ; and, again, those who keep houses of refreshment are permitted to supply the wants of the passing traveller. For the Church, like a tender mother, compassionates the wants of her children, and does not wish to lay upon them a yoke or burden which they are unable to bear. She remembers the words of our Blessed Redeemer, that Almighty God desireth mercy rather than sacrifice,* and, again, that other saying of his, " the Sabbath was made for man, and not man for the Sabbath." †

I will now relate to you a few examples, from which you will see how grievous a sin, in the sight of God, is the profanation of his holy day, and with what severe punishments he often visits, even in

* Matt. xii. 7.   † Mark, ii. 27.

this world, those who are guilty of this heinous crime.

NICANOR AND THE JEWS.

During the struggle which ensued between Judas Machabeus and the Syrian generals of Antiochus, it happened that Nicanor, one of the latter, was on the point of attacking Judas with an overwhelming army on the Sabbath day. The Jews, whom he had forced to serve among his troops, begged of him to respect the Sabbath, and defer the attack till the morrow. Nicanor, in a mocking tone, asked them if He who had commanded the Sabbath to be kept was a God of great might and power, and, on receiving an answer in the affirmative, he blasphemously replied that as he himself was mighty upon earth, it was him they must obey and not God. But God avenged himself on the blasphemer; for, in the engagement which followed, the troops of Nicanor were defeated with great slaughter, and the General himself was numbered with the slain.—*II. Machab.* xv.

THE AVARICIOUS MILLER.

A certain miller in a town in France, in order to increase his gains, was in the habit of pursuing his trade upon every Sunday and festival. While all the villagers were attending the High Mass at the parish church, he might be seen at his mill, employed in his usual avocations, and his irreligious conduct had become notorious in the neighbourhood. One day he went out as usual to his work, but, seeing the people pass by on their way to church, hid himself behind the sails of his mill, which were at that time stationary through want of wind. He had not been there long before a breeze sprung up, and the sails, being suddenly put in motion, caught his body and flung him violently into the air. Alarmed at his prolonged absence, his wife after some hours came to seek him, and found his lifeless body extended on the ground. It presented a fearful spectacle, being pierced in many places with the sharp points of the mill sails, and bruised and shattered with the violence of his fall.—*Instructions of Youth.*

THE AVALANCHE.

In a small village situated on the slopes of the Alps there lived a few years since a man, who was notorious for his open and scandalous profanation of the Sunday. So far from attending Divine service in his parish church, it was his custom, as soon as the Sunday dawned, to set out with some companions, whom he had misled by his evil example, to hunt the chamois and other wild animals on the mountain side.   In vain did his parish priest endeavour, by every means that zeal and charity could suggest, to reclaim him from so unbecoming a practice.   It was all to no purpose, and at length seeing that the miserable man continued obstinate in his wickedness, the zealous pastor threatened him with the anger of God in case he did not desist from scandalising the neighbourhood by his public impiety.

Shortly after, he set out as usual for the chase one Sunday morning, accompanied by two comrades.   A heavy fall of snow had taken place during the night, but this gave the party little concern, as it served to render the traces of the game more visible, and to increase their prospect of a good day's sport.   They had not, however, proceeded far when the two companions of the unhappy man, who were following in his track, perceived to their horror that, wherever he trod, his footsteps were marked with blood.   Unable to account for the strange occurrence, and struck with a secret fear of the impending judgment of God, they both united in imploring him to discontinue the expedition for that day at least, informing him of what they had witnessed.   He refused, however, telling them, with a laugh, that the blood on his track was an omen of a good day's sport.   Whatever may have been the cause of this extraordinary occurrence— whether it proceeded from a natural cause, or was permitted by Almighty God as a mysterious warning—it exercised a wholesome influence over his companions, who, touched by the grace of God and finding that he persisted in his design, began to retrace their steps.   They had not proceeded far when they heard a noise as it were of thunder behind their backs, and looking hastily round beheld the profaner of the Sabbath carried away by an avalanche, which came rolling down the side of the mountain.   They ran with all speed to the village for assistance, and the inhabitants flocked out to search for the unhappy man.   It was not, however, till some days after that his body was discovered in a neighbouring ravine, buried many feet beneath the surface of the snow.*

* This occurrence was related to the writer in 1855 by the Rev. Pere Ermanjaud, the curé of a small village, situated in the neighbourhood of that where the catastrophe had a short time previously taken place.

SEVENTH INSTRUCTION.

The Fourth Commandment. What it commands. Duties of Children to their Parents—namely, Love, Honour and Obedience. The Duties we owe to our Pastors, Rulers, Teachers and Employers. Obligation of contributing to the support of our Pastors.

Q. What is the fourth commandment ?
A. Honour thy father and thy mother.

We have now gone through the first three commandments, which teach us our duty to Almighty God, and we come to speak of the remainder, which instruct us in our obligations to our fellow-men. These seven remaining commandments shew us how to fulfil the second precept of charity, " Thou shalt love thy neighbour as thyself," just as the three which you have learnt teach us how to keep the first precept, " Thou shalt love the Lord thy God with thy whole heart." The commandments which we are coming to are, however, closely connected with those that have gone before, for it is by loving our neighbour that we prove the reality of our love to God. Whence the Apostle St. John says, " He that loveth not his brother whom he seeth, how can he love God whom he seeth not ? *

Among those whom we are bound by the law of charity to love, our parents certainly hold the first place, since it is to them under God that we are

* John, iv. 20.

I

indebted for our birth, our support in infancy and childhood, our education and many other blessings. Hence Almighty God has placed the duty, which we owe to our parents, foremost among all our obligations to our fellow-men, and after instructing us, in the first three commandments, as to what immediately regards his own Divine service, he goes on, in the fourth, to teach us what is due to our earthly parents, *" Honour thy father and thy mother*, that thou mayest live a long time, and it may be well with thee in the land which the Lord thy God will give thee."*

You will notice that to this commandment alone, among all the rest, Almighty God has added a special promise to those who faithfully observe it, namely, the promise of a long life and every happiness. It is true that the keeping of the other commandments will not pass unrewarded both in this life and in the world to come, but it would seem as if God, by making known to us the special blessings which attend the observance of this commandment, desired to impress upon us the particular importance of the duties which it enjoins, and to urge us most powerfully to fulfil them. Remember, then, my dear children, that if you love, honour and obey your parents, Almighty God has promised you, on his own Divine word, a long and a happy life. Disobedient and undutiful children are very often, by the just judgment of God, cut off by death in the flower of their youth, and if spared for a time by the mercy of God, who waits for their repentance, their days are usually full of evil, that is, of trouble and affliction. On the contrary, good and docile children enjoy during this life the special blessing and protection of God ; and if, in his all-seeing Providence, he sometimes takes them to himself while yet young and innocent, it is only in order that they may not lose the purity of their

* Deut. v. 16.

souls by sin, that *it may be well with them* in the next life, and that *they may live a long time*, nay for all eternity, *in the land which he will give them*, namely, amid the joys and delights of his heavenly kingdom.

Q. What are we commanded by the fourth commandment ?

A. We are commanded to love, honour and obey our parents in all that is not sin.

Q. Are we bound to assist our parents in their wants ?

A. Yes, certainly; both in their temporal and in their spiritual wants.

We come now to speak of the different duties which we are commanded by this commandment to practise, and of the manner in which we must discharge them. First of all, the catechism speaks of the duties which children, and those who are under authority, owe to their parents and superiors, and it then goes on to treat of the duties which parents and superiors are required on their part to perform towards those whom God has placed under their charge.

The catechism tells us that we are bound to *love, honour and obey our parents in all that is not sin.* Here, you see, are mentioned three distinct duties which children owe to their parents, namely, *love, honour* and *obedience.* These duties are, indeed, so clearly taught us by reason and the voice of our conscience that even the very pagans, who did not know God, both acknowledged and to a great extent fulfilled them. If you read the history of Greece or of Rome, you will there find related beautiful instances of filial reverence and love, which are sufficient to make the children of many Christian parents blush for their undutiful conduct; and even at the present time, among the Chinese and other infidel nations, the veneration and tender affection which are exhibited by children towards their parents, frequently fill the traveller with surprise and admiration.

The first duty which we owe to our parents, namely, to *love* them, is, as I have said, a sentiment natural to the human heart. There is, indeed, no feeling so deeply implanted in the breast of man as the natural affection which a child bears to those who have given him birth ; that child is justly regarded as a deformity, a monster of nature, who does not love his parents. By this commandment, however, we are taught that we must not love our parents with a mere human affection, like that with which the children of infidels and pagans love those who have brought them into the world, but we must love them because God so wills it, and because they hold in our regard the place of God. Our earthly father should be to us the image of our Heavenly Father, and we should look upon our mother as chosen to nurse and cherish us by Him who loves us with infinitely more than a mother's love, and who, as he himself tells us, though a mother were to forget the child of her womb, still will not be unmindful of us.* Moreover, the love which we bear them must not be a mere sentiment or feeling of the heart, it must be shown also by our outward conduct. Never must we sadden them by any unkind word or undutiful behaviour ; on the contrary, we must show them every mark and token of our affection. Remember that the feelings of parents towards their children are very tender, and that coldness, neglect, or unkindness touches them to the quick. Shew them, then, by every word and action, that you truly love them ; pray daily for their welfare, and do all that you can to promote their happiness. If they are in sorrow, it is your duty to console them ; if they are sick, to

* Isaiah, xlix. 15.

nurse and wait upon them ; if in trouble or in want, to help and relieve them, and when unable to do this, you should at least lighten, as far as possible, the trials which God sends them, by your affectionate and dutiful conduct. When your parents are old and infirm, you should never, if possible, allow them to be dependent on the care and charity of strangers, or to be deprived, in their declining years, of the comforts of a home. You should deem it a pride and a glory, as well as a debt of gratitude which you owe them, to work for their support, to bear with their faults and infirmities, and to tend them with the same loving care which they lavished upon you in your infancy and childhood. If they fall into any serious illness, you should redouble your care and attention, warn them of their danger, and procure for them the helps and consolations of religion. Even after death your love should still follow them, you should mourn over their loss, and do all in your power to assist them by your prayers and Communions, and by the Masses which you should procure for the repose of their souls. Oh, my dear children, how happy will you be if you give these proofs of filial affection to your father and mother ! The love which you shew them will be to you the source of the purest happiness, and will draw down upon you the most abundant blessings of heaven.

We must not, however, be content with *loving* our parents, we must also *honour* them. The importance of this duty is shewn by the very words which Almighty God made use of in giving us the fourth commandment, " *Honour* thy father and thy mother," that is, shew them every mark of respect and reverence. This, indeed, is due to them from the very fact that they hold, in our regard, the place of God ; God has committed us to their care, and appointed them our guardians and protectors. In honouring them, therefore, we honour God; but if we are guilty of treating them with disrespect, we outrage God himself, and are sure to draw upon ourselves his severest punishments. Hence it is that he says, in the Holy Scripture, " Cursed be he that honoureth not his father and mother." * But, on the other hand, he says, " He that honoureth his mother is as one that layeth up a treasure. He that honoureth his father shall have joy in his own children, and in the day of his prayer he shall be heard. He that honoureth his father shall enjoy a long life." † Like the love which we owe to our parents, the honour which is due to them is both interior and exterior, that is, we must both honour them in our hearts, and shew that honour by our outward conduct. We honour them in our hearts when we think of them with reverence, are blind to their failings, and judge favourably of their actions ; we honour them in our conduct when we shew them any mark of outward respect. Thus, for example, we should always speak to them in a respectful manner, listen attentively to what they say, and never presume to contradict them, or argue against them. If they are guilty of faults, we should do our best to conceal them from the eyes of others ; if their character is attacked, we should be eager to defend them, for we should consider their honour as our own, and never should we be so undutiful as to pass any remark which could lower them in the opinion of any one. Finally, we should ever remember that, whatever their conduct or faults may be, they are still our parents ; they still hold the place of God in our regard, and are therefore always entitled to be treated by us with respect. I may add that, if our parents are advanced in years, their grey hairs give them an additional claim to our respectful attention ; for Almighty God himself

* Deut. xxviii. 16.   † Ecclus. iii. 5-7.

teaches us that the aged are always to be treated with reverence, " Rise up," he says, " before the hoary head, and honour the person of the aged man." *

Obedience to our parents is a duty which is a necessary consequence of the love and honour which we owe them, for how can we truly love them if we do what displeases them, or honour them, if we resist their authority ? We are therefore bound by this commandment to submit our will to theirs, and to perform cheerfully, readily and exactly whatever they command us. This, indeed, is just and reasonable, since we are by nature dependent upon them, and are indebted to them, under God, for our very existence and so many other blessings. Moreover, while we are yet young, we are not able to judge for ourselves what is really for our good ; our parents, from their greater age and experience, are far better able to direct us as to what is both for our temporal and spiritual advantage. But the principal reason why we must obey our parents is, because such is the Will of God, who has expressly commanded it. He has given us our parents to be the guides and directors of our life, especially of our infancy and early youth. He has invested them with his own authority ; he has taught us by his holy word and by his own Divine example upon earth to submit our will to theirs in all that is not contrary to the Law of God. Wherefore he says to us, by the mouth of the Apostle, " Children obey your parents in all things, for this is well pleasing to the Lord." † From which words you see that the obedience which we are bound to render to our parents is not only just and reasonable, but that it is also commanded by God, and is most pleasing to his Divine Majesty. Let us now see how we are to practise this important duty.

* Levit. xlix. 82.   † Coloss. iii. 20.

Remember, then, my dear children, that this perfect obedience which you owe to your parents consists in two things—namely, in doing promptly, cheerfully, and readily what they command you, and in faithfully refraining from what they forbid you. No sooner have they spoken, than you should fly to execute their orders, shewing by your cheerful and ready obedience that to do what they tell you is a work of love as well as of duty. Never should you seek to know the why or the wherefore of their commands, much less should you murmur or grumble at what they enjoin, or·shew, by sulky or gloomy looks, that their orders are displeasing or distasteful to you. A good child will even anticipate the commands of his parents, doing what he knows they desire, before they have time to tell him. In all things he will consult their wishes, and be guided by their advice; for example, with regard to the choice of his companions, the employment of his time, &c. Even when he grows older, he will not fail to ask their advice in all matters of importance, and to follow it as far as is possible. In one case only should we refuse to obey our parents, and that is if they order us to do what is sinful, for the obedience which we owe to God is above that which we owe to our parents; hence the catechism says that we must obey them only *in all that is not sin*. For example, if our parents were to command us to steal, tell lies, &c., we must certainly disobey them, for these things are clearly contrary to the law of God. If, however, we merely doubted whether the commands of our parents were lawful or not, we should obey them, for *they* have to answer to God for what they command us; but *we*, unless we know that their orders are sinful, have to answer only for our obedience.

EXAMPLE OF OUR BLESSED REDEEMER.

Our Blessed Lord, who came down from heaven not only to die for our salvation, but also to teach us by his own example the way to heaven, has left us in his own person a perfect model of the fulfilment of the different duties which we owe to our parents. He loved his Blessed Mother and her holy spouse St. Joseph with a tender and devoted affection, honoured them as his earthly guardians, holding towards him on earth the place of his heavenly Father, and was ever obedient to their slightest wish. Behold him as a little infant at Bethlehem in the arms of his mother, submissive to her in all things, though the Lord of all, possessed of all wisdom and power. See him as a child in the cottage of Nazareth, helping his foster-father at his laborious trade of a carpenter, or assisting his mother in the various duties of her little household. At the age of twelve years he went up to Jerusalem for the solemn festival of the Pasch, and, after the days of the festival were ended, remained teaching in the temple, thus entering on the great work which brought him down from heaven, the instruction and conversion of mankind. Mary and Joseph meanwhile sought him sorrowing, and at length, after three days, found him in the midst of the doctors, hearing them, and asking them questions. At their first word he immediately quitted the work in which he was engaged, and returned with them to Nazareth; for, though employed about his Heavenly Father's business, he knew that the will of his earthly parents *was* the will of his Father in heaven. Of his life from the age of twelve to that of thirty the Holy Scriptures tell us but one thing, that he remained subject to Mary and Joseph, a striking lesson for those children who, when they arrive at the age of youth, are only too eager to throw off the control and authority of their parents. Having entered upon his public preaching, our Blessed Lord's first miracle, the changing of water into wine at the marriage feast of Cana, was wrought at the request of his Blessed Mother; for though, as he said himself on that occasion, his hour for working miracles was not yet come, he could not refuse to grant the desire of his mother, expressed in these simple words—"Son, they have no wine." Finally, behold him stretched on the cross at Calvary, suffering the most cruel agony, yet grieving not over his own sorrow, but over the anguish and desolation of his beloved mother, whom he recommends with his last dying words to the care of his disciple St. John.

Oh, my dear children, if ever you are tempted to disobey your parents, or to shew them any slight or disrespect, think of our dear Lord, and how he, who was the Great God of Heaven, became for our sakes subject and obedient to his own creatures.

We have another beautiful example related in the Holy Scripture of the exact fulfilment of the three-fold duty of the fourth commandment—I mean the history of the holy Patriarch Joseph.

JOSEPH THE MODEL OF A GOOD SON.

When Joseph was yet a child, his affectionate attention to his aged father, and his ready obedience to his slightest word, merited for him the special love and favour of Jacob, who, as the Holy Scripture says, "loved Joseph above all his children." The favour of his father aroused, however, the jealousy of his brethren, who sought and plotted his ruin.

On one occasion when his brethren were absent from home in charge of their flocks, Jacob, wishing to hear news of them, called Joseph and said to him, "Behold, thy brethren feed their sheep in Sichem. Come, I will send thee to them." With a cheerful countenance Joseph made answer, "I am ready," and immediately he set out in search of them.

Sold by his cruel brethren as a slave, and carried into Egypt, Joseph never forgot his aged father amid the dignities and honours to which God raised him. His only desire was again to embrace him, to assure him of his safety, to share his good fortune with him, and to be the prop and support of his declining years. When he made himself known to his brethren, who came to Egypt during the famine to buy corn, his first thought and inquiry was for his father. "I am Joseph," said he. "Is my father living? Make haste and go up to my father and tell him, Thus saith thy son Joseph, *God hath made me lord of the whole land of Egypt. Come down to me; linger not. And thou shalt dwell in the land of Gessen, and thou shalt be near me; and there will I feed thee!* And when he was come thither, Joseph went up to meet his father, and seeing him, he fell upon his neck, and embracing him wept."

Though Joseph was raised to so high a post of honour in the kingdom of Egypt, being made governor of that country and second in rank to the king himself, he was not ashamed of the humble occupation which his father followed, namely, that of a shepherd, which was considered by the Egyptians as a mean and servile employment ; "for the Egyptians," adds the Holy Scripture, "have all shepherds in abomination." On the contrary, he took a noble and filial pride in introducing his father to the king, and begged that he would give him a portion of the country to dwell in, that would be favourable for his usual pursuits. And "Joseph," says the holy Scripture, "brought in his father to the king and presented him before him. And Joseph gave a possession to his father and brethren in the best place of the land, as Pharaoh had commanded. And he nourished them and all his father's house, allowing food to every one."

The days of the holy patriarch Jacob were now drawing to a close, but his dying moments were soothed by the tender care of his devoted son, who was eager to render the last duties of filial affection to his beloved father. No sooner had Joseph heard that he was sick than he hurried to his bedside, taking with him his two sons, Manasses and Ephraim, whom he presented to his father to receive his dying blessing. He remained with him to the last, and when he saw that he was dead, says the Holy Scripture, "he fell upon his father's face, weeping and kissing him. And he commanded his servants the physicians to embalm his father. And Egypt mourned for him seventy days."

A short time after, Joseph fulfilled his father's dying wishes by going up from Egypt with a long train of attendants to the land of Chanaan to bury his body in the double cave of Mambre, where the bodies of Abraham and Isaac were already laid.—*Genesis.*

THE SON OF CRŒSUS.

Cyrus the Great, during his war with Crœsus, king of Lydia, laid siege to the city of Sardis, and soon succeeded in carrying it by assault. A body of his soldiers, eager to distinguish themselves by the capture of the king, rushed to the palace of Crœsus, who soon fell into their hands. As, however, he was in disguise, they failed to recognise him. Enraged at their disappointment, one of their number was about to plunge his sword into the breast of their captive, when Atys, son of Crœsus, who had been dumb from his birth, perceiving his father's danger ran to the spot, and bursting by a mighty effort the bonds which nature had imposed upon him, cried out, "Hold thy hand, barbarian, it is the king my father."—*Rollin's Ancient History.*

SIR THOMAS MORE.

The great Sir Thomas More, Lord High Chancellor of England, was remarkable during his youth for his affectionate and dutiful conduct towards his parents. When he had grown up to manhood, and had been raised to the highest dignities of the State by King Henry VIII., he continued to display the same deference and respect towards his aged father, of which he had been so admirable an example when a boy. It is related of him that each morning before taking his seat in the Chancellor's Court, he was wont to repair, clad in his robes of office, to the Court of Queen's Bench. There his father, who was then far advanced in years, sat as one of the inferior judges ; but though far superior in rank and office, the Lord High Chancellor of England was seen each day to come and kneel at the old man's feet to ask his blessing. So admirable an exercise of humility and filial piety drew upon him the choicest blessings of heaven. When Henry VIII. soon after threw off his obedience to the Holy See, and impiously declared himself head of the Church in England, Sir Thomas More firmly resisted every effort which the king made to draw him into his schism, and by his fidelity to the faith merited the glorious crown of martyrdom.—*Life of Sir Thomas More.*

THE AFFECTIONATE CHILD.

The son of a French gentleman in reduced circumstances, having been placed at college for his education through the kindness of a friend, it was remarked that for several days after his arrival he partook of nothing at dinner but dry bread and a little broth. His companions kindly pressed him to eat of the meat and vegetables, and also of the fruit which was served at table ; but, though he thanked them for their attention, he always declined. This strange behaviour came at last to the ears of the president of the college, who sent for him to ask him the reason of it. The young boy at first remained silent, but being encouraged by the kindness of the president, at length said, "It is not because the food is bad, or that I am not hungry, but because I cannot help thinking that my father and mother are now so poor that they have no meat or fruit to dinner like me, but are often obliged to content themselves with dry bread. I would rather eat as they do, than feast when I know they are hungry and in want." "My good child," replied

the president much affected, "you do well to think of your
parents. Eat, however, the same as your companions, and I
will take care that your parents are provided for, perhaps
better than yourself. The worthy president lost no time in
fulfilling his promise. He wrote to the king an account of
what had happened, and his majesty, admiring the noble
conduct of the child, granted his father a pension for life.—
Dict. Hist. de l'Education.

Q. Are we commanded to obey our parents only ?
A. No ; we must also obey our bishops, pastors, magistrates, and masters.

By the fourth commandment we are commanded,
as the catechism says, to obey not only our parents,
but also our other superiors—namely, *our Bishops,
pastors, magistrates, and masters.* For all of these
are placed over us by Almighty God, and the authority which they exercise, is the authority of God
himself. Hence the Apostle St. Paul says, "Let
every soul be subject to the higher powers, for there
is no power but from God, and those that are, are
ordained of God. Therefore he that resisteth the
power, resisteth the ordinance of God. And they
that resist, purchase to themselves damnation." *

In the first place, we must obey our spiritual
superiors, namely, our Bishops, and also our pastors ;
that is to say, those Priests who have the special
charge of our souls. For our Bishop is appointed
by the Pope, who is the Vicar of Christ and the
Universal Bishop of the Church, to rule and govern
the diocese to which we belong, and we are bound,
therefore, to reverence and obey him as the shepherd
of our souls. We owe a like duty to the Priest,
who is sent by the Bishop to administer the Sacraments to us, to teach us the truths of our faith, and
to guide us on our path to eternal life. The Priest
is, indeed, our spiritual father, for it is through *him*

* Rom. xiii. 1, 2.

that we receive our spiritual birth in the Sacrament Baptism. Moreover, it is *he* who feeds us with the Bread of Life in the Holy Communion, who teaches us how to walk on the way to heaven by his sermons and instructions, who heals the wounds of our souls in the Sacrament of Penance, who comforts us in our sorrows, counsels us in our doubts, encourages us in our trials and temptations, and, finally, who visits us on our sick bed and soothes our last moments with the consolations of religion. Hence we are bound to love the Priest as our spiritual father, to honour him as the minister of God, and to obey him as the guide and shepherd of our souls. We should always speak of him with reverence, salute him respectfully, and be guided in what regards our souls by his instructions and advice. Never should we forget that in obeying him, we obey Jesus Christ himself, and in honouring him, we shew honour to our Blessed Lord according to his own words, " He that heareth you heareth me, and he that despiseth you despiseth me." *

There is a beautiful example related in the Holy Scripture of the respect and obedience which we owe to our spiritual superiors. It is the history of the holy prophet Samuel, who, when yet a child, was consecrated to God, and brought up in the temple under the care of the high priest Heli.

THE YOUNG SAMUEL.

"Now the child Samuel," says the Holy Scripture, " ministered to the Lord before Heli, and slept in the temple of the Lord, where the ark of God was.

"And the Lord called Samuel. And he answered, *Here I am.* And he ran to Heli and said, *Here I am, for thou didst call me.* He said, *I did not call thee ; go back and sleep.* And he went and slept.

* Luke x. 16.

"And the Lord called Samuel again. And Samuel arose and went to Heli, and said, *Here I am, for thou calledst me.* He answered, *I did not call thee, my son ; return and sleep.*

"And the Lord called Samuel again the third time. And he arose up and went to Heli, and said, *Here I am, for thou didst call me.* Then Heli understood that the Lord called the child, and he said to Samuel, *Go and sleep; and if He shall call thee any more, thou shalt say, ' Speak, Lord, for thy servant heareth.'* So Samuel went and slept in his place.

"And the Lord came and stood, and he called as he had called the other times, *Samuel ! Samuel !* And Samuel said, *Speak, Lord, for thy servant heareth.*"

Then Almighty God revealed to Samuel the punishments which he had in store for the house of Heli, because the high priest had neglected to correct and chastise his children for their wicked and scandalous conduct. When morning came, Heli questioned Samuel as to what the Lord had said. Samuel, out of respect to the high priest, was at first unwilling to tell him ; but at length, in obedience to the command of Heli, related all that God had revealed to him.— *I. Kings,* iii.

But we must not obey only our spiritual superiors; that is, our Bishops and pastors. We owe the same duty to our temporal rulers, among whom the catechism particularly mentions *our magistrates and masters.* By our *magistrates* we mean those who govern the country to which we belong—namely, the Queen, who is the chief magistrate of the State, her ministers, her parliament, and all the officers and judges appointed by her to preserve public peace and administer the laws of the country. God has invested them with the authority they hold for the public good, for " there is no power," St. Paul says, " but from God, and those that are," that is, that possess authority, " are ordained of," or in other words, receive their power from, " God." * Therefore we should ever treat them with respect, and obey them exactly in all matters to which their authority extends, for the sake of God himself whose

* Rom. xiii. 1.

power they hold.　Hence the Apostle St. Peter says, "Be ye subject to every human creature for God's sake, whether it be to the king as excelling, or to rulers as sent by him;"* and St. Paul expressly declares that those who resist the power resist the ordinance of God, and purchase to themselves damnation.†

From this it follows, my dear children, that we are bound to obey the laws of our country as long as those laws are not in opposition to the law or commandments of God.　Hence we are bound to pay the taxes which are laid upon us by lawful authority for the expenses of government, the support of our armies, and the preservation of the public peace, and this not only from a motive of obedience, but also of justice, for it is just that those who share in the protection of the State should contribute to the expenses of the State.　Hence, also, we are strictly forbidden to resist the authority of the law, by rebelling against our established rulers, opposing the officers of justice, or joining in secret or illegal societies.　And notice, it matters not whether the rulers of a State be good or bad, gentle or cruel, we are still bound to respect and obey them.　And why so?　Because the authority which they hold is the same, whatever their own conduct may be, and is worthy of reverence, since it comes from God, who will require from *them* an account of how they have ruled, but from *us* of how we have obeyed.　Wherefore St. Peter says that we must obey them *for God's sake*.　We read in the history of the Church that the early Christians were grievously oppressed and cruelly persecuted by those monsters of cruelty and wickedness, the emperors of Rome; yet they faithfully observed the laws of their country, and shed their blood freely in its defence.

* I. Peter, ii. 13.　　　　　　　　† Rom. xiii. 2.

Though so numerous, as Tertullian remarks, as to fill the towns, the cities, the camp, the Senate, and the Forum, they preferred to suffer patiently the most barbarous torments and death itself, rather than resist authority or rise in rebellion against their lawful rulers. In one thing only did they refuse to obey, and this at the cost of their lives—namely, in what was forbidden by the law of God. Witness the noble example of St. Maurice and his glorious band of martyrs, which I will now relate to you.

THE THEBAN LEGION.

In the army of the Emperor Maximus was a company of six thousand Christians, who, from having been levied in the neighbourhood of Thebes, a city of Upper Egypt, were named the Theban Legion. Being about to commence a general persecution against the Church, the Emperor celebrated public games, accompanied with sacrifices to his false gods. At the same time he informed his troops that it was his intention to make use of them for the entire destruction of the Christian religion.

At that time his army was encamped on the banks of the lake of Geneva ; but on receiving the Emperor's message, the Theban Legion, under the command of St. Maurice, withdrew to the foot of the mountain now known by the name of the Great St. Bernard. An order soon arrived from the Emperor that they should take part in the public sacrifices, under pain of being decimated ; but they declared with one voice that they would never offer sacrifice to idols, or imbrue their hands in the blood of their fellow-Christians. The lots were cast, and every tenth soldier fell beneath the sword of the executioner. A second message from the Emperor met with no better success, and was succeeded by a fresh decimation. Being a third time summoned to comply with the Emperor's orders, St. Maurice, in the name of the rest replied, " O Emperor, we are thy soldiers, but we are also the soldiers of Jesus Christ. From thee we receive our pay, but from him we receive eternal life. We are ready to fight with thee against the barbarians, but are also ready to die rather than renounce our faith or fight against our brethren." Upon this noble confession of faith, the tyrant ordered the rest of the army to surround the devoted legion and involve them in a general massacre. The Christian soldiers flung away their arms, and, in imitation of their Divine Master, gave themselves up as sheep to the slaughter. Some were trampled down by the cavalry, some were hung on trees and shot with arrows, some were killed with the sword, and St. Maurice, with the other officers of the legion, was beheaded.—*Butler's Lives of the Saints.*

OUR BLESSED LORD AND THE PHARISEES.

"Then the Pharisees," says the Holy Gospel, "going, consulted among themselves how to ensnare him in his speech.   And they sent to him their disciples with the Herodians, saying, *Master, we know that thou art a true speaker and teachest the way of God in truth, neither carest thou for any man, for thou dost not regard the person of men. Tell us, therefore, what dost thou think : is it lawful to give tribute to Cæsar or not ?*

"But Jesus knowing their wickedness, said, *Why do ye tempt me, ye hypocrites ? Shew me the coin of the tribute.* And they offered him a penny.   And Jesus saith to them, *Whose image and inscription is this ?* They say to him, *Cæsar's.* Then he saith to them, *Render therefore to Cæsar the things that are Cæsar's, and to God the things that are God's.*

"And hearing this, they wondered, and, leaving him, went their ways."—*Matt.* xxii. 15-22.

Besides the obligation we are under of shewing respect and obedience to the princes and magistrates, who rule the State and administer the public laws, we are bound also to render the same duties to our *masters ;* that is, to those who have authority over us in private life, either by the will of our parents, or in virtue of some contract or agreement which we have made with them.   Thus children are bound to respect and obey the teachers to whom their parents have entrusted the care of their education. It is their duty to attend punctually at school at the appointed hours, to learn their lessons diligently, and to do their best that the money which their parents expend, and the labour which their teachers bestow on their education, may not be thrown away.

They must also speak to their teachers with respect, submit cheerfully to their reproofs and corrections, listen attentively to their instructions, and be guided by their warnings and advice. In a word, they should look upon their teachers as holding the place of their parents, as their parents hold the place of God in their regard. Never, my dear children, can we be sufficiently grateful to those who train our minds to knowledge and our hearts to the love of God, which is the office of a Christian teacher. While we are young we cannot properly understand the greatness of the service which they render us, but when we grow older we shall feel that they, like the husbandman of the Gospel,* have been sowing good seed in our hearts, which, if it has fallen on good soil, will produce in after years thirty, or sixty, or a hundred fold.

ST. ARSENIUS AND HIS PUPILS.

The holy abbot Arsenius, before he left the world and retired into the desert, led an innocent and saintly life at the court of Theodosius the Great, the Emperor of Constantinople, who had entrusted him with the care of the education of his children. This important office Arsenius discharged with the utmost zeal and fidelity, and the young princes profited no less by the example than by the instructions of their virtuous master.

It happened one day that the Emperor entered the room while the lessons were going on, and found Arsenius standing, while his pupils sat listening to his instructions. Theodosius hereupon reproved his sons as guilty of a want of proper respect to their master, and in punishment took from them for a time their marks of royal dignity. He then bade them rise from their seats, and invited Arsenius to be seated and continue his lesson, begging him to excuse the thoughtlessness of his sons, who had forgotten the respect which must always be paid, even by princes, to those who have the charge of their instruction.—*Butler's Lives of the Saints.*

* Matt. xiii. 3, &c.

Finally, we must honour and obey those into whose employment we have entered, either as servants, workmen or apprentices. For our masters and mistresses are our lawful superiors, and the authority which they have over us comes from God himself. Hence we are bound to execute their lawful commands, to labour diligently in their service, and to speak to them and treat them always with respect. It is our duty also to be *faithful* and trustworthy in their regard, looking upon their interests as our own, guarding their property from injury, turning to the best account what they commit to us to be employed in their service, and never betraying their confidence by exposing their faults or speaking of their private affairs. A servant who cheats his master, wastes his goods, allows others to rob him, or betrays his secret faults, is guilty of a sin of treachery as well as of injustice, since he abuses his master's confidence in order to injure him.

The Apostle St. Paul, in instructing his disciples on this subject, tells them that they should obey their earthly masters not through interest or fear, but for the love of God and because such is the Divine Will. He bids them look upon Jesus Christ in the person of their masters, and labour diligently in their service, since by so doing they are serving God and not men. " Servants," he says, " be obedient to them that are your lords according to the flesh—as to Christ, not serving to the eye, as it were pleasing men, but as the servants of Christ, doing the will of God from the heart, with a good will serving, as to the Lord, and not to men." * Oh how diligently would servants labour, and how much merit would they gain, if they would profit by this beautiful instruction, and do all their work to please, not so much their earthly as their heavenly

* Ephes. vi. 5, 6.

master! The remembrance that His all-seeing eye is ever upon them, and that even the least work done to please Him will not pass unrewarded, would be at the same time a powerful motive to excite them to industry and diligence, and also a sweet consolation in all the labours and trials to which their state and condition are subject.

Q. Is it the duty of the faithful to contribute to the support of their pastors ?

A. Yes ; it is just, and commanded by Christ, for St. Paul says, " The Lord hath ordained that they who preach the Gospel should live by the Gospel."—*I. Cor.* ix. 14.

In this answer the catechism teaches us that it is the strict duty of every Christian to contribute towards the support of his pastors, and this for two reasons—in the first place, because *justice requires it*, and secondly, because it is the will of God and *our Blessed Lord has expressly commanded it.*

In the first place, *it is just.* What, indeed, can be more just and reasonable than that the faithful, who receive so many spiritual blessings through the ministry of their priests, should contribute towards their temporal support ? The priest is, as St. Paul calls him, " a man of God," * that is one who devotes himself entirely to the service of God, and this principally by labouring for the salvation of his fellow-men. Hence though living in the midst of the world he is, as it were, separated from the world ; he does not marry, he does not engage in any worldly business or pursuit, but gives himself up entirely to the worship of God and the care of his flock. He is occupied continually in praying for his people, offering for them the holy Mass, hearing their confessions, instructing them in their duties, administering to them the Sacraments, visiting and consoling them on

* II. Tim. vi. 11.

the bed of sickness or death. He expends his time, his health, his strength in the service of his people, often exposes himself to danger, and not unfrequently, like the good shepherd, lays down his life for his flock. Surely, then, nothing can be more just and reasonable than that the faithful under his charge should cheerfully and readily contribute towards his support.

In the second place, it is, to use the words of St. Paul, expressly *ordained*, or commanded by Christ, *that those who preach the Gospel should live by the Gospel*, that is, should receive all that is necessary for their support, from those to whom they preach. In another place, the same Apostle exhorts his disciples to fulfil faithfully this duty, which they owe to their pastors, " Let him," he says, " that is instructed in the word communicate to him that instructeth him in all good things," * that is, in the good things of this world. If you read the holy Gospel, you will find that our Blessed Lord did not himself disdain to be dependent, in a manner, for the necessaries of life on those to whom he preached. Thus he abode with Martha and Mary, and also with Nicodemus, sat down to eat with Matthew and Simon the Pharisee, and was ministered to by the holy women who followed him during his public preaching. Hence, too, in sending his disciples to the different cities of Israel to announce his coming, he bade them take with them neither purse nor scrip, that is, neither money nor provisions, but remain with those to whom they preached, eating and drinking what was set before them.† In the Old Law it was commanded by God himself, that certain cities and lands should be set apart for the dwelling-place and maintenance of the priests and Levites ; ‡ they were, moreover, entitled, in virtue of their

* Gal. vi. 6.　　　† Luke, x.　　　‡ Jos. xxi.

sacred office, to receive a portion of the sacrifices offered, and also the first fruits, and the tithes which were a tenth part of the produce of the harvests and of the flocks.* In former ages of the Church, when all were united in the one faith, a similar law respecting tithes generally prevailed; money, also, and lands were left by pious benefactors for the support of the clergy. In this country, however, as in many others, the Church has been robbed of all her possessions and endowments by the sacrilegious hand of the spoiler, namely, at the time of the so-called Reformation, and her clergy have been left dependent for their subsistence on the voluntary offerings of the faithful.

You will ask me, perhaps, in what manner Catholics can best fulfil the strict obligation which they are under of contributing towards the support of their pastors. They can do so in many ways, for example, by the payment of entrance money at the church doors, by renting sittings or pews, and by making any private offering or giving to any public collection for this object. They will also help greatly to relieve the burden which often presses heavily on the shoulders of their clergy if they give generously towards the expenses of the mission, the support of the schools, or the paying off of any debt which may remain on the Church. To these objects all are bound to contribute according to their means. If they are rich, they must give liberally, for they are but the stewards of that God who has given them their riches, and who will demand an account of the same; but even if they are poor, they are not excused from giving something out of the little they possess towards the service of God and the support of his ministers. From the example of the poor widow in the Gospel we see that the humble offerings

* Numb. xviii.; Deut. xviii.

of the poor' are often more pleasing in the sight of God than the most valuable gifts of the rich.

THE WIDOW'S MITE.

" And Jesus," says the holy Gospel, " sitting over against the treasury, beheld how the people cast money into the treasury, and many that were rich cast in much.

" And there came a poor widow, and she cast in two mites, which make a farthing.

" And calling his disciples together, he saith to them, *Amen I say to you, this poor widow hath cast in more than all they that have cast into the treasury. For all they did cast in of their abundance, but she of her want cast in all she had, even her whole living.*"—*Mark*, xii. 41, &c.

There is a beautiful history, related in the Holy Scripture, of the hospitality shewn by a poor widow woman to the holy prophet Elias during the severe famine which afflicted the kingdom of Israel in the reign of the wicked King Achab. You will see from this history how pleasing to God are such acts of charity exercised towards his ministers, and how those who receive them and supply their wants, are sure to draw down on themselves the abundant blessings of heaven. Indeed, Almighty God regards as done to himself, what we do to those whom he sends in his name, according to the words of our Blessed Lord to his disciples, " He that receiveth you receiveth me, and he that receiveth me receiveth him that sent me." *

ELIAS AND THE WIDOW OF SAREPHTA.

" The word of the Lord," says the Holy Scripture, "came to Elias, saying, *Arise, and go to Sarephta of the Sidonians, and dwell there, for I have commanded a widow woman to feed thee.*

* Matt. x. 40.

"He arose, and went to Sarephta. And when he was come to the gate of the city, he saw the widow woman gathering sticks, and he called her and said to her, *Give me a little water in a vessel that I may drink.* And when she was going to fetch it, he called after her, saying, *Bring me also, I beseech thee, a morsel of bread in thy hand.*

"And she answered, *As the Lord God liveth, I have no bread, but only a handful of meal in a pot, and a little oil in a cruse. Behold I am gathering two sticks, that I may go in and dress it for me and my son, that we may eat it and die.*

"And Elias said to her, *Fear not, but go in and do as thou hast said, but first make for me of the same meal a little hearth cake, and bring it to me, and after that make for thee and thy son. For thus saith the Lord God of Israel. ' The pot of meal shall not waste nor the cruse of oil be diminished until the day wherein the Lord will give rain upon the face of the earth.'*

"She went, and did according to the word of Elias, and he eat, and she and her house, and from that day the pot of meal wasted not, and the cruse of oil was not diminished, according to the word of the Lord.

"And it came to pass after this, that the son of the woman fell sick, and the sickness was very grievous, so that there was no breath left in him. And she said to Elias, *What have I to do with thee, thou man of God ? Art thou come to me, that my iniquities should be remembered, and that thou shouldst kill my son ?*

"And Elias said to her, *Give me thy son.* And he took him out of her bosom, and carried him into the upper chamber where he abode, and laid him upon his own bed. And he cried to the Lord and said, *O Lord my God, hast thou afflicted, alas, the widow with whom I am after a sort maintained, so as to kill her son ?* And he stretched and measured himself upon the child three times, and cried to the Lord and said, *O Lord my God, let the soul of this child, I beseech thee, return into his body.* And the Lord heard the voice of Elias, and the soul of the child returned into him, and he revived.

"And Elias took the child and brought him down from the upper chamber to the house below, and delivered him to his mother, and said to her, *Behold thy son liveth.* And the woman said to Elias, *Now by this I know thou art a man of God, and the word of the Lord in thy mouth is true.*"—*III. Kings,* xvii.

EIGHTH INSTRUCTION.

The Fourth Commandment continued. Duties of Parents—first, as regards the bodies; secondly, as regards the souls of their children. Duties of masters and other superiors. What the Fourth Commandment forbids. Contempt, stubbornness, and disobedience.

Q. And what is the duty of parents and of other superiors ?

A. To take proper care of all under their charge, and to bring up their children in the fear of God.

In the last instruction I explained to you the duties which children and those who are under authority owe to their parents and superiors. We come now to speak of the obligations of parents, and of the duties, which those who are placed in authority over others, owe to those under their charge.

There is nothing more important, my dear children, than that parents should clearly understand, and faithfully fulfil the important duties which God has entrusted to them. It is the ignorance and neglect of parents which are the cause of the greater part of the evils that we see in the world, and of the eternal loss of innumerable souls. To parents God has committed a most precious charge, namely, the spiritual and temporal care of those little ones whom he has created to his own image and likeness, whom he loves with the tenderest love, and for whom he has shed his own most Sacred Blood. And for what purpose has he confided to them these children whom he loves so dearly? That they may nourish and support them in their infancy and childhood, guard them from evil, whether of soul or body, and train them up in virtue and piety. Hence the catechism says that parents are bound *to take proper care of the children under their charge, and bring them up in the fear of God.* At the day of judgment Almighty God will demand of parents a strict account of the manner in which they have fulfilled these important duties. If they have discharged them faithfully, their reward will be exceeding great; but if they have neglected them, their punishment will be most severe, for their children will bear witness against them, and God will regard those negligent parents as guilty of the spiritual murder of those whom they have brought into the world.

Let us now consider what are the special obligations of parents in regard to their children. It is useful that you should know them, for then you will understand better why it is that the conduct of your parents towards you sometimes appears strict and severe, and you will see how unreasonable and wrong it is for you to murmur at or disobey them, since they only do what they are strictly obliged to do by the command of God, and do it, moreover, for your good.

The duties which parents owe to their children partly regard their bodies—in other words, their life and wellbeing here below; and partly relate to their souls—that is, to that eternal life for which God has created them. We will first speak of those duties which regard the temporal interests of their children.

In the first place, parents are bound to watch over the safety and preservation of their children, to provide them with food and clothing, and supply their necessary wants while they are in the state of infancy or childhood, unable to take care of themselves, or to labour for their own subsistence. The father must provide for their support by his labour and industry; the mother must nurse them, feed them, clothe them, tend them in sickness, and guard them by continual watchfulness from those dangers and accidents to which children are so often exposed. If the father, through his own neglect, leaves his family without the means of support, spending his time in idleness, or wasting and squandering his earnings at the public-house, he is guilty of grievous sin. If, on the other hand, the mother allows her children to run uncared-for in the streets, exposes them by her negligence to the danger of being scalded or burnt, while she is, perhaps, gadding about or gossipping with her neighbours, or, if she, through her own fault, leaves them in rags or without proper nourishment, she, also, is grievously guilty in the sight of God.

As children grow older, it becomes the duty of their parents to send them to school, or to provide them, in some other way, with such instruction as is suited to their position in life. Even the poorest should take care that their children are taught at least to read and write. Parents who neglect this duty, and allow their children to grow up in ignorance, or who fulfil it but partially, by sending them irregularly to school, and keeping them at home on the slightest pretexts, offend Almighty God, and do their children a serious injury, in depriving them of knowledge, which is of great importance for their future advancement in life. A good parent will always be most anxious to second the efforts of the teacher. He will take care that his children attend regularly, and at the appointed hours, also that they learn at home the tasks which are set them, and, finally, he will keep them at school until they have finished their education. How often it happens that children are taken away from school at a very early age for the sake of the trifling wages they are able to earn, and are thus deprived of instruction at the very time when they are most capable of profiting by it! The loss which they suffer is one which will be deeply felt, but can hardly be supplied in later life.

Finally, parents are bound, as far as they are able, to provide their children when they grow older with the means of obtaining a livelihood, either by apprenticing them to a trade, or by procuring for them some suitable employment. In this they should look not to what will bring them the highest wages for the time, but to what will be of the most lasting advantage; they should, moreover, take care that the employment which they procure for their children is one which does not interfere with the practice of their religion, or expose them to any danger of sin.

We come now to speak of the obligations of parents in regard to the *souls* of their children. These obligations are of course far higher and more important than those which simply regard their temporal interests.

In the first place, parents are bound to see that their children are baptised soon after their birth; indeed, if possible, within the first few days. Without Baptism no one can enter heaven, since we are all born in sin, and nothing defiled can enjoy the sight of God. Those parents, therefore, who delay the Baptism of their children for any length of time without strict necessity, are guilty of grievous sin, because they expose their children to the danger of dying in a state of sin, and of being for ever excluded from the kingdom of heaven. Parents cannot be too particular on this point, for new-born infants are exposed to many dangers and sudden diseases ; indeed a very large proportion of the children who are born, die within the first few months of their existence.

In the second place, parents are bound to instruct their children in the great truths of religion, and their daily prayers. As soon as their children are able to lisp, they should teach them to pronounce with reverence the holy names of Jesus and Mary, and to sign themselves with the sign of the cross. They should often speak to them of that good God who made them, who watches over them with the tenderest love, and who gives to them, by the hands of their parents, their food, clothing, and all that is necessary for their daily wants. They should try to inspire them with a lively horror of sin, and with a love of truth, purity and every virtue. They should set before them the example of the child Jesus, who, though the great God of heaven, was obedient to his own creatures—Mary and Joseph. Parents are also bound to teach their children their prayers, and see that they say them regularly, morning and evening. As their children grow older, they must take care that they hear Mass upon Sundays and Holidays, also that they attend Sunday School and catechism, in order that they may be instructed under the care of their priest, and prepared at the proper age for Confession and Holy Communion. Nor must parents think that they have done all that is necessary when their children have been admitted to their first Communion. They must do their utmost to help to preserve the grace of it in their hearts by keeping them at instruction, sending them regularly to their duties, and seeing that they are in due time prepared for the Sacrament of Confirmation. Oh, how happy are those children whose parents fully understand and faithfully discharge these important duties !

In the third place, parents are bound to correct their children when they do wrong, either by warning and reproving, or, if necessary, by punishing them. Do not think that your parents are very good and kind if they never scold you for your faults, or chastise you when you deserve it ; on the contrary, they are your worst enemies, for if your passions are not checked and your faults corrected when you are young, they will be the cause of much misery to you in this life and perhaps of your eternal damnation. Hence the Holy Scripture says, " He that spareth the rod hateth his son, but he that loveth him correcteth him betimes." *   What, indeed, can be more injurious to children than the foolish indulgence of those weak parents, who give way to all the whims and fancies of their children, and can never bear to reprove or punish them ?   No wonder that their children grow up wayward, unruly and stubborn, the cause of many a bitter hour and many a tear to their parents in after life, according to the words of the wise man, " Bow down his neck while he is young, and beat his sides while he is a child, lest he grow stubborn and regard thee not, and so be a sorrow of heart to thee ;" † and again, " The rod and the reproof give wisdom, but the child that is left to his own will bringeth his mother to shame." ‡ On the contrary, some parents err through over severity, or by punishing in anger or passion. Slight faults should be corrected with slight punishments, a look or a word of reproof will often be enough ; but serious faults against the commandments of God should be punished more severely, only with prudence and temper, so that the child may see that the correction is not inflicted through passion or revenge, but through a true love for him and desire of his good.

* Prov. xiii. 24.   † Eccles. xxx. 12.   ‡ Prov. xxix. 15.

The fourth duty which parents owe to their children is to watch over them and guard them as far as possible from all danger of sin. The greatest danger to which children can be exposed is that of bad company; for nothing has more influence over the young than example, and innocent children are soon corrupted by wicked companions. Parents, therefore, are strictly bound to watch over their children in this respect, and to allow them to play with those only whose conduct they know to be innocent and virtuous. They should not permit their children without necessity to be out after dark except in their own company, and should keep them carefully from all sinful and dangerous amusements. Even at home they must still continue to exercise a prudent watch over the conduct of their children, in order that they may not be exposed to any danger of evil. If their children are able to read, they should never allow them to waste their time in perusing those foolish novels, journals and romances which only serve to weaken the mind and inflame the passions, but should provide them, as far as they are able, with books that are both innocent and instructive. Finally, they should never forget that our nature is corrupt through the sin of our first parents, and that, however good and innocent their children may appear, they are still prone to evil and, as soon as they come to the use of reason, are exposed to the temptations of the devil, who will leave nothing untried to rob them of the precious treasure of their innocence.

In the fifth place, parents are bound to set their children good example; for if, as I have said, the example of companions has so powerful an influence over the conduct of the young, how much greater influence has the example of their parents, to whom they look up as their teachers, and whom they are naturally inclined to imitate. Oh how grievous in the sight of God is the conduct of those wicked parents who curse and swear, who get drunk, who quarrel and fight even in the presence of their children ; or who stay away from Mass, neglect the Sacraments, or break the days of fasting and abstinence, thereby destroying, by their own wicked example, the effect of all that their children may have learnt at school or catechism ! If, as our Blessed Lord says, he that scandalises any one of his little ones had better have been cast with a millstone about his neck into the depths of the sea, what will be the punishment of those wicked parents who, by their own bad example, are the spiritual murderers of their own children ? A good parent, on the contrary, will teach his children by his own example to love virtue and fulfil faithfully the duties of religion. His children will learn from him to be attentive to their prayers and their Sunday's Mass, regular in frequenting the Sacraments, truthful in word, upright in their dealings, masters of their own temper, tender of their neighbour's character, charitable to the poor, in a word, faithful in the discharge of all their duties to God, their neighbour, and their own souls. Trained, when young, in the way in which they should walk, by the powerful influence of the example of their father and mother, they will not depart from the right way when they grow old, but will leave in turn to their children the same pattern of Christian virtue, which they have received as a most precious inheritance from their own parents.

Finally, parents are bound to pray for their children, in order to draw upon them the blessing of God, for, as holy David says, " unless the Lord build the house, they labour in vain that build it, unless the Lord keep the city, he watcheth in vain that

keepeth it." * We read in the Holy Scripture that
Job offered sacrifices for his sons and his daughters,
"lest perhaps they had sinned." † So should parents
each day pray for the Divine blessing on their children, both in their daily prayers, and also whenever
they hear Mass or approach the Holy Communion.
What they are not able to effect by their words and
advice, they may often succeed in effecting by their
prayers, for God gives a special blessing to the
petitions which parents offer with fervour in behalf
of their children.

These, my dear children, are the principal duties
of your parents in regard to your temporal and
spiritual welfare. They are great and important
duties, and they are often difficult and trying, but
God will give your parents the necessary grace to
discharge them faithfully, if they earnestly implore
it. Do you, on your part, try to lighten their labour
by your docility and obedience. Imitate the young
Tobias in the respect with which he received the
counsels of his aged father, and the fidelity with
which he copied the example of his virtues. You
will then grow up, as he did, the joy and consolation
of your parents, and when you are parted from them
by death it will only be to meet them again in
another life, to add by your own happiness to the
joy and splendour of their crown.

PUNISHMENT OF HELI.

The High Priest Heli, as the Holy Scripture relates, had
two sons, Ophni and Phinees, who, by their sinful lives, pro-
faned their sacred office, and were the cause of grievous
scandal to the people. In vain were complaints of their bad
conduct made to their father ; a weak and sinful indulgence
prevented him from correcting these abuses and chastising
the offenders. At length the anger of God was aroused, and
he announced to the holy child Samuel, who was then living

---

* Ps. cxxvi. 1,   † Job, i. 5.

in the temple under the care of Heli, the terrible judgment which was about to fall upon the High Priest and his family, *because he knew that his sons did evil and did not chastise them.* Heli, informed by Samuel of the approaching calamity, humbly resigned himself to the Will of the Almighty, "It is the Lord," said he, "let him do what is good in his sight."

Soon after, the Philistines declared war against the Israelites, who were defeated in a great battle. Thereupon, to draw down on their arms the protection of God, and to inspire their troops with confidence, the Israelites brought to the camp the Ark of the Covenant, the most sacred object that they possessed. In their next encounter it was carried to the field of battle, attended by Ophni and Phinees, the two sons of Heli; but their presence was more likely to draw down the anger of God than to avert it. The battle was lost, the Ark of the Covenant fell into the hands of the Philistines, twenty thousand Israelites were left dead on the field, and Ophni and Phinees were among the slain.

Meanwhile the High Priest, now old and blind, sat at the door of his house, anxiously awaiting news of the battle. At length a man of the tribe of Benjamin, fleeing from the general slaughter, came to the spot. Heli eagerly inquired what tidings he brought. The soldier replied, that Israel had fled before the Philistines, that there had been great slaughter of the people, that his two sons, Ophni and Phinees, were dead, and that the Ark of God was taken. At these last words Heli fell backwards from the stool on which he was sitting, broke his neck, and died.

Thus did the vengeance of God fall, the same day, on the two wicked sons, and the weak and indulgent father."— *I. Kings*, ii., iii., iv.

QUEEN BLANCHE.

Queen Blanche, the mother of St. Louis, King of France, brought up her son in the most tender sentiments of piety, and in the most happy innocence. Above all things, she strove to impress upon his soul the most lively horror of sin, and a particular love of holy purity. Often . when a child did she take him to her knee, and address him in these touching words, which became indelibly imprinted on his heart, " I love you, my darling son, with all the tenderness that a mother is capable of, but I would rather see you dead at my feet than that you should ever commit a mortal sin." In after life St. Louis was heard to say that not a day had passed in which these words had not been present to his mind, and served to preserve him from sin.—*Butler's Lives of the Saints.*

ST. MONICA AND ST. AUGUSTIN.

The great St. Augustin, Doctor of the Church, who died about four hundred years after our Blessed Lord, was a native of Tagaste in Africa. He was blessed with a good mother, the virtuous St. Monica, who strove to instil into the mind of her son, from his earliest infancy, sentiments of piety and religion. But the foolish indulgence, and evil example of his father Patricius, who was a pagan, destroyed the effect of his mother's teaching. Wicked companions completed the ruin of St. Augustin ; he fell into many sinful disorders, and at length embraced the errors of the Manichees, who taught that there are two Gods, one the author of good and the other of evil. St. Monica bitterly deplored the misfortune of her son, and never ceased to weep and pray for his conversion. With this view she prevailed on many pious and learned men to reason with him, in order to convince him of his errors, but all their efforts were of no avail. Having one day earnestly implored a certain holy Bishop to attempt the same task, the latter excused himself on the ground of Augustin's youth and self-conceit, which rendered him incapable of listening to reason. As St. Monica still persisted in her request, the Bishop dismissed her, saying, "Go thy way ; it cannot be that a child of those tears should perish." These words greatly consoled the good mother, who redoubled her sighs and prayers to God.

Not long after, St. Augustin, wishing to advance himself in his profession which was that of rhetoric, left home privately to escape his mother's importunity, and sailed for Italy. St. Monica, on learning her son's departure, was at first inconsolable. She regarded that as the greatest of misfortunes which God, in his wonderful Providence, made use of in order to grant her prayer. Meanwhile her son had journeyed to Rome, and thence to Milan, where he gave public lessons in the art of rhetoric. At that time the great St. Ambrose was Bishop of Milan, and St. Augustin, hearing of his extraordinary learning and eloquence, visited him and went to hear his discourses. The words of the holy Bishop made a deep impression upon his mind. Touched by the grace of God, he at length, after a severe struggle with himself, renounced his errors, and received Baptism from the hands of St. Ambrose.

Meanwhile his holy mother, St. Monica, led by the hand of God, had followed her beloved son to Milan, where she witnessed the fulfilment of all her desires, his conversion and Baptism. Soon after she died peacefully in the arms of St. Augustin, whom she left behind her as the fruit of her prayers, to defend the Church by his learning and edify it by his virtue and sanctity."—*Butler's Saints' Lives.*

The following history, related by St Augustin, affords an awful warning to disobedient and rebellious children, while at the same time it conveys a useful lesson to those parents who allow themselves to be so far carried away by the violence of passion as to invoke curses on the heads of their own offspring.

THE MOTHER'S CURSE.

In the city of Cesarea in Cappadocia there lived in the time of St. Augustin a widow woman with ten children, of whom seven were boys and three girls. All of them were, unhappily, greatly wanting in the duties of filial respect and obedience. It happened on one occasion that the eldest of the family so far forgot himself as not only to load his mother with abuse, but even to raise his hand and strike her. Meanwhile the rest looked on in silence, without uttering a word of remonstrance or exerting themselves in any way in her behalf. The unhappy woman, cut to the quick by their undutiful and cruel conduct, instead of praying to God, as she should have done, to convert and spare her guilty children, cursed them in her heart, and invoked the Divine vengeance on their heads. Then repairing to the Baptismal Font, where God had adopted them for his own, she prostrated herself on the ground, and implored of him to strike her children with some strange and terrible disease which should make them an object of horror to all beholders, and to scatter them over the face of the world as a warning to all who should be guilty of like conduct. Almighty God, to punish at the same time the unnatural mother and her undutiful children, heard the words of her prayer, and fulfilled them. In a moment the whole of the ten children, both boys and girls, were seized with a terrible trembling of their limbs, which filled all who beheld them with amazement and horror. Ashamed any longer to appear in presence of those who had previously known them and were acquainted with their crime, they abandoned their home and their mother, and dispersed throughout the various provinces of the Roman Empire.

The great St. Augustin relates that two of these children—one of whom was named Paul, and the other, his sister, Palladia—visited the city of Hippo in Africa at the time when he occupied the Episcopal chair. There they earnestly besought the Divine mercy through the intercession of the holy martyr St. Stephen, whose relics had been lately translated from Palestine, and were daily glorified by God with numerous miracles. The young man Paul, after many days of earnest supplication, was cured in presence of all the people on Easter Sunday. Upon the following Tuesday St. Augustin mounted the pulpit, and pointing to Paul and Palladia, who stood beside him, related to the people the history of this unhappy family. Then conjuring the faithful to unite in earnest prayer in behalf of Palladia, who still remained afflicted, he led her to the chapel of St. Stephen and recommended her to the intercession of that holy martyr. Thereupon she fell into a refreshing slumber, and on awakening found herself completely cured.

St. Augustin then reascending the pulpit, addressed to the people an earnest exhortation, warning children to obey and respect their parents, and parents to refrain from heaping upon the heads of their children unnatural curses, of which they would repent when too late. "Learn, oh children!" said he, "learn, oh fathers and mothers! what you owe to each other, and what you have to fear from God if you neglect your duties. A mother prays bad prayers on her children, because she has received from them a grievous injury, and her prayers are heard by a just and angry God. But what benefit does she receive from her prayers? On the contrary, she is herself punished in her children. Ask then of God what you have no reason to fear, should he grant it; otherwise he will hear your prayer for your own greater chastisement."—*Histoires Édifiantes.*

I must now say a few words about the duties which masters and other superiors owe to those whom God has placed under their charge. Their obligations resemble in many respects those of parents, as all superiors are bound, each in his own sphere, to promote the spiritual and temporal welfare of those under their care. And first, with regard to the duties of *Masters.*

The Apostle St. Paul, in speaking of the obligations which every one owes to his own household, says, "If any one hath not care of his own, and especially those of his house, he hath denied the faith, and is become worse than an infidel." * From these words you see that St. Paul considers that a master, who neglects his duties to his servants, is guilty in some manner of the grievous crime of denying the faith, since he does not act up to its teaching; moreover, that he is worse than an infidel, since there are many who have not the light of the true faith, and yet fulfil exactly, as far as they know them, the duties which they owe to their dependents. How necessary, then, is it for masters to be well instructed as to what their duties are, and to apply themselves faithfully to discharge them!

In the first place, it is the duty of a master to act *justly* towards his servants. To defraud labourers of their wages is, as the Holy Scripture tells us, one of those heinous sins which cry to heaven for vengeance. Now every master who does not act fairly by his servants or apprentices, either by not paying them their wages or delaying to do so, by exacting a greater amount of work than they are paid to render, or by not teaching them their trade, if bound to do so by contract—that is, by previous agreement—is guilty of injustice, and will have to give a strict account of it to Him who is lord of both master and servant. Hence the Apostle says, "Masters, do to your servants that which is just and equal, knowing that you also have a Master in heaven." †

In the second place, a master is bound to treat his servants with gentleness and kindness. He

* 1 Tim. v. 8.   † Col. iv. 1.

should never forget that they are his brethren, children of the same Heavenly Father, and redeemed by the Precious Blood of the same Saviour; moreover, that they are fellow-servants with him of the same Divine Master. Hence St. Paul, speaking of the gentleness with which masters should treat their servants, says, " Know that the Lord both of them and you is in heaven, and there is no respect of persons with him." * For all are equal in the sight of God, rich and poor, princes and subjects, masters and servants; or rather it is the little, and humble, and poor of spirit, in whatever station of life they may be, who are alone great before God. A good Christian master remembering this, and viewing, also, in the person of his servants, Him who became the servant of all in order to save all, will avoid all hasty and overbearing conduct. He will not be, as the Holy Scripture says, " like a lion in his own house, terrifying and oppressing his servants;" † but, on the contrary, ever kind and considerate, making allowance for ignorance, inexperience, and human weakness, and acting towards his servants in all, as he would wish to be done by, if he were in their place. In one word, he will be, as he was formerly called,‡ a father rather than a master to those of whom he has charge.

In the third place, a master is bound to watch over the conduct of his servants, and to exhort, reprove, and correct them as occasion requires. A master is very guilty in the sight of God who allows cursing and swearing, obscene language, drunkenness, or other scandalous vices among those of whom he has charge. He should shew his great displeasure at such conduct, and do all in his power to put a

* Eph. vi. 9.   † Eccles. iv. 35.
‡ The master was anciently called Paterfamilias, that is, " Father of his household." Compare IV. Kings, v. 13.

stop to it. If he cannot remedy the evil, he should dismiss the offender for the sake of those of his fellow-servants, who might be led into sin by such wicked example. Above all, a master should be very careful never himself to do or say anything that could scandalise his servants, for if they are liable to be led astray by the example of each other, how much more by the example of one who is placed in authority over them!

In the fourth place, a master is bound to allow his servants time to fulfil the duty which they owe to God; namely, to hear Mass on Sundays and holidays, attend instructions, and approach from time to time to the Holy Sacraments. With respect to those servants or apprentices who form part of his household, his duty is still stricter, for he is bound to see, as far as he is able, that they fulfil the necessary duties of religion. He should never forget that God has the first right to our service, and that to deprive his servants of the opportunity of fulfilling their religious duties is not only an injustice to them, but an outrage to God himself.

Finally, masters owe a debt of gratitude to those servants who have been long in their employment, and who have fulfilled their duty to them with fidelity. The Holy Scripture bids us look on a faithful servant as a friend rather than a servant, nay even as a brother. "If thou have a faithful servant," says the wise man, "let him be to thee as thy own soul: treat him as a brother." * Surely, then, it is the duty of a master to take a kind interest in the welfare of such a servant, to relieve him in his wants, if it is in his power, and to assist him in his declining years.

These, my dear children, are the principal obligations of masters and mistresses in regard to their

* Eccles. xxxiii. 31.

servants, especially in regard to those who form part of their household, and to whom they are bound by closer ties than to those who simply work in their employment. The neglect of these duties will be severely punished, but the faithful discharge of them will merit from the lips of our Divine Lord at the last day those consoling words addressed in the Gospel to the faithful steward of his master's goods, " Well done, good and faithful servant: because thou hast been faithful over a few things, I will place thee over many, enter thou into the joy of thy Lord." *

In conclusion, all superiors, whether princes or pastors, teachers or guardians, &c., are equally bound by this commandment to take proper care of all under their charge, and to fulfil faithfully the duties of their respective offices. They should ever remember that the power which they possess comes from God, that it is given them to be exercised for the good of those who are placed under their care, and that God will require a strict account from them of the manner in which they have employed it.

Q. What does the fourth commandment forbid ?
A. The fourth commandment forbids all contempt, stubbornness, and disobedience to our parents and lawful superiors.

We come now to speak of the sins which are forbidden by the fourth commandment. The Catechism only mentions three, namely, *contempt, stubbornness,* and *disobedience;* but there are others which, like these, are opposed to the different duties that we are commanded by this commandment to practise.

To *contemn* or despise our parents is a grievous crime, since we are bound, as we have seen, by every motive to shew them all honour and reverence. Those who are guilty of this sin are accursed by

* Matt. xxv. 23.

God. " Cursed," says he, in the Holy Scripture, " be he that honoureth not his father and his mother." *
The curses of God, my dear children, are not like the curses of men; they are never spoken without being deserved and without being fulfilled. Hence that child who shows contempt for his parents will assuredly, unless he sincerely repents, experience the terrible judgments of God, probably even in this life, but most certainly in the next. Let us now see in what manner we may be guilty of this sin. There are many ways, more or less grievous, for example—

1stly, By speaking rudely to our parents, giving them back answers, saying *we do not care*, &c., or at least murmuring against them in our hearts.

2ndly, By calling them names, either before their face or behind their back.

3rdly, By mocking or laughing at them, mimicking their defects, or ridiculing their infirmities. Of this grievous sin the Holy Scripture says, " The eye that mocketh at his father, and that despiseth the labour of his mother in bearing him, let the ravens of the brook pick it out and the young eagles eat it." †   And again, " Glory not in the dishonour of thy father, for his shame is no glory to thee." ‡   It was by laughing at the infirmity of his father Noah, and exposing it to his brothers, that Cham drew on himself and his posterity the curse and severe anger of God.

4thly, By cursing our parents. By the command of God in the Old Law the child who had arrived at such a height of impiety as to dare to curse his father or mother, was ordered to be put to death without mercy. "He that curseth his father or mother shall die the death." §   And again Almighty

* Deut. xxvii. 16.
‡ Eccles. iii. 12.
† Prov. xxx. 17.
§ Exod. xxi. 17.

God says, " He that curseth his father and mother, his lamp shall be put out in the midst of darkness ;" * that is to say, not only shall he be put to death, but he shall die accursed and abandoned by God.

Finally, a child is guilty of the highest degree of contempt to his parents, when he is so impious and unnatural as to strike them. This heinous crime was also, by the command of God, punished with death in the Old Law,† and has justly been looked upon with the greatest horror by all nations, even by those which were buried in the darkness of idolatry. In the early ages of the Church a child, who had been guilty of this sin, had to atone for it by the performance of a severe public penance for the space of seven years, during all which time, besides the observance of a strict and severe fast, he was not permitted to enter the door of the church, but had to remain without during the time of public service, weeping and bewailing his sin.

The sin of *disobedience* is the next sin which we come to speak of. To this we may join *stubbornness*, which is a dogged obstinacy in resisting the commands of our superiors. Both these sins are opposed to that prompt, cheerful and entire obedience which we are bound by this commandment to render to our parents and to all whom God has placed over us.

Disobedience and stubbornness are sins most hateful to God, for they are, in fact, a rebellion against his authority, since all power, as the Apostle tells us, is from God, and those that hold it are placed over us by God himself. Both these sins spring from pride, for it is pride which causes us to set up our own will in opposition to the authority established by God, and to say, like Lucifer and the rebel angels, " I will not obey." Hence we find

* Prov. xx. 20.　　　　　† Exod. xxi. 15.

that Almighty God in the Holy Scripture speaks of the sins of disobedience and stubbornness as crimes most grievous in his sight, and worthy of the severest punishments. It was the disobedience of our first parents in eating the forbidden fruit which caused them to be driven from the garden of Paradise, and condemned with all their descendants not only to a life of labour and suffering, but also to both temporal and eternal death. In the Old Law we find that the severest punishments were enjoined by God himself against disobedient and unruly children. If any man had a stubborn and unruly son who would not obey his parent's commands, and after being corrected still persisted in his disobedience, he was directed to take and accuse him before the ancients sitting in judgment, after which all the people should stone him to death, that so great a scandal might be removed from among them.* Let us never forget, my dear children, that the sin of disobedience, against which so terrible a punishment was pronounced in the Old Law, is the same now in the sight of God as it was then, and is worthy of the same severe chastisement. It is true that the punishment of death is no longer enjoined by the public laws on the disobedient child, but no doubt the secret judgments of God fall upon him with equal severity both in this and in the next world. His life is full of misery and affliction, frequently he is cut off by the hand of the Almighty in the midst of his days, and if he is spared by the mercy of God, who waits for his repentance, he usually experiences in later life from his own children the same ingratitude and undutiful conduct with which he embittered the days of his parents.

Though disobedience is a sin so hateful in the sight of God and worthy of such severe punishment,

* Deut. xxi. 18, &c.

I must remark, however, that all acts of disobedience are by no means equally grievous. To disobey in some small matters is evidently not so great a sin as to disobey in things of great importance. Thus it is a much less fault to break a rule made to preserve order, than it is to disobey a command the object of which is to keep us from falling into sin, such as when we are told not to play with some bad companion or not to go to certain dangerous places of amusement. Those children, however, who accustom themselves to disobey in little things, grow up so wayward and self-willed that soon they rebel against all authority, and bring upon themselves the anger of God and the curse which never fails to follow, even in this life, the stubborn and disobedient child.

There is a terrible example related in the Holy Scripture of the anger with which God regards and the severity with which he punishes the sin of disobedience. I mean the history of the reprobation of Saul, the first king of Israel.

THE DISOBEDIENCE OF SAUL.

Almighty God, having raised Saul from a low station in life to the throne of Israel, ordered him by the mouth of the prophet Samuel to march against the Amalecites and utterly destroy their nation, without sparing either man or beast. Saul accordingly went out to battle and gained a complete victory ; but he neglected to carry out the instructions of the prophet, and spared both Agag the king of Amalec and the best and fattest of the flocks. Soon afterwards Samu l, at the command of God, came to the camp; and, hearing the bleating of the sheep and the lowing of the cattle, asked Saul what the sound meant. The king replied that it was a portion of the spoils, which they had preserved to offer in sacrifice. "What!" said Samuel, "doth the Lord desire holocausts and victims, and not rather that the voice of the Lord should be obeyed ? For obedience is better than sacrifices, and to hearken better than to offer the fat of rams.

Because it is like the sin of witchcraft to rebel, and like the crime of idolatry to refuse to obey." He then went on to tell him that because he had rejected the command of God, God had rejected him, and would take away his kingdom from him and give it to another.—*Kings*, xv.

From this example we may easily see the heinousness of the sin of disobedience. God himself compares it to the sin of witchcraft and the sin of idolatry, two of the greatest crimes we can conceive. We may also see that all the prayers we offer, and good works we perform, are of little value if not accompanied with an humble and a docile heart; for obedience is better than sacrifice, and to hearken —that is to listen and obey—is better than to offer the richest gifts. The following is another example from Holy Scripture of the terrible and visible judgments with which Almighty God sometimes punishes the sin of disobedience.

THE DISOBEDIENT PROPHET.

When Jeroboam, king of Israel, was one day offering incense before the golden calf which he had erected at Bethel, a prophet was sent by God to announce to him the punishment which awaited his impiety. The king, enraged, ordered the man of God to be seized, but the arm which he raised against him was in a moment withered up and hung useless by his side, until it was restored by God at the prayer of the prophet. Hereupon Jeroboam earnestly entreated the holy man to stay and dine with him ; promising to bestow upon him the richest presents ; but the prophet, who had been strictly ordered by God not to eat or drink in that place, excused himself and set out upon his return home.

Meanwhile another prophet, advanced in years, who dwelt at Bethel, hearing what had happened, saddled his ass and went in pursuit of the man of God, whom he overtook upon the road resting under the shade of a tree. Having saluted him with respect, he begged that he would return and eat with him. As the prophet of Juda continued to excuse himself on account of the command which God had given him, the other declared that an angel had appeared to him and commanded him in the name of God to bring the stranger back to eat with him. Hereupon the latter yielded to his entreaties, and returned with him to his house ; but while they were at table the prophet of Bethel, inspired by God, foretold him that, inasmuch as he had disobeyed the Divine command, his body should never be laid in the tomb of his forefathers. And so it happened ; for he had not travelled far on his return, when a lion sprang upon him and devoured him. The old prophet, hearing of the disaster, came and took his body and laid it in his own sepulchre.—*III. Kings*, xiii.

A JUST RETRIBUTION.

A certain father, who led a sinful and scandalous life, had a son who, in consequence of his evil training, was as wicked and abandoned as himself. The father was drunken and degraded ; the son wilful, passionate and rebellious. One day when the father reproached his son for his undutiful conduct, the latter in a fit of fury seized his father by the hair of his head, threw him on the ground, and dragged him to the very door of the house. Having arrived at the threshold, the old man raised his voice and cried out, "Stop, wretched son ; when I was of your age I never dragged my father further than this." Thus did the unhappy father acknowledge the Justice of God, who permitted his son to treat him as he had treated his own parent.—*Anecdotes Chretiennes.*

THE UNDUTIFUL SON.

A gentleman of property had an only son whom he loved tenderly. Upon his son's marriage he gave up all he had to him on condition that he would afford him a home for the rest of his life. The old man soon became infirm, but instead of bearing patiently with the infirmities which often accompany old age, his daughter-in-law expressed herself highly disgusted with him for his want of cleanliness and propriety in taking his meals. One day, when they were to have company, she went so far as to tell her husband that she would not sit down to table unless the old man was made to take his dinner in the kitchen. Her husband was so weak and unmindful of what was due to his aged parent as to consent to this heartless proposal, and he accordingly bade his father go for that day to dine with the servants. The old man was cut to the quick at his son's unfilial conduct ; he wept bitterly, and declared that he would sooner go and beg his bread than remain any longer with such undutiful children. The little grandson hearing what he said, and seeing him go up-stairs to fetch a blanket to put over his shoulders, for it was in the depth of winter, ran to his father and told him that grandpapa was gone to get a blanket to wrap himself in that he might go and beg his bread. "Let him go, if he likes," replied the unfeeling son. "But don't let him take more than half the blanket," said the child. "And why so?" asked his father, "Because I shall want the other half for you, father," replied the boy, "when you grow old and I turn you out to beg your bread." These words went to the heart of the father, and fearing that his undutiful conduct might one day be imitated by his own son, he ran after the old man, humbly begged his pardon, and ever after treated him with proper respect and affection.—*Mrs. Herbert.*

NINTH INSTRUCTION.

The Fifth Commandment. What it forbids. Sins which tend to destroy the life of the body—Wilful murder, fighting, quarrelling, injurious words, anger, hatred and revenge. Sins which tend to destroy the life of the soul—Scandal and bad example. What the Fifth Commandment commands.

Q. What is the fifth commandment?
A. Thou shalt not kill.

We come now to speak of the fifth commandment, which is, *Thou shalt not kill.* God alone, my dear children, is the Supreme Master of life and death. It is he who has given us our life, and it is he only who has a right to take it. By this commandment he teaches us that whoever, without his authority, takes away or does what tends to take away the life of man, usurps his place, and is guilty of a grievous outrage against him. Such a one, moreover, commits a crying injustice against him whose life he takes; for as there is nothing that we usually esteem of greater value than our life, so there cannot be a greater injury done us, than for any one by violence to deprive us of it. The fifth commandment is given us by God to protect and enable us to preserve this precious gift.

You might perhaps think, from the wording of this commandment, "Thou shalt not kill," that wilful murder is the only sin which it forbids; but this is far from being the case. It forbids not only the unjust taking away of human life, but also all those acts, and words, and thoughts which, by their very nature, tend to lead to the commission of that great crime—such, for example, as wounding, striking, calling injurious names, giving way to feelings of envy, hatred, or desire of revenge. For murder is not a sin which a person commits all at once. He is usually roused to it by hatred or envy, or he has received some real or fancied injury from another and thirsts for revenge, or he has quarrelled with some one, and from angry words has come to blows, and in a fit of passion has inflicted a deadly wound. Hence all these sins are forbidden, as well as the sin of murder, by the fifth commandment; for though, of course, they are not always followed by the commission of this dreadful crime, yet they often are so followed, and, if not checked in time, may perhaps lead to the taking away of human life. Wherefore our Blessed Lord, in explaining the fifth commandment to the Jews, says in the Gospel, "You have heard that it was said to them of old, *Thou shalt not kill;* but I say to you not to be angry with your brother,"* &c.; thus plainly shewing us that the lesser sins of anger, injurious language, &c.,

* Matt. v. 21, &c.

are no less forbidden by this commandment than the heinous crime of wilful murder.

Besides these sins which naturally tend to the taking away of the life of the body, we are also forbidden by this commandment to do anything to kill or to injure the soul. For besides our *natural* life, which consists in the union of the soul with the body, our soul has also a *supernatural* life of its own, a life by which it lives now in the sight of God, and will live for all eternity in heaven. This life is the grace and friendship of God, and, since it is eternal, it is of far more value than this bodily life with its brief existence. Whoever, therefore, destroys that life of the soul by leading another into mortal sin is guilty of a spiritual murder—a crime which is as strictly forbidden by the fifth commandment as is the wilful murder of the body.

Q. What does the fifth commandment forbid?
A. The fifth commandment forbids all wilful murder, fighting, quarrelling, and injurious words.

Q. Does it forbid anger?
A. Yes ; as also hatred and revenge.

In these two answers, my dear children, you have a list of seven sins which are forbidden by the fifth commandment. The first is *wilful murder*, and the other six—namely, *fighting, quarrelling, injurious words, anger, hatred* and *revenge*—are sins which all tend to lead to the commission of that crime. We will speak of these different sins one by one.

By the crime of *wilful murder*, we mean the taking away of human life, unless it be done by lawful authority or in lawful self-defence. In these two cases to kill is no crime, since it is permitted by Almighty God. Hence the soldier, who slays the enemies of his country on the field of battle ; the executioner, who carries out the public law on notorious criminals; the traveller who, when attacked by robbers, to save his own life takes that of his assailant, are not guilty of murder, nor indeed of any sin against the law of God. We are not, however, permitted to take human life to preserve ourselves from a trifling injury either in person or property, for the life of our neighbour is of far greater value than any slight loss or injury to ourselves. Thus, for example, it would not be lawful, usually speaking, to kill a robber, who simply demands our purse but does not seek to take away our life.

I need hardly tell you, my dear children, that of all sins wilful murder is one of the most grievous. For he who takes away human life destroys one of God's noblest works, defaces the image of God—that is, man himself created to God's image and likeness—and offers the most horrible outrage to God, who alone has a right to fix the moment and manner of our death. Moreover, the murderer inflicts the most grievous injury on his fellow-man, and sends his soul, often, alas! unprepared and without a moment's warning before the judgment-seat of God. Hence Almighty God himself tells us in the Holy Scripture that murder is one of those heinous crimes which cry to him for vengeance. "The voice of thy brother's blood," said he to the murderer Cain, "crieth to me from the earth." * And he goes on to pronounce him accursed on the face of the earth, which had sucked in the blood that he had shed. This terrible curse of God follows the murderer wherever he goes. Tormented by the remembrance of his crime and the bitter remorse of his conscience, he knows no longer happiness or peace. The image of his murdered victim haunts him both by day and by night. He seems ever to see before

* Gen. iv. 10.

his eyes his bleeding form, and to hear his voice crying for vengeance upon his murderer. Nor is that vengeance long delayed, even in this life; for seldom does it happen that the murderer escapes that terrible penalty of a violent and shameful death which God himself in the Old Law, and which the laws of almost every nation on the earth, have pronounced against those who are guilty of this heinous crime. Not unfrequently, indeed, do we see the murderer, through anguish and distress of mind, give himself up of his own accord to the officers of justice, in the hopes of appeasing thereby the bitter reproaches of his conscience. A painful and disgraceful death seems better to him than the life of misery he leads.

The crime of suicide, which is the taking away of our own life, is no less forbidden by this commandment than the murder of our neighbour. For we are the creatures of God, and it is from him we have received our life, to be employed in doing his adorable will; we cannot, therefore, lay it down when we please, but only at the moment and in the manner which he appoints. The folly of suicide is equal to its wickedness, for he who kills himself to escape from pain, disgrace, or any of the ills of life, knows that he thereby casts himself into the flames of hell, which infinitely surpass all that man can endure in this world. He flies from temporal evils, which soon pass away, and which, if borne with patience, are the source of eternal joy, into the midst of cruel torments which can never profit him, but which he must needs endure for endless ages. Could there be a greater folly and madness?

Notice, moreover, my dear children, that we are not only forbidden to take away our life, but to do anything that will naturally tend to injure or destroy it. For life is a precious gift of God of which we must take reasonable and ordinary care, that we may be able to use it for the intentions of the giver. Hence you will see that gluttony, drunkenness, and indeed excesses of every kind, are strictly forbidden by this commandment, since by them thousands are injured irrevocably in mind and body and hurried to an early grave. We shall, however, have occasion to speak of these sins in another part of the catechism.

Now, can any of you tell me which was the first murder that was ever committed, and who was the first murderer? Yes, it was the murder of the innocent Abel, one of the sons of Adam, and it was his brother Cain who killed him. The history of this dreadful crime is related as follows in the Holy Scripture.

CAIN AND ABEL.

" Abel was a shepherd," says the sacred writer, "and Cain a husbandman. And it came to pass that Cain offered of the fruits of the earth gifts to the Lord. Abel also offered of the firstlings of his flock, and the Lord had respect to Abel and to his offerings. But to Cain and his offerings he had no respect : and Cain was exceedingly angry, and his countenance fell. And the Lord said to him, *Why art thou angry ? and why is thy countenance fallen ?*

" And Cain said to Abel his brother, *Let us go forth abroad.* And when they were in the field, Cain rose up against his brother Abel, and slew him. And the Lord said to Cain, *Where is thy brother Abel ?* And he said, *I know not : am I my brother's keeper ?* And he said to him, *What hast thou done ? The voice of thy brother's blood crieth to me from the earth. Now, therefore, cursed shalt thou be upon the earth, which hath opened her mouth and received the blood of thy brother at thy hand. When thou shalt till it, it shall not yield to thee its fruit: a fugitive and a vagabond shalt thou be upon the earth.* And Cain said to the Lord, *My iniquity is greater than that I may deserve pardon.* And the Lord set a mark upon Cain, that whosover found him should not kill him.—*Gen.* iv.

The sin of *fighting* is the next which is mentioned in the catechism. It comes after the sin of murder, because it often leads to it. A quarrel arises, blows are struck, the passions are inflamed to a pitch of frenzy, some deadly weapon is seized, and in a moment one of the parties lies a bleeding victim on the ground. It is true that all fights do not end in so horrible a crime, but they often do, and when our angry passions are aroused, we know not what may be the end. How often do we hear of children even, who, while fighting with some playmate, in the heat of passion have struck a deadly blow. They have seized a stone, perhaps, which lay near, and hurled it at their companion, without heeding the consequences, or perhaps they have drawn a knife at him and inflicted a mortal wound. And now he lies a corpse upon the ground ; all their bitter tears, and the anguish and remorse which will accompany them to the grave, cannot restore the life which they have taken. Oh ! my dear children, avoid the wicked habit of fighting, which is so contrary to Christian charity, and often leads to such terrible consequences. If any one strikes you, do not strike him back, but rather forgive him from your heart, and return him good for evil. This is true courage, to be able to bear an injury patiently and to conquer your angry passions.

FATAL EFFECTS OF UNRESTRAINED PASSION.

A melancholy instance of the sad effects which often arise from a trifling quarrel, and from a blow struck in a moment of passion, was lately recorded in the newspaper. Two boys of the names of Davies and Roberts, aged respectively eleven and nine years, had gone out to amuse themselves on the sea shore. They had always been on good terms with each other, and had been frequent playmates and companions. While they were at play, Roberts, for some reason or other, kicked Davies on the knee. Davies, in a great passion, cried out, " Why did you do that ?" and immediately drawing from his pocket a large knife, opened it and hurled it at his companion. The blade of the knife penetrated the head of the unfortunate boy to the depth of two inches. With a loud cry he fell back upon the ground, and in a few minutes expired. The boy Davies, who shed many tears at beholding the sad consequences of his ungovernable temper, was taken up by the police and committed for trial on the charge of manslaughter at the Chester Assizes.—*Liverpool Mercury.*

The next sin spoken of is the sin of *quarrelling*, which often leads to fighting, as fighting, in its turn, leads to the crime of murder. By quarrelling we mean wrangling and angry disputing, which are very contrary to Christian charity and most displeasing to Almighty God. For the God whom we serve is the God of peace, and, if we are truly his children and disciples, we also should be lovers of peace. Love, therefore, to be always at peace with every one, especially with your brothers and sisters, also with your playmates and companions. Let there be no disputing or quarrelling amongst you, but speak gently and kindly to one another. If any one contradicts you, do not contradict him back; if any one speaks to you unkindly, answer him mildly and lovingly, and you will make a friend instead of an enemy. "A mild answer," says the wise man, "breaketh wrath, but a harsh word stirreth up fury."* Be also kind and good-natured in your conduct towards others, not proud and self-willed, always wanting your own way, but ready to give up your will to theirs as long as you can do so without offending God. For, if they want you to do anything wrong, such as to steal, disobey your parents, say bad words, &c., you must never give way to them, no matter what they say or do to you. Finally, do your best not only to keep peace yourselves, but also to promote it among your companions. Stop a quarrel when you can by kind and gentle words, or by saying or doing something that will turn the

* Prov. xv. 1.

thoughts of those who are angry to a fresh subject. Thus shall you merit that special blessing that is promised to peace-makers in the eight beatitudes, and shew yourselves true children of your Heavenly Father. " Blessed," says our Lord, " are the peace-makers, for they shall be called the children of God." *

Next to the sin of quarrelling comes that of *injurious words*, for seldom does a quarrel take place without abusive words or rude and insulting nicknames being bandied to and fro. Indeed it is the bad habit of calling names which often leads to quarrelling and fighting, for he who is insulted soon retorts, and the passions being aroused, angry words are quickly followed by blows. Our Blessed Lord, in his Sermon on the Mount, speaks of this sin in very severe terms, telling us that all abusive names are forbidden by the fifth commandment, and are worthy of the severest punishment. " You have heard," says he, " that it was said to them of old, *Thou shalt not kill, and whoever shall kill shall be in danger of the judgment.* But I say to you, that whosoever is angry with his brother shall be in danger of the judgment. And whosoever shall say to his brother, *Raca*, shall be in danger of the council. And whosoever shall say, *Thou fool*, shall be in danger of hell fire." † From these words we see that injurious names, if they are such as to be a very grievous insult to the person we address, may even amount to the guilt of mortal sin which is punished with the eternal fire of hell. Thus, among the Jews, to call a person a *fool* was considered the greatest insult you could offer him, and was therefore a great crime. Among us it is not looked upon in the same light, nor would it usually amount to the guilt of grievous sin, unless it were spoken to a parent or superior.

* Matt. v. 9.   † Matt. v. 21, 22.

There are some children who are so unkind and full of malice as to take a pleasure in calling their companions ugly nicknames, in order to tease them and put them in a passion. Sometimes they are so mean as to take advantage of the bodily infirmities of others to vex and annoy them, for example, of their being lame, or blind, or ill shaped, &c. Those who act thus are generally great cowards, for they only do it to those who are weak and helpless, while they themselves are strong. But they should remember that by teasing and annoying others, they act the part of the devil, who desires nothing so much as to arouse our angry passions and cause a quarrel. To be fond of teasing and vexing others is the sign of a bad heart, for no one, who is kind and charitable, can take a pleasure in causing his neighbour pain and annoyance.

THE SCOLDING BOY, A STORY FOR CHILDREN.

Little George Markland was a well-meaning boy, but had an unfortunate habit of saying rude and unpleasant things to his companions, and even to his sisters and brothers. This bad habit led him into many a quarrel, and these angry disputes sometimes ended in blows. One day as he was playing down by the river side he began to cry out in a singing tone, "Ho, ho! ho, ho!" To his astonishment he heard a voice from the neighbouring wood mimicking him, and singing out, "Ho, ho! ho, ho!" in like manner. "What are you mocking me for?" cried he, in an angry tone. "What are you mocking me for?" said the voice quite as angrily. "You foolish fellow," said George. "You foolish fellow," replied the voice. "I'll come and beat you," said George, in a passion. "I'll come and beat you," replied the voice. George could restrain himself no longer. He rushed into the wood, fell over the stump of a tree, hurt himself severely and, finding no one, came home crying. His mother, seeing him all bruised and scratched, asked what had happened. "It is that bad boy," said George, "in the wood, who called me names, and when I ran into the wood to beat him, I tumbled and hurt myself." "But what did you say to him first!" said his mother. Hereupon George told her the whole story; for, though he was often rude and quarrelsome, he always spoke the truth. "George," said his mother, when he had finished, "it was not a boy that answered you, but the echo, which often repeats sounds that are made near woods and rocks. If you had spoken kind and pleasant things, it would have answered the same. And so it is, my dear child, in speaking with our fellow-men. Gentle and courteous words breed peace and pleasantness; but angry words provoke anger, and lead to quarrels and dissensions."

ST. MACARIUS AND THE IDOLATER.

One day as St. Macarius was walking in the desert with one of his disciples, the latter went on a little in advance. He had not gone far before he met a heathen priest, running with a heavy log of wood upon his shoulders, whom he thus accosted, "Where art thou going, thou devil?" The idolater, being much enraged, took the log, gave him a severe beating with it, and left him half dead upon the ground. He then put the wood back on his shoulders and went on his way, running as before. Soon after, he met St. Macarius, who thus addressed him, "God save thee, poor labouring man." "You do well," replied the pagan, "to salute me in a friendly manner." Upon which the saint rejoined, "I saw that you were tired, and were, nevertheless, running hastily, so I greeted you in order that you might stop and rest yourself awhile." The heathen priest, hearing these words, cried out, "From this I know you to be a true servant of God." Then, casting himself at his feet, he implored St. Macarius to instruct him in the Christian religion and receive him into the number of his disciples."—*Lives of the Fathers of the Desert.*

INJURIOUS WORDS THE CAUSE OF A SOUL'S DAMNATION.

Two gentlemen who had been for a long time on the most friendly terms, had a violent quarrel, and became known in the town where they resided as declared enemies. Their hatred had lasted many years, when one of the two fell dangerously ill, and lay at the point of death. His friends earnestly entreated him to send for his confessor and settle the affairs of his soul, to which he at length consented. The priest, on his arrival, knowing well the circumstances of the case, represented to the sick man the necessity of being reconciled with his enemy before he could be admitted to the holy

Sacraments.   His penitent consented to the proposal, and
the other party was sent for; meanwhile the priest proceeded
to hear his confession.

His enemy, having at length arrived, was introduced into
the chamber of the sick man, who asked his pardon for the
offence he had given, and begged that they might be reconciled.
The other party consented and soon after took his leave, but,
on quitting the room, was heard to exclaim to some one at
the door, "The coward is afraid."   At these words the dying
man sat up in his bed, and cried out in a violent passion, "No,
I am not afraid, and, as a proof of it, I return you all my
former hatred."   So saying, he fell back and expired.—
Mrs. Herbert.

The next sin that we come to speak of is the sin
of *anger*, which is a feeling of displeasure at some
real or supposed injury, with a desire of punishing
the offender.   Anger is called in your catechism one
of the seven deadly sins, because it is a sin which, if
not checked in time, is sure to bring death to the
soul.   It does not follow, however, that anger is
always a mortal sin; sometimes it is only venial,
and sometimes it is no sin at all.   Hence St. Paul
says, "Be angry and sin not.   Let not the sun go
down upon your anger." *   You will wonder, perhaps, how a person can be angry and not commit
any sin.   I will shew you what I mean by an
example.

Let us suppose that one of your companions has
hit you a blow in the face.   You feel very angry,
and you cannot help feeling angry at first, for the
blow has hurt you.   There is no sin so far, because
it is only natural for us, being made of flesh and
blood, and not of wood or stone, to feel angry when
we are hurt.   But the next moment your Guardian
Angel whispers to you to bear the blow patiently for
the love of Jesus, who for us was buffeted and struck
upon the face, yet bore it like a meek and gentle
lamb without opening his mouth.   Immediately you

* Eph. iv. 26.

try to check your angry feelings, you say a little prayer, in your heart, to our Blessed Lord, and speak good-naturedly or do a kind turn to the boy who struck you. Here you have done exactly what the Apostle tells you, you have been angry and yet you have not sinned ; on the contrary, you have gained a victory over yourself and over the devil, and have merited a great reward hereafter.

Now let us suppose that you have acted quite differently. The blow has put you in a passion, and you have not tried to overcome it. You speak angrily to the boy who struck you, you call him names, you try to hit him back. You do not wish to do him any great harm, but to hurt him a little as he has hurt you. In this case you have been angry and sinned, but your sin is a venial sin, and not a mortal one.

But perhaps the blow you have received has put you in a very great passion indeed, through your not trying at all to check or control your temper. You call your companion the worst names you can think of, and blinded by rage you seize whatever is at hand to strike or throw at him, careless what injury you do him, as long as you can only revenge yourself. In this case there is great reason to fear that your anger will amount to the guilt of mortal sin.

You see now how anger may be either a mortal sin, a venial sin, or no sin at all, according to the manner in which we indulge or resist it.

Anger, my dear children, when it is not checked, is the fruitful source of innumerable crimes. Quarrelling and fighting, cursing and swearing, revenge and hatred, bloodshed and even murder, are often the terrible consequences of this detestable passion. Hence we cannot watch against it too carefully, or fight against it too earnestly. For anger is like a viper which, if we cherish it in our bosom, may at any time turn against us and inflict a mortal wound. So does our passion, if we are in the habit of indulging it, often hurry us, when we least think of it into the most frightful crimes. Moreover, it is the cause of great misery and unhappiness, for the passionate man is a torment to himself and a torment to every one about him. He is not, indeed, fit for the company of men, for he is no longer a reasonable being, but is guided like a brute beast only by the blind impulse of his rage. No wonder that he is an object of ridicule to every one about him, and is shunned and avoided by all that know him. Have you ever seen a child in a fit of passion? His eyes start from their sockets, and glare like the eyes of an angry cat; his cheeks become pale and livid, his face ugly and deformed, so that you would hardly know him. He shouts at the top of his voice like a madman; he stamps on the ground; it is dangerous for any one to come near him, for he knows not what he strikes at, and is sometimes so foolish as to break and destroy all that he lays his hands on. Finally, he generally ends by a passionate fit of crying. Can you imagine a more pitiable and ridiculous object?

In order to preserve yourselves from the fatal consequences of the sin of anger, you must fight against it while you are still young. Like every other bad passion, it grows stronger and stronger the older you get and the more you indulge it, while, on the contrary, if you generously strive against it, it grows weaker and weaker, and gives you less trouble each succeeding day. And how are you to strive against it? In the first place, you must earnestly ask of God to help you in the combat, both when you say your daily prayers, hear Mass, or frequent the Sacraments, and also, in the moment of danger, that is, when you are beginning to feel vexed or impatient. Then you must join to the grace, which God will certainly give you, your own good efforts, keeping back the angry word which flies to your lips, and trying to speak gently and kindly to him who has injured you, or not to speak at all till your anger is gone by. Finally, you should set before your eyes the example of our dear Lord, who bore with such infinite patience the greatest injuries from his own creatures, allowing himself to be insulted, buffeted, spit upon, scourged and nailed to the cross without so much as uttering a single word of reproach. Follow these three rules, my dear children, and you will soon obtain a glorious victory over the passion of anger, a victory which God will reward with many blessings here, and with the crown of eternal life. Do not be discouraged if you are naturally hot and hasty, for, though it may cost you more efforts to overcome your anger than it does those who are of a contrary disposition, the victory will be all the more glorious and the reward greater. Thus St. Francis of Sales, who was naturally hasty, became, by the victories he gained over himself, a model of meekness and an illustrious saint.

"LET NOT THE SUN GO DOWN UPON YOUR ANGER." [*]

It is said of St. John the Patriarch of Alexandria, commonly called the Almoner on account of his extraordinary charities, that he conquered all his enemies by his meekness, and by his sweet and amiable disposition converted his bitterest opponents into his warmest friends and supporters.

Upon one occasion he had recourse to Nicetas, the governor of the city, in behalf of the poor of his flock, who were in danger of being grievously afflicted by an oppressive tax which it was proposed to levy on them. He was, however, received with great coldness and even insult, for the governor, being prejudiced against St. John by certain calumnies which had reached his ear, instead of listening to him with the respect to which his sacred character and eminent virtue

[*] Ephes. iv. 26.

entitled him, flew into a passion and abruptly turned his
back upon him. The holy man, however, shewed no signs
of indignation or displeasure, but when evening was come,
reflecting with sorrow on what had passed, sent a friend to
the house of Nicetas with this short message—"The sun is
about to set." The governor, touched with the allusion to
the words of Holy Scripture, "Let not the sun go down upon
your anger," instantly rose and went to meet the patriarch,
at whose feet he cast himself, confessing his fault and earnestly imploring his pardon. St. John tenderly embraced
him, and assured him that he was already forgiven. This
happy reconciliation caused the greatest edification to all the
citizens, who knew not which to admire most, the humility
of Nicetas or the meekness of their holy Archbishop.—*Butler's
Lives of the Saints.*

TRUE GREATNESS OF SOUL.

A certain missionary, one of the companions of St. Francis
Xavier, was preaching one day in a city of the East, when a
man out of the lowest dregs of the people came up as if to
speak to him and spat in his face. The holy priest, without
saying a word or betraying any signs of emotion, took out
his handkerchief to wipe his face, and then went on with his
discourse. Every one was filled with astonishment at such
heroic meekness, and those who had been the first to laugh
at the insult, found their feelings soon changed to admiration.
One of the most learned doctors in the city who was present,
upon reflecting on what he had witnessed, said to himself,
"This stranger may well assert that the doctrine which he
announces to us is a heavenly doctrine. A religion which
inspires such courage and greatness of soul, and which enables
its followers to obtain so perfect a victory over themselves,
can only come from heaven." No sooner was the discourse
completed than he publicly acknowledged that the virtue of
the preacher had convinced him. He then implored the
grace of Baptism, which was conferred upon him with due
solemnity. His conversion was followed by that of many
others, and is a proof that the virtue of meekness has power
not only to soften the heart, but also to convince the understanding.—*Anecdotes Chretiennes.*

We come now to speak of the sin of *hatred*, which
is, of all other sins, the one most opposed to Christian
Charity. For Charity teaches us to love our neigh-

bour as ourselves, whereas hatred leads us to abhor and detest our neighbour; it makes us feel sorry at his happiness and glad at his misfortune. He that has given himself up to this detestable sin no longer knows peace or happiness. The object of his hatred is ever before his mind, his heart is full of rancour and bitterness, and he becomes gloomy, restless, and miserable.

The sin of hatred is, moreover, most heinous in the sight of God, who is a God of love, and who, though he meets with so many injuries and outrages from his ungrateful creatures, loves them all, as the Holy Scripture says, and hates nothing of those things which he has made.* In this he teaches us to follow his own Divine example, bidding us to love our neighbour and even our enemies for his sake. Without this love we cannot please God; all our works of piety or virtue, our prayers, our Communions, our fasts, our almsdeeds, our mortifications, will not avail us if we cherish in our hearts feelings of hatred against our fellow-man. Hence the holy Apostle St. John says, "If any man say 'I love God,' and hateth his brother, he is a liar; for he that loveth not his brother whom he seeth, how can he love God whom he seeth not?" † And in other places the same Apostle, to shew us the evil and the terrible consequences of the sin of hatred, compares it to the heinous crime of wilful murder. "Whosoever hateth his brother," he says, " is a murderer;" ‡ that is, he is a murderer in his heart, since his hatred, if not checked, will lead him to that sin, or at least to desire and rejoice at his neighbour's death.

Notice, however, my dear children, that there is a great difference between *hating* and simply *disliking* a person. To dislike another is not always a sin, for we cannot help disliking those, for example, who

* Wisd. xi. 25.　　　　† I. John, iv. 20.　　　　‡ I. John, iii. 15.

are proud, selfish, or quarrelsome. But then we must not give way to our dislike, or shew it by our black looks or by any unkind word or action. On the contrary, we must try to check it, to put away uncharitable thoughts and suspicions, and to speak to and act towards those whom we dislike with charity and kindness. If we find that, instead of resisting, we indulge our dislike, that we are often brooding over it, and take every opportunity of shewing it, let us redouble our efforts and pray earnestly to God to enable us to overcome these dangerous feelings, which if not checked, will sooner or later lead us to the grievous crime of hatred. The following history from the Lives of the Saints will shew you how the sin of hatred serves to harden the heart and shut out from the soul the grace of Almighty God.

SAPRICIUS AND NICEPHORUS.

Sapricius and Nicephorus were two Christians who dwelt in the same town during the persecution of the Emperor Valerian. For many years they entertained for each other the affection of brothers, till at last an unhappy quarrel took place between them, and their former love was succeeded by the most bitter hatred. After some time Nicephorus, entering into himself and touched with remorse for the past, conceived a great desire to be reconciled to Sapricius. He accordingly applied to some friends of the latter to procure a meeting between them, but in vain. He then went in person to the house of Sapricius, and, throwing himself at his feet, besought him to consent to a reconciliation ; but Sapricius refused to listen to the proposal.

Meanwhile a violent persecution broke out against the Church, and Sapricius, who was known to be a Christian, was seized and brought before the judge. Although cruelly tortured in many ways, he persisted in his profession of the faith, and declared that he would rather die than sacrifice to false gods. Upon this confession he was condemned to lose his head.

Nicephorus, hearing of what had passed and that Sapricius was actually on the way to execution, ran from his house as fast as he could, and met him at the end of a street. There casting himself upon the ground, he besought him more earnestly than ever to pardon him ; but the heart of Sapricius was hardened by hatred, and he turned away his head. Nicephorus, almost broken-hearted, ran to the place of execution by another road, and there throwing himself on his knees before Sapricius cried out, "Martyr of the true God, pardon me, I conjure you !" but the wretched Sapricius refused to listen. At that moment Sapricius, by a just judgment of God, was seized with a terrible fear of death, and when told to lay his head upon the block, cried out trembling, "Why would you put me to death ? I am ready to offer sacrifice." Nicephorus, grieved to the heart at the apostacy of the wretched Sapricius, and feeling himself animated with a courage which God bestowed upon him in reward of his charity, cried aloud that he was a Christian, and ready to die for his faith. The Roman judge instantly condemned him to be beheaded, and thus in a moment he received the glorious crown of martyrdom, which Sapricius had deservedly lost.—*Butler's Lives of the Saints.*

The next sin mentioned as forbidden by this commandment is the sin of *revenge*. Revenge is the desire or act of returning evil for evil, whereas we are bound by the law of God to return good for evil, after the example of our dear Lord, who prayed on the cross and shed his blood for those who persecuted and put him to death. Revenge is the daughter of anger, for, when we are angry with any one, our first thought frequently is to say something unkind to him, or to speak ill of him, or to strike or otherwise injure him. If we give way to think of returning evil for evil, we are guilty of revengeful thoughts, and if we actually do the evil we think of, we are guilty of revengeful actions. When we come to confession we should confess whether we really took revenge, and in what way, or whether we only desired it.

Our Blessed Lord, in explaining the fifth commandment, strictly forbids the sin of revenge, whether it be committed in deed or in thought only. "You have heard," said he, "that it hath been said *An eye for an eye and a tooth for a tooth.* But I say to you not to resist evil." And again—"I say to you, Love your enemies, do good to them that hate you, and pray for them that persecute and calumniate you, that you may be the children of your Father who is in heaven, who maketh his sun to rise upon the good and the bad and raineth upon the just and the unjust." * From these words we see that to return good for evil is the revenge of a Christian, the only one that is permitted him by the law of God. If any one has injured us, he is accountable to God, and God will certainly punish him if he does not repent. "Revenge is mine, and I will repay them in due time," says the Lord.† But, on the contrary, he will punish us if we do not forgive our enemy from our heart, much more if we seek to revenge ourselves upon him. Wherefore the wise man says, "He that seeketh to revenge himself shall find vengeance from the Lord, and he will surely keep his sins in remembrance." ‡ And our Blessed Lord expressly tells us that if we forgive others their offences, our Heavenly Father will forgive us our offences; but if we will not forgive others their offences, neither will our Heavenly Father forgive us our offences.§ If ever, then, my dear children, you are tempted to revenge yourselves, think of these words of your Blessed Redeemer; remember the great debt which you owe to God by your sins, and that you cannot hope for mercy from him if you do not shew mercy to others. Pray, also, earnestly to God in those moments of temptation; he will calm the storm that rages within' your breast, and when by his grace you have overcome your angry passion, and made your victory still more perfect by praying

* Matt. v. 38, 39; 44, 45.   † Deut. xxxii. 35.
‡ Ecclus. xxviii. 1.   § Matt. vi. 14, 15.

for and doing good to your enemy, you will feel in your soul a sweet peace and joy of heart, which are but the foretaste and a pledge of that eternal reward which God has in store for the meek and humble.

The following history is handed down to us by St. Francis of Sales, the holy Bishop of Geneva. The event which he relates occurred at Padua, where he made a portion of his studies.

THE STUDENT OF PADUA.

At the time when St. Francis was studying in the city of Padua, the students of the University indulged in the dangerous and wicked practice of parading the public streets at night time, armed with swords. Whomever they met they questioned as to his name and business, and if he refused to reply, they drew their swords upon him. On one occasion it happened that a certain student, meeting one of his companions whom he did not recognise, put to him the usual question, and, on his refusal to reply, stabbed him to the heart. Fearing the consequences, the murderer immediately took refuge in the house of a widow, whose son was his intimate friend, and, confessing what he had done, begged of her to conceal him in some secret place until the matter was hushed up. The good woman consented, and conducted him to a private room ; but what was her grief and astonishment when, a few moments after, her own son was carried home, a bleeding corpse ! She at once perceived that the youth whom she had secreted was his murderer, and running to the place where he lay hid, she asked him what her son had done that he should treat him so cruelly. The student, little thinking that it was his friend whom he had slain, was almost beside himself with grief, and, instead of begging for mercy, besought her to deliver him up to the officers of justice, that he might atone for his crime with his life. The poor mother, however, being very charitable, would not hear of it. "No," said she, "I do not wish to avenge my son's death with your blood. All I ask of you is that you should repent of your sin, and promise to change your life." The young man readily promised, and shortly after she furnished him with all he required, and assisted him to make his escape beyond the reach of pursuit. This act of mercy was so pleasing to God, that he permitted the soul of the deceased youth to appear to the mother, and assure her that thereby she had procured his release from purgatory, where he would otherwise have been long detained.—*Life of St. Francis of Sales.*

I have now explained to you the sins which are forbidden by the fifth commandment as tending more or less directly to the taking away of human life; that is, the life of the body. But, as I have said, we have another life far more precious than that of the body, which we are equally forbidden by this commandment to injure or destroy, namely, the life of the soul, which consists in the union of the soul with God by sanctifying grace. Whatever, therefore, tends to deprive our neighbour of sanctifying grace, and thus to destroy that spiritual life by which he lives in the sight of God, is a sin against the fifth commandment. Tell me, then—

Q. What else is forbidden by the fifth commandment?
A. Giving scandal and bad example.

Yes, *scandal and bad example* are the two sins which tend to take away the life of our neighbour's soul by inflicting on it the deadly wound of mortal sin, and thereby depriving it of the grace of God. By *scandal* we mean any word or deed which is calculated to lead another into sin, so that *bad example* is really a kind of scandal; for when we commit a sin in the presence of others, there is great reason to fear that they may be led by our example into the same fault. But there are many ways of giving scandal besides bad example, for instance, when a person induces another to commit sin by his advice or entreaties. And this is a far worse kind of scandal than mere bad example, for by it we become not only the *occasion*, but the direct and wilful *cause* of our neighbour's crime; hence we make ourselves actually answerable for the sins which we have led him to commit, just as if they were our own.

You will, perhaps, understand better what I mean by an example. Let us suppose that a boy in the presence of his companions steals an apple from a garden. Another boy, who sees him do it, gets over the hedge and also takes an apple. Here the first boy has given scandal to the other, and led him to steal by his bad example, but he did not tell him to steal; perhaps he is even sorry when he sees what his bad example has led to. But let us suppose that, after he had stolen the apple, he called some of his companions, told them what he had done, and advised them to go and fill their pockets. In this case you see the scandal he has given is of a much worse kind, for he has actually caused them to go and steal through his advice and encouragement. Hence he is answerable for what they have done just as if he had done it himself, and if they do not restore what they have taken, he is bound himself to make good the damage.

The catechism in another part mentions nine ways in which we may be guilty of this worst kind of scandal, namely, by advising, commanding, provoking, or encouraging another to do wrong, by joining in his crime or sharing the fruits of it, by not preventing it when it was our duty to do so, by concealing or defending it. Thus masters are guilty of the sin of scandal who make their servants do servile work on Sundays or holidays without necessity, parents who do not reprove or punish their children when they do wrong, boys who put others up to fight or quarrel, servants who allow their employers to be robbed without trying to prevent it, shopkeepers who buy stolen goods, &c. In all these cases the person who gives the scandal is as bad as, and often worse than he who commits the sin, and has to answer for the consequences of it both to God and man.

Secondly, we are guilty of the sin of scandal in the way of *bad example* when we say or do anything wrong in the presence of others, and this although we may have no intention of leading them into the same sin. For evil example is as contagious as fever or small-pox; and a sin committed in presence of others, especially of children and young people, is but too often the occasion of their falling into a like offence, not perhaps immediately, but in some future moment of temptation. Hence it follows that the greater the number of those who hear or see us do wrong, the more grievous does our sin become, since more are likely to be injured by our bad example, and thus by one sin we may be the cause of the ruin of many souls. For this reason, when we come to confession we ought to mention as near as we can the number of those to whom we have given scandal or bad example. I may add that though these two sins come strictly under the fifth, you will generally find it more convenient to accuse yourselves of them under the other commandments as the case may be; for instance, if you have to confess missing Mass under the third commandment, you might mention at the same time whether you kept any one else away; if you have to accuse yourselves of speaking bad talk under the sixth, you might say how many heard you; and so of the rest.

I need not tell you that scandal and bad example are most grievous sins in the sight of God. For if Almighty God, as we have already seen, regards with such horror any injury inflicted on our neighbour's body, how much more angry will he be at any injury which is done to his soul! Again, if wilful murder, which destroys the life of the body, be so great a sin in his sight that it is said in the Holy Scripture to cry out to him in heaven for vengeance, how much more heinous must be the murder of our neighbour's soul, which we are actually guilty of when we draw him into mortal sin! Ah! my dear children, have always a great horror of the grievous sin of scandal. Remember that our dear Lord shed the last drop of his Precious Blood for the salvation of that soul which you destroy by leading it into sin. What mercy, then, can you expect from him at the day of Judgment, when he calls yon to account for the murder and eternal ruin of that soul which he died to save?

Our Blessed Lord, in warning his disciples against the sin of scandal, speaks in terrible words of those who are guilty of this grievous crime. " Woe," he says, " to the world because of scandal, for it needs must be that scandal come, nevertheless, woe to that man by whom the scandal cometh. He that shall scandalise one of these little ones, it were better for him that a mill-stone should be hanged about his neck, and that he should be drowned in the depth of the sea." * Notice these last words of our Blessed Redeemer. It were better, he says, that you should die a violent and shameful death than scandalise one of his little ones. And why so ? Because the death of your body is a little evil compared with the death of your own and your neighbour's soul which you cause by leading him into sin.

Another terrible thought, which should fill us with an extreme horror of the sin of scandal, is that we never know where the evil may stop. Those whom we have led into sin by our encouragement or bad example, may in their turn corrupt others, and these, again, others perhaps yet unborn ; so that the mea-

* Matt. xviii. 7, 6.

sure of the sins committed, in consequence of our first bad act, may never be filled up till the day of judgment. And of all these sins, as far at least as we have or ought to have foreseen them, we shall have to give a strict account to Almighty God. Well might the holy psalmist David, filled with terror at this dreadful thought, cry out earnestly to God to deliver him not only from his own sins, but also from the guilt of those which he had caused others to commit, and which perhaps were hidden from his sight, " From my secret sins cleanse me, O Lord, and from those of others spare thy servant." * Alas! my dear children, we have enough sins of our own to answer for without burdening ourselves with the sins of others by giving scandal and bad example.

It sometimes happens that an act good in itself, or at least harmless, may be the occasion of scandal to our neighbour, if, for example, it has the appearance of evil in the eyes of others. This is what is called *the scandal of the weak*, because those who take it shew a certain weakness in judging by appearances and not putting, as they ought to do, the best construction on our actions. In these cases it is better for charity's sake not to do the act which may give scandal unless, indeed, there is some important reason for performing it. Thus, for instance, if you had a dispensation to eat meat on Fridays, but were in company with others to whom it would give scandal, it would be better, in most cases, to abstain from eating it.

There is another kind of scandal, however, which we are not obliged to avoid, I mean when we do any good act which others, through their own malice and wilful obstinacy, pronounce to be bad, and pretend to be scandalised at. This is the kind of scandal which the Pharisees took at the miracles of our

* Ps. xviii. 13.

Blessed Lord, because he healed the sick upon the Sabbath; hence it is usually called *Pharisaical scandal.* Our Lord did not in these cases pay any regard to the scandal which his good actions caused; on the contrary, he reproved the Pharisees for their conduct, and shewed them that what they pretended to be tenderness of conscience was in reality nothing better than hypocrisy.* In like manner, those who differ from us in religion often pretend to be scandalised at Catholics because they shew respect to sacred images, pray to our Blessed Lady, wear crucifixes, scapulars, &c. To give up these pious practices simply because others take scandal at them, would not be charity, but weakness and cowardice.

The following example will shew you what terrible judgments sometimes fall, even in this life, upon those who are guilty of the grievous sin of scandal.

THE TWO LIBERTINES.

Some years ago there lived in one of the villages of France two young men, who disedified the whole neighbourhood by their wicked and dissolute conduct. The Curé of the parish, finding that his good advice and repeated warnings were treated by them with contempt, addressed himself to their parents, hoping that they would assist him by their authority to bring their sons to a sense of their duty. Instead of doing so, however, they blamed him for interfering unnecessarily in the concerns of their families, and insolently told him that they knew how to bring up their children without his advice. The good priest meekly replied, that whoever despised the advice of his pastor was guilty of an act of contempt against God himself, which certainly would not remain unpunished.

The next day, which was Sunday, was spent as usual by the young men at the public house, where they openly boasted of their insolence to their pastor, and declared that they set him at defiance. Meanwhile a dreadful thunderstorm gathered in the air, and, bursting over the village, filled every one with terror and consternation. The two young libertines, accompanied by two other youths, ran to the church tower to sound

* See Matt. xii. 1-13; Luke, xiii. 11-16; xiv. 1, &c.

the consecrated bells, as is usual in Catholic countries on such occasions.   While they were thus engaged, a dreadful peal of thunder resounded through the air immediately above their heads, which filled them with such alarm that they all hastily ran down the steps of the tower to seek some place of greater security.   A vivid flash of lightning, however, entering at the same moment by the loopholes of the tower, passed down the stairs as if in pursuit of the fugitives. Descending in a zigzag form, it struck and killed on the spot the second and the fourth of the company, who were the two libertines ; their two companions escaped without injury.   The lightning then descended into the church where the people had begun to assemble, and picking out the mother of one of the youths, dashed her violently against the wall.   This awful judgment of God produced the deepest impression upon the guilty parents, who came to the curé with tears in their eyes, to beg pardon for the disrespect they had shewn him.

Finally, the fifth commandment not only forbids us to do anything that tends to injure or take away the life either of the body or the soul, it also *commands* us to do all that we can to promote and maintain it. We are commanded, therefore, by this commandment to live at peace with all men, to forgive injuries, to take reasonable care of our own life, to help our neighbour both in his corporal and spiritual necessities, and to set him an example of every Christian virtue.   This last is one of the most important duties of fraternal charity, for, as nothing is of greater power in drawing men to evil than the example of the wicked, so nothing has greater effect in leading them to the practice of virtue than the example of the good.   Hence our Blessed Lord says, " Let your light shine before men, that they may see your good works, and glorify your Father who is in heaven." *   We must not, however, do good *for the sake* of being seen by men, for this would be vain glory which our Lord reproves in the Pharisees, telling them that they have already received their reward,† but we must do

* Matt. v. 16.   † See Matt. vi. 1, &c.

it to please God, who in his Providence will make use of our good actions to edify others, and lead them to the practice of virtue.

TENTH INSTRUCTION.

The Sixth and Ninth Commandments. The grievousness of impurity. What these Commandments forbid—Adultery and all impurity in deed, look, word, thought or desire. Preservatives against impurity. Sources of impurity—namely, bad company, dangerous amusements, immodest books, love of dress, &c. Advice in temptation. What these Commandments command.

Q. What is the sixth commandment ?
A. Thou shalt not commit adultery.
Q. What is the ninth commandment ?
A. Thou shalt not covet thy neighbour's wife.

We come now to speak of the sixth commandment, *Thou shalt not commit adultery,* to which we may join the ninth, *Thou shalt not covet thy neighbour's wife;* for as these two commandments relate to one and the same subject, they may be explained together. The sixth and ninth commandments are given us by God to preserve us both in soul and body from the shameful sin of impurity. The sixth commandment directs our outward conduct, the ninth regulates the interior of our hearts according to the rules of holy chastity; for while the sixth commandment forbids us to be guilty of any immodest *word*, or *look*, or *action*, the ninth forbids us to allow our *thoughts* to dwell on any unchaste object.   Thus you see that God is not satisfied with a mere outward observance of his Divine Law, but as he is the Creator and Lord of our souls as well as of our bodies, he requires that not only our words and actions, but even our very thoughts and desires, should be innocent and pure.

I need not tell you, my dear children, that the detestable sin of *impurity*, or *lust* as it is sometimes called, is most heinous in the sight of God.   It is one of those seven deadly sins which are mentioned in a later part of the catechism, and which are sometimes called the capital vices, because they are the root or parents of all other sins.   Impurity consists in the love and indulgence of those sinful pleasures of the flesh which are forbidden alike by our right reason and by the law of God.   There is no sin which degrades man more and reduces him more to the level of the beasts than this shameful crime; for he who, forgetting the noble nature which God has given him and the sublime end for which he has created him, gives himself up as a slave to the passion of lust, is like a senseless beast that, having no knowledge of God or his Divine Law, seeks only its own pleasure and the indulgence of its own appetites.   Moreover, the sin of impurity seems of all others the most opposed to the Holiness and Purity of God, which we are bound to imitate as far as we are able, since we are the creatures of God, made to his image, and made for the eternal enjoyment and possession of God.   Hence Almighty God said to the Jews in the Old Law, "Be ye holy, because I, the Lord your God, am holy." *   But there is another reason why we are still more strictly bound.

<hr>

* Levit. xix. 2.

under the New Law to practise the beautiful virtue
of holy purity, and this is because by Baptism our
souls and bodies have become the very temple of
the Holy Trinity ; while by Holy Communion and
Confirmation they are made the special dwelling-
place of Jesus Christ and of the Holy Ghost. Oh,
how great must be the sin of him who defiles the
temple of God, the dwelling-place of the Son of God
and of the Holy Ghost, the Spirit of Purity, with
the filthy abominations of lust! The Apostle St.
Paul, struck with horror at the thought, cries out,
" Know ye not that you are the temple of God, and
that the Spirit of God dwelleth in you ?   But if any
man violate the temple of God, him will God destroy.
For the temple of God is holy : which ye are." *
And again, " Know ye not that your bodies are the
the members of Christ? Shall I then take the members of Christ and make them the members of a
harlot ?"—that is, by polluting them with the filthy
sin of impurity—" God forbid." † Ah! my dear
children, let us have a great horror of this detestable
sin which offers so great an outrage to the three
Persons of the Adorable Trinity, and which daily
fills hell with innumerable souls. Even in this life
there is perhaps no sin, which draws down upon
those who are guilty of it, more signal chastise-
ments from Almighty God. Witness the whole of
mankind, one family excepted, swept away by the
waters of the deluge ; witness Sodom and Gomorrah
destroyed by a rain from heaven of fire and brim-
stone in punishment of this sin ; witness the terrible
diseases, the premature death, which are so frequently the dismal consequences of this shameful
vice. And yet these temporal punishments are as
nothing compared to the eternal torments which await
the impure in the world to come.

* I. Cor. iii. 16, 17.   † I. Cor. vi. 15.

Q. What does the sixth commandment forbid !

A. The sixth commandment forbids all sins of uncleanness with another's wife or husband.

Q. What else is forbidden by the sixth commandment?

A. All other kinds of immodesties, by kisses, touches, looks, words, or actions.

Q. What does the ninth commandment forbid ?

A. The ninth commandment forbids all lustful thoughts and desires, and all wilful pleasure in the irregular motions of the flesh.

These three answers, my dear children, tell us what the chief sins are which are forbidden by the sixth and ninth commandments. For when Almighty God says, " Thou shalt not commit adultery," and " Thou shalt not covet thy neighbour's wife," he does not forbid merely the sin of adultery and the desire of that sin, but also every thought, or word, or look, or deed that is contrary to the holy virtue of purity ; just in the same way as when he says, " Thou shalt not kill," in the fifth commandment, he forbids not only murder, but all that tends to lead to the commission of that crime.

The sin of *adultery*, which is the first here mentioned, and under which we include *all sins of uncleanness with another's wife or husband*, is one of the most grievous acts of impurity of which man can be guilty. It is most grievous not only because it is so contrary to the sanctity of the married state, but also because it is a crying injustice to our neighbour, since it wrongs him in a most tender point by violating the fidelity which husband and wife have mutually pledged to each other. Hence it is a crime of which Almighty God in the Old Law speaks in the most severe terms, ordering those who were guilty of it to be put to death without mercy, that so great an evil might be taken away from the midst of the people.* It is true that our Blessed Lord in

* Levit. xx. 10; Deut. xxii. 22.

the New Law would not allow the adulterous woman to be stoned to death, according to the custom of the Jews; but this was not because her sin did not deserve death, but to reprove the Pharisees for their hypocrisy, and to shew that he had come to seek and to save the lost sheep, and would never refuse to receive back the poor sinner if truly penitent.*

We must not, however, think that the sin of adultery or the desire of it are the only mortal sins which we can commit against these two commandments. On the contrary, every sin of impurity even of thought only, is, if fully consented to, grievous in the sight of God, and brings eternal death to the soul. Hence the Apostle says, " Know ye this and understand, that no fornicator or unclean person hath inheritance in the kingdom of Christ and of God." † And again, " The works of the flesh are manifest, which are fornication, uncleanness, immodesty, luxury, &c. ; of the which I foretell you as I have foretold you, that they who do such things shall not obtain the kingdom of heaven." ‡ You see here St. Paul plainly tells us that no unclean person, that is who is guilty of any sin of impurity, shall ever enter into eternal life. From which we may gather that all indecent liberties either with ourselves or others, all unchaste looks, immodest talk, impure thoughts and desires, are, *if fully and deliberately consented to*, mortal sins, which grievously offend God, and, unless they are blotted out by a sincere repentance, deprive us of the hope of heaven, and condemn us to the eternal torments of hell.

Take notice, also, my dear children, that in confessing any sin against the sixth and ninth commandments it is not sufficient to accuse yourselves of impurity in general, but it is necessary to mention the very sin you have committed; for example,

* John, viii. 3-11.   † Ephes. v. 5   ‡ Gal. v. 19, 21.

O

whether it was by look, by word, by deed, by desire, &c. For a sin of look differs in kind from a sin of speech, and both of them differ from sins of action and from sins of thought or desire. Again, it is necessary to confess whether a bad action was done by oneself or with another, and if with another, whether that person was of the same or of the other sex—whether single, married, a relation, &c.; for all these circumstances change the nature of the sin. In like manner it is necessary to say how many persons we have scandalised by our bad example or wicked conversation. Sometimes young people, through a false shame or fear, try to pass over the sins they have committed against these commandments as lightly as possible For example, they will say they have had bad thoughts, when they have not only *had* them but consented to them, and perhaps even committed impure actions as well. Again, they will accuse themselves of speaking bad words, which may mean anything, instead of saying that they have been guilty of talking immodestly, and before how many people. Others, perhaps, say nothing at all about these sins; they are possessed by a dumb devil, who keeps their mouths shut. They go through their little daily offences very exactly, but say nothing about the great loathsome wound of impurity that is festering in their hearts. In so doing they are. guilty of a grievous sacrilege, for they trample on the Blood of Jesus Christ in the Sacrament of Penance by receiving it unworthily. Moreover, they tell a lie to the Holy Ghost, and heap upon their own souls a heavy burden of sin, which will one day weigh them down to the bottom of the abyss. Alas, how many souls does not the devil thus lure on to their eternal ruin ! Whenever, therefore, you come to Confession, earnestly implore the grace of God and the assistance of our Blessed

Lady and your good Angel, that you may have not only light to know your sins, but courage to accuse yourselves of them with humility and perfect sincerity. If you find extreme difficulty in confessing any sin, ask the priest to assist you, for he will always understand and know how to compassionate your weakness.

The following history will shew you how the sin of impurity serves to harden the heart and render the soul deaf to the voice of Divine grace.

THE BLEEDING CRUCIFIX.

It is related in the life of St. Francis Borgia that a certain Spanish gentleman, who was addicted to the sin of impurity, was stricken in the flower of his age by a mortal distemper. St. Francis, having heard of the circumstance, was inspired by a holy zeal to make every effort to bring him to a sense of his sad condition and move him to repentance. Before going to visit him, he first went and threw himself at the foot of the crucifix, earnestly beseeching Almighty God to bless his endeavours and grant him the salvation of this unhappy soul. "Go," said our Blessed Lord to him interiorly, "go to the sick man and exhort him to repentance. I promise you that my grace shall not be wanting to him." St. Francis set out on his errand of charity, and obtained admittance to the sick man's bedside. In moving terms he represented to him the sad condition of his soul, and exhorted him to make his peace with God by a good confession ; but at the mention of confession the dying man turned away and declared that he would never consent to it. St. Francis returned home, and again throwing himself before the crucifix, earnestly implored our Divine Lord to soften the hardened heart of the sinner. "Return to him," replied our Lord, " and take with thee the crucifix. Can he resist the sight of a God dead on the cross for his salvation ?" The Saint immediately returned to the dying man, and shewing him the crucifix, urged him in burning words to repent and confess his sins, placing all his trust in the mercy of a God who had shed the last drop of his Blood upon the cross in order to save him. At the same moment, by a prodigy of grace, the sacred image appeared torn with wounds and covered with blood. Alas ! the hardened sinner still remained insensible to the voice of Divine grace. Having cast one look upon the crucifix, he turned to the wall and died in despair.—*Life of St. Francis Borgia.*

In order, my dear children, that we may preserve our souls from the detestable stain of impurity, it is necessary that we should keep a constant guard over our senses—that is, over our eyes, our tongue, our ears, &c.—which are, as it were, the doors by which the unclean spirit enters into our hearts. How often does it not happen that an unguarded glance, some unbecoming story listened to with pleasure, or a too great freedom of behaviour, is the beginning of some terrible fall, and even of the eternal damnation of the soul! The devil is always watching for some opportunity of tempting us, knowing well the weakness of our corrupt nature ; we ought, therefore, to be always on our guard, ever watchful and prudent. Holy Job tells us that he made a covenant—that is an agreement—with his eyes never to think of any dangerous object, for he well knew that if he did not keep his eyes from dangerous looks, he could never preserve his heart from impure thoughts and desires.* Hence our Blessed Lord himself tells us that " whosoever shall look on a woman to lust after her, hath already committed adultery with her in his heart." † Witness the sad example of King David, who, though before so innocent and beloved of God, was led, by looking curiously at a woman who was bathing, into the double crime of adultery and murder. It was, on the contrary, by observing a continual watchfulness over their eyes and other senses that a St. Aloysius, a St. Stanislaus, &c., became like very angels upon earth in their spotless purity. Imitate, my dear children, their bright example, and if ever your eyes rest by chance on any dangerous object, turn them

* Job. xxxi. 1.　　　　　† Matt. v. 28.

away at once and say some short prayer in your heart to our dear Lord or his Blessed Mother. Listen to what happened to the great St. Bernard.

ST. BERNARD'S VICTORY OVER TEMPTATION.

It is related of the chaste St. Bernard, that on one occasion he allowed his eyes to rest for a short time with some degree of curiosity on a person of the other sex. Although he was not conscious of anything more than a passing curiosity, he had no sooner reflected on his fault than he was touched with remorse on considering the danger he had run, and severely reproached himself for his indiscretion. Whereupon, to punish himself for this fault, as well as by way of remedy for the future, he ran at once to a pool of water, and, though it was the depth of winter, cast himself into the half-frozen pond, where he remained so long, that the natural heat of his body was well nigh extinguished by the cold. This generous act was well rewarded by Almighty God, who from that moment not only extinguished in him all motions of concupiscence, but bestowed upon him the gift of that tender and ardent love of Jesus and Mary which breathes forth in all his words and writings.—*Life of St. Bernard.*

We must not, however, be contented with watching over our *eyes* that they may not rest on dangerous objects; we must use a like vigilance as regards the *tongue* that it may not utter, and as regards the *ears* that they may not listen to any indecent word or expression. What can be more unworthy of a Christian than that the tongue, which is made to sing for ever the praises of God, and which is consecrated with the Blood of Jesus Christ in the Holy Communion, should be polluted with filthy and obscene language? And what can be more dangerous to the soul than that the ears, by which wicked thoughts so easily enter into the heart, should be open to the voice of the devil, speaking the foul language of hell by the mouths of his children? For those, who are in the habit of speaking immodest talk, are truly the children of the devil, since they

are continually employed in his work of corrupting
and destroying souls. Avoid carefully the company
of those who give way to this detestable habit, for
depend upon it, if you go with them you will soon
become as wicked and as shameless as they are. If,
however, you hear any immodest word by accident,
or among those in whose company you are obliged
to work, turn a deaf ear to it, and raise your heart
by some short prayer to Jesus or your Blessed Mother.
Often it is well to begin to speak of some other
subject, by which you both shew your dislike of such
wicked talk and are able to prevent our dear Lord
from being offended.

I cannot, my dear children, impress upon you too
strongly the necessity of avoiding all *evil companions*,
if you wish to preserve the precious treasure of holy
purity. Alas, how many are there now in hell who
owe their eternal damnation to the bad advice or
wicked example of some false friend, whom they
now curse as the author of their ruin ! Our Blessed
Lord, to shew us the absolute necessity of avoiding
all bad company and, indeed, every occasion of sin,
however near and dear it may be to us, says, " If
thy hand or thy foot scandalise thee, cut it off and cast
it from thee. It is better for thee to go into life
maimed or lame, than having two hands or two
feet to be cast into everlasting fire. And if thy eye
scandalise thee, cut it out and cast it from thee. It
is better for thee having one eye to enter into life,
than having two eyes to be cast into hell fire." *
Learn from these words of our Lord to make any
sacrifice, however much it may cost you, to keep
out of bad company and the occasion of sin. If you
have a friend or companion, who is as dear to you
as your eye, or your foot, or your hand, but who is,
or who is likely to be an occasion of sin to you, shun

* Matt. xviii. 8, 9.

him as you would the devil himself. It is better for you to go without him into eternal life, than to be condemned along with him to everlasting torments.

Listen and I will now relate to you some examples, which will shew you on the one hand the fatal consequences of a want of vigilance and firmness in keeping away from bad companions, and on the other the blessings with which God rewards those who are faithful in shunning such dangerous occasions.

THE ISRAELITES AND THE MADIANITES.

When the Israelites were on the point of entering the promised land, Almighty God strictly commanded them to avoid all communication with the wicked inhabitants of the country into which he was leading them. "Beware," said he, "thou never join in friendship with the inhabitants of the land, which may be thy ruin. Thou shalt not enter into league with them. Let them not dwell in thy land, lest perhaps they make thee sin against me." * Unmindful of the Divine commandment, the Israelites allowed the Madianite women to enter their camp, and were seduced by them into the commission of grievous sin—the double sin of fornication and idolatry. Upon this occasion a terrible punishment was inflicted by God both on the Israelites and their seducers. Of the former, twenty-four thousand were slain by the hand of God ; while the Madianites, as the authors of the evil, were almost utterly exterminated at the Divine command by the swords of the Israelites.† Almighty God then repeated his command to the Jews in the strongest terms, warning them of the terrible consequences which would ensue in case they disobeyed him. "Destroy," said he, "all the inhabitants of that land. But if you will not kill the inhabitants of the land, they that remain shall be unto you as nails in your eyes and spears in your sides. And whatever I had thought to do to them, I will do to you." ‡

THE VIRTUOUS JOSEPH.

When the holy patriarch Joseph had been sold by his brethren as a slave and carried into Egypt, his innocent and

* Exod. xxxiv. 12 ; xxiii. 32, 33.   † Numb. xxv. xxxi.
‡ Numb. xxxiii. 52, 55.

virtuous life gained for him the confidence of his master Putiphar, who raised him to the office of his steward, and entrusted him with the charge of his entire household. In this position the holy youth was exposed to a great temptation, for his mistress being carried away by a guilty passion, sought his consent to a grievous sin. Joseph was struck with horror at the proposal, and declared that he would never be guilty of so heinous an offence against God and so great an act of ingratitude to his master. The wicked woman, however, persisted in her efforts, and one day finding him alone, caught hold of his garment and pressed him to consent. The prudent youth knowing well that flight is the best security in moments of temptation, ran away from her presence leaving his garment in her hands. Hereupon his mistress, blinded with rage and the desire of revenge, raised a loud cry, and having alarmed the household, accused Joseph of having offered violence to her, producing his cloak as a proof of the truth of her story. On this false charge the virtuous youth was cast into prison, where he remained a long time in confinement. But "the Lord," says the Holy Scripture, "was with Joseph, and gave him favour in the sight of the chief keeper of the prison, and made all that he did to prosper."—*Genesis*, xxxix.

"WOE TO MY SEDUCER."

A certain student in one of the French colleges, who had always been remarkable for his virtuous life and sincere piety, had the misfortune to fall into the company of a depraved youth, whose wicked conversation and loose behaviour soon served to corrupt his soul and rob him of the treasure of his innocence. Having once fallen, he plunged deeper and deeper into sin, until at length a sudden and alarming illness came to interrupt his course of crime. In this extremity his friends spoke to him about his soul, and exhorted him to make his peace with God, but an obstinate and gloomy silence was the only answer that he gave them. Soon after, waking up one night from his sleep, he began to fill the house with frightful cries. His attendants ran to his bedside and asked him the cause of his alarm, but they could obtain no answer. The priest was at once sent for, who came without delay, and earnestly exhorted him to think of God and beg pardon for his sins, but all in vain. Still the good priest continued to encourage him with many moving considerations to hope in the Divine mercy, when suddenly the dying youth turned to him with a ghastly look, and in a voice of terror exclaimed, " Woe to my seducer ! woe to my seducer ! It is in vain for me to hope for pardon, for I see hell open to receive me."   So saying, he fell back and died in despair.—*John Gerson.*

TEMPTATION OF ST. THOMAS AQUINAS.

St. Thomas of Aquin, who, on account of his exceeding purity and sublime learning is surnamed the *angelic doctor,* was inspired in his youth with the desire of devoting himself to the service of God in the order of St. Dominic, but had to undergo the most formidable opposition from his friends and family.   Among other artifices they sought to undermine his virtue, in order that having once fallen into mortal sin he might abandon the worship of God in disgust.   With this view they one evening introduced a wicked woman into his chamber, promising her a considerable sum of money if she succeeded in seducing him into sin.   No sooner, however, had she entered the apartment and begun to make her wicked proposal, than the holy youth, overcome with horror, snatched from the fire a burning brand, and, calling on God for assistance, drove her contemptuously from the room.   Then, falling on his knees, he with many tears thanked God for his deliverance, and implored him to give him grace never to forfeit the precious jewel of his purity.   At the same time, he consecrated himself once more to the service of God by renewing his vow of perpetual chastity.   Soon after he fell into a deep slumber, during which he beheld two angels approach his bedside and gird him about the loins with a cord, to signify his deliverance from all impure temptations, with which he was never afterwards molested.—*Butler's Saints' Lives.*

Q. What ought we to think of immodest plays and dances ?
A. They are also forbidden by this commandment; and it is sinful to be present at them.

We come now to speak of certain other fruitful sources of impurity which we are bound by the sixth commandment to avoid.   Among these the catechism mentions in a special manner *immodest plays and dances,* telling us that *they are forbidden by this commandment, and it is sinful to be present at them.* What indeed can be more dangerous to the purity of the soul than to witness the representation of conduct which is in itself sinful, or to take part in amusements which inflame the passions, and are calculated to fill the heart with impure affections and the mind with sinful imaginations ! The play house and the dancing room are, indeed, too often the schools of satan, where the souls of the young and innocent are robbed of the fresh bloom of holy purity, and become gradually corrupted and hardened in vice. How many a young girl, first led by curiosity or seduced by evil companions, has entered these abodes of sin under the pretence of innocent amusement, and though at first shocked at the unbecoming jests and bold and shameless behaviour of those around her, has in a short time been carried away by the excitement of the dance or the play, and learnt before the close of the evening to laugh at and enjoy, nay to take part in that at which she had at first blushed ! Again and again does she return to throw herself into the danger, each time her heart becomes more hardened to grace, her passions more inflamed, until she finishes by forming some wicked connection which ends in her shame and her ruin. And how many an innocent youth is first seduced in these haunts of vice into some grievous sin, which is the beginning of a long career of profligacy and crime ! Such, alas ! is the true history of the greater part of those who frequent the low play house, or the singing or dancing saloon. And no wonder, since God himself has expressly warned us that " he that loveth danger shall perish in it." * No, my dear children, God will not work a miracle of grace to preserve those from sin, who willingly and knowingly place themselves in the occasion of it. Be always firm, therefore, in resisting every invitation to visit such dangerous resorts. It is better to bear with the scoffs and

---

* Ecclus. iii. 27.

jeers of false friends, than to lose your innocence and incur the terrible anger of the Almighty.

The great St. Augustine has handed down to us the sad example of a young man who, by a weak compliance in remaining at a sinful spectacle, was not only corrupted himself but became the corrupter of others. The history is as follows :—

ALIPIUS AT THE ROMAN SPORTS.

Alipius, who was a bosom friend of St. Augustine, was in his youth much opposed to the cruel games and criminal amusements of the Roman amphitheatre. Frequently was he solicited by his friends to accompany them to these sinful spectacles, but he always steadily refused. One day, however, they would take no refusal, but, holding him in a friendly way by the arms, led him to the amphitheatre, where the games were about to commence. "What matter," said he, "if you drag my body with you ! You cannot compel me to fix my eyes or my thoughts upon the shows."

Wrapped in a fatal security, Alipius took his seat by the side of his companions. At first he resolutely closed his eyes, and refused to gaze for a moment on the cruel sports. "Would to God," says St. Augustine, "that he had closed his ears also !" A loud shout arose from the spectators, and Alipius, impelled by curiosity, opened his eyes to ascertain the cause. "Immediately he was struck," adds the Saint, "with a more grievous wound of the soul than the gladiator, whom he desired to behold, had received in the body. What more shall I say ! He continued to gaze, he shouted like the rest, he was inflamed with excitement, and carried away with him a mad passion, which impelled him not only to return again himself, but to draw others along with him."—*St. August. Confess.* vi. 8.

HUBERT AND LOUIS.

In a small town in France lived a young man named Hubert, whose piety and good conduct were an example to all persons of his age. It happened on one occasion that a public entertainment, accompanied with fireworks, dancing and other amusements, was given in a neighbouring village, and Hubert took a walk in that direction by way of recreation. On his way he was joined by a young man named Louis, who was noted in the country for his immorality and impiety. Hubert, instead of making a civil excuse for quitting his company, weakly allowed himself to be drawn into conversation, and after they had talked for some time on indifferent subjects, Louis, following up his advantage, began to rally his friend on his piety, and to paint to him the pleasures of a gay life in glowing colours. Hubert at first felt some displeasure at his conversation, but continuing to listen, he began to feel ashamed of what his companion called a want of knowledge of the world. Having arrived at the fair, Hubert was introduced by Louis to several wicked associates, and after visiting together the principal objects of attraction, the whole party entered into one of the booths to refresh themselves with wine. Heated with liquor, and inflamed by the wicked conversation of his companions, Hubert yielded to the tempter, joined in their dissolute conversation, and was led on to the commission of a still more grievous sin. Scarcely had he thus offended his God, when part of the building, which had been erected for the occasion, gave way, and the unhappy youth was buried beneath the ruins.

Louis, who escaped, was so touched with remorse at the untimely fate of Hubert, that he entered shortly after into a neighbouring monastery, and spent the remainder of his life in the practice of the most severe penance. Until the day when he was seized with his last illness, as often as the monks entered in procession into the church, he prostrated himself before the door, that they might step over him, and repeated the following words, " Beg of God to have mercy on a poor wretch who once destroyed the soul of a brother."— *Mrs. Herbert.*

Q. Does the commandment forbid us to read immodest books ?

A. Yes ; for such reading is very dangerous and generally sinful.

Another source of impurity is the reading of *immodest books*, which the catechism tells us *is very dangerous and generally sinful.* Indeed, it is always a sin *knowingly* to read any book that is calculated to fill the mind with impure thoughts and expose us to the danger of offending God. Among such books we may include not only those which are absolutely indecent, but those which treat of impure love, and

which tend to inflame the passions.   Such, alas! is
the case with a great part of modern novels and
romances, as well as with many of the cheap weekly
and monthly magazines. The writers of these works
seek nothing else but their own gain, and as man is
more inclined to evil than to good, they pander to
the vicious and morbid taste of the multitude in
order to obtain a greater sale.   Even the very news-
papers are often full of accounts of abominable crimes,
the very mention of which should make us blush,
and of which the Apostle says that they should not
so much as be named among Christians.*   Amid this
universal corruption how necessary it is, my dear
children, that you should exercise the greatest vigilance as to what you read!   In regard to this, your
parents and your confessor will be your best advisers.
Consult them in all cases of doubt, and never ask or
accept the loan of a book unless you know that it is
one which you can read with safety.   I would also
advise you to read such books as will not only
entertain but improve the mind, for example, books
of history, travels, &c., also Catholic magazines and
Catholic stories, which generally contain some instruction or useful moral lesson.   The constant
reading of novels and love tales, even of those which
have in them nothing immoral, cannot but serve
to weaken the mind and unfit it for serious pursuits,
besides often exciting the passions and filling the
head with foolish and dangerous imaginations.   We
have a remarkable instance of the evil effects of such
reading in the person of the great St. Theresa.

ST. THERESA.

St. Theresa was brought up by her virtuous parents in the
practice of fervent piety.   At a very early age she took great
delight in reading the Lives of the Saints, the perusal of

* Ephes. v. 3.

which strongly incited her to the imitation of their virtues, so that she grew up a perfect model of goodness and piety. At the age of twelve she lost her excellent mother, and about the same time fell into the dangerous habit of reading love tales and romances, in which she was encouraged by a young cousin, who had come upon a visit to her father's house, and who was much addicted to such reading. Every day the young Theresa gave a greater portion of her time to the perusal of these dangerous books, and consequently had less to devote to study, prayer and useful employment. The consequence was, that in a short time she became idle, worldly and fond of dress, and would no doubt have fallen deeper had not her father, perceiving the change which her dispositions had undergone, placed her in a convent of Augustinian nuns, where, removed from the occasion of sin, she after a time recovered her former fervour. She often thanked God in after life for delivering her from so great a peril, and in her writings she warns all parents to guard their children carefully against such dangerous reading, which had well nigh proved the instrument of her own ruin.—*Butler's Lives of the Saints.*

Another fatal source of impurity among young women especially, is that *excessive love of dress* which is frequently their ruling passion. This dangerous propensity springs from a foolish vanity ; they long to be admired, and fancy that gay ribbons, showy frocks and smart hats will set them off to advantage, and secure for them the admiration they covet. They forget that modesty and simplicity, both in dress and behaviour, are the most beautiful ornaments of the female sex. Isaac was more pleased with Rebecca in the simple garb of a shepherdess, carrying her empty pitcher on her shoulder to the well, than if she had been decked out in showy and costly garments. And so it is ; those who rely upon dress as a means of pleasing, may indeed secure the flattery and dangerous attentions of the dissolute and designing, but they will never obtain the love and esteem of the sensible and virtuous. How often, alas ! does it happen that girls whose heads are turned by this foolish passion for dress, fall an easy prey to the seducer, who well knows how to obtain an influence over them by flattery and false promises. It is, indeed, to this silly vanity and love of finery that many poor unhappy girls can trace their shame and their ruin. Do you then, Christian mothers, do your best, both by word and example, to preserve your daughters from so dangerous a passion. Dress them always with simplicity and in a manner becoming their station, and teach them that true beauty does not consist in smart clothes or in a pretty face, but in a pure and innocent soul, and in modest, amiable and gentle manners. And do you girls, when you grow up and begin to earn for yourselves, spend your earnings not in what is showy and gaudy but in what is useful and lasting, and, moreover, suited to your state and employment. Lay by, too, what you can for a *rainy day*, that is, to help you when you happen to be sick or out of employment. Above all, do not forget that it is your duty, when your parents grow old and infirm, to assist them to the utmost of your power, and to devote a portion of your earnings to procuring for them the help and comforts they require.

Finally, my dear children, it is our duty not only to watch over our senses and to avoid those occasions which lead to the sin of impurity, but also to *guard our thoughts* from dwelling on any unchaste or dangerous object. For immodest thoughts freely indulged in soon lead to impure desires, and these, again, to the actual commission of the sin. We cannot, indeed, help being tempted with bad thoughts, for the devil—who is, as our Blessed Lord tells us, an " unclean spirit " *—is never weary of filling our minds with his filthy imaginations, in order to rob us, if possible, of the inestimable treasure of holy

* Mark, v. 8, &c.

purity. All that God requires of us is not to listen to the tempter, but to put away at once his wicked suggestions. And how can we put them away? By thinking of some good thought, such as the presence of God, the hour of our death, the torments of hell, the sufferings of our Lord, &c., and by raising our hearts to God with some short prayer. "O Lord, save me or I perish; Jesus and Mary, help me; my good Angel, assist me;" these or such like aspirations will be sure to draw down from heaven the grace which we require. It is also very useful to wear about our necks some blessed cross or medal, to kiss it in time of temptation, to sprinkle ourselves with holy water, to make the sign of the cross, &c. Above all, we should frequently go to Confession and approach the Holy Communion. As long as you make use of such means to overcome temptation, the devil will have no power to hurt you, and all his efforts will but increase your crown. Almighty God often allows us to be tempted for our greater spiritual good, in order that, being made sensible of our own wretchedness, we may become more humble and watchful, and that by our fervent prayers and generous resistance we may merit a greater reward. The Saints of God during their mortal life were not free from such temptations, but they became Saints by manfully overcoming them. Even the great Apostle St. Paul tells us that he himself was grievously tempted with a sting of the flesh for his greater humiliation and spiritual profit. "Lest the greatness of the revelations," he says, "should exalt me, there was given me a sting of my flesh, an angel of Satan, to buffet me. For which thing thrice I besought the Lord, that it might depart from me. And he said to me, *My grace is sufficient for thee; for power is made perfect in infirmity.*"* You see that Almighty

* II. Cor. xii. 7-9.

God did not grant the prayer of the Apostle for deliverance from the temptation, but he gave him grace to resist it.   Thus was the power of God more clearly manifested and the virtue of the Apostle more solidly established.   Do not, therefore, be discouraged if the temptation still continues to trouble you after you have prayed fervently.   Only be faithful to God's grace by continuing to fight bravely, and he, who witnesses your combat, will not fail to reward it and to turn all to your greater good.   God is never wanting to those who trust in him, as you will see from the following beautiful examples.

SUSANNA AND THE ELDERS.

During the time of the captivity there lived among the Jews at Babylon a certain rich man named Joakim, whose wife Susanna was distinguished no less for her extraordinary beauty than for her admirable virtue and piety.   Now it happened that two of the ancients of the people, who held that year the office of judges, conceived an impure affection for her, and only sought some opportunity to gratify their passion.   Accordingly one day when she went down to bathe in her husband's orchard, and had dismissed her maids, they suddenly presented themselves before her and solicited her to the commission of a grievous crime, threatening, in case of her refusal, to accuse her before her husband and the whole people as an adulteress.   Whereupon the chaste Susanna, calling to mind in this her cruel temptation the all-seeing presence of God, exclaimed with a sigh, " I am straitened on every side, for if I do this thing, it is death to me, and if I do it not, I shall not escape your hands.   But it is better for me to fall into your hands without doing it, than to sin in the sight of the Lord."   Having said this she cried out loudly for assistance, but the wicked elders called out still more loudly, declaring that they had found her in company with a young man, who, on perceiving their approach, had escaped by flight.

On the following day the innocent Susanna was summoned to the tribunal and publicly accused of the grievous crime of adultery.   Upon the testimony of the two elders she was found guilty, and condemned to be stoned to death; but

God, who never deserts his faithful servants, sent to her a deliverer in the person of the prophet Daniel. This holy youth, who was then but a boy, though endowed with supernatural wisdom and discernment, meeting her as she was being led to execution, cried out with a loud voice, "I am clear from the blood of this woman. Return to judgment, for they have borne false witness against her." Hereupon the execution was stayed, and Daniel was invited to take his seat with the ancients of the people. By his directions the two elders were then separated, and questioned apart as to the circumstances of the crime which they had witnessed. The one declared that it had been committed under a mastic tree, while the other asserted that it had taken place under the shade of an oak; upon which manifest contradiction Susanna was triumphantly acquitted, and the two false witnesses were executed in her stead.—*Daniel*, xiii.

THE TEMPTATIONS OF ST. CATHARINE OF SIENNA.

The great St. Catherine of Sienna, that favourite spouse of our Blessed Lord, who bore in her body the stigmata or marks of his Sacred Wounds, was at one time of her life subject to the most violent temptations of Satan. That wicked spirit, envious of the angelic purity of her soul, was wont to fill her mind with filthy imaginations, and to assail her heart with the most impure temptations. Unceasingly did she call on God for help, but she seemed to receive no answer. Her mind was obscured with frightful darkness, and she seemed on the very brink of the precipice. Often, indeed, she was unable to distinguish between temptation and consent, but an invisible hand always preserved her from falling. Upon one occasion after her temptations had ceased, our Blessed Lord came to visit her, filling her with heavenly consolations. "Ah, my Divine Spouse," she cried out, "where wast thou when I lay in such an abandoned and frightful condition?" "I was with thee," he replied. "What," said she, "in the midst of the filthy abominations with which my soul was filled?" "Yes," answered our Lord, "for these temptations were most displeasing and painful to thee. By fighting against them thou hast gained immense merit, and the victory was owing to my presence." Thus did St. Catharine learn that God is never nearer to us than when we appear the most desolate and abandoned, and that he is never wanting to those who call upon him with humility and confidence.—*Butler's Lives of the Saints.*

In conclusion, we are *commanded* by the sixth and ninth commandments to be decent and modest in all our thoughts, words, looks and actions, and carefully to preserve the purity of our soul, which is the greatest treasure and most beautiful ornament of man.

ELEVENTH INSTRUCTION.

The Seventh Commandment. What it forbids. First, the unjust taking away of what belongs to another ; Secondly, the unjust keeping of our neighbour's goods. Obligation of restitution. The Tenth Commandment. What it forbids. What these two Commandments command.

Q. What is the seventh commandment ?
A. Thou shalt not steal.

Q. What is the tenth commandment ?
A. Thou shalt not covet thy neighbour's goods.

The seventh and tenth commandments, my dear children, may be explained together for the same reason as the sixth and ninth—namely, because they both treat of the same subject. The one forbids us to *steal*, the other to *covet*, the goods of our neighbour ; in other words, the one forbids all *acts* and the other all *thoughts and desires* which tend to deprive him of his lawful possessions. Almighty God has given us these two commandments to secure to us the use and peaceful possession of the temporal goods which he has bestowed upon us. For what-

ever man has, is from God, though it may appear to
us the fruit of his own labour and industry, or even
the result of chance, as people sometimes foolishly
say, forgetting that there is no such thing as chance
in the world, but that everything is ruled and directed
by the all-seeing Providence of God.   He it is who
gives to man the health, the strength, the ability,
the opportunity to earn, and it is his Providence
which ordains that one should be born of poor and
another of wealthy parents.   Therefore whatever
man has is the gift of God, who bestows on one
more, on another less, according to his own wise
designs. The goods of this world are so many talents
entrusted to us by God to be employed for his honour
and the good of our fellow-men, and every one will
have to give a strict account to God of the manner
in which he has employed them.   From this you
see the particular hatefulness of the sin of theft,
which is a rebellion against God's Providence, and
an effort to overturn the order which he has established. The thief declares, not in words but by his
deeds, that it shall not be as God has ordained ; he
usurps to himself what God has given to his neighbour.   By so doing he not only inflicts a grievous
wrong on his fellow-man whom he deprives of what
is justly his, but he also offers an extreme outrage
to God in resisting his divine appointments, and
violating the first principles of justice, which is one
of the most admirable perfections of the Almighty.
Hence the Apostle declares that both theft and
covetousness are most grievous sins, and such as will
exclude us for ever from the kingdom of heaven.
"Do not err," says he to us, " neither idolators, nor
thieves, nor covetous, nor extortioners, shall possess
the kingdom of God." *

* I. Cor. vi. 9, 10.

Q. What does the seventh commandment forbid ?

A. The seventh commandment forbids all unjust taking away or keeping what belongs to another.

Q. What else is forbidden by the seventh commandment ?

A. All manner of cheating in buying and selling ; or any other way of wronging our neighbour.

We come now to speak of the sins which are forbidden by these two commandments. And first, as regards the seventh, the catechism says that it forbids *all unjust taking away or keeping what belongs to another.* Under these two general headings are comprised all the various sins of dishonesty which are here forbidden. Notice, however, that the catechism only speaks of the *unjust* taking away or keeping of our neighbour's goods, for it may happen that a person may *justly* be deprived or kept out of the use and enjoyment of what belongs to him. Take for example the case of a person who has broken some public law, for which he is liable to pay a fine to the State. If he refuses, the money may lawfully be taken from him by the public officers in the manner the law prescribes. Take, again, the case of a madman who demands from his friends possession of some deadly weapon which belongs to him, but which he would probably use for his own destruction. Not only may it lawfully be kept from him, but it would even be a sin to place it in his hands. In these and such like instances no sin is committed in taking or detaining what belongs to another, but in all other cases we are strictly forbidden by the seventh commandment to deprive our neighbour of what God has given him, or, if it happen to be in our hands, to keep him from the use and possession of it. Let us now see what are the principal ways in which we may commit this injustice.

First of all, those are guilty in the highest degree

of unjustly taking away what belongs to another, who are guilty of *theft accompanied by violence;* for example, those who knock down people and rob them, who break into and plunder houses, who by threats of personal violence extort money from the timid and feeble. This kind of robbery is more grievous than ordinary sins of theft, on account of the violence employed, and the terror, anxiety, or personal injury caused to the person who is plundered. Hence the punishment inflicted by the law on those who commit these crimes is usually far more severe than that which is enjoined in cases of simple dishonesty.

Another species of theft which carries with it a special guilt is that which is *accompanied with a breach of confidence.* For example, a master entrusts to one of his servants a sum of money for some particular purpose, or puts certain goods under his charge. Now the servant, seeing the confidence which the master places in him, takes advantage of it to pilfer the money or make away with the goods for his own profit. A shopkeeper sends round one of his men whom he considers trustworthy to collect the accounts due to him. The collector, however, is a rogue, who keeps back part of the money paid, or, like the unjust steward in the Gospel, knocks off a portion of the bills for the sake of a present bestowed upon him, or else in the hopes of some future advantage. A servant girl is sent by her mistress to purchase some goods in a shop. She does not go where she can make the best bargain, but where she is likely to receive a gift from the dealer in return for her custom—a bribe which her mistress will have sooner or later to pay for by the increased charge made in the bill or the inferior value of the goods purchased. Again, a cook happens to have some friends or relations whom she goes to visit, and to whom she takes the dripping or scraps of meat which she can get together without her mistress's knowledge. Perhaps she is misled by a mistaken charity to the poor, and gives half a loaf to one, a little tea or sugar to another, and the remains of a joint of meat to a third, without ever asking her mistress's consent. She says, "Oh, it will never be missed!" or, "Surely the mistress can well afford it;" but she forgets that to give alms at another's expense is not charity, but theft. Or perhaps it is the housemaid, who disposes of the cast-off clothes, which she finds lying about, to some travelling pedler in exchange for a smart ribbon or a few pence. Again, a servant man is hired for a certain sum to work for a fixed time or to perform certain duties. Instead of setting to his work earnestly and industriously, he wastes his time, neglects the duties he has undertaken to perform, or does them in an imperfect and slovenly manner. My dear children, let us not deceive ourselves, all these are sins of dishonesty; and though they vary in enormity in proportion to the amount of injury inflicted on the employer, yet they have all a special guilt of their own, on account of the abuse of that confidence which is placed by every master or mistress in those who are engaged in their service. Hence sins of theft committed by servants on employers, like those which are accompanied with violence, are usually punished with additional severity by human laws.

The third kind of dishonesty of which we may be guilty is *simple theft* without violence or abuse of confidence. For example, there are some who get their livelihood by stealing from open shops or by picking pockets; others by robbing gardens, market stalls or ships' cargoes, others, again, by stripping clothes-lines or taking whatever they find lying about exposed and unprotected. Travelling pedlers and gipsies who, under pretence of selling their wares, plunder back yards and kitchens, boys who rob orchards, children who pilfer sugar or preserves, or who steal the playthings and sweetmeats of their companions, come under this class of thieves.

The fourth kind of theft, and this is one which is especially mentioned in your catechism, is *cheating in buying or selling*. By *cheating*, we mean over-reaching our neighbours by some trick or artifice. Shopkeepers who give short weight or measure, who adulterate their goods—that is, mix them up with something inferior, for example, sugar with sand, milk with water, &c.—are guilty of this sin. The same may be said of those who tell lies about their goods to deceive the customers as to their value or quality, who sell them for more than they are really worth allowing for their own trouble and risk, who keep back part of the change which they may have to give on receiving payment, who send in bills already paid or charge for more than they have sold, &c. On the other hand, buyers are guilty of this sin when they take advantage of a shopkeeper's mistake as to the quality or price of the goods purchased, who pass bad money, or who seek in any way to defraud those with whom they deal. These sins of cheating, whether it be on the part of buyer or seller, are of course nothing less than downright robbery. Hence, Almighty God said to the Jews in the Old Law, "Thou shalt not have divers weights in thy bag, a greater and a less. Neither shall there be in thy house a greater bushel and a less. Thou shalt have a just and a true weight, and thy bushel shall be equal and true. For the Lord thy God abhorreth him that does these things, and he hateth all injustice." * And again he says to us by

* Deut. xxv. 13-16. See also Levit. xix. 35 36, and Prov. xx. 23.

his Apostle, "This is the will of God, that no man overreach or circumvent his brother in business, because the Lord is the avenger of all these things " *

The fifth way of wronging our neighbour is by *imposition*, which is indeed a kind of cheating, though not necessarily in the way of buying and selling. Those who beg without necessity, or who tell lies to excite compassion, are guilty of this sin. They wrong those from whom they obtain an alms, for the latter would not give if they knew the truth; and they wrong the deserving poor, who often have to go without relief on account of the great number of imposters. Those who order goods without the means of paying, who forge the names of others, or pretend to be acting for them in order to obtain money, goods, or credit; in a word, all those who try to get anything under false pretences are guilty of this sin. Indeed the ways adopted by the dishonest for imposing upon others are as numerous as the fertile inventions of the human brain.

The sixth way of taking unjustly what belongs to our neighbour, and one which is especially grievous, is by *extortion*. Those are guilty of this sin who take advantage of the necessity of others to exact extravagant interest for the loan of money, or who in times of famine hoard up corn and provisions, refusing to sell except at unreasonable and ruinous prices. This does not, however, prevent a shopkeeper from raising the price of his goods to a certain amount, according to their scarcity and the public demand.

Finally, we are guilty of wronging our neighbour in the way of *wilful damage* whenever we wilfully destroy or injure his property. For example, if any one through spite were to set fire to his neighbour's stack, to trample down his corn, or kill his poultry,

---

* I. Thess. iv. 3, 6.

he would be guilty of this kind of dishonesty. The same would be the case if the damage were not done through spite but through gross carelessness, for we are bound to use ordinary care that our acts should not be the cause of injury to others.

These are the seven different ways in which we may sin against this commandment by the *unjust taking away* of our neighbour's goods. Now let us see in what manner we may be guilty of sin by unjustly *keeping what belongs to another*.

And, first of all, we sin *when we do not restore what we find* to the rightful owner, provided we know or are able to discover him. Supposing, for example, that one of you in going to school were to find a muffler or satchel by the roadside. If you know whose it is, you can easily see that it is your duty to give it back to the owner as soon as possible, and that it would be stealing if you were to take and keep it for yourself. But what if you do not know to whom it belongs? You must do your best to find out. Perhaps one of your schoolfellows has gone along the same road before you. You can easily enquire among them, and if none of them owns it, you should ask the neighbours or any one you think likely to know. But if, after all, you cannot find the owner, would it be a sin to keep it? No, it would not. Take notice, however, that the greater the value of the article you find, the greater pains you should take to discover to whom it belongs; so if you were to find a watch or a purse of money, you ought to put an advertisement in the paper about it, or leave word at the police office, where people generally go to enquire when they have lost anything of value. If, after you have done all in your power, you are still unable to find the owner—although, as I have said, it would not be a sin to keep it—yet it would be far the best to give the money, or the value of the article you have found, or at least a portion of it, in alms to the poor, or to have Masses said with it for the intentions of the owner. And why so? Because this is what he would most likely wish to be done with it, since he would thereby get the benefit of what he had lost. And Almighty God would not fail to reward the finder abundantly for his charity and self-denial.

The second way of keeping unjustly what belongs to another is *by not returning what is lent to us or placed in our charge.* If any one, for example, were to lend you a book to read and you never returned it, you would really be stealing it from him, or something very like it. Again, if some one were to lend his neighbour a hundred pounds for a week, and he were to keep it for a year, the borrower would be guilty of an act of injustice, for he would be keeping his friend out of the use of his money for that space of time. Persons, also, who have money *in trust*—that is, placed in their charge for special purposes—and who neglect to employ it for those objects, are guilty of this kind of injustice.

Before we go on to speak of the other two ways of unjustly keeping what belongs to our neighbour, which are mentioned in the next answer of your catechism, namely, *not restoring ill-gotten goods* and *not paying our debts*, I will tell you two stories to amuse and instruct you. They will shew you the truth of two old and homely proverbs, namely, that "Honesty is the best policy," and "When thieves fall out among themselves, honest men come by their own."

THE QUAKER AND THE COUNTRYMAN.

A Quaker passing one day through a market, stopped at a stall to inquire the price of some pears. "I will not charge you much for them," said the fruit dealer, "but I am afraid that they will not suit you, for they are old and have lost their flavour." Thank thee, friend," said the Quaker, "I will go to the next stand. Hast thou any good fruit to-day?" said he, addressing the next dealer. "Certainly," replied the dealer, "excellent fruit. See, here are some of the finest pears of the season. They are small, but they have the richest flavour." "I will take some, then, friend," rejoined the Quaker. Count me out a quarter of a hundred and send them to my house." The pears were accordingly sent, but they proved miserably poor and tasteless.

The next day the Quaker again entered the market. He was immediately accosted by the dealer who had sold him the pears, and who said that he should be very happy to serve him, as he had a choice selection of fruit. "Nay, friend, thou hast deceived me once," said the Quaker, "and though thou mayest be telling the truth this time, yet I cannot trust to thee. Thy neighbour here dealt truthfully with me, and he shall have my custom. Thou wouldst do well to remember this, and to learn that a falsehood is a base thing in the beginning, and a very unprofitable one in the end."

THE THREE ROBBERS.

A certain merchant, who was travelling through a forest with a quantity of jewels and gold and silver ornaments, was attacked by a party of banditti, who stripped him of all he possessed and beat him severely. Having done so, they carried off the treasure which they had stolen into their cave, and sent the youngest of their number into the neighbouring town to buy wine and provisions.

During his absence the two robbers said to one another, "Why should we be obliged to share all this treasure with that boy? As soon as he returns let us make an end of him." Meanwhile their young companion thought within himself as he journeyed to the town, "What a grand thing it would be if all that gold and silver belonged to me! And why should it not? for I can easily poison my two comrades and take it all for myself." Accordingly when he had reached the town and bought the provisions, he purchased some poison and put it into the wine; he then set out on his return.

No sooner had he reached the cave than his two companions set upon him and murdered him with their daggers. They then ate heartily and drank the poisoned wine. In a short time they died amid agonies of pain, and the dead bodies of the three were soon after discovered beside the treasure, which was restored to the rightful owner.

Q. Must we restore ill-gotten goods?
A. Yes, if we are able, or else the sin will not be forgiven; we must also pay our debts.

We come now to speak of the third way of wronging our neighbour by keeping what belongs to him, and that is *when we do not restore ill-gotten goods.* The restitution of what we have stolen to the rightful owner is a strict duty, for the neglect of which millions are now burning in hell, and it is therefore most necessary that all should be well instructed as to the strict obligation of it and the manner of making it.

Remember, therefore, my dear children, throughout life, that there is no pardon from God for any injury which you have *knowingly* and *willingly* inflicted on your neighbour, unless you repair that injury to the utmost of your power. This is equally true of injuries which regard the property and those which affect the character of your neighbour; but it is of those which regard his property that we are here speaking, those which concern his character will be treated of under the eighth commandment. Remember, then, that if you have stolen from your neighbour, cheated him in any way, or wilfully damaged his property, you are strictly bound, as a necessary condition of obtaining pardon, to make good the loss. Moreover, the loss which we have to make good is not the bare amount or value of what we have stolen or destroyed, but it is the *entire loss* which our neighbour has undergone, and which we might have foreseen that he would be in danger of undergoing from our unjust action. For example, let us suppose that a thief has stolen a hundred pounds from a shopkeeper. To supply the loss, the poor tradesman has to borrow another hundred pounds to enable him to preserve his credit and carry on his business. You can easily see that the thief has injured him not only to the amount of the hundred pounds which he stole, but also to the amount of the interest which the tradesman has to pay for the money which he has been obliged to borrow; therefore the thief is bound to make this good also. Take, again, the case of a person who has stolen a workman's tools. The poor man is unable to get employment without his tools, and remains for some days or weeks idle. The thief is obliged to restore not merely the value of the tools, which may be trifling, but the loss which the workman and his family have suffered in consequence. In a word, a thief is always bound in justice to repay all the losses and expenses as well as the direct injury which has been caused by his theft. Hence we find Zaccheus in the Gospel restoring to those, whom he had wronged, fourfold the amount of that of which he had unjustly deprived them, no doubt in order to make full atonement for all the losses which they might have suffered in consequence of his dishonesty. And our Blessed Lord praised him highly for so doing, and assured him that his excellent dispositions had obtained his pardon.*

So far we have been speaking of restitution in cases where a person has himself actually committed the theft or wilful damage by which his neighbour has suffered loss. But what shall we say of him who finds that he is, without any fault of his own, in possession of a stolen article or any property which in justice belongs to his neighbour. For example, a person inherits a fortune which he afterwards finds out to have been unjustly acquired, and to be really the property of another. In this case

* Luke xix. 8, 9.

he must at once, when he has undoubted proof as to the ownership, give it up to the real heir. Again, supposing that you have purchased a watch or any other article which you learn afterwards has been stolen; you must give it up at once to the rightful owner, for he does not lose his right to his own property by the fact of you having been deceived in buying it. In this case, however, you could justly claim the money you had paid for it from him from whom you had bought it.

We next come to speak of those who, though they do not actually commit the theft or do the damage with their own hands, are equally guilty of it in the sight of God. I mean those who *co-operate* in the injustice; in other words, who have a share in doing it by being, in part at least, the cause of it. For example, they may have *advised* another to commit a theft, or even *commanded* him to do so if he happened to be under their authority, as in the case of a master and servant, or of a parent and child. Again, they may have joined with others in some plan for injuring their neighbour, thus *consenting* to the wrong, though possibly it may not have been inflicted by their own hands. Or they may have *provoked* some one by sneers and threats, or encouraged him by *praise and flattery* to injure another. They may also have undertaken to *hide* or *conceal* the stolen goods until they could be divided without danger, or to go shares and *partake* in the spoil in case the theft was committed. Again, they may have preserved *silence*, when it was their duty to speak, as in the case of servants who have the charge of certain goods, but allow their masters to be plundered without opposition. Finally, they may have become sharers in the crime by promising protection and *defence* to those who commit it. These, my dear children, are the nine ways of co-operating or partaking in another person's sin which are mentioned in a later part of the catechism, and when that sin happens to be a sin of injustice, those who partake of it not only incur the guilt of the sin, but also the obligation of restitution. For this, however, it is necessary that they should really have been, though perhaps in part only, the cause of the injury having been committed. For example, a person might shelter a thief after he had committed a crime, and though he might do wrong, he would not bo obliged to repair the injury the thief had done, unless he had actually induced him to commit the theft by the promise of giving him shelter. In all cases of theft we must remember that whoever has the stolen property in his possession, is the first person obliged to restitution; but if he neglects, the obligation falls on all those who have had a share in the deed in any of the ways I have mentioned— each is bound to make good the loss in proportion to the part he has taken in the crime. If all the rest neglect, then the obligation of repairing the entire loss will fall upon each one of the number. The best plan to take in all such cases is to consult your confessor, both as to the extent of your obligation and the best manner of discharging it.

But some one will ask, what must I do if I have wronged my neighbour but am unable through poverty to make restitution? Will not Almighty God forgive the sin in that case? He will, provided that you have the sincere intention of repairing the injury as soon as ever it is in your power. If you are able to restore a portion of the amount though not the whole, you must restore now that which you are able, and the remainder at the first opportunity. Meanwhile you must avoid all unnecessary expense, lay by a portion of your weekly earnings, and make restitution by degrees until the whole of the debt is discharged. But what do you think of a man who has wronged another, and declares to his Confessor that he is too poor to restore, but still continues to frequent the public house, and spend money on his own pleasure and amusement, putting off the duty of restitution from day to day? Such a one is undoubtedly mocking Almighty God, but, though he may deceive his Confessor, he will not deceive God, who sees the real dispositions of his heart, and who strictly requires that restitution should be made without delay and to the utmost of the means in our power. To put off restoring what we owe when we have the means of doing it, is a fresh sin of injustice; it is like a fresh theft committed, for our neighbour has a right this very day to that of which we have deprived him. Hence it is often the duty of a Confessor to defer giving absolution to a penitent, or to put off his Communion until restitution has actually been made. By so doing he really acts with the greatest charity towards his penitent, for the latter is thereby better prepared to receive the grace of the Sacrament, and is preserved from the unhappy fate of so many thousands who promise their Confessors to make restitution, but by putting it off from day to day are in the end surprised by death, and eternally lost through the neglect of this essential duty. Listen, my dear children, to the following awful example on this subject related by St. Alphonsus Liguori.

FATAL NEGLECT OF RESTITUTION.

A certain father, who had committed many acts of injustice during his lifetime in order to enrich his family, finding his death approach, sent for a lawyer to make his will. As soon as he arrived, the dying man exclaimed, "Write down the following bequests:—I leave my soul to the devil." Hereupon his wife and children cried out, "Alas! alas! the poor man is delirious." He replied, "I am not delirious. Lawyer write, I leave my soul to the devils that they may carry it to hell in punishment of the thefts I have committed. I also leave to the devils the soul of my wife, who encouraged me to steal that she might indulge her vanity. I also leave to the devils my children, who have been the cause of my thefts." The Confessor who had heard his confessions during life, and was then assisting him, was struck with horror, and earnestly exhorted him not to despair, but to hope for everything from the Divine Mercy. But the wretched man again addressing the lawyer, said, "Write, I leave to the devils the soul of my Confessor, because during life he always absolved me and did not oblige me to make restitution." So saying, he fell back and expired.—*St. Liguori on the Commandments.*

From what I have said you see, my dear children, the absolute necessity we are under of making restitution to the last farthing for every act of injustice committed against our neighbour, if we ever hope to enter the kingdom of heaven. But to whom must the restitution be made? Will it do if I give that which I have stolen to the poor, or devote it to the building of a church, or get Masses said with the money for the poor souls in purgatory. No, it certainly will not do, unless it is quite impossible to make restitution to the person you have wronged, for example, through not knowing who he is or where he lives, or for some other cause. For you must always remember that it is your neighbour whom you have wronged, and not the poor, nor the Church, nor the souls in purgatory, and therefore it is to your neighbour that the restitution must be made. You have no right, without his leave, to give away *his* money in charity, for he might probably wish to employ it in some other way. If, however, he is not to be found, then you must do with his money what you think will do him most good, by devoting it, for example, to some pious or charitable work for the good of his soul. The Apostle St. Paul, in speaking on this subject, says, "He that stole, let him now steal no more, but rather let him labour, working with his hands the thing which is good, that he may have something to give to him that suffereth need." *   Here the Apostle suggests alms to the poor as an excellent way of making restitution in certain cases.   You will notice also, from the words of St. Paul, how strict is the obligation of restoring to the utmost what we have stolen, since he says that we must, if necessary, labour with our hands in some honest employment, in order that we may obtain the means of fully discharging our debt, if no other way is possible, at least by works of charity to the poor.

We come now to speak of the last way in which we may wrong our neighbour by keeping what belongs to him, and that is when we neglect to pay our just debts.   Hence the catechism says, *we must also pay our debts.*   Remember then, my dear children, that when you have bought anything, and it has been delivered up to you, the price you agreed to pay is no longer yours but belongs to him from whom you have purchased the article. It is *his* money, not your own, which you have in your purse. If, then, you go and spend it on something else, and leave your debt unpaid, you wrong your neighbour as much as if you had stolen from him. Even if you put off paying for an unreasonable time you still wrong him, for no one willingly consents to be kept out of what belongs to him. It is this delay in the payment of bills which brings on tradespeople so many troubles, losses, and often total ruin. Under this class of dishonesty comes that grievous sin which is mentioned in the catechism as one of the four crimes which cry to heaven for vengeance, namely, *defrauding labourers of their wages.* Those masters and mistresses are guilty of this sin who cheat their servants of their just hire, and those also, though in

* Ephes. iv. 28.

a less degree, who delay to pay them for a long time, and thus expose them to want or inconvenience.

I have now explained the different ways in which we may sin against the seventh commandment either by unjustly taking away from our neighbour or keeping what belongs to him. You will ask, perhaps, whether to do this is always a mortal sin, or whether it may not sometimes be only venial. This, my dear children, depends partly upon the amount which we steal, and partly upon the injury which we inflict upon the person whom we wrong. If the amount be great or the injury a serious one, then the sin is mortal; but if the amount be only trifling, then the sin is usually a venial one because but a slight injury is inflicted on our neighbour. Thus it would be a venial sin to steal an apple or an orange, or even a small sum of money unless it were from a very poor man, for the loss of a sixpence or a shilling might be a serious one to him. But notice, that if you often steal little things from the same person, it may come in time to be a mortal sin, for little things mount up and soon make a considerable sum. Indeed, if from the first you intended to go on stealing, it would be a mortal sin to begin with, for you have the intention of taking what will soon become a large amount, and may inflict a serious injury on your neighbour. Thus, for example, a shop boy who intends to steal a sum of money from his master, but only takes sixpence or a shilling at a time for fear of it being missed, is guilty of a mortal sin of theft when he takes the first sixpence on account of his wicked intention. Nay, even if you were to pilfer many little things from different people, the sin after a time would be mortal, because the total amount of the thefts would be large, though perhaps no particular person would be seriously injured. You would like to know, I daresay, how much would be considered such a serious amount as to make the theft a mortal sin. My dear children, it is impossible to tell you. If a number of little things be taken from different people, or even from the same person at different times, no doubt it requires a larger amount to be a grievous theft than if it all be taken at once from the same man, because the injury to our neighbour is less serious. But what exact amount is required in each case to make it a mortal sin God only knows. You must not therefore ask yourselves whether to take this or that is a mortal or a venial sin, but whether it is a theft or not. Those who accustom themselves to steal little things under the pretext that they are only trifles, show very little love to God, for they know that even this offends him. Besides they will always be in extreme danger of passing the line and committing mortal sin, for when the habit of pilfering is once formed, the thief goes on from little things to greater and finds the temptation to steal, when a good opportunity presents itself, too strong to be resisted. And depend upon it that a thief, though for a time he may escape detection, is sure to be found out in the end. Some day or other, suspicion will fall on him, he will be watched and caught in the act, or some way or other the theft will be brought home to him. Then what becomes of him? His character is utterly ruined; he is looked upon as a mean contemptible creature whom no one can place the slightest confidence in, and he is pointed at by all with the finger of scorn. But, worst of all, he has incurred the anger of God and merited his severe punishments. Oh what true friends to their children are those parents who bring them up in the strictest honesty, and chastise them severely if ever they are guilty of petty thefts! If it is true of other things, it is, above all, true of stealing, that to spare the rod is to spoil the child.

Do you parents, then, be always firm in chastising severely the least theft of which your children are guilty. If it is from others that they have stolen, see that they go back with what they have taken and restore it at once, no matter how trifling its value is. And do you, children, be grateful to your parents if they are strict with you on this point; for, by acting thus, they are preserving you from much misery and sin. In conclusion, if ever you are tempted to steal, say a Hail Mary to our Blessed Lady, to preserve you from such a crime, and go at once out of the way of temptation. Listen now to a true story I am going to tell you about a poor Irish servant girl who was tempted to steal her master's money.

THE IRISH SERVANT GIRL.

A few years ago there lived in London a gentleman who was extremely prejudiced against our holy religion, and never lost an opportunity of laughing at and ridiculing its practices. Upon one occasion, however, when Catholic doctrines became the subject of conversation and ridicule, it was noticed that he preserved a grave silence. He was asked the reason, upon which he related to the company the following story :—

"You wonder," said he, "why I no longer join with you, as I used to do, in scoffing at Catholic practices, I will tell you. A few days ago I was busy writing in my room, when I had occasion to leave my desk in order to fetch a certain paper from an inner apartment. While I was so engaged, the servant girl, who is an Irish Catholic, happened to enter the room to mend the fire, for, as I had not answered to her knock, she imagined that I had gone out. Now, I had left by chance upon my desk a large sum of money, and I could see that as soon as she entered the room she was attracted by the glitter of the gold. I determined to watch her narrowly, for I was in a position to observe all her movements, though she had no knowledge of my presence. On perceiving the gold she dropped the coal box, and advanced eagerly to the table. She then stretched out her hand, and was on the very point of clutching the money, when, to my astonishment, she suddenly withdrew her arm and made with her hand the sign of the cross, saying aloud, "The Cross of Christ be betwixt me and my master's money!" She then turned her back and fairly ran out of the room, leaving her brush and coal box on the floor. Now I am convinced from this that the pious practices of the Catholic religion, so far from being idle and superstitious, are most holy and pleasing to God, since they are means of raising the heart to him, and drawing down grace in moments of strong temptation.—*The Lamp.*

Listen now to another story which I will tell you of a wise and prudent father, and of a son who knew how to profit by the correction which he received.

THE GOOD FATHER.

When St. Francis of Sales was a little boy not quite seven years old, he was one day playing in a room at his father's castle, when he noticed lying on the floor the waistcoat of a workman who was employed at some work about the place. Attached to it was a silk ribbon of different colours which immediately attracted the child's attention. No sooner did he see it than he longed to have it, and looking round and seeing no one near he took and hid it. After a short time the workman came back for his waistcoat and perceived at once that some one had stolen his ribbon. He made inquiries among the servants but to no purpose, for they all denied that they had touched it.

At length the matter came to the ears of the Count of Sales, the father of Francis, who sent for his child and asked him whether he knew anything of the workman's ribbon. The truthful boy acknowledged at once that he had taken it, and falling on his knees expressed his sorrow with many tears, and begged his father's pardon. All who beheld him were touched alike by the child's candour and his genuine sorrow, and joined in entreating his father to forgive him this his first offence, but the latter, knowing well that petty thefts, when left uncorrected, lead to greater ones, and, judging like a wise and prudent parent, that it was his duty, even at the expense of his own feelings, to do all in his power to inspire his son with a horror of so serious a fault, sent for a rod and chastised him on the spot. From that time so far was Francis from falling into a like sin that he grew up a model of innocence and virtue.—*Life of St. Francis of Sales.*

There is another well-known story which is handed down to us by an ancient Greek writer, and though we cannot be sure about it being a true one, yet it shews us that even pagans understood how wicked and cruel is the conduct of those parents who permit, and much more of those who encourage petty thefts on the part of their children.

THE BAD MOTHER.

A certain boy had the habit of stealing trifling articles from his neighbours which he brought home to his mother, who never chastised or reproved him. When he grew older he went on stealing things of greater value, and became a confirmed thief. At length he was discovered in the act and, being taken by the officers of justice, was brought before the judge, who condemned him to death. When he had arrived at the place of execution, he perceived his mother among the crowd shedding many tears, and bewailing his fate, upon which he begged leave to speak to her once more before he died. Permission being granted, his mother drew near, and he bent his head as if he would whisper something to her, but, instead of doing so, he caught her ear between his teeth and bit it off, regardless of her shrieks and reproaches. Hereupon the judge reproved him severely for his unnatural conduct, upon which he said, " I have only treated her as she deserved, for it is she who has brought me to this. Had she punished me in my childhood for my petty thefts, I should not when I have grown up been condemned to die on the gallows."—*Æsop.*

We come now to speak more particularly of the tenth commandment which, as I have told you, is closely connected with the seventh. Tell me then—

Q. What does the tenth commandment forbid ?
A. The tenth commandment forbids all covetous thoughts and unjust desires of our neighbour's goods and profits.

The seventh commandment forbids us to injure our neighbour in his property by any act or deed; the tenth forbids us to wrong him even by thought. This we do when we *covet* his goods, in other words, when we inordinately desire to possess what belongs to him. Such desires are often very dangerous, for the wish to possess any object is soon followed by the thought of how to obtain it, and if no easy and honest way of getting it comes to our mind, the devil is not long in suggesting to us some plan that is unjust and dishonest. In fact, coveting is the high road to stealing. If there were none who coveted their neighbour's goods, there would be no longer any thieves. Hence Almighty God forbids, in the tenth commandment, *all covetous thoughts and unjust desires of our neighbour's goods and profits.*

You will ask me, perhaps, my dear children, if it is *coveting* when you simply wish for something nice that you see. No; not if it is a mere passing wish, though such desires are both foolish and useless. It is when you keep thinking over the object of your wish, when you feel discontented and miserable because you have not got it, and desire to have it no matter by what means, it is then that it becomes coveting. This is what we mean by desiring *inordinately*, because such desires are contrary to the order established by Almighty God. Indeed, they are a kind of repining against God for not having given you what you long for, and hence such thoughts are most displeasing to him on account of your want of submission to his Holy Will. Besides, you commit an injustice against your neighbour if you desire to possess what belongs to him, rather than that he should have it, for it is just that he should have what God has given him. If ever such thoughts and desires come into your mind, put them away at once with a little prayer, and try to think of something else; thus will you keep your souls in peace, and preserve them from much sin and unhappiness. Those who give way to those thoughts are always full of trouble and uneasiness; they cannot even enjoy what they have, for they are always longing for what they have not. The history of Achab and Naboth in the Holy Scripture is a striking example of this, and of the dreadful crimes which are often the consequence of giving way to the sin of covetousness.

NABOTH'S VINEYARD.

"Naboth," says the sacred writer, "had a vineyard near the palace of Achab, King of Samaria. And Achab spoke to Naboth saying, *Give me thy vineyard that I may make me a garden of herbs, because it is nigh and joining to my house, and I will give thee for it a better vineyard; or, if thou think it more convenient for thee, I will give thee the worth of it in money.* Naboth answered him, *The Lord be merciful to me and not let me give thee the inheritance of my fathers.*

"And Achab came into his house angry and fretting because of the word which Naboth had spoken. And casting himself upon his bed, he turned his face to the wall and would eat no bread. And Jezabel his wife said to him, *What is the matter that thy soul is so grieved, and why eatest thou no bread?* And he answered her, I spoke to Naboth and said to him, '*Give me thy vineyard and take money for it, or if it please thee, I will give thee a better vineyard.*' And he said, '*I will not give thee my vineyard.*' Then Jezabel said to him, *Thou art of great authority indeed, and governest well the kingdom of Israel. Arise, eat bread and be of good cheer, I will give thee the vineyard of Naboth.* So she wrote letters in Achab's name, and sealed them with his ring, and sent them to the ancients and the chief men that were in the city and that dwelt with Naboth. And this was the tenor of the letters, *Proclaim a fast and make Naboth sit among the chief of the people. And suborn two men, sons of Belial, against him, and let them bear false witness that he hath blasphemed God and the king; and then carry him out and stone him, and so let him die.*

"And the men of his city did as Jezebel had commanded them. They proclaimed a fast and made Naboth sit among the chief of the people. And bringing two men, sons of the devil, they made them sit against him, and they like men of the devil bore witness against him before the people, saying, *Naboth hath blasphemed God and the king.* Wherefore they brought him forth without the city and stoned him to death. And they sent to Jezabel saying, *Naboth is stoned and is dead.*

"And it came to pass when Jezabel heard that Naboth was stoned and dead, that she said to Achab, *Arise and take possession of the vineyard of Naboth, for Naboth is not alive but dead.* And when Achab heard this he arose and went down to the vineyard of Naboth to take possession of it.

"And the word of the Lord came to Elias the Thesbite, saying, *Arise and go down to meet Achab; behold he is going down to the vineyard of Naboth to take possession of it. And thou shalt speak to him, saying, 'Thus saith the Lord, Thou hast slain, moreover also thou hast taken possession. In this place wherein the dogs have licked the blood of Naboth, they shall lick thy blood also. And the dogs shall eat Jezabel in the field of Jezrahel.'"—3 Kings, xxi.*

I have now explained to you the various sins of deed and of thought which are forbidden by the seventh and tenth commandments. But every commandment, as I have told you, *commands* as well as forbids. What then are the duties which these two commandments enjoin? They are principally two, namely, to give to every one his due, which is the perfect practice of justice, and to be content with our own condition and state of life.

TWELFTH INSTRUCTION.

The Eighth Commandment. What it forbids. False testimony, rash judgment, lies, calumny, detraction, and backbiting. Obligation of restitution. What the Eighth Commandment commands.

Q. What is the eighth commandment?
A. Thou shalt not bear false witness against thy neighbour.

The Apostle St. James tells us, my dear children, that the tongue is a little member, but that it is the cause of innumerable evils, defiling the whole body, inflaming the passions, and infecting the soul with a deadly poison.* I have already explained to you some of the terrible evils which spring from the abuse of this unruly member. False teaching, cursing, swearing, blaspheming, injurious words, impure talk, bad advice, &c., are all sins of the tongue, but there are many others, for example, all words which tend to ruin the character and destroy the good name of our fellow men. It is of these that we now come to speak under the eighth commandment—*Thou shalt not bear false witness against thy neighbour.*

This commandment is given us by Almighty God to preserve our character from the unjust attacks of malicious men, in the same way as the fifth commandment is given us to protect the safety of our person, the sixth to guard our purity, and the seventh to secure our earthly goods from the violence and injustice of others. Were it not for the eighth commandment our good name—which, as the wise man tells us, is far more precious than great riches †—would be ever at the mercy of envious and designing men. Let us now see what are the particular sins which are here forbidden.

Q. What does the eighth commandment forbid ?

A. The eighth commandment forbids all false testimony, rash judgment, and lies.

Q. What else is forbidden by the eighth commandment ?

A. All calumny, detraction, and backbiting, or any words which injure our neighbour's character.

In these two answers are mentioned seven distinct sins, which all tend more or less to the taking away of our neighbour's character, and which are therefore forbidden by the eighth commandment.

* James iii. 5-8. † Prov. xxii. 1.

By *false testimony*, we mean bearing false witness against any one in a court of justice. This is the most grievous of all the sins here named, because by it we offer the greatest outrage to God, and inflict the greatest injury upon our neighbour. You know, I daresay, that when any one is called as a witness before a public tribunal, he is always examined upon oath. A copy of the New Testament is placed in his hand, and he swears upon that, which is the Word of God, to answer with perfect truth the questions put to him. If, therefore, he answers falsely, he has called upon the God of Truth to bear witness to that which is a lie. This, as I have before explained to you, is the crime of *perjury*, and it is a perjury of the most grievous kind, both on account of the public and solemn manner in which it is committed and on account of the injury thereby inflicted upon society. Indeed, if the words of witnesses thus solemnly pledged to speak the truth could not be depended upon, there would be an end of all public justice, and every one would be at the mercy of the malice and rapacity of his enemies. Moreover, the injustice committed against him whose character is thus defamed is almost beyond remedy, for besides the imprisonment or other punishment inflicted upon him in consequence of this false evidence, the public disgrace which is attached to the sentence accompanies him throughout life, and often falls likewise upon his family and nearest connections. Of those who are guilty of this heinous sin, some are prompted by sheer malice, like the Jews who accused our Blessed Lord before Pilate as guilty of blasphemy and sedition, or the two elders who out of revenge publicly charged the chaste Susanna with that very crime which she had refused to consent to. Others give false testimony through interest, for instance those who swear against their neighbour in order to remove blame from their own shoulders. Finally, there are many who commit this sin through a criminal negligence, because they do not consider well what they say. They speak at random, exaggerate what they have seen or heard, give their suspicions as facts, or represent as certain what is only doubtful. This kind of false testimony is less grievous than that which is prompted by malice or interest, but still it cannot be excused, where the negligence is great, from the guilt of mortal sin and the obligation of restitution. For a witness is strictly bound, both out of respect for his oath and regard for the rights of justice, to weigh well what he says, and to state nothing but what he knows to be the exact truth.

The second sin against this commandment is *rash judgment;* that is, condemning a person in our own mind as guilty of a fault upon slight and insufficient grounds. If we have good grounds for believing him guilty, then our judgment is not *rash;* though charity, " which thinketh no evil but hopeth all things," * as St. Paul says, would rather incline us not to judge him at all, but to leave all judgment to God. Moreover, how liable we all are, even the wisest amongst us, to be deceived and misled by appearances ! The golden cup of Joseph, which was found in the sack of Benjamin, seemed in the eyes of all a convincing proof of his guilt, and yet he was perfectly innocent.† So it is continually in the judgments formed by men, for God alone can see all things, and he alone knows not only the acts but the secret motives and dispositions of each one. " Man seeth those things that appear," says the Holy Scripture, " but the Lord beholdeth the heart." ‡

But we must not only have a horror of rash judgments, we must also, as far as we can, avoid

* I. Cor. xiii. 5, 7.   † Gen. xliv.   ‡ I. Kings xvi. 7.

even rash *suspicions*, for it is unjust not only to condemn, but even to *suspect* a person of wrong without cause. Moreover, we should strive always to act by that golden rule of charity, " Do as you would be done by." Now which of you would like to be even suspected of being a thief or a liar on very slight and insufficient grounds, or perhaps without any grounds at all. Would you not think it exceedingly unjust and uncharitable in those who suspected you, and much more so if they actually formed a judgment about you and condemned you in their own minds? Avoid then, my dear children, in your own conduct that which you would so much blame in others. Turn your thoughts, rather, to your own faults which are so many and so great, but to which you are often so blind. " Why seest thou the mote that is in thy brother's eye," says our Blessed Lord, " and seest not the beam that is in thy own eye?" * And again he says, " Judge not and you shall not be judged, condemn not and you shall not be condemned. For with what judgment you judge, you shall be judged, and with what measure you mete, it shall be measured to you again," †

The following short histories will shew you how easily we are apt to fall into the sins of rash judgment, and how displeasing it is in the sight of God.

THE ABBOT AND THE ANGEL.

It is related in the Lives of the Fathers of the Desert that the Abbot Isaac, being one day present at an assembly of the religious, formed a bad opinion of one of the monks whom he met there, and, from some trifle or other which he noticed, judged him to be worthy of correction. Upon his return to his cell he found an Angel waiting at the door, who opposed his entrance. Filled with awe, the Abbot humbly begged to know the object of his mission. "I am come from our Blessed Lord," replied the Angel, "to inquire from you what

* Matt. vii. 3. † Luke vi. 37; Matt. vii. 2.

you wish to be done with that monk whom you have already condemned in your own mind?" The holy Abbot at once cast himself upon the ground, acknowledged his fault, and implored pardon of God. "Go," said the Angel, "God pardons you; but in future be more careful about judging your brethren, and condemning those whom God himself perhaps has not condemned."—*Lives of the Fathers of the Desert.*

TOTILA AND THE BISHOP.

In the days of Totila, king of the Goths, there lived at Narni in Italy a holy Bishop named Cassius. It happened that Totila, seeing him one day, formed a bad opinion of him, on account of his red and fiery complexion. "This man," said he to himself, "is certainly a drunkard." But Almighty God undertook upon the spot the defence of his servant. At the same moment he permitted a devil to enter into the person of Totila's sword-bearer, who became grievously tormented by the evil spirit. The bystanders in the greatest alarm carried the poor possessed man to the feet of the holy Bishop, who at once delivered him by simply making over him the sign of the cross. Thereupon Totila retracted his unfavourable judgment, and ever after esteemed and reverenced Cassius as a saint.—*St. Gregory the Great.*

The next sin which we come to speak of—that of telling *lies*—is one against which I am particularly anxious to warn you, both because it is, unhappily, very common among children, and because it is the root of many other vices. To tell a lie, is to say what we believe to be untrue. If we believe that we are speaking the truth, and happen to be mistaken, it is not a lie; on the other hand, if we say what we believe to be false, and it turns out to be true, it is really a lie in the sight of God.

All lies are sinful, because they are all directly opposed to Divine Truth, which is one of the most admirable Perfections of Almighty God. Moreover, they are an abuse of that most excellent gift of speech, which God has given us to enable us to make our thoughts known to our fellow-men; whereas the liar uses his speech to conceal his thoughts and deceive his neighbour. But though all lies are sinful, they are not all equally sinful; some are much more grievous than others. The worst lie of all is that which is told in confession by him who conceals a sin, for such a lie is a *sacrilegious* lie, a lie told to God himself, and is the profanation of a most holy Sacrament. The lie next in guilt is that which is told to injure our neighbour's character : for example, when a person gives false testimony in a court of justice, or when he spreads abroad calumnies against his neighbour, accusing him of crimes which he has never committed. Such lies are called *malicious lies*, because they are told through malice on purpose to injure others, and they are very grievous sins. But there are other lies which are much less in guilt, namely, *lies of excuse* and *lies of jest*. These lies are sometimes called by foolish people *white lies*, as if that which is black in its very nature could ever become white. It is true that they may not cause our neighbour any injury, but still they are displeasing to God and hurtful to the soul. They displease God, because he is the very Truth, and as the Holy Scripture says, " Lying lips are an abomination to the Lord." * They are hurtful to the soul, not only on account of the wound they inflict upon it at the time, but also because a habit of lying is thereby formed, which is the foundation of many vices. If a child is a habitual liar, depend upon it that, if he is not cured of this vice in time, he will grow up both a hypocrite and a thief, for truth is the twin sister of candour and honesty. " Shew me a liar," says the proverb, " and I will shew you a thief." Moreover, to tell a lie to excuse yourself is an act of cowardice, and shews a certain weakness of character and principle, which may well

* Prov. xii. 22,

R

cause us to fear that so feeble and timid a soul will soon fall a prey to its evil passions and the temptations of the devil. Be always, then, my dear children, most exact in speaking the truth, and pray to God to give you a great love of this excellent virtue which is so pleasing to him. Remember that if you love and always speak the truth, you are in a special manner the children of God, who is the Divine Truth. On the contrary, if you have a habit of lying, you are the children of the devil, who is, as our Blessed Lord says, a liar and the father of lies. *
You must not tell the smallest lie even to save the whole world, for it is better that the world should be destroyed than that God should be offended. Much less, then, should you tell a lie to save yourself from a scolding or a beating, which are soon over, and, moreover, are intended for your good. If you have done wrong, be sorry for it and own it, then you are soon forgiven both by God and your parents; whereas if you try to hide it by a lie, you are guilty of a fresh sin, and one often much greater than the fault you first committed. Listen to these two lines of one of our own poets on this subject; they are well worth remembering—

> " Dare to be true, nothing can need a lie ;
>   The sin that needs it most grows two thereby." †

Yes, *dare to be true.* Be *brave* enough to speak the truth, for it is an act of true courage. Your parents or teachers may punish you, but they will respect and trust you, the Saints and Angels will look down on you with approval, God will hear and will reward you. *Nothing can need a lie*, because nothing can excuse it. Moreover the sin you have committed, and that seems to *need it most, grows two thereby*, since you offend God doubly, and thus make it far more

* John, viii. 44.   † George Herbert.

difficult to obtain his pardon. And depend upon it, sooner or later the liar will be found out in his lies, for, as the proverb says, "truth will out." In conclusion, what is more contemptible than the character of a liar, whose word is never taken, whose denials are never believed, whose promises are never trusted? On the contrary, what is more noble, what more amiable, than the character of a child who is always candid, truthful and sincere? Such a one, wherever he goes, carries with him the esteem, the confidence, the respect of every one.

The following examples will shew you how a true Christian should be ready to lay down his life rather than consent to the least falsehood, and how severely Almighty God sometimes punishes those who are guilty of this sin.

THE BISHOP AND THE SOLDIERS.

It is related in Church History that upon one occasion the emperor Maximinian, a cruel persecutor of the faithful, despatched a troop of soldiers to apprehend and cast into prison Antony, the venerable Bishop of Nicomedia. It happened that, without knowing it, they came to the house of the holy Bishop, and being hungry, knocked at the door and begged for some refreshment. He received them with great kindness, invited them to sit down at table, and set before them such food as he had at his disposal. When the meal was ended, the soldiers entered upon the subject of their mission, and requested him to inform them where they could meet with the Bishop Antony. "He is here before you," replied the Saint. The soldiers, full of gratitude for his generous hospitality, declared that they would never lay hands upon him, but would report to the emperor that they had not been able to find him. "God forbid," replied the Saint, "that I should save my life by becoming a party to a lie. I would rather die a thousand times than that you should offend Almighty God." So saying, he gave himself into their hands, and was conducted to prison.—*Catechisme de Perseverance.*

DEATH RATHER THAN A LIE.

During the great French revolution, at the end of the last century, the Catholic churches were everywhere pillaged throughout the country and closed for public worship. The priests were also proscribed, and forced to conceal themselves in private houses, or even to seek shelter in the thickets of the forests or in the caves and fastnesses of the mountains. It happened about this time that a young girl, named Magdalen Larralde, of the village of Sare, on the borders of Spain, fearing to have recourse to her own parish priest in his place of concealment, was wont to cross the mountains whenever she desired to approach the Sacraments, in order to seek spiritual assistance from the Capuchin Fathers at the convent of Vera, on the Spanish side of the Pyrennees. One day, however, in returning from the convent, she fell in with an outpost of the French army, which was then stationed along the frontier, in consequence of the war which raged between the two countries. The soldiers immediately seized her as a spy and dragged her before the general, who questioned her as to the object of her presence in Spain. Magdalen answered simply and without a moment's hesitation that she had been to confession. The officer, touched by her youth and innocent bearing, and anxious, if possible, to save her, quickly replied, "Unfortunate woman, do not say that, for it will be your sentence of death. Say, rather, that the advance of the French troops frightened you, and drove you to seek shelter on Spanish ground." "But then I should say what would not be true," answered the girl, "and I would rather die a thousand times than offend God by telling a lie." In vain did the general urge and solicit her to yield, her firmness never gave way, and she was conducted before the tribunal of St. Jean de Luz. Before her judges Magdalen again with unflinching courage refused to save her life by a lie. She was therefore condemned to the guillotine, and as she walked to the place of execution her step never faltered, and she ceased not to invoke the assistance of God and to sing the Salve Regina in honour of the Queen of Heaven.— *The Month.*

THE IMPOSTOR STRUCK DEAD.

St. James, Bishop of Nisibis, was one day travelling through the country, when he was accosted by a beggar who appeared to be in deep distress. On approaching the Saint he implored him with earnest supplications to bestow an alms upon him to enable him to bury his companion, who, as he said, had just expired by the roadside. The holy Bishop readily gave him what he asked, and then went on his way praying earnestly for the soul of the deceased. The beggar, laughing at the thought of having succeeded so easily in imposing upon the Saint, meanwhile ran back to his companion, whom he had left lying upon the ground at a little distance pretending to be dead. On coming to the spot he called out to him to get up, as the trick had been successful, but he received no answer. He approached nearer, and took his companion by the hand in order to arouse him, but what was his horror at finding that he was really dead ! Immediately with loud cries and lamentations he ran after the Saint, and throwing himself on his knees before him, acknowledged the deceit which they had practised, and implored his pardon and intercession. The servant of God, having first reproved him for his sin, betook himself to prayer, and the unhappy man, who had provoked Almighty God to deprive him of life, was restored at the prayers of the Saint and became a sincere penitent.—*Theodoret.*

We come now to speak of the sin of *calumny*, by which we mean a lie, told to injure our neighbour's character. It is sometimes malice, sometimes self-interest, which leads people into this sin ; for example, a person may falsely accuse another of theft through spite and revenge, or he may do so to get him turned out of his employment, in order that he himself may step into his place. In either case the sin is very grievous, for, as I have told you, there is nothing, except life itself, of such value to us among temporal goods or which we prize so much as our good name. Our means of employment, the peace and happiness of our lives, and frequently that of those who are dear to us, depend in a great measure upon our bearing an unblemished character. Hence he who unjustly robs us of this, inflicts on us the greatest of injuries. To deprive us of our earthly goods, or to cause us some bodily injury, is generally a less evil than to blacken our character in the eyes of our fellow-men.

The next sin here mentioned, namely, *detraction*, consists in taking away our neighbour's character by publishing his secret faults. You see it is a different thing from calumny, which is telling lies of our neighbour. The detractor tells the truth, but then he has no right to tell it, for every one is entitled to his good name unless he has forfeited it by some public crime. There are, however, certain cases in which it is our duty to make known the bad conduct of others to those whose office it is to advise and correct them. For example, if we knew that any boy or girl was keeping very bad company, or going secretly to some dangerous place of amusement, it would not only be lawful, but it would be our duty, to make it known to the parents or guardians of the child. Silence in such a case would be a sin, for it might easily be the cause of the eternal loss of a soul. But this is very different from the case of a detractor, who no sooner hears of any one having done wrong than he goes about to publish it. "Have you heard," he says, "what such a one has done? I could not have believed it, yet I fear it is too true. Come, I will tell it you as a secret." And so the *secret* goes about from one to another, until the poor victim of the detractor's malice has lost his good name in the eyes of all that know him.

Sometimes, my dear children, the calumniator and detractor succeed in destroying the character of their neighbour without actually charging him with any crime, but by running down his good deeds, or by artfully hinting that there is something which people do not know which would quite change the good opinion they have of him. "Oh!" they will say, "such a one is not so good as he looks. For my part—but I will say no more, for the least said is soonest mended." And so their hearers go away under the impression that the person, whom they have been speaking about, has been guilty of some secret crime, which the detractor is too good-natured to mention—an error which can never be removed, as no special sin has been laid to his charge. Could anything be meaner, more ungenerous, and more cruel than such conduct? It may well be compared to that of the midnight assassin, who lurks under cover to stab his enemy in the dark. Of such and of all detractors the Holy Scripture truly says—"They have whetted their tongues like a sword." * "Their words are smoother than oil, and the same are darts." † And again, "They have sharpened their tongues like a serpent, and the venom of asps is under their lips." ‡

The last of the sins against the eighth commandment mentioned in the catechism is *backbiting*. The difference between backbiting and the two vices we have just been speaking of is, that in backbiting you do not tell *lies* of your neighbour, which would be calumny; neither do you publish his *secret sins*, which would be detraction; but you simply take a pleasure in speaking of *his faults and failings which are known to every one*. But is there any harm in doing this? Yes, certainly; for such a practice is quite contrary to Christian charity, which bids us to love our neighbour as ourselves, and do to others for the love of Christ what we would wish them to do to us. Now which of us would like our own faults to be made the subject of conversation? If we *are* passionate, or untruthful, or greedy, do you think we should like these failings of ours to be discussed over a tea table or by the fireside, and all the lies we have told, and the passions we have been in, and the times we have eat or drunk too much, recalled to mind and talked about? Well, then, if we should not like it ourselves, it is clear that charity forbids us to do it to others. Yet, alas, how common is

* Ps. lxiii. 4. † Ps. liv. 20. ‡ Ps. cxxxix. 4.

this vice among mankind! Seldom do people meet together but the faults of their neighbours form the chief subject of their conversation, and well is it if they only speak of their public faults, and do not fall into the still more grievous sins of detraction and calumny. My dear children, have throughout life a great horror of the mean and ungenerous vice of backbiting. If you find yourselves in company where your neighbours' faults are discussed, take no part in such conversation. On the contrary, discourage it as much as you can; begin to speak of something else, or at least shew by your silence that you are not pleased. According to the advice of the wise man, "by the sadness of the countenance the mind of the offender is corrected." * Happy, indeed, will you be when you come to die, if you have within you the sweet and consoling reflection that throughout life you have kept your tongue from all uncharitable conversation, and have been as jealous in guarding your neighbour's character as you would be in protecting your own.

THE SLANDERER REBUKED.

It is related of St. Augustine, the illustrious Doctor of the Church, that he had an extreme horror of all uncharitable conversation. To prevent any discourse of this nature from being held in his presence, he caused the following inscription to be painted in large letters upon the walls of the room where he usually entertained his friends—

> " Slanderer beware, this is no place for thee ;
> Here nought shall reign but truth and charity."

It happened one day that some of his guests began to speak in his presence of the faults of an absent neighbour. The holy Bishop, with a grave and severe look, immediately reproved them, saying, " My friends, you must either cease to speak on such a subject, or it will be necessary for me to have those verses blotted out from the walls of my room."— *Catech. de Perseverance.*

* Eccles. vii. 4.

Before we go on to the next question, I wish to speak to you of two other sins against the eighth commandment which are not mentioned in your catechism, but against which it is very necessary to warn you. The first of these is the sin of *talebearing*.

By *talebearing* we mean the habit of carrying tales backwards and forwards from house to house, from person to person. For example, Peter goes to the house of Paul, who happens to say in his presence something unkind about his neighbour John. Peter's next visit is to the house of John, to whom he repeats word for word, and often with additions, what Paul has said of him. Thus does Peter create an ill feeling, and not unfrequently sow the seeds of a lamentable quarrel between two neighbours. Even children often cause trouble in families, sometimes between their very parents, by carrying tales from one to another. Whenever, therefore, you see or hear anything that is likely to cause annoyance to others or create ill feeling, keep it to yourselves, unless it is something which it is your duty to tell, and then tell it only to the proper person. Talebearers are the greatest pests to society; they are the cause of half the quarrels and dissensions which arise among mankind. Moreover, though they may bitterly repent of it, they can seldom repair the evil they have caused or undo the consequences of their own thoughtless words. My dear children, avoid carefully this common but most mischievous vice.

But if a talebearer is a contemptible creature, a *prier into secrets* is even more so, though not perhaps equally dangerous. He is ever on the watch to gratify a morbid curiosity by listening at doors, peeping into drawers and boxes, opening and reading letters and secret papers. To do these things is not only mean, but it is actually sinful. Nay, it may even amount to the guilt of a mortal sin, for instance, if you were to open and read a letter that is likely to contain something that the owner would be very much grieved to have known to others. Always resist at the beginning these itchings of curiosity, and go away from the temptation. Look upon it as a mean and contemptible practice, unworthy of a noble and generous soul, to attempt to pry into the secrets of others.

We now come to speak of a very important subject, namely, the obligation which rests upon those who have unjustly taken away their neighbours' character, to repair the injury, with all its consequences, to the utmost of their power. Tell me, then—

Q. What is he bound to do who has injured his neighbour by speaking ill of him ?

A. He must make him satisfaction and restore his good name as far as he is able.

Yes, my dear children, as there is no pardon from God for those who have stolen their neighbours' goods, unless they restore that which they have stolen to the last farthing, so neither is there any forgiveness for those who have robbed their neighbour of what is still more precious, namely, his character, unless *they make him satisfaction and restore his good name as far as they are able.* Whoever by false testimony, or by calumny, or by detraction, has deprived his neighbour of the confidence and esteem of his fellow men, has inflicted upon him a grievous injury, and justice therefore requires that he should do all in his power to restore to him that of which he has robbed him. To do this he must retract his false accusation, and must do it in presence of those before whom the *calumny* has been spoken. Nay more, if the story has spread abroad and become public he must retract it in public. In every case he must see that those, to whose ears it has reached, are informed that there is no ground for the charge which has been made.

But what, you will say, must he do who has taken away his neighbour's good name by revealing his *secret sin;* in other words, who has been guilty of *detraction?* It is clear that he cannot retract his words, for he cannot declare a man to be innocent of a crime when he knows him to be really guilty. He must, however, do all that he can in accordance with truth to repair the wrong which he has inflicted. For example, he might make what excuses he can for the guilty person, if the case admits any ; or he should publish his good deeds when opportunity offers, as he has done his bad ones, and make known the good points of his character. By doing this prudently and discreetly he may be able, in some degree at least, to remove the evil impression which his words have made, and to restore to him whom he has wronged the good opinion of others.

This, however, my dear children, is not all that the calumniator or detractor is bound to do in the way of making restitution. It may happen that the false charge which he has uttered, or the secret crime which he has revealed, has been the means of depriving the injured man of his employment, his custom in trade, or his means of subsistence. It may have caused him some serious loss or heavy expense. This also must be set right; the loss must be made good, the injury repaired as far as it is in the power of him who has inflicted it. See then what an awful responsibility these sins of the tongue bring upon the soul. Watch, therefore, carefully over that unruly member, that no word may ever escape your lips which can in any way blacken the character, or destroy the good name of your neighbour. And if ever you err in this respect, through want of prudence or through bad feeling towards any one, hasten to recall your words at once before they are repeated to others and the injury has thus become greater and more difficult to repair.

I will now relate to you an interesting story on this subject which is taken from the Lives of the Fathers of the Desert.

THE STOLEN BOOK.

Among the holy solitaries, who formerly peopled the deserts of Egypt, was a monk named Paphnucius, who for his singular piety, austerity and innocence of life is justly venerated among the saints. His extraordinary virtue and reputation for sanctity excited feelings of envy in the breast of a certain wicked monk, who concealed under the garb of a religious the pride and passion of a worldling. Being determined to destroy the character of St. Paphnucius, he secretly entered his cell one Sunday morning when all the religious had gone out to assist at Mass, and hid his own prayer book under a pile of mats which lay in one corner of the cell. When Mass was ended he complained aloud to the Abbot Isidore, in presence of all the community, that some one had entered his cell and stolen his prayer book. The assembled monks were filled with grief and indignation at hearing of the event, for such a crime had never yet been heard of among the holy solitaries. Meanwhile the wicked monk earnestly besought Isidore to send some of their number to search the cells, and to forbid any one to leave the spot until the return of the messengers. Three monks were accordingly chosen for the purpose, and they at once set out to execute their commission. They searched every cell, and the book was of course found in that of St. Paphnucius. It is impossible to describe the grief and astonishment of the assembled monks at hearing of the result of the inquiry, for St. Paphnucius was both beloved and venerated by all his brethren. The proofs were, however, convincing, and as the saint uttered not a word in his defence, he was adjudged guilty and condemned to a severe penance for the space of fifteen days. Meanwhile the calumniator returned to his cell rejoicing at the success of his scheme.

No sooner was the term of the penance expired, than Almighty God took into his own hands the defence of the innocent Paphnucius and the punishment of his guilty accuser. The wicked monk became possessed by an evil spirit, and went from cell to cell to seek his cure from those who enjoyed the greatest reputation for sanctity. No one, however, was able to afford him the least relief, until at length, throwing himself at the feet of St. Paphnucius in presence of all the solitaries, he confessed his crime, and published aloud the innocence of the Saint. He then implored of the holy man to return him good for evil by obtaining his cure from God ; upon which St. Paphnucius, kneeling down, offered up his prayers in his behalf, and delivered him from the devil who tormented him.— *Cassian.*

So far, my dear children, we have been speaking of the different sins forbidden by the eighth commandment; can you now tell me what are the *duties* which it enjoins? They are principally these—to speak the truth in all things great and small, to think kindly of our neighbour in our hearts, to speak of him always with charity and forbearance, and to guard his good name as we would our own.

As I have already explained to you the ninth commandment along with the sixth, and the tenth along with the seventh, we shall go on in the next instruction to speak of the Commandments of the Church.

THIRTEENTH INSTRUCTION.

CHAPTER V.—*The Commandments of the Church. Their strict Obligation. The First Commandment. The Holydays of Obligation. The Second Commandment.*

Q. Are we bound to obey the Church ?

A. Yes ; because Christ has said to the pastors of the Church, "He that heareth you, heareth me ; and he that despiseth you, despiseth me."—*Luke,* x. 16.

We now come to speak of the *Commandments* or Precepts *of the Church*, which we are as much bound to keep as we are the commandments of God himself. Indeed they *are* the commandments of Almighty God, though he gives them to us by his Church, which he has appointed to guide and direct us in all that regards his Divine service. Hence our Blessed Lord plainly tells us that to obey the pastors of the Church is just the same thing as to obey himself, and, on the other hand, that he will look upon any disobedience to the laws of the Church as an act of disobedience and contempt offered to his own Divine Person. "He that heareth you," said he to the Apostles, who were the first pastors of the Church, "heareth me; and he that despiseth you, despiseth me." And again he says—If any man "will not hear the Church, let him be to thee as the heathen and publican;" * that is, look upon him in the light of an unbeliever and a public sinner, and, as such, avoid his company and friendship.

In accordance with the authority committed to her by our Blessed Lord, the Church has ever from the earliest ages exercised the power of making laws and regulations, binding upon all the faithful. Sometimes her object is to explain more clearly the Divine commandments and to shew how they are to be fulfilled; at other times it is to promote better order and discipline among the various classes of her members. The second precept of the Church, for example, about hearing Mass on Sundays, is to shew us how to keep that sacred day holy, as we are commanded to do in the third commandment of the Decalogue. Again, the third commandment of the Church about fasting and abstaining teaches us how to mortify and subdue our passions, which we are bound to do by the Divine law. On the other hand,

* Matt. xviii. 17.

the sixth commandment of the Church about not solemnizing marriage at certain times refers to a mere matter of discipline, being intended to prevent the faithful from profaning with feasting and public rejoicing those holy seasons, which are set apart for the exercise of penance and prayer.

Q. Which are the chief commandments of the Church ?

A. 1. To keep certain days holy, with the obligation of resting from servile works.

2. To hear Mass on all Sundays and Holydays of obligation.

3. To keep the days of fasting and abstinence appointed by the Church.

4. To go to confession at least once a year.

5. To receive the Blessed Sacrament at least once a year, and that at Easter or thereabouts.

6. Not to marry within certain degrees of kindred, nor to solemnize marriage at the forbidden times.

Yes, my dear children, these are *the chief commandments of the Church;* that is to say, they are the most important among those which concern the faithful in general. There are, however, many other precepts of the Church besides these six, but as some of them relate to matters which seldom occur, and the remainder are only intended for the Clergy and the Religious Orders, they are not put in the catechism, since there is no necessity for you to be instructed in them.

As the Church has authority to make laws for her children, so she has also power to change or do away with them according as occasion or necessity may require. For there is this difference between the commandments of God and those of the Church— that the former never vary, they are always binding, and binding in all places and upon every living soul; whereas the commandments of the Church bind those only who are members of the Church; moreover, they may vary in different ages and different countries.   And what is the reason of this difference? It is because the commandments of God are simply the expression of those principles of right and wrong which are as unchangeable as God himself; whereas the precepts of the Church are laws made to promote the glory of God and the salvation of the faithful, which ends may be accomplished in many different ways.   Thus it could never be right to steal, or curse, or blaspheme, but it might be lawful to eat meat on Fridays and not to hear Mass on the present Holydays of obligation; for instance, if the Church were to enjoin some other way of doing penance, or were to appoint some other days for Divine worship instead of those which are now observed.   For the time, and place, and manner of penance and prayer are matters of discipline, which the Church has power to regulate as seems good to her.   Indeed, our merit in the performance of these good works arises in a great measure from the fact of their being so many acts of obedience to that authority, which God has established to rule and direct us here below.   Hence you will find that the commandments of the Church have undergone various changes at different periods.   For instance, in the first great Council of her Pastors held in Jerusalem, it was commanded, as we read in the Acts of the Apostles, that the faithful should abstain from eating blood and things that were strangled; * but after a time this law was done away with, and it has never since been in force.   Even in our own days there have been changes in the discipline and laws of the Church; thus a few years ago there were certain days kept as Holydays of obligation which are now no longer observed.   You, see, therefore, that the Church can and does change her laws, as she sees to be most conducive to the glory of God and the

* Acts, xv. 29.

good of the faithful committed to her charge. In like manner she can give authority to any of her ministers to excuse her children from the observance of any particular law, when there seems to be a just cause for so doing. This is what is called giving a dispensation. You have, I daresay, often heard of a person having a dispensation to eat meat on Fridays, or not to fast during Lent; in other words, he has been excused from the law of abstaining or of fasting for some good and important reason. The enemies of our holy religion sometimes falsely assert that Catholics can purchase a dispensation from their priest even to commit sin; for example, to tell lies, &c. This, of course, is a wicked calumny, for the Church has no power over the commandments of God, but only over those which she herself has made; nor does she ever excuse any one from the observance of these without some just and sufficient cause.

There are many terrible examples related in the Holy Scriptures of the severe punishments which Almighty God inflicts on those who despise and set at nought the authority of their lawful pastors. The following history shews how true it is that God regards every act of resistance to those, whom he has appointed to represent him upon earth, as a direct rebellion against his own Divine authority.

HISTORY OF CORE, DATHAN, AND ABIRON.

While the Israelites were journeying through the desert on their way to the land of promise, a formidable rebellion broke out against Moses and Aaron, headed by Core, Dathan, and Abiron. They complained that Moses and Aaron had usurped the office of the priesthood, and that they tyrannised over the rest of the people. Two hundred and fifty of the principal Israelites joined in the sedition, and murmured openly against their spiritual leaders. Having tried in vain by mild and gentle measures to recall them to their obedience, Moses, by the command of God, ordered the whole people to separate themselves from the tents of the three ringleaders. Then addressing the multitude he said, "If these men die the common death of men, then the Lord has not sent me. But if the Lord do a new thing, and the earth opening her mouth swallow them up, and they go down alive into hell, then you shall know that they have blasphemed the Lord." No sooner had he spoken than the earth broke asunder under their feet, and opening her mouth swallowed them up alive, along with their wives and children and all their substance.—*Numbers* xvi.

We will now go on to speak of the different commandments of the Church separately.

Q. What is the first commandment of the Church?
A. To keep certain days holy, with the obligation of resting from servile works.

Q. What are these days called?
A. They are called Holydays of obligation.

The first commandment of the Church is *to keep holy certain days* throughout the year, which are usually called Feasts or *Holydays of obligation*, and to abstain on such days from all *servile work* the same as upon Sundays. These Holydays of obligation are days which the Church has set apart to honour special mysteries in the life of our Divine Lord or his Blessed Mother, or to commemorate the lives and triumphs of the Saints. Formerly, when faith was more lively and charity more fervent, these festivals were more numerous than they are at present; but the Church, out of compassion for the weakness of her children and for other important reasons, has done away with several of them. These have now become simply *Feasts of devotion*, that is days which we are *exhorted* to sanctify as much as possible by works of piety and religion, though we are not strictly commanded to do so. For example, the Feasts of the Apostles and the Monday and Tuesday in Easter and in Whit week, with many others, used formerly to be Holydays of obligation, but now they are no longer so, though you still find them in your prayer-books marked as days of devotion. Moreover, the Holydays of obligation differ somewhat in different countries: thus in France four only remain, which are kept on the following Sundays; in Italy, the Feast of the Archangel St. Michael is a Holyday of obligation; in Ireland, that of St. Patrick; &c.

Can any of you now tell me how many Holydays of obligation we have in this country, and what they are? If you count them over you will find that there are eight, and they are as follows:—

1. The Feast of our Lord's Circumcision, which falls upon New Year's Day.

2. The Feast of the Epiphany—that is, of the manifestation of our Lord to the three wise men, who came, guided by the star, to adore him at Bethlehem. This Feast is sometimes called Twelfth Day, because it occurs on the sixth of January, the twelfth day after our Lord's Birth.

3. The Ascension of our Lord, forty days after Easter Sunday. This feast always falls upon a Thursday.

4. The Feast of Corpus Christi—that is, of the Body of Christ. This Feast has been instituted by the Church to honour the real presence of our Lord in the Blessed Sacrament, and is kept upon the second Thursday after Whitsunday.

5. The Feast of SS. Peter and Paul, 29th June, on which day we commemorate the glorious martyrdom of those two great Apostles.

6. The Assumption of our Blessed Lady, 15th August. Upon this Feast we celebrate the glorious entrance of the Mother of God into the kingdom of her Divine Son.

7. The Feast of All Saints, which is kept on 1st November. In this festival the Church honours

the glorious memory of all the Saints of God, even of those who are not canonised, and whose names and good works are perhaps hidden from mankind.

8. Christmas Day, 25th December, which is the day of our Lord's Nativity—that is, of his Sacred Birth in the stable at Bethlehem.

These, my dear children, are the eight Holydays of obligation kept in this country, and we are as strictly bound to devote them to the worship of God as we are the Sunday itself. Hence it is a grievous sin, without great necessity, for women to wash or to sew upon these days, or for men to do labouring work or follow any mechanical trade. But the Church, which is ever a tender mother to her children, allows them to labour upon these days in cases where they would otherwise be put to great loss and inconvenience. This often happens in our country, where Catholics for the most part work under Protestant masters who do not keep these Holydays of obligation, and who would probably dismiss any workman who insisted upon resting on these days. Thus the fear of losing his employment in the case of a workman, or the custom of his employers in the case of a master tradesman, would be considered a sufficient reason for working upon Holydays or for causing others to do so. In the same way buying and selling, which are generally forbidden by the Church on Holydays as well as on Sundays, are in this country permitted to people in business on account of the necessity of the case, for a Catholic shopkeeper could not shut up his shop on these days without losing his custom and incurring serious loss. Notice, however, that a person would not be allowed to work for amusement on a Holyday of obligation, since there would be in this case no real necessity to excuse him; nor would it be at all becoming for a lady to do her shopping on days which the Church has set apart to be employed in the worship of Almighty God. In cases of doubt as to what is permitted, a good Catholic will always have recourse to his confessor for advice, and abide by his counsel and direction.

The following history is handed down to us by St. Gregory, the Bishop of Tours, who lived in the sixth century.

THE MAN WITH THE TURNED HEAD.

At the beginning of the sixth century there lived in France a holy Abbot named Avitus, who died in the odour of sanctity, and was buried at Orleans. A church was soon after built over his tomb, and the feast of St. Avitus was celebrated every year as a Holyday of obligation with great pomp and solemnity. Now it happened one year upon this festival day that a certain inhabitant of Orleans, despising the precept of the Church, took his spade and went to dig in his vineyard, while all the rest of the people flocked to the Church to assist at the solemn office celebrated in the Saint's honour. Many rebuked him for his irreverence, and tried to persuade him to accompany them to the church, but he only laughed at his advisers or answered them with a jest. No sooner, however, had he entered his vineyard and placed his spade in the ground, than immediately, by a just judgment of God, his head was completely twisted round upon his neck, so that he could no longer look before him or continue his work. Filled with terror and remorse, he repaired at once to the church of St. Avitus, where he earnestly implored pardon of God and the cure of his hideous deformity. St. Gregory informs us that his prayers were heard, and that his sincere repentance obtained for him, through the intercession of the Saint, both the cure of his bodily infirmity and pardon for the sinful profanation of which he had been guilty.—*Catholic Anecdotes.*

Q. What is the second commandment of the Church ?

A. To hear Mass on all Sundays and Holydays of obligation.

The second commandment of the Church is *to hear Mass on all Sundays and Holydays of obligation.* You will wonder, perhaps, how it is that the duty of hearing Mass upon Sundays comes under the commandments of the Church, as we have already spoken of it under the third commandment of the Decalogue, " Remember that thou keep holy the Sabbath Day." But notice that, although Almighty God commands us to rest from work upon the Sabbath and to keep it holy, he does not lay down precisely *how* we are to sanctify it, or what works of piety we are to perform on that day. It is the Church (to whom it belongs to explain the Divine commandments) which enjoins the hearing of Mass as the most important means of sanctifying the Lord's Day. Hence the hearing of Mass upon Sundays is one of the commandments of the Church, by which we are taught how to sanctify that day which we are ordered in the Decalogue to keep holy.

But the second commandment of the Church commands us to hear Mass not only upon Sundays, but also on Holidays of obligation; for as there is no higher act of religion than the Holy Sacrifice of the Mass, so there is no better way of honouring the sacred mysteries of man's Redemption, or of celebrating the triumphs of the Saints, than to hear Mass with attention and devotion. Hence the obligation of hearing Mass on Holydays is as strict as that of hearing it upon the Sunday itself. And though the Church sometimes permits her children to work upon these days, as I have already explained to you, on account of the serious loss they might otherwise undergo, yet she by no means excuses them from hearing Mass, if there is any possibility of their attending. Thus, for example, the working man who is obliged to go early to his work upon a Holyday, is bound to rise still earlier, if necessary, that he may be able first of all to sanctify the day by assisting at the Holy Sacrifice. Hence in large towns there is generally a Mass celebrated at five o'clock in the morning, that all may be able to hear Mass before commencing their daily labour.

I will now relate to you a story on this subject which is handed down to us by St. Antoninus, Bishop of Florence.

THE TWO HUNTSMEN.

Two young men had agreed to go out hunting together upon a certain Holyday of obligation, but only one of them took care to hear Mass before starting upon the expedition. They had scarcely been out an hour, when suddenly the sky grew dark, and a fearful storm came on, accompanied by such terrible peals of thunder and such vivid flashes of lightning, that it appeared as if the end of the world was approaching. But what alarmed them most was that, in the midst of the tumult of the elements, they heard from time to time a voice of thunder saying, "Strike, strike." At length the storm began to clear off, and they resumed their way, when suddenly the thunder pealed forth afresh with great fury, and the huntsman who had failed to hear Mass that morning, was struck dead on the spot by a flash of lightning. His companion, beside himself with terror, knew not which way to turn, and his terror was increased when he heard the same voice repeating, "Strike! strike the other also." At these words he was ready to sink upon the ground in mortal anguish, but his courage returned when he heard another voice reply, "I cannot strike *him*, for he has heard this morning the 'Verbum caro factum est. The Word was made flesh.'" These words, my dear children, are, as you know, the concluding words of the last Gospel, at which all the congregation bend their knee in honour of our Lord's Incarnation.—*Rodriguez Christ. Perf.*

FOURTEENTH INSTRUCTION.

The Third Commandment of the Church. Difference between Fasting and Abstaining. Who are bound by this Precept. What the Appointed Days are. Why the Church commands us to Fast and Abstain.

Q. What is the third commandment of the Church ?
A. To keep the days of fasting and abstinence appointed by the Church.

The third commandment of the Church teaches us *to keep the days of fasting and abstinence*, which have been *appointed by the Church*. The catechism first explains to us the difference between fasting and abstinence; it then goes on to tell us what the days are on which we are bound to fast and abstain; and, finally, it explains to us the reason why the Church has laid on us this obligation.

Q. What is meant by fasting days ?
A. Days on which we are allowed to take but one meal, and are forbidden to eat flesh meat.

Q. What is meant by days of abstinence ?
A. Days on which we are forbidden to eat flesh meat, but are allowed the usual number of meals.

From these answers you see, my dear children, that fasting consists in two things—namely, in *taking only one meal* during the day, and in *not eating flesh meat ;* whereas abstaining consists in *not eating flesh meat*, it has nothing to do with the number of meals. You will remember this, if you think of the meaning of the word *abstaining ;* to abstain is to *keep from* something, in this case from flesh meat. Fasting is, therefore, much harder than abstaining, for it includes abstaining from flesh meat and something else besides—namely, the taking only one meal. For this reason the Church, which is a tender and compassionate mother, does not require *you* to fast, for she knows very well that children who are young and growing, and who are generally very hungry little people, stand in need of plenty of nourishment, and that they could not live on one meal a day without doing themselves harm. So she will wait till you have completed the age of twenty-one years, when you will have reached your full growth and strength, and then you will have to fast like the rest. In the meantime you will have only to *abstain* upon fasting days, which you can do without hurting yourselves, for as long as you have plenty of other good food, it will do you no harm to go now and then without meat. In the same way old people who have reached the age of sixty are not obliged to fast, because when people grow old they begin to lose their strength and to become weak and infirm, so that fasting would be injurious to them. All, however, who have come to the use of reason, both young and old, from the child of seven to the old man of eighty, are bound to abstain from flesh meat upon both fasting and abstinence days, unless they are excused for some just and special reason.

But is it really the case that those who are bound to fast are only allowed to take one meal in the day? Yes, my dear children, fasting essentially consists in only taking one full meal. In the early ages of the Church this law was kept so strictly that those who fasted, only tasted food once in the day, and that not till sunset during Lent and the middle of the afternoon on other fasting days. But now the law of fasting is so far relaxed that the meal can be taken as early as twelve o'clock or mid-day, and a little supper, or *collation* as it is called, is allowed in the evening, but not so much as would make a full meal, or else it would be no longer fasting. As to the exact quantity that can be taken at the collation, the general custom allows as much as eight ounces, and custom also allows in the morning a cup of tea or coffee and a small bit of bread or toast, in place of the usual breakfast. At dinner on fasting days in this country any kind of food is usually allowed, as long as it is not flesh meat or what is made from meat, such as broth or gravy. In some countries milk, butter, cheese and eggs are forbidden as well as flesh meat, but they are allowed here by a special dispensation, except on certain days in Lent, when eggs and cheese are forbidden. These things could not, however, be taken at collation, except by those who are not obliged to fast. There is also a special permission in this country to use dripping and lard on all days of abstinence and fasting throughout the year, except Good Friday, and they can be used at collation even by those who are bound to fast.

Like all the other precepts of the Church, that of fasting and abstinence is binding under pain of mortal sin. Hence whoever eats meat without permission on fasting and abstinence days, and whoever, when bound to fast, eats a second full meal, or takes a considerable quantity of food in addition to his dinner and collation on a fasting day, is guilty of a grievous sin. If the amount of meat or other food which he takes is only trifling, then the sin is only venial, unless he eats again and again, so as to make a considerable quantity altogether. To drink between meals on a fasting day is not a sin for those who are bound to fast, unless they were to drink milk, or broth, or something that is in itself forbidden.

The other causes besides age which excuse from fasting, are principally hard labour, poverty, and sickness or infirm health. Thus those who have to earn their bread by manual labour, such as field labourers, joiners, smiths, bricklayers, mill hands, laundry women, &c., are not obliged to fast ; neither are the very poor who depend upon charity for their daily food. The Church allows the latter to eat whatever is given them, as it is seldom that they are able to obtain proper nourishment; she also excuses from fasting women who are nursing, and all who are so weak and poorly that they cannot, without injury to their health, do without their usual quantity of food. In cases where it is quite clear that there is sufficient cause to excuse us from fasting—for example, if we were seriously ill—it would not be necessary to ask for a dispensation, for the law would evidently no longer bind us. If, however, there is any doubt about the matter, it is our duty to consult our confessor and tell him the circumstances of the case ; he will then grant us a dispensation if he thinks it necessary. Indeed, in all cases where it is in our power, it is better to ask his advice, for self-love is very apt to blind and deceive us

With respect to the law of *abstaining*, the same may be said as with regard to fasting. There are some people so weak as to require flesh meat daily, others with whom nothing else will agree. In these cases a dispensation to eat meat both on fasting and abstinence days may be granted by their confessors, or the obligation *commuted*, that is to say *changed*, into some other work of piety. Those who have permission not to abstain must always bear in mind that they are never allowed upon fasting days to eat flesh and fish at the same time.

The following example shews how pleasing to God is the practice of devout abstinence, and what blessings it draws down from heaven on those who faithfully observe it.

DANIEL AND HIS YOUNG COMPANIONS.

Nabuchodonosor, king of Babylon, having taken and plundered Jerusalem, and carried into captivity the remnants of the Jewish race, instructed his chief eunuch Asphenez to select from among the conquered people certain youths, distinguished alike for birth, comeliness and talent, who might abide in the king's palace and learn the language and customs of the Chaldeans. "And the king appointed them," relates the prophet Daniel, "a daily provision of his own meat and of the wine of which he drank himself, that, being nourished three years, afterwards they might stand before the king."

"Now there were of the children of Juda, Daniel, Ananias, Misael, and Azarias. But Daniel purposed in his heart that he would not be defiled with the king's table, nor with the wine which he drank, and he requested the master of the eunuchs that he might not be defiled. And God gave to Daniel grace and mercy in the sight of the prince of the eunuchs. And the prince of the eunuchs said to Daniel, *I fear my lord the king, who hath appointed you meat and drink ; who, if he should see your faces leaner than those of the other youths your equals, you shall endanger my head to the king.* And Daniel said to Malasar, whom the prince of the eunuchs had appointed over Daniel, Ananias, Misael, and Azarias, *Try, I beseech thee, thy servants for ten days, and let pulse be given us to eat and water to drink. And look upon our faces and the faces of the children who eat of the king's meat, and as thou shalt see, deal with thy servants.* And when he had heard these words he tried them for ten days ; and after the ten days their faces appeared fairer and fatter than all the children that eat of the king's meat. And when the days were ended after which the king had ordered they should be brought in, the prince of the eunuchs brought them in before Nabuchodonosor. And when the king had spoken to them, there were not found among them all such as Daniel, Ananias, Misael and Azarias, and they stood in the king's presence. And in all matters of wisdom and understanding that the king inquired of them, he found them ten times better than all the diviners and wise men that were in all his kingdom."—*Daniel,* i.

ANECDOTES OF LOUIS XVI.

It is related of the unfortunate Louis XVI., king of France, who died on the scaffold during the great French revolution, that when he was a youth of twenty years he said one day to his courtiers, " I have not done much in the way of keeping Lent· this year, but next year it will be different, for I shall have to fast."   " Sire," said one of them, " that will be impossible, for you would not be able to hunt." " No matter," replied Louis, " I must give up hunting if it is necessary, for a mere amusement does not excuse any one from obeying the laws of the Church."

Among other abuses, which the young king abolished on coming to the throne of France, was that of serving up both fish and meat at the royal table on the great hunting days when they happened also to be days of abstinence. A certain officer grumbled at the new regulation, quoting the words of our Blessed Lord, " Not that which goeth into the mouth defileth a man." *   " You are right," replied the king, " it is not the meat we eat which injures the body, but the disobedience we are guilty of that kills the soul. Whosoever *will not hear the Church,* says our Lord, *let him be to thee as the heathen and the publican.*† Now, I do not think you would like to be called either one or the other."

The same king, when in prison and in the hands of his merciless enemies, was equally exact in observing the days of abstinence, and was wont to content himself for his meal with a piece of dry bread, when forbidden food was placed before him in derision by his cruel jailer.—*Anecdotes Chrétiennes.*

TRUE OBEDIENCE.

In one of the principal cities of France there lived a young boy, whose parents were so neglectful of the practice of their religion that they used flesh meat on all days alike, without regard to the laws of the Church. When he was being prepared for his first Communion the boy went to confession, and among his other faults accused himself of not keeping the days of abstinence. His confessor explained to him the greatness of the sin of which he had had hitherto little or no idea, and laid down rules for his conduct in future which he promised faithfully to observe.

It was not long before his resolution was put to the test, for on the following Friday nothing was served up for dinner

---

* Matt. xv. 11.   † Matt. xviii. 17.

but the usual forbidden fare. The young boy was helped like the rest, but begged to be excused from taking it. His father was much astonished, and immediately demanded the cause of his refusal. He replied that it was an abstinence day, on which it was forbidden by the Church to eat flesh meat, adding that he was quite ready to make his dinner on the bread and vegetables. His father, enraged at his resolution, took him from the table without allowing him to eat a mouthful, and shut him up in a solitary room, telling him that he should remain there until the following day. The boy made no answer, and submitted to his punishment without a murmur.

In the course of the same evening his mother who, though as negligent about the duties of her religion as her husband, could not help feeling for the privations of her child, came to see him and brought him some food, at the same time reproving him for his obstinacy and disobedience. What was her surprise when he refused to partake of it! "My father," said he, "has condemned me to fast till to-morrow, and as I can obey him in that without sin I would rather not eat what you have been so good as to bring me." The mother, much affected at hearing her child express himself with such sense and modesty, left the room, and went to tell her husband what had passed. The latter was equally struck with the admirable conduct of his child, and agreed with his wife that the boy was much more reasonable than themselves. He at once went to his room, tenderly embraced him, and asked him who had taught him to be so faithful to his duty. Learning that it was his confessor, the father went to visit him without delay, thanked him for the care he had taken of his son, and begged of him to hear his own confession. His conversion was sincere, and was soon followed by that of his wife. The noble conduct of the child was thus the happy means of reconciling his parents to Almighty God."—*Anecdotes Chrétiennes.*

We now come to speak of the days which have been set apart by the Church for the practice of fasting and abstinence. And first, as regards the fasting days.

Q. What are the fasting days?

A. The forty days of Lent; certain Vigils; the Ember days; and, in England, the Wednesdays and Fridays in Advent.

Yes, these are the fasting days which, from the earliest ages have been observed in the Church, though formerly with far greater severity than at present. The greater part of Protestants are wont to deride the practice of fasting as foolish and superstitious; they will, nevertheless, find these very days marked in their prayer books as fasting days, for their own Church Calendar, which was copied from the Catholic Missal, retains both feasts and fasts which they have long since ceased to observe. Thus is heresy itself, through the Providence of God, made to bear witness to the antiquity of Catholic practices and doctrines. We will now speak of the origin and meaning of the different fasts which are mentioned in the Catechism.

First, there are *the forty days of Lent*. These have been observed as a solemn fast since the time of the Apostles, in honour of our Lord's forty days' fast in the desert. This fast is intended by the Church to prepare the soul to celebrate the Passion of our Blessed Lord at the end of Lent, and to keep the solemn Feast of his Resurrection.

Secondly, *certain vigils*, that is, the *eves* of certain great Feasts. They are called *vigils*, because they were spent formerly not only in fasting, but in *watching*, which is the meaning of the word vigil, just as the word vigilance literally means watchfulness. On these days the faithful were wont to repair to the Church to assist at the solemn offices, which were celebrated in preparation for the coming Feast. There they remained *watching* even through the night, until the day of the Festival dawned upon them. In former times the vigils or eves of all the great Feasts were kept as fasting days, but now there are only six in this country which are so observed, namely, the eves of Easter and Whitsunday, Corpus Christi, SS. Peter and Paul, the Assumption of our

Blessed Lady, All Saints and Christmas Day. If any of these vigils falls upon a Sunday it is kept upon the preceding Saturday.

Thirdly, *the Ember days,** namely, the Wednesday, Friday and Saturday in the four Ember weeks, which are distributed through the four quarters of the year. These days are instituted by the Church for the purpose of consecrating to God the four seasons of the year, of returning thanks to him for the various fruits of the earth, and of averting his anger justly merited by our sins. They are also especially intended to implore the Divine blessing on the solemn ordination of Priests and other sacred Ministers, which takes place on these days throughout the Church.

Fourthly, *the Wednesdays and Fridays in Advent*, at least in England, for in some countries they are no longer kept. The season of Advent, which commences on the fourth Sunday before Christmas Day, is set apart as a time of prayer and penance, to prepare our souls to celebrate the birthday of the Divine Infant. Advent is of very ancient institution, and was formerly kept as a second Lent.

Q. Which are the days of abstinence ?

A. All Fridays, except the Friday on which Christmas Day may fall ; and the Sundays in Lent, unless leave be given to eat meat on them.

The days of abstinence, my dear children, are very easily remembered. They are—

First, *All Fridays* in the year ; there is only one exception, namely, *the Friday on which Christmas Day may fall ;* for Christmas Day, being a day of great rejoicing both in heaven and on earth, on

---

* So called, perhaps, from the Saxon word *ymbren* or *circular*, which is the title given to them in the laws of King Alfred, probably because they recur at certain fixed times. Others derive the name from the word *embers* or *ashes*, which have been in all ages a sign of mourning.

account of the Birth of our dear Lord which we celebrate thereon, the Church excuses us on that day from the law of abstinence, the observance of which is a mark of affliction and penance. I need not tell you that the reason why *Friday* is selected by the Church out of all the other days of the week as a day of mortification and penance, is in honour of the Passion and Death of our Blessed Lord which took place on that day. It is fitting that, upon the day on which he endured such cruel sufferings for the love of us, *we* should do penance for those sins which caused him to suffer, and should practice some acts of self-denial for the love of him.

Secondly, *The Sundays in Lent, unless leave be given to eat meat on them,* are, by the general laws of the Church, kept as days of abstinence. But in England the permission to eat meat on these Sundays is now always given by our Holy Father the Pope, and is announced to the people by the different Bishops in their Lenten Pastorals, along with various other dispensations which are usually granted.

Q. Why does the Church command us to fast and abstain? A. That so we may mortify the flesh and satisfy God for our sins.

The twofold object of all fasting, my dear children, is *to mortify the flesh* with its rebellious senses, and *to satisfy* the Justice of *God for the sins* by which we have provoked the Divine anger. Mortification and penance are, indeed, two of the most important duties of every Christian, and the Church, in commanding us to fast and abstain, shews us a most efficacious means of fulfilling them.

In the first place, we must ever remember that, owing to the sins of our first parents, we bear in our bodies the seed of concupiscence, that is, the desire of unlawful gratification. Hence there is a warfare continually going on within us between our carnal appetites and desires, which incite us to rebel against, and our reason and conscience, which teach us to submit to the Law of God. It is of this interior conflict that St. Paul speaks when he says, "The flesh lusteth against the spirit and the spirit against the flesh, for these are contrary one to another." *   Hence the necessity of bodily mortification, by which we subdue the flesh and bring it under subjection to the spirit, accustoming it to the denial of its own pleasure and indulgence. "If any man will come after me," says our Blessed Lord, "*let him deny himself.*" †   Now the Church, knowing our natural unwillingness to practise the painful but necessary duty of self-denial, has provided in some measure for the fulfilment of it by setting apart certain days throughout the year as days of public fasting and abstinence. On these days she teaches us all to unite in fulfilling that duty of bodily mortification which is prescribed by our Blessed Redeemer, and is, at the same time, so necessary for purifying the heart and obtaining a perfect victory over our corrupt passions. The more the flesh is subdued, the more is the spirit exalted above earthly things, and the better are the mind and heart disposed to converse with God by prayer, and to receive the impressions of Divine grace. Hence the Archangel St. Raphael revealed to Tobias that prayer is especially pleasing to God when accompanied with fasting.‡   And our Blessed Lord, in explaining to his Apostles the cause of their failure to cast out a devil from a possessed child, assured them that it was because they had not made use of this powerful means of grace, "This kind of devil," said he, "can go out by nothing but by prayer and by fasting.§

---

* Gal. v. 17.
‡ Tobias, xii. 8.
† Matt. xvi. 24.
§ Mark, ix. 28.

Another important reason why the Church commands us to fast is, that thereby *we may satisfy God for our sins.* Sin, as I have told you, though truly repented of and pardoned by God, still renders us liable to a certain amount of punishment either in this world or the world to come. This punishment is a kind of debt which we owe to the Justice of God, and we must discharge the last farthing of this debt before we can ever enter into the kingdom of heaven. I told you that one way of paying this debt is *by gaining indulgences;* for, when we gain an indulgence, the sufferings and good works of our Lord, the B. Virgin and the Saints, are applied to our souls in the way of satisfaction for what we owe to the Justice of God. Another way of paying this debt is *by bearing patiently the trials and sufferings of this life,* and a third way is *by doing works of penance,* such as keeping the days of fasting and abstinence. There is, moreover, this advantage in keeping the fasts of the Church, that we have the merit of *obedience,* which makes our works of penance doubly pleasing to God and profitable to the soul.

But tell me now about yourselves, what do *you* do in the way of fasting? It is true that you are not yet twenty-one years old, and therefore you are not bound to observe the fasts of the Church. But ought you not to do something in the way of fasting? Have you not got a rebellious flesh to subdue, and sins to make atonement for? Yes, certainly, and therefore you ought to practise such acts of mortification and self-denial as are suited to your tender age, and are not likely to be hurtful to your bodily health. For example, you might, on fasting and abstinence days, refrain from eating and drinking between meals, deny yourself something nice at meal time, and, instead of spending your halfpence on cakes and sweets, bestow them on the poor and needy. It was thus that

the Saints of God, even in their very childhood, were
wont to exercise themselves in the practice of Christian
mortification, and laid the foundation of that spirit
of self-sacrifice which made them so holy and so dear
to God, and capable of performing such heroic deeds
in the Divine service.

Among all the practices of our holy religion, there
is hardly any that is more frequently inculcated in
the Holy Scriptures, both by word and example,
than that of fasting. Were the Jews in danger from
the enemies who surrounded them, they fasted to
secure the Divine protection; had they fallen into
sin and drawn upon them the anger of God, they
sought his pardon by fasting and other works of
penance; did they desire any extraordinary favour
from God, they proclaimed a solemn fast as the most
certain means of obtaining it; and, indeed, they
never failed to obtain what they asked, when their
prayers were accompanied with fasting and humiliation. Witness the fast of the holy king Josaphat
and his people, which was followed by the destruction of Sennacherib and his mighty army; witness
the fasts of Judith and Esther, which resulted in
the deliverance of the Jews from impending ruin.
Even the very pagans experienced the power of
fasting in averting the anger of Almighty God, as
we learn from the following history of

THE REPENTANCE OF THE NINIVITES.

" And the word of the Lord came to Jonas saying, *Arise
and go to Ninive, the great city, and preach in it the preaching
that I bid thee, for the wickedness thereof is come up before me.*
And Jonas arose and went to Ninive according to the word
of the Lord : now Ninive was a great city of three days'
journey. And Jonas began to enter into the city one day's
journey : and he cried, and said, *Yet forty days and Ninive
shall be destroyed.*
And the men of Ninive believed in God, and they pro-

claimed a fast, and put on sackcloth from the greatest to the least. And the word came to the king of Ninive : and he rose up out of his throne, and cast away his robe from him, and was clothed with sackcloth, and sat in ashes. And he caused it to be proclaimed and published in Ninive from the mouth of the king and of his princes, saying : *Let' neither men nor beasts, oxen nor sheep, taste anything : let them not feed nor drink water. And let men and beasts be covered with sackcloth, and cry to the Lord with all their strength, and let them turn every one from his evil way, and from the iniquity that is in their hands. Who can tell if God will turn and forgive : and will turn away from his fierce anger, and we shall not perish ?* And God saw their works, that they were turned from their evil way : and God had mercy with regard to the evil which he had said that he would do to them, and he did it not."—*Jonas.*

But it is not from the history of the Jews only that we learn the great advantages to be derived from fasting and abstinence; frequent mention of the same holy practice, of the manner of fulfilling and the graces attending it, is to be found also in the New Testament. Thus, our Blessed Lord, in instructing his disciples on this subject, warns them against the vanity and hypocrisy of the Pharisees. " When you fast," he says, " be not as the hypocrites, sad. For they disfigure their faces that they may appear unto men to fast. Amen I say to you, they have received their reward. But thou, when thou fastest, anoint thy head and wash thy face : that thou may appear not to men to fast, but to thy Father who is in secret, and thy Father, who seeth in secret, will repay thee." * Moreover, he has given us the most powerful of all motives to fulfil this duty—namely, his own Divine example, which should ever be the rule and model of our lives. Accordingly, before entering on his public ministry, he retired into the desert and there observed a strict fast of forty days and forty nights,

* Matt. vi. 16-18.

as the evangelist tells us.* The forty days' fast of Moses on Mount Sinai, by which he sanctified himself while conversing with Almighty God,† and the similar fast of Elias, by which he prepared his soul to fulfil the important mission with which God had entrusted him,‡ were figures of this fast of our Blessed Redeemer; but there was this difference, that *they* fasted in order to purify their hearts and prepare them better to receive the Divine favours, whereas our Lord had no need of purification, but fasted simply to set us an example, and to atone for our sins by his own voluntary penance. And though we do not find that he imposed any special fasts on his disciples during his lifetime—for he bore their burdens in his own innocent person—yet he warned them that the day would come, after he should be taken from among them, when they also should have to practise the duty of fasting.§

The following little history will shew you with what strict fidelity the laws of fasting and abstinence were observed by the early Christians.

MARTYRDOM OF ST. FRUCTUOSUS.

You do not perhaps know, that in the early ages of the Church, Friday was kept not only as a day of abstinence, but as a fasting day in honour of our Blessed Lord's death, nor was it permitted to touch food until three o'clock in the afternoon, the hour at which he expired. Now it happened that St. Fructuosus, Bishop of Taragon, in Spain, being condemned to death for refusing to adore the false gods, was led to execution on a Friday morning along with two of his deacons, Saints Augurius and Eulogius. They had been condemned to be burnt alive in the public amphitheatre, and as they were conducted thither they were attended by vast crowds of people, eager to receive the last dying blessing of the holy Bishop, who was beloved alike by Christians and pagans. Some offered him refreshments on the way, and

---

* Matt. iv.   † Exod. xxxiv. 28.
‡ III. Kings, xix. 8.   § Mark, ii. 18-20.

begged him to take at least a cup of wine to strengthen him before his last combat. "I thank you," replied he, "for your charity, but it is Friday, and it is as yet but the tenth hour of the day." The martyrs were fastened to wooden stakes, and the flames consuming the bands with which they were secured, left their arms at liberty, which they extended in the form of a cross. In this posture they expired before the flames touched their bodies, and at the same moment the heavens were seen to open, and their happy souls to enter therein crowned with bright diadems of glory.—*Butler's Lives of the Saints.*

FIFTEENTH INSTRUCTION.

The Fourth and Fifth Commandments of the Church. At what age children are bound to go to Confession. At what age they are bound to receive Holy Communion. Sixth Commandment of the Church. The Impediments of Matrimony.

Q. What is the fourth commandment of the Church ?
A. To go to confession at least once a year.

Q. What is the fifth commandment of the Church ?
A. To receive the Blessed Sacrament at least once a year, and that at Easter or thereabouts.

The fourth commandment of the Church is *to go to Confession at least once a year;* and the fifth *to receive the Blessed Sacrament at least once a year, and that at Easter or thereabouts.* Whoever, therefore, remains a whole year without going to Confession, or who neglects to make his Easter Communion, is guilty of a grievous act of disobedience to the law of the Church.

In the early age of the Church, when the light of faith and the fire of charity burned brightly in the hearts of Christians, there was no need to remind them of the obligation of making frequent use of those means of grace which our Blessed Lord had left behind him to help us on our way to heaven. But as time went on, and men grew careless and lukewarm, and so occupied in worldly and temporal concerns as to forget the far more important interests of their souls, and the end for which God had made them, it became necessary to put before them by a strict command the absolute necessity of approaching at certain times to the Holy Sacraments of Penance and the Blessed Eucharist. Accordingly in the fourth Council of Lateran, held in the year 1216, it was solemnly enacted that the faithful of both sexes, after they have arrived at the years of discretion, should confess their sins at least once a year, and receive at Easter or thereabouts the Sacrament of the Blessed Eucharist.

Such, my dear children, is the law of the Church ; but there are many who fulfil it, who go to Confession once a year and never miss their Easter Communion, but who are still guilty of grievous sin in not approaching more frequently to these holy Sacraments. For the law of God certainly commands us to preserve his love and friendship, and to make use of those means of grace which will enable us to do so. What, then, would you think of one who, having become the enemy of God by giving way to mortal sin, continues for weeks or even months in his rebellion, without ever coming to Confession to implore the Divine pardon. Meanwhile he braves the anger of God, and exposes himself to the imminent danger of being eternally lost, should his life be cut short by some sudden sickness or unforeseen accident. And what would you say of one who, when violently assailed by his passions and in danger of yielding to the continual assaults of temptation, refuses to nourish his soul and renew his strength with that lifegiving bread, the source of all grace— namely, the Body of our Blessed Lord in the Holy Communion?   Surely, in such cases, to neglect deliberately these powerful means of salvation must be a grievous outrage against the Divine Goodness.

The following history will shew you the dreadful danger to which those are exposed who live on in sin, deferring their confession from day to day in the hope of a deathbed repentance.

" IT IS NOW TOO LATE."

The Venerable Bede relates in his Saxon Chronicles, that the pious king Coinred had at his court a nobleman to whom he was much attached, on account of his good qualities and faithful service.   Unhappily this poor man neglected the duties of his religion, and remained for years without approaching the Sacraments, continually deferring from day to day, notwithstanding the earnest entreaties and remonstrances of Coinred. At length he was attacked by a dangerous malady, and the king went to visit him, urging him to delay no longer, but to send at once for his confessor. Some days after the king went a second time, and finding him at the last extremity, besought him in the most moving terms to have pity on his own soul, and send at once for the priest. But he, turning upon the king a look of anguish, exclaimed, "It is now too late. There is no more time now for confession. I am lost ; hell is my portion." So saying, he fell back and expired.—*Catholic Anecdotes.*

You will notice that these two commandments differ from one another in this respect, that the exact time of the annual Communion is fixed for the Feast of *Easter or thereabouts,* whereas the time of the annual Confession is not determined.   In the case of those who are bound to receive Holy Communion, the Confession must of course be made at Easter time, as Confession is ordinarily a necessary condition for the devout reception of the Blessed Sacrament. By *Easter or thereabouts*, we understand in this country the whole time which intervenes between Ash Wednesday and Low Sunday. In many other countries the time for making the Easter Communion is more limited, extending only from Palm to Low Sunday. The annual Confession may be made to any Priest who has faculties from the Bishop to hear Confessions; but the Easter Communion should, if possible, be received in our parish church, though in England this is not of obligation as it is in most countries.

Q. How soon are children bound to go to confession?
A. As soon as they come to the use of reason, so as to be capable of mortal sin.

Q. When are children generally supposed to come to the use of reason?
A. About the age of seven years.

All are bound by the law of annual Confession who have *come to the use of reason*, for it is then that man becomes capable of offending Almighty God by mortal sin. A little child of four or five years old may do what is in itself sinful—for example, fight, or steal, or repeat bad words—but he is not accountable for what he says or does, for he has not yet sufficient sense to distinguish right from wrong. His parents, it is true, punish him if he does wrong, and with reason—not, however, because he has really committed a moral fault, but because the punishment will help him by degrees to distinguish good from evil, and meanwhile will teach him to avoid that for which he has been chastised. But when the child grows older and his mind begins to unfold, he learns by the light of reason and the voice of his conscience, as well as by the teaching of his parents and instructors, that to fight, steal, and say bad words are things wicked in themselves and displeasing to that Good God from whom he has received his being. Then it is, and not till then, that he becomes answerable to God for his actions, and capable of offending him; for if he still does those things which he knows to be displeasing to God, it is plain that he wilfully rebels against him in refusing to submit to his Divine Law. At what exact age a child arrives at sufficient sense to know the evil of sin, so as to be capable of offending God grievously, it is impossible to say; indeed the age differs greatly in different children, since some are by nature, and some by their training, far quicker and more forward than others of the same or even a greater age. *The age of seven years* is, however, usually considered to be about the time when reason is sufficiently developed in children to enable them to distinguish clearly right from wrong, and to bring them under the obligation of the fourth commandment of the Church. It is, therefore, the duty of all parents, when their children arrive at that age, to see that they are prepared for their first Confession, and henceforward to send them to Confession regularly at the times appointed by their pastors.

Q. How soon are Christians bound to receive the Blessed Sacrament?

A. As soon as they are capable of being instructed in that sacred mystery.

The age at which children are bound to receive the Blessed Sacrament is not when they come to the use of reason, but when *they are* sufficiently *capable of being instructed in that sacred mystery,* so as to be able to understand the sublime nature and great importance of the act which they perform. A much greater degree of instruction, and consequently a more advanced age, are necessary for receiving Holy

Communion than for simply going to Confession. It is true that in the early ages of the Church children of very tender years were admitted to Holy Communion; indeed we read that even infants were communicated with a few drops of the Precious Blood from the consecrated chalice. But this arose from the circumstances of the times, which were times of persecution, when children and even babes were sometimes called upon to lay down their lives in defence of the Faith. Therefore, in order that they might not want the sustaining power of this holy Sacrament, or lose that additional degree of glory which shall adorn those in heaven who have been made one with Jesus Christ on earth by Holy Communion, the Church at that time permitted children to partake of the Heavenly Banquet before their instruction was completed, and sometimes even before it was commenced. Now, however, that this necessity has passed away, she requires that children should be fully instructed before they are admitted to this Holy Sacrament.

But at what age is it that children may be considered sufficiently capable of being instructed for their first Communion? This is a matter which will depend entirely on their capacity, their dispositions, and the prudent decision of their confessor. Some children who are brought up in innocence and piety, and who have been carefully instructed from their infancy, may be admitted to their first Communion at as early an age as nine or ten years; with others who have been less carefully trained, and who are, perhaps, naturally less intelligent, it may be prudent to defer it to the age of twelve or thirteen. But, ordinarily speaking, eleven is about the age when children may be admitted to the first Communion class. It will soon be seen from their attendance, their behaviour, and their progress in instruction, whether they can be admitted to Holy Communion, or whether this privilege must be deferred for another year. In Catholic countries, these instructions are usually continued for twelve months before the great event, becoming more frequent as the time approaches. Meanwhile the children come monthly to Confession, while their pastor makes frequent inquiries as to their conduct at home, at school, in the church, and in the public streets. This he does that he may be able to form a better judgment as to whether they are really trying to correct their faults, and to acquire those habits of obedience, gentleness, truthfulness, purity, &c., which form the most important part of the preparation for first Communion. Parents are bound to watch over their children with special care during this period, to send them regularly to instruction and to Confession, to correct their faults, and to strive to form them to habits of virtue. Oh, my dear children, if you properly understood how much depends upon the dispositions with which you receive our Blessed Lord for the first time, you would begin from this very day, and do all in your power to prepare your hearts to receive so great a guest. A good first Communion is the foundation of a virtuous and holy life, and is a strong pledge of eternal salvation. Say, then, a little prayer to our Blessed Lady every day that she may obtain for you this happiness. Above all, try to purify your hearts from sin by correcting your faults and fighting against your bad passions, for He whom you are to receive is Holiness and Purity itself, and the fruits and joys of your first Communion will be in proportion to the efforts you have made to cleanse your hearts from sin and make them worthy to be his dwelling-place. And you, my dear children, who have already received our Blessed Lord in Holy Communion, thank him frequently for the wonderful gift he has bestowed upon you, and shew how much you value it by frequently and devoutly approaching to the Holy Table. Let not a month pass, if possible, without receiving this Food of the strong, this Bread of Angels. The oftener you partake devoutly of this Heavenly Banquet, the more will you relish its hidden sweetness, and the more will you be inflamed with the fire of Divine Love, while you will feel in your hearts with holy David * how true it is, that better is one day spent in union with Jesus, than a thousand in the vain and empty pleasures of the world.

ST. FRANCIS AND THE OLD MAN.

We read in the life of St. Francis of Sales that he was one day giving Communion in a country Church, when an old man, whom he had communicated early in the morning, approached a second time to the altar rails. "My good friend," said St. Francis, "I have already given you our Blessed Lord ; you must not come to receive him again." "Oh, my father," said the old man, "give him to me again, I beseech you ; I felt so happy in his company." St. Francis could not help admiring the fervour and simplicity of the good old man, and as he could not grant his request he said to him, "Well, my friend, go away this time, but take care to come again to-morrow morning, and I promise you that I will give you our Blessed Lord once more." The old man went away consoled, and was punctual in returning again next morning, when he had again the happiness of receiving his God.—*St. Francis of Sales.*

THE FIRST COMMUNION VEIL.

A certain young girl, who had been brought up by virtuous and pious parents, had the happiness to make her first Communion with exceeding fervour and in the most excellent dispositions. The remembrance of the happy day on which she first received our Lord continued for a long time ever present to her mind, and became a powerful motive to encourage her to the practice of virtue. Every month she returned again to the Divine Banquet, and on her Communion

* Ps. lxxxiii. 11.

days it was her frequent custom, when in private, to clothe herself again with the veil and wreath that she had worn on the occasion of her first Communion, in order that she might renew the sweet emotions which she had then experienced.

It happened, however, that as time went on, her fervour and piety relaxed. She grew lukewarm and slothful, careless about her prayers, and negligent in approaching the holy Sacraments, until she at last fell away by degrees into a worldly and sinful life. The sight of the garments which she had worn on the day of her first Communion now became hateful to her, for they never failed to awaken in her the voice of conscience, until at last, to avoid their continual reproach, she shut them up in a drawer which she seldom opened. Here they continued unnoticed for many years, during which this once innocent and holy soul fell deeper and deeper into the abyss of sin.

At length it pleased Almighty God to look upon her with eyes of mercy. Going one day by accident to the drawer where the veil and wreath had been laid by, she came upon them unexpectedly. Her first motion was one of impatience. "Cursed veil," said she, casting it on the ground, "can I never banish you from my sight! And yet," she added, for Divine grace began now to work in her heart, "how happy was I when first I wore you! Where is the innocence which then adorned my heart, where the robe of grace with which my soul was clad on that blessed morning when first I went to receive my God?" So saying, she knelt down and fervently kissed these tokens of her early innocence and piety. Then bursting into tears, she implored our Blessed Lord to pardon her many crimes and her past ingratitude, and restore her once more to his love and friendship. From that moment she quitted her evil life and became a sincere penitent.—*L'Homond.*

The following history, related by St. Cyprian, the illustrious Bishop of Carthage, who died a martyr to the Faith in the third century, shews us what was the practice of the early Church with regard to infant Communion, and at the same time conveys a useful lesson.

THE INFANT COMMUNICANT.

During the cruel persecution raised against the Church by the Roman Emperor Decius, a certain Christian and his wife, to secure their safety, fled from their house in the city of

Carthage, leaving behind them their little girl of twelve months old in charge of the nurse. The latter, unwilling to be burdened with the care of the child, took her to the pagan magistrates of the city, who, out of hatred to the Christian religion, caused her to be fed with bread soaked in wine that had been offered to idols. The persecution soon after abating, the parents returned to Carthage, and the little girl was restored to her mother. She, not knowing what had happened, took her with her to the house where the Christians were assisting in secret at the holy Sacrifice of the Mass. When the time of the Consecration arrived, the little child began to struggle violently, and appeared as if she sought to explain by signs what had passed before the magistrates. At length the moment of Communion came, and the Deacon of the Mass, after communicating the rest of the faithful, brought the consecrated chalice to the little girl, seeking to administer to her a few drops of the Precious Blood, according to the custom of the time. She, however, violently resisted, turning her head away and seeking to push away the chalice with her little hand. At length, however, he succeeded in communicating her, but no sooner had she swallowed the consecrated wine than she began to vomit, and threw up all that she had taken. The Precious Blood of Christ could not remain in a heart which had been defiled with the presence of wine that had been offered to idols. From this we may learn how necessary it is to purify our hearts from sin by sincere contrition and a good confession before receiving our Blessed Lord in Holy Communion, for far more hateful to him is the presence of sin in the soul, than that of any superstitious food within the body.—*Catholic Anecdotes.*

Q. What is the sixth commandment of the Church ?
A. Not to marry within certain degrees of kindred, nor to solemnize marriage at the forbidden times.

Q. Which are those forbidden times ?
A. From the first Sunday of Advent till after the Epiphany, and from Ash Wednesday till after Low Sunday.

The sixth commandment of the Church relates to the sacrament of Matrimony, and is divided into two parts. The first tells us *who* are able to contract marriage, and the second *at what time* it may be solemnized.

In the first place, the Church forbids marriage *within certain degrees of kindred;* in other words, relations are unable to marry within certain forbidden limits, and should they attempt to do so, the marriage would be a grievous sacrilege, and null and void in the sight of God. These limits are four degrees for blood relations, and for those also who are relations by marriage. I will explain what I mean by an example. Your sisters and brothers, your uncles and aunts both on your father and mother's side, your cousins and their children, are your blood relations. Your sisters and brothers are in the first degree of relationship, your first cousins in the second, being further removed, while your second and third cousins are in the third and fourth degree. Now, with all these, marriage is forbidden either by the Divine law or the law of the Church; therefore you could not marry even your third cousin, unless you had received a *dispensation;* that is, unless the Church had, for some good and weighty reason, granted you a special permission to do so. The object of this prohibition is to protect the purity and sanctity of family life, and to prevent innumerable evils which would otherwise arise. For the same cause, marriage is equally forbidden between relations by marriage within the same limits; so, for example, a man can not only not marry his deceased wife's sister, but not even her third cousin, and the same holds good in her case with regard to her deceased husband's relatives. But this hindrance to marriage, or *impediment,* as such hindrances are usually called, only exists between the wife and her husband's relations, and between the husband and his wife's relations, not between the relations themselves in regard to each other; so that the husband's brother, for example, could lawfully marry the wife's sister, or indeed any of her relatives. Remember always, my dear children, that in all that regards the Sacrament of Matrimony, as well as the other Sacraments, it is the Church only which has power to make regulations, to establish impediments, or, if she thinks fit, to remove them. Civil governments often seek to usurp this power, but they have no commission from our Blessed Lord, and all that they do, as far as regards the Sacrament itself, is null and void. They may pretend to remove by law impediments to marriage, but the marriage, if forbidden by the Church, will be an empty form ; they may declare marriage null when certain conditions are not fulfilled ; but as long as it is performed according to the laws of the Church, it is binding in the sight of God, though it may expose those who contract it to certain legal penalties.

In the second place, the Church forbids us in this commandment *to solemnize marriage at forbidden times,* and the catechism goes on to explain that those forbidden times are the holy seasons of Advent and Lent, along with Christmas and Easter time. For Advent and Lent are set aside by the Church for the exercise of prayer and penance, while Christmas and Easter are seasons of spiritual jubilee and thanksgiving. Now it is not fitting that that which is a time of mourning should become one of temporal rejoicing, nor that seasons of spiritual joy should be occupied in those vain festivities of the world which usually accompany the celebration of marriage. Hence it is that the Church has forbidden her children to *solemnize* marriage at these times ; that is, to celebrate it with the usual tokens of joy and festivity. She does not absolutely forbid people to marry, for the Sacrament of Matrimony is always sacred and holy, besides it is not always possible to defer it, as in the case of those who are setting out on a long voyage. In such cases the marriage should be celebrated in as quiet and private a manner as possible. Every good Catholic will, however, except in cases of extreme necessity, defer his marriage, out of respect to the mysteries which the Church is celebrating, until the public solemnization of it is permitted.

A MARRIAGE BLESSED BY HEAVEN.

During the time of the Crusades, a young English gentleman, named Gilbert, undertook a journey to the Holy Land, accompanied by his servant Richard, in order to fight against the Infidels, who were at that time in possession of the Holy Places. Both, however, were soon taken prisoners, and fell into the hands of a Saracen prince, who treated Gilbert with some degree of consideration on account of his superior education and excellent qualities.

In this state of slavery the virtues and piety of Gilbert attracted the attention and admiration of his master's daughter, who took every opportunity of conversing with him unobserved. She questioned him regarding his country and religion, and the evident interest which she took in his answers, encouraged him to unfold to her by degrees the various truths of our holy Faith. One day he spoke to her with extreme fervour of the happiness of loving and serving Jesus Christ. "But tell me," said the Princess," who was deeply touched by his discourse, " since you love Jesus Christ so much, would you be willing to suffer death for his sake ?" "Gladly," replied he, with ardour ; "the greatest happiness that could befall-me would be to sacrifice to him my life and the last drop of my blood." This generous answer so moved the Princess that she took a resolution to embrace the Christian religion at any cost, whenever the opportunity occurred.

Meanwhile a plan of escape was secretly formed among the Christian slaves, and Gilbert and Richard found themselves once more at liberty after a captivity of eighteen months. The young Princess wept bitterly when she found herself deprived of Gilbert's instruction and advice, and detesting from her heart the superstitions of Mahomet, took a generous resolution of seeking out Gilbert in the land of his birth, in order to procure through his means the grace of Baptism. Accordingly she fled secretly from her father's house, and embarking in an English vessel, arrived at length, destitute and friendless, in the city of London.

Almighty God did not abandon a soul which had so generously corresponded with the call of Divine grace. As the Saracen maiden was wandering in great distress through the busy streets of London, unable, on account of her ignorance of the English language, to make any inquiries as to the object of her search, she suddenly recognised among the crowd the form of Richard, the servant of Gilbert, who had been sent out on some message by his master. Overjoyed at this providential meeting, she eagerly acquainted him with the object of her journey, and implored him to conduct her to his master, that he might complete the work of her conversion. Gilbert, being informed of her arrival, caused her to be conducted to the house of a pious lady of his acquaintance, where, on the following day, he went to visit her. The young maiden, throwing herself at his feet, besought him with many tears to procure for her that priceless gift of the Divine friendship, which in his captivity he had declared to be more precious than life itself. Gilbert was deeply moved at her lively faith and generous dispositions, and not only promised to do his utmost to obtain for her what she asked, but felt himself inspired by God to make her the offer of his hand, in order that he might be able, with a better title, to devote himself to the work of her instruction. His resolution was approved of by the Bishop, whom he consulted on the subject, and shortly afterwards she was baptised under the name of Matilda, and then solemnly espoused to Gilbert in the presence of the Bishop, who himself gave the nuptial benediction to the holy couple.

Soon after their espousals, Gilbert, to fulfil a vow which he had taken, returned to the Holy Land, where he served for three years and a-half against the infidels. Matilda herself encouraged him in his generous undertaking, assuring him that God, who had watched over and protected her so visibly when yet an infidel, would not abandon her now that she was a Christian. During Gilbert's absence, his faithful servant Richard remained with Matilda to watch over her safety and minister to her wants. His time of service completed, Gilbert returned to England to the great joy of his virtuous spouse, and Almighty God blessed their union by giving them a son, who was no other than the great St. Thomas à Beckett, Archbishop of Canterbury, who received the crown of martyrdom under Henry II. in defence of the liberties and privileges of the Church.—*Histoires Edifiantes.*

LAUS DEO, HONOR MARIÆ.

END OF VOL. II.